Wendy Perriam

was expelled from a strict convent boarding-school and escaped to St Anne's College, Oxford, where she read History. After a stint in advertising and a succession of more offbeat jobs, ranging from the bizarre to the banal, she now writes full time.

Her previous novels, which include *Absinthe for Elevenses*, *Born of Woman*, *Fifty-Minute Hour* and *Breaking and Entering*, have been acclaimed for their provocative mix of the sacred and the profane, and their extraordinary power to disturb, amuse and shock.

She is currently working on a collection of short stories. Her new novel, *Second Skin*, is due for publication soon.

WENDY PERRIAM

Coupling

Flamingo
An Imprint of HarperCollins*Publishers*

Flamingo
An Imprint of HarperCollins*Publishers*
77–85 Fulham Palace Road,
Hammersmith, London W6 8JB

Published by Flamingo 1997
9 8 7 6 5 4 3 2

First published in Great Britain by
Flamingo an Imprint of HarperCollins*Publishers* 1996

Author photograph by Jane Bown

Grateful acknowledgement is made to J M Dent
for lines from 'Fern Hill' in *The Poems* by Dylan Thomas

ISBN 0 00 649870 1

Set in Baskerville

Printed and bound in Great Britain by
Caledonian International Book Manufacturing Ltd, Glasgow

For Patricia Parkin,
dear friend and valued editor

(Sir Walter Raleigh said it better)

I

1

'Right, this is it!' the tractor-driver shouted as he swung left off the road, then phut-phutted laboriously through the elaborate wrought-iron gates. A heraldic crest soared overhead and proud stone lions reared on either side. 'I'll take you up to the house, shall I? It's still a fair old haul, by the looks of it.'

'No, I think I'd better . . .' Beattie's words were shredded by the wind. She abandoned all attempts to speak and clung grimly to the side of the trailer as it bumped and rattled up the drive. Her other hand clutched her makeshift hood – an old fertilizer bag the man had offered her as protection against the elements. The rain was drumming down as relentlessly as ever, drenching her best clothes; her once-blue skirt now darkening into black.

A sudden hooting made her jump. A chauffeur-driven Mercedes, immaculately white, had nosed up behind them and was trying to overtake. She ducked down out of sight – too late. The passengers had spotted her and were bound to gossip about the dishevelled girl they'd seen, delivered at the Grange by trailer like a bale of sodden straw.

Once the car had passed, she raised her head and peered out at the formal landscaped gardens sweeping down to an ornamental lake, complete with statuary and fountain. Ashley Grange was *grand* – which made it all the more ridiculous to turn up draped in plastic sacking with a weatherbeaten yokel as her chauffeur. She kept wanting to laugh – or cry.

The tractor negotiated the final bend and spluttered to a halt outside the house. It was every bit as imposing as the grounds: row upon row of windows, a green-domed roof, and an entrance flanked by fluted marble columns. A second set of supercilious stone lions stood rampant at the bottom of the steps and another pair guarded the front door – lean and sinewy beasts, looking as ravenous as she was, as if about to devour the heraldic shields they held. Perhaps they'd come as a job lot, she thought – a whole pride of lions going cheap. Nothing else was cheap, least of all the cars, parked in snooty rows outside the house: Rolls-Royces and Range Rovers, a vintage Jaguar and several long, low, restless sports cars chafing at the bit.

The man clambered down to help her out of the trailer. 'How the other half live, eh?' he muttered, with an attempt at a smile.

She leaned on him and jumped, landing with a thud, feeling the hardness of the gravel through her flimsy white suede shoes. She was dressed for this morning's sunshine, not the Noah's Flood which had erupted after lunch.

The man heaved her suitcase down for her, shaking the rain from what little hair he had. 'Want a hand with this inside?'

'No, honestly, I'm fine now.' She wasn't a snob – far from it – but she was already very late, and the last thing she wanted was to walk into this mansion accompanied by a tattooed and balding chaperone in streaming oilskins and mud-caked rubber boots. She was being observed as it was. A scarlet Lotus had pulled up alongside and its two female occupants (impeccably turned out – and *dry*) were staring at the tractor in astonishment. Beattie hunched over her bag, unearthed her purse and pushed a five-pound note into the tractor-driver's hand. 'Thanks – you saved my life!'

Before he could respond, she was running towards the entrance and up the marble steps. As she reached the top, she heard the tractor revving up to leave, and for a moment she was tempted to dash after it.

No *way*, she told herself. Don't be so pathetic. Get in there and go for it!

Decisively she walked inside; cold greyness giving place to bright lights and near-tropical heat.

She found herself in an elegant reception hall with floor-length velvet curtains and a marble fireplace surmounted by a flamboyant antique mirror. A bevy of gilt cherubs beckoned from its frame. She took a step towards them, caught sight of her reflection and quickly looked away. Her suit was clinging wetly to her body, and her expensive hair-do had been reduced to dripping rats' tails. Selfconsciously she wiped her feet, aware of a group of women lounging on a sofa, talking with that loud assertive confidence born of wealth and breeding. And mounted on the wall behind them was a display of large signed photographs: celebrities who had stayed at Ashley Grange. Perhaps you *had* to be rich and famous to be admitted here at all.

She edged towards the reception desk. 'Beattie Bancroft,' she mumbled, aware that the name sounded bogus – which it was. 'I . . . I'm sorry I'm so late. My car broke down, miles from anywhere, and I couldn't find a phone-box. Is there a garage I can contact?'

'Don't worry, madam. We'll take care of that. If you could just tell me where you left the car and let me have the keys . . .'

Beattie suppressed a grin. She couldn't quite imagine her battered, fourth-hand 2CV, with its dented bumpers and rusting bodywork, sitting intrepid amidst the pedigree cars outside. Still, she had no wish to leave the poor thing stranded in some lonely country lane all night. She handed over the keys, then filled in the registration form.

'Thank you, Miss Bancroft. You're in the Bluebell Room – just off the Grand Staircase. The porter will show you up. I'm afraid you've missed your consultation, but we can slot that in tomorrow.'

'Consultation?'

'With Matron.'

Beattie pushed a strand of wet hair out of her eyes. Had she come to the wrong place – a boarding school or hospital?

'We like our guests to have a brief medical check-up on arrival, to monitor their blood pressure and so on, before we schedule any treatments. And talking of treatments, I see you were booked to have a massage at five, with Julie, but I'm afraid you've missed that too. All the staff will have left by now.'

'Oh bloody hell! I could really use . . .' Beattie broke off in embarrassment. Bad language seemed a crime in these surroundings. Two haughty-looking women were standing just behind her and must have overheard. Max might have done better to have given her a subscription to the RAC, rather than a weekend at an exclusive health farm.

'I'll see what I can do for you, Miss Bancroft.' The receptionist glanced up from her appointments book with a lacquered smile which failed to reach her eyes. 'If you'd like to go to your room and change, I'll phone the treatment suite to see if anyone's still there. You might just be lucky, you never know.'

'Thanks, that's great. I really would appreciate it.'

5

She followed the porter – and her damp-stained case – along a stretch of corridor and up a curving staircase. Everyone she passed seemed to be female and in pairs. She wished *she* had come with someone, but none of her friends could have afforded the inflated prices, and Max himself would never fit in here. Max was to blame for her language: *he* swore all the time and she had picked up the habit almost without noticing. She didn't actually disapprove of swearing (it was only words, after all – a combination of syllables which meant nothing very much), but it annoyed her that he should influence her so strongly. He had also paid for her new slinky suit, which she now realized was out of place. The Ashley Grange dress-code was studiously casual: designer tracksuits; no make-up beyond a natural healthy glow.

The porter stopped to unlock a panelled door and ushered her inside. She wondered if she should tip him, and how much. Health farms were probably a law unto themselves. She slipped a pound coin into his hand, quickly scrabbling for a second coin when his inscrutable expression failed to thaw into a smile.

Once he'd gone, she stood gazing at the room: bluebells every-where – and *frills*. The frilled bluebell-patterned bedspread matched the ruffled bluebell curtains, and there were more bluebells on the wallpaper and more frills on the lampshades (which were mercifully plain blue). The room was so large it was a fair trek to the window, which looked out over miles of mist-swathed countryside – majestic, even in the rain. What an ungrateful bitch she was, turning her nose up at the bluebells, when this was the most luxurious place she'd ever *been* in – a world away from her London flat, where nothing matched at all and which overlooked a row of dreary garages. Perhaps she should ring down to reception and order an improvement in the weather. It was only the first week of September, and only ten to six, but instead of golden lushness it was as murky as a wet November night.

She rubbed the misty windowpane and watched the wind slap the shivering poplars, freckled with their first brown leaves. She had seen Christmas cards already in a shop in Westbourne Grove. Ninety-six shopping days to Christmas. No, she mustn't think of Christmas – it posed too many problems, such as how to put the 'happy' in it, where to spend it, and who with.

She walked briskly back to the bed and unlocked her case. This was meant to be a *break*, for heaven's sake, and anyway it was pointless worrying about Christmas four months in advance. Far better to unpack and change her clothes.

Her stomach rumbled suddenly as she kicked off her wet shoes. She should have brought emergency supplies: a litre of Bacardi, a crate of Crunchie bars. She hunted through her handbag, but found only a lone toffee, which she unwrapped guiltily. Sweets were bound to be forbidden at a health farm – as were alcohol and smoking, according to the brochure. What if there were hidden video cameras, spying on her right now? Well, one Creamline toffee was hardly an indictable offence.

She drifted into the bathroom, wincing at the array of mirrors. No cherubs here to recoil from her; just that unflattering reflection staring back again. Her hair still looked unspeakable and she'd clearly overdone the henna. It might be an idea to have a shower – wash off some of that vulgar red; wash off the last two hours.

She was just unzipping her wet skirt when the phone rang. Max! He said he'd ring at six. She ran to pick up the receiver, her skirt sliding to her ankles. 'Darling,' she said, speaking indistinctly through the toffee. 'This place is quite amazing! I've even got . . . Oh, sorry. I thought . . .' She dislodged the toffee from her teeth, hastily spitting it into her hand. 'Gosh, thanks. Where do I go? And – oh – what am I supposed to wear?'

A robe? She hoped her towelling dressing-gown fitted the description. Slippers she'd forgotten, so it would have to be bare feet.

Ask for Steve? A *man*? She hadn't thought in terms of male masseurs. In fact, she had never had a massage in her life, but had assumed it would be given by one of that glamorous breed of females who staffed most beauty parlours – all hair and bones and eyelashes. The idea of Steve was somehow disconcerting, as if he were appraising her already, judging her too fat, too naff.

'I thought you said you'd booked me with . . . er, Judy?'

'*Julie.* Yes, but I'm afraid she left at half past five. Don't worry, Steve's absolutely first rate – one of our best masseurs. You'll be in very good hands, I assure you.'

'Okay,' she said nervously, reaching for her 'robe' and sucking the last sinful trace of toffee off her teeth. 'I'll be right down.'

7

2

'*Relax*!' urged Steve. 'You're incredibly tense.'

'Sorry,' Beattie murmured, her face pressed into the couch. Though why should she apologize for a stiff back and knotted shoulders? Anyway it was impossible to relax when she kept worrying that her body might smell sweaty. She should have had that shower.

'Just let go. That's better. If you tense your muscles, it's more difficult for me to work.'

She shifted on the couch. Odd to think of it as work. Steve might be working – battling with her recalcitrant muscles – but *she* just had to lie there beneath thick white fluffy towels. The room was frilled again and blue again (though delphiniums this time, not bluebells) and partitioned into cubicles, each lit with blue-shaded lamps. All the other cubicles were empty; the only sound Steve's soothing voice and some schmaltzy music playing in the background.

'How long are you here for, Miss Bancroft?' He accompanied the question with a slow sweeping movement down her spine.

'Just the weekend.'

'And have you been to Ashley Grange before?'

'No. Never.' It sounded rather abrupt. He was only trying to be friendly, after all. 'Actually, it was a birthday present,' she added, her voice muffled by the couch. She needn't say *which* birthday. She dreaded being thirty – the official end of youth, that terrifying watershed dividing the successes from the failures. If you hadn't made it by thirty, you probably never would. She wondered how old Steve was. It was difficult to tell. His formal manner and starched white uniform were at odds with his boyish figure and exuberant fair hair.

'Aha!' he laughed. 'A present from your boyfriend, I bet.'

How on earth had he guessed? Why not from her mother? Except

8

her mother was dead, and would have given her bath salts, or a box of 'useful' notepaper, not a weekend of indulgence.

'Sort of,' she hedged. Max was far too old to be called anybody's boyfriend. He said he was forty-nine, but she suspected he'd been forty-nine for a couple of years at least. He seemed touchy about his age, so she didn't like to question him too closely, especially as she'd only known him three months.

'Is that painful?' Steve was asking, as he pressed a knobbly bone in her spine.

'Ouch! Yes.'

'I'm not surprised. You've tensed again. Do try to relax.'

'Look,' she said irritably, 'it's not *easy* to relax. I've had a hell of a day. I got hopelessly lost on the way here and landed up in the back of beyond. Then my car broke down and . . .' Suddenly she was pouring out the whole demoralizing saga.

'God! It sounds horrendous.' His hands had moved to the back of her neck, and were slicking deftly out across her shoulders. 'Never mind – now you're here, you can take it easy. This is the perfect place to unwind.'

Obediently she let her body sink into the couch; tried to stop herself from thinking altogether and just enjoy the first massage of her life. She closed her eyes and surrendered to the sensations: the fragrant smell of massage oil, the soft blue glow of light, Steve's firm, confident touch. She wished he wouldn't talk so much – it was an effort to keep having to reply – but masseurs were presumably trained, like hairdressers, to avoid silence at all costs.

'Have you come far, Miss Bancroft?'

'No, only from London. Just off Westbourne Grove. I've always lived in London – well, except for my first sixteen years, which I spent in dreary old Croydon. Mind you, I suppose even that's considered part of London now.'

'Croydon? Really? That's where my parents live.'

'Gosh, I'm sorry – I hope I didn't sound rude. Which part?'

'Highfield Road.'

'Oh, yes, I know it. *We* weren't quite so grand.' She could see the house quite clearly in her mind: a poky terraced house which seemed always to be dark and cold, even in the summer. And somehow always empty – her father away, her mother ill upstairs. As a child, she had invented her companions; transforming the bad-tempered kitchen boiler into a rumbustious grandfather, spitting words and flames, and then cancelling him with a candy-floss-haired grandma who made her currant buns. Weird how she could remember tiny details – her mother's china chamber pot with its yellow crusted scum inside; the purple knitted tea-cosy coddling the brown teapot; the way the bathroom door squealed, as if it were constantly in pain.

'Right, Miss Bancroft, if you'd like to turn over . . .'

She opened her eyes, annoyed with herself for wasting time in Croydon, breathing in boiler fumes instead of scented oils. Steve held the towels discreetly over her while she rolled over onto her back. All along he'd been meticulous about covering the parts of her body he wasn't actually working on. None the less, it was rather an unsettling experience to be lying completely naked, alone with a strange man in a remote wing of an unfamiliar house. The massage must be halfway through, yet still she hadn't managed to let go. She took in a deep breath, exhaling with a long yawning sigh.

'Tired?' Steve asked sympathetically.

'Yeah, I must admit I am. I've been working late all week. *And* last weekend. And I got up at the crack of dawn this morning, so I could leave the office early.' Dammit – she was here to forget the pressures. There were two delicious days ahead without a deadline in sight. She wrapped the thought around her like a luxurious goose-down duvet and at last felt her body relax. It was more comfortable in any case lying on her back. Her face was no longer squashed against the couch, and the crick in her neck had gone. She hardly even cared now about not having had a shower, but simply lay contentedly, savouring the sense of peace, the cosseting. Steve was massaging her foot, gently kneading the ankle, devoting time and trouble to each toe. Bones she didn't know she had were being discovered and defined; her whole body stirred by his expert touch. *Max* never touched her like this – he was too concerned with his own pleasure – but Steve was a professional. He was also damned attractive, in a different league from Max; his body lean and muscly, and conspicuously defined by his closely-fitting jacket and white trousers.

'And what work is it you do, Miss Bancroft?'

'Look, do call me Beattie. It makes me feel so . . . *ancient* when people use my surname.' She blushed, wondering if she had sounded over-familiar, but it was hard to keep up the formalities now she was beginning to see him not just as a masseur but as a *man*. She noticed the fair hairs glinting on the backs of his hands, and tiny drops of perspiration beading his top lip, which she found peculiarly exciting.

Once, she caught his eye, and looked away, embarrassed. His eyes were slatey-blue, with a serious expression, as if he regarded his work as some solemn sort of ritual.

He completed the right foot and folded back the towel to start on her leg – firm kneading movements up and down the calf. His hands moved higher still, gliding up the inside of her thigh. She felt her nipples stiffen; her legs ease surreptitiously apart. God! She mustn't react, or it would show on her face. Massage had nothing to do with sex (well, in Soho strip-joints, maybe, but not in a genteel place like this). Besides, it was disloyal to Max, who was paying for this treatment; paying for the entire weekend. Determinedly she switched her mind to mundane things – stalled engines, rainswept roads – but Steve's hands were only inches from her groin and the tension was electrifying. She let out an involuntary sound: a sort of muffled gasp of pleasure, which she tried to conceal with a laugh. 'I . . . I'm feeling better already, Steve.'

'I'm glad to hear it, Beattie. But do relax. I can feel your muscles tightening again.'

How *could* she relax? She was caught in an impasse, simmering between indulgence and frustration, tension and release; her mind saying one thing, her body another. And anyway she wasn't used to lying back, just accepting and enjoying. Her normal role – with Max, at least – was to give pleasure, not to take it. Yet those ingenious fingers on the inside of her thigh were weakening her resistance. And so was the whole atmosphere: the soporific heat and lulling music, the warm caress of the towels. She wished her face was covered. Surely Steve could see the effect he was having? Her eyes had closed and her neck curved languorously back, as if she were abandoning all control.

She willed him never to stop, to inch his sensuous fingertips higher and higher up her thigh, until they slipped beneath the towel. In her mind it was happening – her legs edging further apart, her whole body arching up, as she whispered, 'Yes, go *on*, Steve.'

Then suddenly she realized that he was no longer working on her legs at all. He had moved from the foot of the couch and was now standing by her head. She opened her eyes, to find him looking at her. She didn't glance away this time; instead held his gaze for what seemed dangerously long. It was he who broke the contact, as he transferred his hands to her shoulders and began smoothing out the stiffness there.

11

'You're very knotted up, Beattie. I hope this isn't hurting.'

'Yes, it is a bit.' She smiled at him – a suggestive smile. 'I prefer the . . . gentler stuff.'

He gave one last sweeping movement along her shoulders, then placed his hands on her collarbone, just above her breasts, pressing firmly against the skin. It felt almost more tantalizing than if he'd touched the breasts themselves. Yet his expression was still solemn and intent, and the towel still irreproachably in place (though she longed to push it off, to seize his hands and force them against her nipples). The same steady pressure continued – provocative, exquisite. Was this a standard part of the massage, or was he arousing her deliberately?

'Steve,' she whispered. 'You're making me feel . . . wonderful.'

He appeared not to have heard. She could see the tip of his tongue just showing between his teeth – he was obviously absorbed in what he was doing; totally preoccupied. More seconds passed, until she was exploding with the tension, then finally, unbearably, he removed his hands and stood upright, with a quick glance at his watch.

'I'm afraid we have to finish now, but your back and shoulders need a lot more work. I haven't managed to break down all those bad adhesions.' He traced a line with his finger from one shoulder to the other, to indicate the problem. 'But I could fit you in later on this evening, for' – he paused – 'a more intensive treatment.'

'I . . . intensive?'

'Yes.'

Was she imagining the come-on? His voice was as professional as ever, but that pause had undermined it; a tiny lethal bombshell still reverberating in her mind.

'I think you'd find it helpful, Beattie. You see, we can only do the basics here, but I've got these special oils in my room . . .'

'No, really, Steve, I . . .'

'You actually *need* a longer treatment. I could tell as soon as I started.'

The blood rushed to her cheeks. 'Look, you mustn't think . . .'

'And especially after that frightful journey. Breakdowns are so stressful, aren't they? And if you say you've been overworking, on top of everything else, well you see, all that chronic tension causes acid wastes to build up in the muscles, and you're left with shortened fibres . . .'

She felt thoroughly confused. He was giving out contradictory

12

messages: part lecher, part masseur. Perhaps she *did* need extra treatment. Yet . . .

'So I'll see you tonight, then, Beattie?' His voice was soft, persuasive.

'*No*. Well, yes . . . I . . . I'm not sure.'

'Shall we say nine o'clock?'

She hesitated a moment longer, not daring to meet his eyes, then nodded guiltily.

'You're doing the right thing,' he murmured. 'With a bit more work, we can get rid of most of that tension. And it'll be more relaxing in my room. It's just across the courtyard in the stable block. Go out of the main door, turn immediately left, and you'll see a . . .'

Suddenly the phone shrilled, cutting off his words. Beattie clutched the towels in panic, pulling them right up to her chin. Someone must have heard – *Matron*, or . . .

Steve seemed unperturbed. 'Excuse me,' he said coolly, picking up the receiver. 'Yes, Miss Bancroft's just about to leave. I'm running a little late . . . Oh, I see . . . Yes, of course. I'll tell her. Thanks, Lorraine.'

Beattie lay rigid beneath the towels. They must be going to kick her out. For agreeing to a private session with one of their masseurs. Of *course* he'd intended more than just a massage. And she'd agreed with barely a second's hesitation; practically begged for it, for Christ's sake. Word would get around – it was bound to – once Steve had sniggered with his colleagues about the randy girl who could hardly keep her hands off him. The whole of Ashley Grange would know of her disgrace by the time she'd been banished into the night.

Steve turned to her again. 'Someone's been trying to get you on the phone, Beattie. A Mr Max Gillespie. He's rung three times, but says he can't . . .'

She sprang up from the couch, scattering the towels. 'I . . . I'll phone him now. Thank you, Steve – for everything.'

'Beattie, wait!' he called. 'What about our appointment?'

Without replying she grabbed her dressing-gown, fled to the door and went pounding up the stairs, back to the chaste safety of her room.

3

Beattie sat up in alarm, the sheets tangled around her legs. She had been trapped in a tiny car all night, crawling along a deserted country road with no street-lamps, no way out; every exit blocked by high black walls. She freed herself from the bedclothes and stumbled to the bathroom. She had deliberately left the light on there, so that she wouldn't wake up in darkness. It was shameful being afraid of the dark – acceptable at three, maybe, but certainly not at thirty.

She switched on all the other lights and inspected herself in the mirror. Her cheeks looked hectically flushed, as if she really had spent the night with Steve. The whole massage seemed distasteful now, and Steve's come-on was undoubtedly her fault. She had encouraged him quite shamelessly, gazing into his eyes like that and arching up her body under his hands. Any normal, decent woman would never have been so cheap. But she didn't *feel* like a normal woman; she wanted things too violently: food, sex, money, men. It was ironic really, when she was constantly on a diet, usually over-drawn, and most of her relationships with men had ended in disaster.

She returned to the bedroom and stood by the window, peering out at the sky. The clouds were still moving restlessly, half-shrouding the puny moon. The intense silence made it seem that no one else existed in the world, though she knew that scores of other people were sleeping in the house. She wondered if Max was asleep, or lying thinking of her, as he said he sometimes did. It had been callous to compare his body with Steve's – worse than that, she'd been willing to betray him, with barely a second thought.

She let the curtain fall. The room felt far too big for her, and *cold*. She ran her hand across the radiator, now chilly to the touch. It had been boiling hot last night when she'd sat here on the window-seat, sweating with sheer nerves as she watched the hands of her alarm clock creep round to eight, then nine. There had been no call from Steve, thank God, but she was so scared of running into him, she had missed dinner altogether. And anyway, she hadn't found the courage to venture alone into that formidable-looking dining room, with its chandeliers, its dark oak-panelled walls.

The woman on reception had offered to send a tray up to her room, but she'd said she wasn't hungry. Not hungry! She was famished. Breakfast had been half a slice of toast, and there hadn't been time for lunch before she left. It suddenly occurred to her that, if other guests had had supper in their rooms, there might be a few left-overs outside – a bread roll or a piece of cheese discarded on a tray. She buttoned up her dressing-gown and crept out to investigate.

Two long corridors later she had salvaged only a cream cracker, a tomato slice and a wilting sprig of parsley. She continued along the passage and down a flight of stairs, searching for the kitchen, where she might be able to help herself to something more substantial. She only hoped she wasn't caught. Her list of offences was growing by the minute: useless car mechanic, easy lay, and now common thief. In fact, she *did* feel like a burglar as she tiptoed through the shadowy house, surveying all the treasures on display: gilt-framed portraits, alabaster vases, an antique clock with two buxom shepherdesses painted on the dial. Yet, despite its opulence, the house seemed hollow at the core, empty of all heart.

She stopped to look at a picture of a Victorian family group: the mother in a crinoline, surrounded by four children; her young and handsome husband leaning over protectively to fondle a small head. She stared into the mother's smug blue eyes. Mrs Virtuous Mother-of-Four would never have agreed to a shag with her masseur.

She crept on through the Tapestry Hall, with its Persian rugs and Bechstein grand. No hope of sustenance there. The rooms were helpfully labelled, but when at last she found the kitchen, it was locked. She stood with her hand on the doorknob, struck by a sudden longing to go home. She was only forty miles from London, and in familiar Sussex countryside, yet she felt as if she'd been deposited in some far-off foreign land, deprived of food and human contact. The shepherdess clock had said twenty-five to three: another five hours to breakfast. The thought of returning to her room and sitting till dawn amidst the bluebells held no appeal whatever. She turned another corner, passing a door marked 'Art Room', then doubled back and pushed it open. She could paint her *own* flowers: poison ivy, thistles.

'Hello.' The voice was soft and well-modulated.

Beattie jumped, surprised to find the lights on and someone else awake. A middle-aged woman, small and rather delicate-looking, was sitting in the corner, modelling clay. Although her accent was spot-on for Ashley Grange, her clothes most definitely weren't. She was wearing a shabby candlewick dressing-gown over blue-striped men's pyjamas, and her salt-and-pepper hair was pulled back into a haphazard sort of ponytail.

'Er, hello,' Beattie mumbled, poised for a quick getaway. The woman sounded welcoming enough, but she could turn out to be a bore. The conversations she had overheard so far seemed to centre on people's ailments. She didn't fancy listening to a long litany of symptoms, or the full-frontal details of some gruesome operation.

'Can't you sleep?' the woman asked.

'No,' said Beattie tersely. If she could sleep, she'd be in bed.

'Why don't you have a go at making something? I find messing about with clay is marvellously relaxing.'

Beattie tensed – that was *Steve*'s word. Nothing would be relaxing in her present state of mind.

'Come and sit down.' The woman pulled up a second chair, smiling at her encouragingly.

Beattie could hardly claim a prior engagement at three o'clock in the morning. She walked over with bad grace, refusing the lump of damp brown clay the woman was holding out. It looked repulsive, almost faecal.

'Well, how about a cigarette instead?'

'No thanks. I don't smoke.' One of her few virtues.

'Do you mind if I do?'

'Not at all,' said Beattie. Secretly she rather admired smokers. It took courage in this day and age to defy the po-faced anti-smoking brigade. And smoking at a health farm was even more heroic; an audacious flouting of the rules. 'What's your name?' she asked, feeling decidedly less hostile.

'Elizabeth.'

'That's my name too.'

'Well, nice to meet you, Elizabeth.'

Beattie watched her light a cigarette and exhale a coil of smoke. 'No, I'm Beattie now. In fact I've never been Elizabeth. I was christened that officially, but my mother called me Betty and my father called me George.'

'George? Why?'

Beattie shrugged off the painful memory. 'Oh, just a pet name,' she said vaguely. 'Then, when I left school, I did a bit of modelling and I wanted a new name. Betty Cook sounded rather frumpy, so I changed the Betty to Beattie and the Cook to Bancroft. So now I'm Beattie Bancroft, which has more of a ring about it. The only problem is, it doesn't really *feel* like me. I suppose I've had too many names. Even when I was little, I used to call myself exotic things like Natasha or Camille.'

'So what d'you *like* to be called?'

'Oh, Beattie. I can't go back to Betty or Elizabeth – they're even less like me.'

'And George?'

Beattie shook her head. 'What are you making?' she asked, determined to leave George dead and buried.

'Oh dear, can't you *tell*? It must be pretty hopeless then! It's meant to be a cat.'

'Yeah, I can see its tail now, and isn't that a paw curved round its head?'

'Mm. I'm afraid I haven't got the knack yet, but one good thing about clay is that if you don't like what you've done, you can always squash it down and start again. Why don't you have a try? You'll find it's very soothing.'

'It's soothing just to watch. You finish your cat and I'll admire.'

'I'd rather finish my cigarette.'

'Are you allowed to smoke in here?'

'I doubt it. It's forbidden everywhere else, even in your room. They do allow it in the cellar bar, but there's never anyone down there, so you feel like a pariah.'

'Bar?' said Beattie hopefully. 'You mean they actually serve drinks?'

'Not any longer, I'm afraid. They used to have a party every Saturday night, but the guests got so wild and rowdy, they had to put a stop to it. Apparently the whole cellar used to shake!'

Beattie laughed. Instead of arthritis and colostomies, she was being regaled with booze and rave-ups. And yet Elizabeth *did* seem frail; a small-boned type, as fragile as papier-mâché, easily crushed by a careless hand. Her skin was fair and delicate and hadn't worn too well; yet her eyes were a deep striking blue (and her most attractive

17

feature). The untidy hair was silky-fine, and that teenage ponytail, so out of keeping with her dreary mummish night-clothes, did at least suit her girlish build. Beattie felt clumsy in comparison – constructed on too large a scale, with thick assertive hair, eyes defiantly dark, and a voice which couldn't rival Elizabeth's plummy tones.

'You sound as if you're a regular here,' she said, trying to polish up her vowels.

'No, I've only been once before. How about you?'

'I'm a new girl. I arrived last night, and too late for anything.' Except to be propositioned by a masseur, she added sotto voce. Impulsively she leaned across and helped herself to a piece of clay. She'd make an effigy of Steve, then do as Elizabeth had said and squash him down again into an anonymous brown lump.

Elizabeth put her cigarette on the old tin plate she was using as an ashtray, and continued shaping her cat. 'What are you going to make?' she asked.

'I . . . I'm not sure.' Beattie mangled the clay aggressively, wondering where to start – with Steve's dangerous hands, maybe. No, hands would be too difficult, and anyway was the wretched man really worth the effort? She kicked him from her mind and concentrated instead on the cool, firm texture of the clay. Elizabeth was right – it *was* surprisingly soothing, once she'd overcome her venomous feelings. Even its messiness was satisfying: the way it slurped between her fingers, oozed beneath her nails. She recalled the Victorian family portrait and decided to make her *own* family, beginning with her father. His head came out like a pumpkin, and when she tried to do his nose, she found she couldn't quite remember what it looked like. It had been so long since she'd seen him, his features had become fuzzy in her mind. In any case, it was probably over-ambitious to try to do people at all, especially as her family offered very little scope – no brothers or sisters, no cats or dogs, not even a headstone on her mother's grave.

She sat pummelling the pumpkin head, cupping her hands around its gratifying weight and wishing it was a big hot buttered bun: the sort her imaginary grandma used to make. Perhaps she could make a bun herself – that should be easy enough. She re-formed the embryo nose into a currant, then added a few more.

'What's that?'

'A currant bun.'

Elizabeth laughed. 'You must be hungry!'

Beattie nodded, suddenly terrified she might cry. Hungry was such an empty word – hollow and deprived.

'I've got some biscuits in my room. Or we could always raid the kitchen.'

'I've already tried. It's locked.'

'No, there's a smaller kitchen for the staff. It's usually left open for the night porter.'

'Won't he see us, though?'

'I doubt it. He's meant to stay in reception to deal with any calls. And anyway, he won't object. He's a mild-mannered sort of chap.'

'Okay. Lead on!'

She followed Elizabeth along the passage and through a baize swing door. Instantly the thick-pile carpet gave way to functional lino, and the ceiling was much lower and less ornate. Elizabeth turned off into a dingy room – frankly little more than a cubbyhole, with plain white walls, a tiny plastic-topped table and two simple wooden chairs. It housed the basic kitchen equipment: a kettle on a gas ring, a compact fridge below it and two shelves above, stocked with cereal packets, biscuits and caddies of tea and coffee.

'There you are,' said Elizabeth. 'A feast!'

'It still feels like we're stealing.' Beattie glanced over her shoulder, as if the night porter might pounce at any moment, handcuffs at the ready.

'When you consider what we're paying, I'm sure they won't begrudge us the odd ginger nut. Or would you prefer a bowl of cornflakes?'

'What I'd really like is something hot. I'll settle for steak and chips.'

'I'm afraid that would take a miracle. The best I can suggest is porridge.'

Beattie made a face.

'Don't you like it?'

'I've never had it.'

'Never had porridge? You're joking!'

'I'm not. It's the kind of thing that mothers make, and my mother wasn't the cooking type.' Beattie knew she was being disloyal. Her mother hadn't cooked because she was ill – endlessly, depressingly ill.

Elizabeth took the packet down and checked its sell-by date. 'It's funny you should associate it with mothers. I remember I used to

19

get a craving for porridge whenever I went into labour. The pains would start and instead of rushing to the hospital I'd reach for the Quaker Oats.'

'How many children have you *got*? You make it sound as if it happened every year.'

'Well for four years it did. I had four daughters in succession.'

A brood of four, like Mrs Virtuous Crinoline's, Beattie thought enviously. And probably a handsome protective husband thrown in as well.

'Shall I make a pot of tea?' Elizabeth asked.

Beattie shrugged. 'If you want.'

'What's wrong?'

'Nothing.'

'You sound a little low.'

'I'm sorry.'

'Can I help at all?'

'Not really, unless you can stop it being Sunday.'

'Why? What's happening on Sunday?'

'I'll be thirty, and I'm dreading it.'

'Oh dear.'

'You're laughing at me.'

'No, I'm not. Every new decade's always rather daunting – well, perhaps not twenty, but certainly all the rest. And even twenty has its perils. I'm reading this biography of Lord Byron, and he said at twenty-three the best of life was over.'

'Well, at least he'd *achieved* something. And so have you – four children.'

'Some people might accuse me of overpopulating the planet.'

'Well *I* wouldn't. I'm not even married.'

'Nor am I, actually,' Elizabeth admitted with a smile.

'What? You mean you're a single parent four times over? God! That must take some guts.'

Elizabeth laughed, but quickly changed the subject. 'Look, let me make that porridge. If *you* don't want it, I do!'

'You're not going into labour again, I hope? I'd make the world's worst midwife.'

'Don't worry, there's absolutely no danger of that!'

Now it was Beattie's turn to laugh. This woman was good company. She also seemed kind-hearted; the type of sympathetic person you could relax with, to use Steve's dreaded word. Beattie watched her measure milk into a saucepan, then spoon in porridge oats. She moved with a sort of grace, as if she were perfectly at home in this apology for a kitchen.

Elizabeth looked up from the pan. 'Actually, I've just had a birthday myself,' she confided. 'I was fifty in August – another of those milestones, like your thirtieth. The strange thing was, though, I didn't really mind. Perhaps getting older is something of a relief. Several of my friends have said the same. You tend not to mind so much what people think. And you *accept* things more. I suppose you realize you can't change them, so you might as well submit with good grace.'

'I can't see *me* doing that,' Beattie said, helping herself to a biscuit from one of the packets on the shelf.

'So you won't even submit to the porridge?'

Beattie grinned. 'Okay.'

'Thank goodness! Otherwise I'd have to eat it all myself and I seem to have made enough for the whole of Ashley Grange.'

Beattie licked her spoon clean and laid it in the empty bowl. 'Are you *sure* I haven't shocked you?'

'Of course not.'

'I didn't really mean to tell you, but I've been in such a state about it, it just . . . came out.'

'That's perfectly all right, Beattie. And from what you say, I don't think there's any need to worry. It sounds as if it was *Steve's* fault.'

'But I told you – I encouraged him.'

'Well, maybe so, but he shouldn't have taken advantage. And anyway, nothing happened, did it?'

'Yes, but it *would* have done, if the phone hadn't rung.'

'You can't be sure of that, Beattie.'

Oh no? she thought, unwilling to admit how often she landed up in bed with men she didn't know from Adam (and then loathed herself for being so cheap). Why did she keep *doing* it? Perhaps to make men like her. Sometimes, sleeping with them seemed the only way.

'D'you know, I . . . I think one of the reasons I dread being thirty is that I still haven't met the right guy – even after all these years. It makes me feel such a failure. I mean, I ought to be madly in love by now, or flashing a huge diamond ring.'

'There's no rush, Beattie dear. You've got plenty of time. One of

21

my most attractive friends didn't get married till she was thirty-nine, and she still had three lovely children.'

'In her forties, you mean?'

'Yes. The last one at forty-six.'

'Oh, well, I suppose that gives me a *few* years!' Beattie laughed, feeling a definite sense of relief. Elizabeth had proved to be a wonderful listener and didn't seem the slightest bit shocked by anything she'd told her. Admittedly she hadn't mentioned Max (*or* her previous bloke, the unspeakable Dominic), but she had said things she'd never revealed to anyone else. 'I'm not sure I even *want* children,' she added. 'I'm so mixed up, I don't know what I want.'

'Well, at least you've given the subject some thought, and that's extremely valuable in itself – the beginning of wisdom, as they say.'

Beattie took another biscuit and sat crumbling it distractedly. 'God! I'm anything but wise. I always seem to mess things up. Take this evening, for example. Instead of enjoying a fancy dinner and being waited on hand and foot, I stayed huddled in my room like a prisoner, jumping at the slightest sound, in case it was Steve on the prowl.'

'But that's quite understandable. And anyway this place *is* rather daunting, especially when you first arrive. I felt much the same last year. But after a day or two you realize it's much less grand than it seems.'

'But I haven't *got* a day or two,' Beattie protested wryly. 'I'm leaving Sunday lunchtime.'

'Well, we'll have to speed the process up and help you to enjoy it straight away. How about more porridge, for a start?'

'Okay. Why not? I'm still hungry, would you believe.'

'No wonder, if you missed dinner.' Elizabeth got up and peered into the saucepan. 'I'd better reheat it. It's gone all cold and gluey.'

Beattie rocked back on her rickety chair and surveyed the shabby kitchen. 'This place is a bit of a come-down after my huge great swanky bedroom. It's practically the size of Wembley Stadium and covered in bluebells – millions of the things.'

Elizabeth laughed. 'Oh really? I'm in the Daffodil Room, and I must admit they have gone overboard. I wouldn't say *millions* of daffodils, but thousands certainly. And it does seem a bit unseasonable. I keep feeling it should be spring – outside as well as in.'

Beattie poured more tea for them both, showering sugar into hers.

'Elizabeth, I know you say it isn't grand here, but to me it's almost as posh as Buckingham Palace.'

'Well, it's true, the house is grand, but the guests are very friendly.'

'That's not the impression *I* get. In fact, I'm terrified of going into breakfast and having to face them all.'

Elizabeth ladled porridge into Beattie's bowl, then left the saucepan to soak. 'Would you like me to come and fetch you? Then we could go down together and sit at the same table.'

'Yes please – that would be great. And if Steve shows up I'll leave *you* to sort him out.'

'Thank you kindly! But don't worry, we're quite safe. The staff never set foot in the dining-room. And anyway, you're perfectly entitled to change your masseur, you know. You can ask for anyone you like. I have rather a sweet girl called Simone. Why not book with her, or one of the other girls, then you won't need to see Steve again. And he'll also get the message that you don't actually *want* to see him.'

'Oh, Elizabeth, you're brilliant! You seem to be solving *every*thing. I feel so much better – you can't imagine.'

'Good. I'm glad. Now don't let your porridge get cold.'

Beattie picked up her spoon. 'I think I'll add a dollop of chocolate-spread this time.'

'Chocolate-spread on porridge? It'll go the most revolting colour.'

'No worse than that clay of yours. Hey, Elizabeth, when we've finished our midnight feast, can we go back to the Art Room and do some more modelling? Thanks to you, I feel positively inspired – ready to make a masterpiece!'

4

Beattie lay with her eyes closed in the warm white dripping fug, rivulets of perspiration trickling slowly down her body. Matron had recommended the Steam Room for the relief of catarrh and chesty coughs, and – again – as an aid to relaxation. It was certainly wonderfully relaxing, lying naked on a padded wooden bench, draped in a soft towel and dozing in the sultry heat. Clouds of steam billowed languidly across the room, reducing everything to a haze. She breathed in the scent of pine, imagining herself in some fantastic tropical rain forest, where no one bothered with clothes, or had to do boring jobs, and luscious fruits dropped from the trees whenever you were hungry.

She had already gorged herself on tropical fruits. Breakfast this morning had been nothing like the ordeal she'd feared. Instead of regulation muesli served with low-fat milk, there had been guavas and lychees, mangoes and papaya, as well as the more usual fruits – all laid out on a central buffet table. And huge glass bowls of fromage frais and raspberries, marbled pink and white, and every type of yogurt, and home-made rolls, served crusty hot. (Breakfast at home was usually coffee on the run.) She and Elizabeth had disgraced themselves by eating more than anyone else, and had also talked non-stop. Well, *she* had talked and Elizabeth had listened. Elizabeth was the perfect listener, and seemed to be genuinely interested in everything she said; even the tedious stuff about her childhood and her family. She had felt *safe* in that imperious panelled dining-room with Elizabeth beside her; her new friend a sort of buffer against haughty waiters or pretentious fellow guests.

She turned over on her tummy, enjoying the sensation of her body gently melting in the cocoon of swampy warmth. Perhaps she'd stay at Ashley Grange for ever; refuse to go home tomorrow after all, but relish a lifetime's pampering instead.

Suddenly the door opened and two shadowy figures made their way through the fug. Beattie almost resented the intrusion – this was her private domain. It was even more annoying when they sat down somewhere opposite and began discussing their weight; a subject she wasn't keen to think about.

'I've only lost two pounds all week, so Matron's put me on a fast.'

'You poor thing! How long for?'

'Three days.'

Beattie made a mental note to avoid Matron from now on – *she* was looking forward to lunch, and the formal four-course dinner.

'Listen, Katy, you know that MP's wife . . .'

Beattie strained her ears. The voice had dwindled to a whisper, just loud enough to arouse her curiosity but not to satisfy it.

Protracted murmurings followed, then the second woman spoke in a slightly louder voice. 'Julian's just as bad though. Apparently he brought his *mistress* here last year, and then . . .'

Beattie grinned to herself. Hearing snippets about other people's failings made her feel less guilty about her own. Actually, she had almost stopped worrying about Steve. He hadn't been in evidence this morning, and she'd enjoyed a marvellously uneventful massage with Simone.

She heard no more about Julian's transgressions. They had moved on now to someone else.

'D'you know, that Arab chap's complained again about his . . .'

About what? she wondered, recalling the young Arab who had sat alone at breakfast, refusing all the food on offer and drinking a small glass of some sludgy grey concoction.

There was more whispering, even giggling, then the louder voice continued: '. . . and have you met that woman Elizabeth Hargreaves – small and rather dowdy-looking?'

Beattie was instantly alert. *Her* Elizabeth! She bridled at the unflattering description. Admittedly, that's what *she* had thought of Elizabeth, before they'd spent half the night talking. But now she saw her differently: small, maybe, but special.

'She's a psychiatrist, you know.'

Beattie's hand tightened on the bench. She must have misheard. Elizabeth – a *shrink?*

'Yes, she's quite well known – at least her husband is. Or ex-husband, I should say. She used to be married to . . .'

Beattie hardly dared breathe, in her determination to catch what they were saying. She had missed the husband's name, but . . .

'Yes, he got the CBE or something and then went off with an actress half his age. God, Katy – I'm practically melting! I can't take any more of this. I think we're only meant to stay in here ten minutes.'

'Okay, let's cool off in the shower.'

Beattie lay rigid on the bench, furious that they should go at such a crucial juncture. But what little she had heard was enough to leave her burning with embarrassment. So Elizabeth was divorced – not the courageous single mother she had joked about so flippantly. In fact, now she thought about it, *every*thing she had said last night must have seemed crass and out of place. If she'd been less absorbed in her own troubles, she might have stopped to wonder why Elizabeth couldn't sleep. It had never crossed her mind that the poor woman might be miserable as well. But why hadn't she *said*? She had given nothing away except that she had four daughters and two cats, and that she didn't mind getting older.

She covered her face with the towel, wishing she could hide her shame as easily. Elizabeth would have sussed out all the weaknesses in her story. They weren't lies exactly – only exaggerations – but a psychiatrist would probably spot them a mile off. She didn't trust psychiatrists. Max's son had been to one and apparently it had really screwed him up. She would never have confided in Elizabeth if she'd known that every word she said would be analysed, dissected.

She groped her way to the door with a growing sense of anger added to the shame. Elizabeth had *deceived* her. In spite of her kindness last night and her friendliness this morning, she had actually concealed everything that mattered. In reality she was someone grand and snooty – not just a psychiatrist, but the ex-wife of some celebrity or other.

She stumbled into the shower, grimacing at the shock of ice-cold water. Without bothering to dry herself, she threw on her towelling dressing-gown and set off to find Elizabeth. First she checked the clinic reception, then scanned the chairs and loungers by the pool – half a dozen people were there, but no five-foot-nothing woman with a ponytail. Next she tried the exercise room, the boutique and beauty shop, and eventually tracked her down in the coffee lounge, sitting reading on her own.

Beattie stormed up to the table, surprised at the strength of her feelings – why the hell should she mind so much when she barely knew the woman? 'You might have *told* me you were a shrink!'

'What?' Elizabeth sat up with a start.

'I've just heard some people discussing it. There's a woman here who knows you.'

'No one knows me here, Beattie. Except you.'

'But that's just it – I *don't* know you. You didn't tell me anything last night. And now I discover you're a psychiatrist, for God's sake!'

'Well, actually I'm not.'

'You mean they got it wrong?'

'Not entirely, no. I'm a psychotherapist.'

'What's the difference?'

Elizabeth smiled. 'Quite a lot. But look, I'm really sorry you're upset, Beattie. You mustn't take it personally. I tend *not* to tell people what I do for a living. Otherwise they either clam up straight away and refuse to say another word, or they go to the other extreme and buttonhole me for hours with their problems.'

'Like *I* did, you mean?'

'No, that's different – we're friends.'

'Are we?'

'Yes, of course.'

Beattie subsided into a chair and started fiddling with the belt of her dressing-gown. 'Well, if we're friends, why didn't you *say* you were divorced, and that your husband was famous and everything?'

'Someone *has* been talking,' Elizabeth murmured with a frown. She took a cautious sip of orange juice. 'We haven't known each other long, Beattie.'

'Maybe not, but – hell! – I told you everything. I feel stupid now. And selfish, going on about *me* all the time. Anyway, how on earth do other people know these things if you say you keep yourself private?'

Elizabeth continued sipping her juice, her face giving nothing away.

'Elizabeth, do *tell* me. Otherwise how can you say we're friends?'

'Well . . .' Elizabeth closed her book and held it in her hands as if assessing its weight. 'I . . . I'm afraid the divorce was in the papers, Beattie, so now it's public knowledge. You see, my husband was a heart surgeon, and at the time he was chairing a committee on the safety of a new surgical technique. It was something rather contro-versial, so naturally it aroused a lot of interest, and . . .'

Beattie saw the pain on Elizabeth's face. No wonder, if her husband had gone off with some bimbo and the whole affair was splashed all over the press. She had no right to be probing. Apologizing would be more in order.

'Elizabeth, I . . . I'm terribly sorry. I feel even worse now, boring you with my trivial little problems, when . . .'

'Beattie, of *course* you didn't bore me. I enjoyed our talk immensely and it got us through the night. In fact, we have something in common I didn't mention then: *you*'re here as a present for your thirtieth birthday, which you'd rather didn't happen, and *I*'m here to avoid what would have been my thirtieth wedding anni-versary.'

'Oh Elizabeth, how ghastly for you.'

'No, it's the best place I could be. My eldest daughter arranged it – to stop me moping around at home, she said. She made the booking and paid for it, arranged to feed the cats, then packed me off with a new swimsuit and half a dozen books.'

'She sounds a bloody saint.'

'Oh, I wouldn't go *that* far!' Elizabeth drained her glass. 'Look, can I get you a fruit juice, or a rosehip tea or something?'

Beattie shook her head. Elizabeth was keen to change the subject – that was pretty clear. If only she'd open up; confide in *her*, in return.

'Or you can have hot chocolate if you prefer.'

'Hot chocolate at a health farm?'

'Oh, yes. They serve more or less everything, but with all the calorie-counts attached. It's nil for black coffee and five hundred-odd for hot chocolate with whipped cream on top.'

'I'd better have black coffee then.'

'Why? You don't need to count calories.'

'Oh, Elizabeth, I *do*!'

'But there's almost nothing of you!'

Beattie stared in disbelief. No one had ever considered her *thin* before. Max had once alluded to her 'child-bearing hips', which depressed her doubly: not only did it make them sound gigantic, it also reminded her that she didn't have children (and probably only wanted them because of some vague idea that motherhood made you a bona fide woman). Perhaps a psychiatrist – psychotherapist – could help her sort *that* out.

'What sort of psycho-whatsit *are* you?' she asked. 'You don't look like one at all.'

Elizabeth laughed. 'What are they meant to look like?'

'Oh, male, I suppose, and rather sinister, with little goatee beards and mid-European accents.'

'You're about fifty years out of date! Maybe Freud was like that, but things have changed enormously since his time.'

'But do they actually do any *good?*'

Elizabeth paused before she spoke, frowning to herself. 'That's a very fair question, Beattie. And it would probably take all day to answer. In fact, I'm trying to write a book about it.'

'Wow! I *am* impressed. I couldn't so much as write my name if I'd just gone through a divorce. I think I'd simply fall apart.'

'I very nearly did. Which is why I started the book. You see, I took a two-month break from my patients around the time of the divorce, and that left me with nothing much to do but think about myself. So I began writing as a kind of therapy.'

'And did it work?'

'Well, yes and no. The book's proving frightfully difficult. If I criticize the profession, it makes me feel disloyal, but if I don't, then I seem to be condoning various abuses and inadequacies which ought to be exposed. Oh, dear, I never *did* get you that drink. Have you decided what you'd like?'

'What I'd *like* is hot chocolate with three sugars and whipped cream, but what I *should* have is sugarless black coffee. The conflict's killing me!'

'Compromise. Have coffee with two sugars.'

'Okay.' She watched Elizabeth walk over to the counter. She was relieved that she had broken through the older woman's reserve and that they were now talking on more equal terms. It was stupid to have got so het up in the first place. Just because Max's son had had a bad experience with a shrink, it was hardly fair to damn the lot of them. She had to admit she found Elizabeth wonderfully calming. *And* kind. *And* tolerant. And after all, she wasn't Elizabeth's patient (or client, or whatever they were called), just her friend. She had wanted a friend at Ashley Grange, and was lucky to have found one. They had already planned to sit together at lunch, and then go to the keep-fit class afterwards. Why didn't she just relax (as everyone was so fond of telling her), and stop fretting about what she had or hadn't said?

She lolled back in her chair. The coffee lounge was much more casual in style than the dining-room, and had pretty wicker furniture, and walls painted primrose yellow (though without a primrose in sight). She liked the little touches: the framed cartoons of famous fatties on the walls; the selection of glossy magazines on every table. She was even becoming reconciled to the *frills*, for heaven's sake, and would have felt almost disappointed if the yellow curtains had been free of ruches and ruffles.

She looked up as two girls came in; one wearing a silk robe, the other a kimono. It did seem odd to be undressed all day. Apparently you could even wear your dressing-gown for dinner. Beattie pulled her belt tighter. She was used to clothes providing a sort of armour – both to enhance her image and hide her inner self – so she felt vulnerable without them. The same with make-up. She had resisted the urge to put any on this morning, even the tiniest dab of mascara, and still felt naked without her mask (though admittedly more comfortable).

The girl in the kimono sat down at an adjoining table. 'Lousy weather, isn't it?' she remarked.

'I've scarcely noticed, to tell the truth.' Beattie turned to look out of the window. Gentle rain was pattering on the flowerbeds; puddles gleaming on the impeccably swept paths. 'It doesn't seem to matter, when there's such a lot to do inside.' She liked the fact that every conceivable pleasure and diversion had been laid on under one roof, so there was no need to brave the elements at all.

'Your coffee, *madame*!' Elizabeth set it on the table – a dainty yellow cup with a gold rim.

'Tell me about your book,' urged Beattie. She wanted Elizabeth to talk about herself, for a change.

'Do you mind terribly if I don't? It's a bit too much like work.'

'Oh, I'm sorry.'

'That's all right. Tell me some more about *you* instead. You're much more interesting.'

'I should think you've heard enough of me by now.'

'Not at all.' On Elizabeth's lips the cliché sounded convincing. She sat placidly in her chair, but her blue eyes were alert with interest.

'Well actually, I've always wanted to write myself. Oh, not *your* sort of stuff – a nice, fat, juicy blockbuster would do me, so long as a string of film producers were fighting over the rights! Believe it or not, I *did* write a novel once. I was all of fifteen and still at school. It was about this father and daughter – based on me and my Dad, of course. They ran away together.'

'And did you ever think about getting it published?'

'Heavens, no! It was way over the top. Funnily enough, I dug it out recently and re-read it. You see, there's this guy I know who . . .' Beattie broke off. She still hadn't mentioned Max, or only very vaguely as the 'someone' who was paying for her stay here. But she needn't say she was having an affair with him (*or* that he was married). 'He . . . he's a newspaper man – quite high up – what's called an executive editor. He used to work for *Today*, but ten minutes after it closed one of the top brass from the new *Daily Herald* was on the phone with an offer. In fact' – she laughed – 'they more or less dragged him across Docklands to make sure they got him on board before someone *else* snapped him up.' She enjoyed boasting about Max – with no real achievements of her own, she could bask in *his* success. 'Apparently the city suits who put up the money knew nothing about showbiz or supermodels, except that they sell papers. Which is why they wanted Max – you know, to jazz things up a bit. Anyway, I met him at this party and he was telling me all about it. And then I told *him* I was dying to be a writer, and he asked me if I'd done anything already, and if so, could he see it? Well, we arranged to meet the following week and I handed over my bundle of ink-splodged exercise books.'

'And what did he think?'

'Oh, he hasn't read it yet. He's always incredibly busy. And it's probably rubbish anyway. It's just that I'm so sick of frittering my life away – well, we went through that last night. I won't bore you with an encore. D'you know, while I was lying in bed, I added up all the different jobs I'd had and it came to a total of thirty-three.'

'Yes, but that's not necessarily a *bad* thing. It means you've had a lot of valuable experience. And look how much you've seen of the world.'

'Hardly the world.'

'Well, you said you worked all over the country. And you've done exciting things in London with people *I* would never meet in a thousand years. You made me feel quite humbled.'

'Humbled? I thought you'd be shocked.'

'Why shocked?'

'Well, the kissagrams, and posing for that lurid magazine.'

'I imagine that took courage – *and* talent. And anyway, you're

31

ignoring all your other achievements. What about that great complicated typescript for the management consultants, and those brochures for the leisure centre?'

'Oh, they were only temp jobs. I loathe working as a secretary – it makes me feel tied down. In fact, I only agreed to do a secretarial course because my father was so insistent that I had some kind of training. He wanted me to stay on at school to do A-levels, and when I refused to even consider it, he paid for me to go to Pitman's. I hated every moment, to be honest, but I stuck it, for *his* sake. His own life was so rootless, I suppose he hoped I'd be more settled.' She smiled ironically as she helped herself to sugar.

'And how did he feel when you moved up north?'

Beattie stared down at the table. 'Well, I . . . I didn't really move there. I just did sort of . . . day-jobs.' Last night she had exaggerated shamelessly. 'Working all over the country' had a certain ring about it, whereas the reality was drab in the extreme: sporadic jobs at some dreary south-coast conference or Midlands motor show. 'You see, I was dying to get out of Croydon. It's such a nothing sort of place – neither London nor the country, and so ugly and . . . Oh, *shit*!' she said suddenly. 'Here I am rabbiting on about me, me, me, again. You must be sick to death of it.'

'Beattie, my love, I find it very interesting. Why do you keep running yourself down?'

'I . . . I don't know.' Beattie took refuge in her cup. Elizabeth had called her 'my love', and it seemed more than just a casual phrase. It could have sounded condescending, but it hadn't in the slightest. There had been real affection in the words, which made her feel accepted and approved of. 'I suppose I feel my life's so . . . aimless. I mean, I'm not saving whales, or fighting in Somalia or . . .'

'Yes, but nor are *most* of us.'

'I know, but it seems so awful to die without achieving anything big.'

'Beattie dear, thirty may seem ancient to you, but it's not quite the brink of extinction.'

Beattie laughed. 'Okay, I'm getting morbid – put it down to lack of sleep. Oh, God!' she exclaimed. 'I've just noticed the time. I've got a mud-pack at eleven-thirty.'

'Don't worry. They usually run a little late. Is that your last treatment this morning?'

'Mm.' Beattie gulped her coffee, one eye still on the clock.

'Well, shall we meet again before lunch and try out the jacuzzi? It's really rather super – big enough for a tribe.'

'I'm afraid I forgot to bring my swimsuit.'

'Borrow mine. I've got two.'

'They wouldn't fit.'

'The new one will – it's stretchy. And anyway, we're not that different in size. You keep making out that I'm a gnat and you're an elephant.'

'Well, aren't I? Or perhaps a hippopotamus, as I'm about to have a mud-pack!' Beattie abandoned her coffee and jumped up. 'I'll see you in the jacuzzi at twelve-thirty. I can always wear my leotard.'

She arrived out of breath at the treatment rooms, and was ushered into a cubicle by a girl in a pink overall with a badge marked 'Melanie'. Thank God it wasn't a man, she thought, as she stripped off to the skin.

'Make yourself comfortable,' Melanie smiled. 'Lie face-down on the couch and just relax.'

Beattie grinned to herself. If she'd been given £50 for every time she'd heard that word, she would be rich enough by now to buy a villa in Las Palmas. Melanie was slathering hot brown mud across her shoulders and, yes, it did feel relaxing – fabulously so. 'What does the mud *do*?' she asked, luxuriating in the warmth.

'It eases painful muscles and stiff backs. And it's also good for the skin – it draws out the impurities.'

'Mm . . . just what I need,' Beattie murmured, as the thick and soothing poultice was spread right along her back. It seemed to obliterate last night's massage and any lingering traces of Steve. She was feeling really happy, and it wasn't just the treatment. Elizabeth's words had moved her. She had never thought of herself as interesting, let alone talented or courageous, and it was still difficult to believe that a famous surgeon's wife could actually be 'humbled' by her string of low-grade jobs. And yet she knew Elizabeth had meant it – it had been obvious from her face.

She closed her eyes, allowing Elizabeth's generous praises to warm her, like the mud.

5

'Happy birthday, Beattie!' Annette called, jogging past the swimming pool on her way to an aerobics class.

Beattie waved a hand from the water, glad to be so fêted. The news of her birthday had spread – as all news did at Ashley Grange – and most of the guests had wished her many happy returns; some had even given her cards. She felt very much at home now, and had made a host of new acquaintances in just a day and a half. (And mercifully she'd seen no more of Steve.) Elizabeth had been right about the place not being as grand as it appeared. She'd met some perfectly ordinary people with mundane, even boring, jobs and no pretensions to wealth or fame, and she'd be genuinely sorry to say goodbye to them. Her suitcase was already packed and waiting in reception, and she was enjoying this last swim before returning to London and reality. (Even her car had enjoyed a weekend of pampering, and had been delivered back by the garage not just repaired but miraculously clean.)

She struck out in an energetic crawl, almost colliding with Barbara, who was surfacing from a dive. 'Sorry!' she gasped, slowing to a less anti-social pace. She was still wearing Elizabeth's swimsuit. She had intended to buy one in the boutique, but the prices were horrendous, and anyway she'd grown strangely fond of the simple grey-blue costume with its decorous high neck. When she had it on, she felt she could almost slip into Elizabeth's identity: become a calm professional person who helped others solve their problems; a mother of four with the proper maternal feelings; the owner of a big house in Kent with six bedrooms and a conservatory.

Despite their completely different backgrounds, she felt more drawn to Elizabeth than to the people her own age here, even

Annette, who'd been thirty last month, and lived within a mile of her in London. It was Elizabeth, not Annette, she had sat next to at every meal; Elizabeth she sought out between treatments. And they'd spent the whole of yesterday evening together, talking in the lounge. Once again, *she* had done the lion's share of the talking, but that was more or less inevitable when Elizabeth made listening almost an art-form. She hadn't realized how rare a gift it was. Most people hardly listened at all, but were for ever interrupting or letting their attention wander. Whereas Elizabeth really *concentrated*, absorbing everything you said, as if the words were some rare species of plant which needed nurturing with water, food and light.

She turned over on her back, floating indolently and gazing up at her reflection in the mirrored mosaic ceiling. One more minute, then she'd better get out – Elizabeth was waiting for her. She could see her lying on a lounger in her old unglamorous navy swimsuit, which looked like something from a 1930s boarding school.

She swam towards the shallow end, splashed up the marble steps, then threw herself, dripping, on the chair next to Elizabeth's.

'Aren't you going to have a shower?' Elizabeth asked, smiling as she closed her book. (It was still the biography of Byron – four hundred pages of close print.)

'Can't be fagged! I'm too lazy even to dry myself. Gosh! I'll miss these swims.'

'Haven't you got a pool nearby?'

'Yes, but not like this. It's freezing cold and full of screaming kids.'

'Don't talk about screaming kids! I've got my grandsons coming tomorrow. One's just learned to crawl and the other's a trainee terrorist.'

'Well, make the most of your last half hour of peace! That's it – close your eyes.'

Elizabeth closed them obediently, and Beattie stole a look at her. She was fascinated by the older woman's body – not that it seemed older. There was no ounce of spare flesh, no visible trace of four successive pregnancies. The word girlish came to mind again: small breasts, slim hips, smooth skin. Her legs were dusted with golden down, the sort of faint fair hair you saw on children's limbs. Beattie glanced at her own legs: coarse dark hairs were beginning to sprout through again, although she'd waxed them only three weeks ago. And the scarlet polish on her nails looked overdone and garish compared with Elizabeth's unvarnished natural pink. She fidgeted

35

in her chair. There were hundreds of questions she was dying to ask Elizabeth, especially about her work. It must be such an intriguing job: to be closeted in a room with her patients' pain and passion; distraught, chaotic people living on a knife-edge, who might have tried to kill themselves – or someone else. And yet Elizabeth appeared so *calm*. Did none of that emotion rub off on her, and was *she* never tempted to kick over the traces?

Beattie scrutinized the tranquil face. She would never know the answers because Elizabeth refused point-blank to discuss her patients, and seemed equally unwilling to talk about herself, despite everything she'd been through. Christ almighty! If it was *her* who'd been abandoned for some so-called actress, she'd be plotting wild revenge – like hacking the bitch into bite-sized chunks and grilling them on a spit with garlic butter. She let out a sudden laugh.

'What's the joke?' Elizabeth opened one eye.

'Oh, nothing. Go back to sleep!'

'I wasn't asleep.'

'Well, you should be. D'you realize, Elizabeth, we didn't get to bed last night till two? And the night before we had hardly any sleep at all.'

'I don't feel tired, though. Do you?'

She didn't answer. She *wanted* Elizabeth to sleep, so they could continue dozing by the pool till dinner-time, then saunter into the dining-room and order another sumptuous meal – low in calories maybe, but high in artistic presentation. (Even the garnishes at Ashley Grange were so exquisitely crafted you could practically frame them and hang them on the wall.) All she had in her fridge at home was half a carton of coleslaw and a staling piece of mousetrap. Elizabeth, presumably, would be going home to dinner with one or other of the daughters. She had heard more about those precious girls than anything else in Elizabeth's life: Caroline, Emma, Sarah and Harriet. She grimaced at the names, so correct and upper-class. She disliked them already – they were bound to be spoilt brats. Well, hardly brats. Caroline, the oldest (the mother of the two tearaway boys), was only five years younger than she was. This time tomorrow, Elizabeth would be fussing over her grandsons; absorbed once more in her busy life, her own blue-blooded circle of family and friends.

Beattie reached for her towel and rubbed her wet hair. She would probably never see her again. It was always the way with people you met on holiday: you exchanged addresses and promised to keep in touch, then forgot their names within a week. She and Elizabeth hadn't even exchanged addresses. All she had gleaned was Kent – the commuter part, with fast trains into Charing Cross – and she was reluctant to probe further. She could see no earthly reason why Elizabeth should bother to keep up with her.

As if she had read her mind, Elizabeth sat up on the lounger and looked at her watch. 'We'd better make a move. It's almost ten to two.'

Beattie didn't stir. She felt like a child, pleading silently but desperately, 'Just one more minute, one more page of the story!' She had a job fixed up for Monday (only temping again, but at least it was with a fashion house), and there'd be Max to see – and repay – and she and Annette had arranged to go to a film together, followed by an Indian meal. Yet all those things seemed vague and out of focus; only *Elizabeth* was sharply defined.

'I'll see you in reception,' Elizabeth said, gathering up her things.

'Okay. Give me twenty minutes.' Not that she would need that long. There seemed little point putting on make-up or fussing with her hair. She simply dressed and rinsed the swimsuit, put it in a plastic bag and was back in reception with it ten minutes later. Elizabeth wasn't there yet – only a queue of people waiting to settle their bills and a huddle of guests crowding round the sofa, saying their farewells. Sunday was change-over day, and a few new arrivals were already straggling in, making their way through those departing.

'Goodbye, Beattie!' Barbara smiled. 'Keep in touch, won't you?'

'Yes, of course.'

'Hey, Beattie,' called another voice. 'I've only just found out it's your birthday. Annette told me in aerobics. Many happy returns!'

'Thanks, Ruth. Though I'm doing my best to forget it.'

'Wait until you're forty,' Debbie groaned. 'That's the really hairy one! By the way, are you coming back next year, Beattie? Jill and I have booked again for January, to work off the Christmas pudding and mince pies.'

'I . . . I'm not sure.' Beattie envied them their certainties – just to know you'd be in funds in four months' time, or to know there'd be mince pies for Christmas. 'Have you seen Elizabeth anywhere?' she asked.

'I think she's left already,' Barbara said. 'I saw her by her car.'

Beattie dashed out to the car-park. Elizabeth's green Volvo was still there, but no sign of its owner. She trudged back inside again, and became embroiled in more goodbyes, though the queue for paying bills was now reduced to three. Neither she nor Elizabeth had a bill to pay – one of the few things they had in common. She had been trying to think of *other* things, but could only come up with the fact that each of them was an only child, and they both hated aubergines.

And both were rotten time-keepers, she thought, her eyes fixed on the door. No, that wasn't fair. Elizabeth had never kept her waiting before, not even a few minutes. It made her feel quite panicky. Saying goodbye was bad enough in itself, but for Elizabeth to vanish without a word . . . But of *course* she hadn't done that – she would never be so rude. She was probably just making a phone call or finishing her packing. Anyway, it was ridiculous to get in such a state. It wasn't as if she was parting from a lover. And yet it *did* feel rather like that: she was being wrenched away from someone vitally important, whose absence would leave a scar. Elizabeth was special – more special than she cared to admit.

She marched out to the garden again and walked restlessly up and down until she suddenly caught sight of her, strolling across the lawn towards the house.

'Where on earth have you been?' she demanded.

'Oh, hello, Beattie. Sorry if I've kept you. I was dying for a cigarette, so I sneaked out to the shrubbery!'

'Well . . . here's your swimsuit. Thanks.' It sounded ungracious, even rude. All the things she'd planned to say – the light-hearted, grateful, cheery things – somehow died on her lips.

Elizabeth took the swimsuit with a smile. 'Drive safely, Beattie, and do take care. Oh, and good luck with that job on Monday!'

Beattie nodded dumbly. Elizabeth was about to go, to walk out of her life, and she felt dangerously close to tears. She still couldn't understand it. She had always preferred men's company to women's, and even at school had never been one for 'best friends'. But perhaps that was the whole point. For the first time ever she felt *close* to a woman; had found a friend she could confide in without fear of being laughed at or betrayed.

She managed to blurt out a goodbye, then turned away from Elizabeth and strode over to her car. She started the engine with a jolt and accelerated down the drive, refusing to look back. Some witless DJ was babbling on the radio, so she tuned through the various stations until she found some suitable music – desolate but defiant.

Okay, so it was over, but she had *other* friends, hadn't she? Her own life to lead, for heaven's sake? Determinedly, she hummed to the music as she turned left into the lane, then left again for the main road. At least it had stopped raining; the first sun of the weekend seeping weakly through the clouds. Perhaps *next* weekend she and Max could drive down to the coast, if he could dream up some excuse to get away. A sudden toot made her jump. She looked in the mirror and saw Elizabeth's green car behind, evidently heading for the London road.

Impetuously she slammed on the brakes, jumped out of the car and flagged the Volvo down. Elizabeth swerved to a stop and put her head out of the window in alarm. 'What's wrong, Beattie?'

'I'm sorry, but I've just remembered something. I'm having a party next weekend – you know, for my birthday. Nothing special, a few odd friends, that's all. Why don't you come too?' It sounded perfectly plausible. And she could always *make* it true: invite the friends, lay on food and wine.

'I'd love to, Beattie, but I'm afraid I'm busy next weekend.'

'Well, forget the party and come and see me on your own. How about Thursday? Or Friday? We'll have a private celebration. I'll even cook you porridge. Porridge and chocolate-spread!'

A car behind them hooted impatiently. They were causing an obstruction on the narrow road. Beattie flashed a smile at the driver, then turned back to Elizabeth. 'It's not that far, I promise. When your train gets into Charing Cross, all you do is change onto the District Line and . . .'

'Look, phone me,' Elizabeth said. 'I'm not sure what I'm doing next week, but give me a ring tomorrow.' She scribbled her number on an empty cigarette packet and passed it through the window. 'Au revoir,' she called, as Beattie scrambled back into her car.

'Au revoir,' Beattie echoed, turning up the music to a roar. Au revoir was a definite advance on goodbye.

6

Beattie flicked swiftly through her *Can't Cook Cookbook*, then tossed it back into the cupboard. Every recipe seemed to be based on cans of soup – condensed mushroom poured over sweetcorn, condensed celery shrouding tuna, cream of tomato to enhance plain pasta shells. They all sounded quite revolting and anyway she had no pasta, corn or tuna in the place. She went to fetch her jacket and her bag. It would have to be Marks & Spencer food, and she'd have to get a move on. Elizabeth was due at seven and it was already half past five. Her friend had finally rung – though only late last night – saying she had to be in London for a seminar today, and perhaps they could meet briefly after that. It would only be a lightning visit, with no time for a meal, and anyway Beattie would be too tired after work.

'No, I won't,' she had retorted, though actually she *was* tired, and not feeling all that well. She suspected she was going down with cystitis, but ill or no, she couldn't expect Elizabeth to turn up so close to dinner-time and not give her something to eat.

Originally she had planned a simple snack – a cheese sandwich or a salad – but as the day progressed her ideas had grown in scale and grandeur until now she felt she couldn't greet the ex-wife of a famous heart surgeon with anything less than a three-course meal.

She set off down the road for Marks & Spencer's, finding the food hall crowded with shoppers; infuriating fusspots who blocked her way while they stood scrutinizing the labels on every smallest item. She too was dithering, running round in circles from ready-meals to vegetables to wine; her head aching from the noise and neon glare. Did there *have* to be so much choice? Paupiette of chicken or *poussin Normande* (which had virtually the same picture on the packet)?

Mange-tout or ratatouille? Asparagus or globe artichokes? And which of the half-dozen different types of pea?

The contents of her trolley were mounting up alarmingly, and when she reached the check-out she was shocked by the size of the bill. Far cheaper not to cook at all. Most of the local pizza places offered as much as you could eat for less than a fiver, and bread and cheese at home cost even less. Damn! She'd forgotten the cheese, but it was too late to buy it now. She must get back and hide the cartons, so that Elizabeth would think she had produced this spread herself, in the calm collected hour between strolling home from work and putting the finishing touches to the table. (The table would need more than finishing touches. It was a hideous thirties monster from a junk-shop, and she didn't even own a tablecloth to hide its stains and scratches.)

As she unlocked the drab brown door and stepped into the dingy hall, she tried to view the place through Elizabeth's eyes. It wasn't exactly impressive. The hall wallpaper was patterned not just with faded flowers, but with scribblings from the two Tobin boys, who lived on the ground floor. The staircarpet was badly worn, and no one (herself included) ever bothered to dust the banisters. She continued on and up, wrinkling her nose at the smell of curry wafting from the first-floor flat. Vince lived on his own and seemed to exist on a diet of takeaways, but *must* he choose the most virulent of vindaloos the very night she was 'cooking' for Elizabeth?

She unloaded the shopping in the kitchen and set about decanting the food into dishes, cramming the cartons into the bottom of the bin. She boiled water for the vegetables, put the chicken in the oven, then did a quick tour of inspection. The sitting-room was a mess – every chair a different style and colour, and that cheapjack table too bulky for the space. The bedroom wasn't much better and boasted so few drawers and cupboards that her clothes spilled everywhere. She made a half-hearted attempt at tidying up. Here, it wasn't incriminating Marks & Spencer wrappings which needed instant disposal, but Max's latest *Penthouse* and the packet of multi-coloured condoms by the bed. (Not that he used condoms: he merely bought them as proof of his belief in safe sex, then complained about the palaver of actually putting them on.)

She pushed both offending items under the bed, then returned to the sitting-room and plumped up the cushions on the sofa. The reek of curry was growing more insistent, blasting up two flights of stairs. Vince must be cooking it himself, and had certainly overdone the spices. She would have to buy some air freshener, which meant going out again, but it was terribly important that Elizabeth got the right impression. She had waited long enough for the visit – these last ten days had seemed ten *months*.

She ran downstairs and turned the other way this time, towards the corner-shop. Passing Bits and Bobs, she noticed the familiar tray of dusty books outside. There were scarcely any books in the flat, apart from the odd Jeffrey Archer and an ancient Catherine Cookson, yet she was entertaining a woman who read Byron. She poked among the hardbacks, eventually picking out the collected poems of someone with the daunting name of Edna St Vincent Millay. At only 50p for close on a thousand poems, it was obviously a bargain. In addition, she found a Doris Lessing novel (torn, reduced to 15p) and a history of Greece with a pock-marked cover but rather fetching illustrations. All three books cost under a pound, so once she'd bought the air freshener, she still had money left for parsley, lemons and radishes. They would do for garnishes, although she could hardly rival those at Ashley Grange. The health farm seemed so distant now – another age, another world. She kept worrying that Elizabeth might be *different* here in London, or even annoyed at being pestered into coming. She had rung her four times in Kent. Twice she'd got the answerphone; twice Elizabeth was 'busy'. She was beginning to wonder now if Elizabeth had only agreed to come as a way of preventing further bombardment. Well, if so, all the more reason to do everything she could to make the evening a success.

She checked the oven and the table as soon as she got back, then put the books on show on the coffee-table. The musty smell of the volumes suddenly reminded her of the second-hand clothes she had worn as a small child. How she'd *loathed* those clothes – the way they'd arrived screwed up in plastic bags with other children's stains on them, other children's smells. She had never been allowed to choose anything herself. It was all to do with her mother being ill: only able-bodied parents could bustle round the shops; an invalid's child had to take what it was given.

She strode abruptly towards the mirror over the mantelpiece and inspected her appearance, as if afraid she'd find herself in cast-offs even now. No. Her mask and her armour were safely back in place, and the shoulder-padded scarlet jacket was her own choice – and expensive. If anything, she looked *too* smart, but there wasn't time to change. She removed her extravagant earrings and continued staring in the mirror, wondering who she was exactly, and why she didn't spend less money on swanky jackets and more on furnishing the flat.

She went back to the kitchen and put the vegetables on. While they were heating, she tried her hand at garnishes *à la* Ashley Grange: radish flowers and lemon twists, a parsley arabesque. Her efforts all looked amateurish, but then she wasn't any good at domestic trivia. Even as an adolescent, she'd been scornful of the sort of women who sat happily at home decorating fairy cakes or polishing the brass. She had identified with *men* – men who broke in horses, or crossed the Atlantic single-handed; men like her father, who had never stayed in one place long enough to let it bore or tame him. She chewed a piece of lemon peel, wincing at its sharpness; glanced up at the clock. Six minutes to seven.

At precisely one minute past, the doorbell rang. She quickly smoothed her hair, stole one last glance in the mirror, then ran downstairs and flung open the door. In her nervousness, she began to talk too fast, swamping poor Elizabeth in an incoherent babble of greetings and apologies, and even getting things the wrong way round – offering her wine before they'd so much as walked upstairs.

It was only after she'd poured the wine that she paid any real attention to Elizabeth's appearance. She was wearing old blue jeans, which seemed peculiar garb for a psychotherapist, especially one who had just attended a seminar. Beattie felt a twinge of resentment: she might have made an effort – if not dressed up, then at least worn something less casual. Her hair hung loose and straggly round her shoulders, and her red-and-white checked shirt looked positively hick, as if she'd dropped in on her way to a barn dance. And yet her voice was so distinguished. It wasn't simply the pukka accent, but the caressing way she spoke; never harsh or over-emphatic.

'Well, how are you, Beattie?' she asked, taking a sip of wine and nodding appreciatively at its bouquet.

'I'm fine,' said Beattie, trying to moderate her own voice. 'Well, actually, I'm not. I think I've got cystitis. I've been rushing to the loo every half an hour.'

'Oh, how rotten for you, my dear. It's so painful, isn't it? Perhaps you shouldn't be drinking, though? Alcohol's the worst thing for cystitis.'

Beattie cupped her hands around her glass. 'I don't think it makes much difference. I used to get it badly as a child, when all I drank was water, or Pepsi as a treat. Anyway, you're a fine one to talk! What about your smoking?'

Elizabeth laughed. 'I see you haven't forgotten my ashtray,' she said, gesturing to the saucer by her glass. She unzipped her shoulder-bag and extracted her cigarettes and also a small package wrapped in tissue. 'And I mustn't forget your present. I've brought you a little something. I was browsing round the antique shop in the village and I found this elephant. It reminded me of you – the way you keep insisting you're a great big hulking creature when you're actually so slim. Well, this chap is small as well, and most attractive, I think. I hope you'll like him, anyway.'

Beattie unwrapped the tissue, to reveal a tiny jade elephant carved in exquisite detail, from its diminutive tail to the markings on its ears. She was touched by the gift, not just because it was obviously expensive, but on account of Elizabeth's words, which had made her 'slim' and 'most attractive'.

'Gosh, thanks!' she said. 'It's beautiful.' She set it on the mantel-piece beside the photo of her father; stood gazing at them both before returning to her chair.

'So how's the job?' Elizabeth asked, lighting a cigarette and relaxing back on the sofa. 'The one with the fashion house.'

'Oh, that's all over and done with. It was only a three-day wonder. I'm working for a quantity surveyor now, which is boring boring boring. The only good thing is that I can usually leave early. Like I did today. It meant I had time to cook, you see. I've made us a chicken thing. In fact I ought to go and check on it – I don't want it to burn.'

'But Beattie, dear, I told you I couldn't stay for supper.'

Beattie froze at the door. 'You didn't.'

'I did, most definitely. I've got to get back for Harriet. She's . . .'

'B . . . but I've spent hours and hours getting everything ready.' Beattie heard the tremor in her voice. Elizabeth *couldn't* go and leave her with all that food. She wasn't even hungry herself, and anyway, it had been intended as her *own* present – not as precious as the elephant, but special none the less.

'Look, please don't be upset, Beattie. I remember saying quite specifically it would have to be a lightning visit.'

'Okay – you did, but I thought at least you'd have time to *eat*. I've

44

been begging you to come for days and days, and when at last you get here, you have to rush away again almost straight away.'

'Hold on! I haven't got to go yet. We can finish our wine together. Come and sit down and tell me all your news.'

I haven't any news. Beattie bit the words back. If she sounded as churlish as that, Elizabeth would *want* to rush away. 'Supper won't take long,' she insisted, still hovering at the door. 'It's only a quick snack.'

'All right then, let's eat.'

'Great! I'll go and fetch it.' She hurried into the kitchen. She'd better forget the starter and serve just the *poussin* and the raspberry cream pavlova. It all seemed far too grand now; not the simple snack she'd promised, but a pretentious wasteful blow-out. She tipped the garnishes in the waste bin, burnt herself trying to manoeuvre the chicken from the oven and let out a flustered curse.

'Beattie, are you all right? Can I help at all?'

'*No!*' The last thing she wanted was Elizabeth coming in here and catching sight of the pavlova before she'd decided whether to ditch it, along with the avocado mousse. She turned off the three gas-rings and drained the vegetables – enough to feed the whole of West-bourne Grove. She mixed the mange-tout with the ordinary peas in the hope that they'd look less, and was just carrying them in when the phone rang.

'Shall I get that?' Elizabeth asked.

'No!' said Beattie, more flustered still. It might be Max, ringing her from France. (He was thinking of buying a house in Provence and had gone to inspect a couple of properties.) She was terrified he'd scandalize Elizabeth with some vulgar greeting or raunchy comment. She clattered the dishes onto the table and picked up the receiver.

'Hi, Beattie. It's Sal.'

'Oh . . . I'm sorry, Sal, I can't talk now.'

'You okay?'

'Yes, of course.'

'Your voice sounds different – sort of posh.'

'Don't be stupid.'

'It *does*. I hardly recognized you. Are you entertaining royalty?'

'Look, I'll phone you back. All right, Sal?'

'No, it's *not* all right. I'm bloody miserable. John's just given me the push.'

'Oh God! How awful. Why?'

'Well, he . . .'

Beattie tried to listen to Sal whilst keeping her eye on Elizabeth, who was mouthing 'Shall I go?'

'No!' Beattie whispered desperately. Elizabeth probably only meant go into the other room, but she didn't want to risk her leaving altogether.

'What do you mean – "no"?' demanded Sal.

'I wasn't saying "no" to you. I . . .'

'So you *have* got company. Okay, I get the message. I'll ring you later on.'

Sal hung up, sounding close to tears. Beattie stood clutching the receiver, equally upset.

Elizabeth came over to her. 'Look, Beattie, don't mind me. If you need to speak to your friend, I can always disappear.'

'No,' said Beattie, 'it's quite all right. She . . . she's not really a friend, just another temp I met once on a job. She only rings me when she's in trouble.' Beattie left the receiver off the hook, wondering why she was being so disloyal. She and Sal were actually quite close, but she just couldn't cope with any more interruptions. Things were going badly enough as it was – she had seen Elizabeth glance surreptitiously at her watch, the meal was getting cold, and she was dying for another pee.

She dashed from the bathroom to the kitchen, forcing a determined smile as she carried in the chicken. 'Okay. Supper up!'

Elizabeth exclaimed at all the dishes as she sat down at the table (transformed for the occasion with a purple sheet and matching paper serviettes). 'Oh, Beattie, you've gone to so much trouble . . .'

'It's nothing. I threw it all together in five minutes.'

'Well it looks perfectly delicious, and what exotic vegetables!'

Beattie served the chicken, already feeling better – mentally at least. Perhaps now they could sit quietly and do justice to the meal, although she didn't have much appetite.

'Aren't you going to take more than that? You've given me twice as much as you.'

'No, I'm afraid I'm not feeling too good. It's probably the cystitis.'

'You ought to see your GP, you know.'

'I haven't got a GP.'

'Oh Beattie! That's not wise.'

Beattie swallowed a sliver of asparagus, lapping up Elizabeth's advice: how she must find herself a doctor and have some proper tests; what she should and shouldn't eat to help her bladder; how a hot water bottle could be comforting if the cystitis gave her stomach cramps. It was marvellous being fussed. Throughout her childhood she'd had to be the well one – the great big strapping elephant – while her mother monopolized the role of invalid.

'Couldn't you take some time off work, if you're feeling under par?'

'I can't afford it! Temps don't get sick pay. Actually I'm planning to do *more*, not less. I thought I might find myself a Saturday job, or even take a stall on the Portobello Road. I've always wanted to sell antique clothes. And I know where I can pick them up for a song.'

'Gosh, you do have initiative! I wouldn't know where to start.'

Beattie warmed to her theme. 'Even as a child, I used to sell things to the other kids at school.' Things I'd nicked, she omitted to say. 'I had these stupid dreams, you see. I wanted to be a Somebody, and that meant being rich.'

'And what happened to the dreams?'

Beattie laughed. 'They're a bit bruised and bashed about, but still more or less intact, I suppose. I'm pinning all my hopes on Max now.'

'Who?'

'That newspaper man I told you about. He said if I could write a couple of pieces which really had some bite, he might get them accepted. Imagine seeing my by-line in the *Herald*!' Beattie sat back in her chair, glancing with satisfaction at Elizabeth's plate, empty but for the chicken bone. She had eaten with real relish and, better still, she hadn't consulted her watch again, nor mentioned going home. The wine must have relaxed her. With any luck they'd have time for the pavlova, even for the After Eights.

'There's just a bit of pudding,' she said. 'If you've got time, that is. We can always skip coffee, but I would like you to try my meringue.'

'I love meringues! They're quite my favourite pudding. However did you know?'

'I guessed. People who hate aubergines always love meringues.'

They laughed together and the last tension seemed to dissipate. Beattie cleared away the plates, and went to fetch the pavlova, carefully roughing its pristine surface so it would look convincingly home-made.

'Beattie, that's a work of art!'

47

Beattie shrugged dismissively. 'Meringues are so easy, aren't they? They practically make themselves.'

'Well, I've been cooking for thirty years and I still find them rather tricky. These are really professional.'

Beattie ate a mouthful proudly. Things were definitely improving. Elizabeth's praises were as welcome as her sympathy. Both had always been in short supply. She didn't meet the sort of people who complimented her on 'works of art', or spent twenty minutes pouring out advice on her health. Perhaps she could persuade her friend to visit every week.

'Do you have these seminars often?' she asked. 'I mean, when are you next . . . ?'

Her words were cut short by the doorbell. Blast! It was probably the old chap from the house across the road. Jack was always trying to borrow things – did she have a corkscrew or some 50ps for the meter?

'Excuse me a second, will you? I expect that's my neighbour – Jack the lad. He's eighty if he's a day, but I think he fancies me. Any excuse and he's round here.'

She ran downstairs and opened the front door, staring in astonishment at the camel coat and suntanned face. It was Max the lad, not Jack.

'I . . . I thought you were in France?'

'I came back early, sweetheart. Both the houses I went to see were a load of expensive crap. I tried to ring you from the airport, but first there was no reply and then it was engaged. Well aren't you going to give me a kiss? Christ, I've missed you! Let's go upstairs and make up for lost time.'

'Max, I . . . I'm sorry but I'm not feeling all that well. I've got cystitis.'

'No wonder after last weekend! It must be honeymoon cystitis. God, you were amazing!' He closed the door and began nudging her upstairs. She stood her ground, dodging back as his hand groped for her breast.

'Look, I really do feel ill, Max. I was just about to go to bed.'

'Great! I'll come with you. Whatever's wrong, I'll kiss it better. Though I can't say you look ill to me – you're positively glowing. Anyway, one little kiss won't hurt.' His hands crept beneath her jacket and he drew her close against his chest and tried to slip his tongue into her mouth. She pulled away, wiped her lips.

'What's wrong with you, for Christ's sake? Do I smell of garlic, or are you playing hard to get? You'll be telling me you've got a headache next.'

'Well, actually I have.'

'Is this the brush-off then? I go to France for forty-eight hours, rush straight here from Heathrow, and you slam the door in my face.'

'Don't be stupid, Max. I just don't feel very well, that's all.'

'It doesn't seem to have stopped you drinking, I notice.'

'I . . . I haven't been drinking.'

'Come off it, sweetie-pie! I can always tell when you're lying. It takes one to know one.' He laughed, and gave her a teasing nip on the neck. 'I'm pretty sure you haven't got cystitis, but you *have* got someone else upstairs. And I'm going up to bash his fucking brains in.'

Beattie grabbed his arm. 'Max, *no!*'

He gave a snort of triumph. 'Aha! That proves I'm right. You don't want me to see him.'

'It's a *her*, not a him, if you really want to know.'

'Oh yeah? You expect me to believe that?'

'It happens to be true.'

'Fine! I'll go up and say hello to *her*.' He made the 'her' sarcastic, as he pushed past her up the stairs. Beattie charged after him, but as she reached the landing, he was already striding through her door into the sitting-room. 'Mmm – something smells good!' he observed, stopping short as he saw Elizabeth.

Both of them were taken aback, Max straightening his straight tie while Elizabeth stumbled to her feet. 'Yes,' she said uncertainly. 'Beattie's cooked me a delicious meal.'

'*Really?*' His face expressed total disbelief. 'Well, congratulations, that's all I can say.'

'She's just made the best meringues I've ever tasted.'

Max threw himself on the sofa, tossing the cushions out of his way. 'In that case, I've obviously come to the wrong house. *My* Beattie has trouble boiling an egg.'

'Shut up, Max!' Beattie hissed, wishing the floor would swallow her up. And bloody Max as well. This was the man who had the power to make her dreams realities, yet, with Elizabeth here, she somehow felt ashamed of him. He had never looked so old before: crinkly little lines around his eyes, his paunch straining against his shirt, his hair well cut but over-long. He kept it long on purpose, because he thought it made him look boyish, yet it contrasted oddly with the formal suit and camel coat. All his clothes were just a fraction too new and smart: shoes too highly polished, tie expensive silk, gold cufflinks ostentatious. And did he *have* to wear two rings? The wedding ring was downright hypocritical when he'd been cheating on his wife since the week after their honeymoon (or so he'd admitted once), and the signet ring was set with a ruby – naff, despite its cost. As for his voice, it always sounded slightly 'estuary', even to her untutored ear, but compared with Elizabeth's velvet tones, it was bordering on pleb. But there was no way she could avoid introducing him. Elizabeth was still standing by the table, looking bemused and rather spare.

'Er . . . this is Max Gillespie,' she mumbled. 'He's just come back from France.' She was desperate to steer Max away from the subject of her cooking skills and onto something less embarrassing, such as the relative merits of the Var and the Lubéron. (She had never heard of either when Max first mentioned them, but Elizabeth's geography would probably be less hazy.)

Max, however, refused to be diverted. Having exchanged the briefest of pleasantries with Elizabeth, he announced that he was starving. 'All they gave us on the plane was a piece of pâté no bigger than a frog's eye, and a biscuit-thing which tasted like a Brillo pad. As you've suddenly become such a brilliant cook, my sweet,' he said with heavy irony, 'could you rustle up a little something?'

She swore under her breath. She could hardly refuse in front of Elizabeth. 'There's some chicken left,' she muttered. 'And loads of vegetables.'

'Fantastic! And how about a glass of vino so we can drink to your first cordon bleu meal?'

Beattie ignored the barb and went to fetch the food, though she was loath to leave Elizabeth with Max. God knows what he'd say to her. She could hear his voice booming from the sitting-room, and then a sudden explosive laugh. She rushed back with the chicken to find Elizabeth on her feet, buttoning up her coat.

'I'm afraid I must be on my way now, Beattie. I'm terribly late as it is. I've only just noticed the time.'

'Okay,' said Beattie, torn between relief and disappointment. She'd been hoping Elizabeth might stay till nine or ten, but a three-some was a completely different matter.

'There's no need to see me out, Beattie.' Elizabeth was already at the door.

'Of course I will! You're my guest.'

'And I'm just the gas man,' Max retorted. 'Who doesn't even warrant a knife and fork.'

Beattie ignored him and hurried Elizabeth down the stairs. 'Look, I'm sorry . . .' she began, as they stood awkwardly in the hall.

'What for? I've had a lovely evening, and a really first-class meal.'

'There's no need to be sarcastic.'

'But I'm *not*, Beattie. I wouldn't dream of it.'

'Okay, I didn't cook it *all* myself. There wasn't actually time, you see. I had to do the shopping first and . . .'

'It doesn't matter whether you cooked it or not. You still went to a lot of trouble. I feel honoured, honestly.'

'Now you *are* taking the mick.'

'Beattie, you're impossible! Whatever I say, you don't believe me.'

'No, I do, I *do*! Just promise me you'll come again. Soon. Next week or . . .'

'I'm afraid I can't promise that – not until Harriet's better. But I'll *phone* you next week. All right?'

'All right,' said Beattie grudgingly, opening the front door and watching her friend growing smaller smaller smaller, until she vanished altogether into the dusk.

7

'Relax, darling,' Beattie urged. 'You're making things worse by getting so het up.'

Max rolled over in bed and shoved a pillow behind his back. 'It's that bloody woman's fault.'

Yes, thought Beattie, Elizabeth *did* seem to have put a jinx on him. Max might be a selfish lover, but never before had he failed to get an erection, least of all when she was trussed up in her suspender-belt and matching black lace basque. Despondently, she nudged a black-stockinged leg against his thigh. She had worked through her whole repertoire, and got absolutely nowhere. If only he'd give up and let her go to bed – to sleep.

'I honestly thought you had some horny guy here and it's put me off my stroke.'

'Yes, but I *didn't*, Max, so everything's okay.'

He pummelled the pillow savagely. 'It's *not* okay. I want to fucking please you.'

'You are. You do. Let's just cuddle up.' Beattie put her arms around him, but he refused to be placated.

'I can't think why you had to invite her anyway.'

'I've *told* you, Max, I . . .'

'I mean, spending a fortune on food, when you always say you're . . .'

'Oh Christ! Not that again. Why d'you have to get so paranoid about a pathetic piece of chicken?' She stopped. She couldn't afford to quarrel. Max was the most important man she had ever been to bed with. He had a string of credit cards, drove a BMW 5 Series, and belonged to a ritzy health club with three fountains and a waterfall as well as a huge pool. Not that she was a gold-digger, or simply out for what she could get. It was Max's *power* she valued rather than his money. On her own, she was nothing, but when he took her to the sort of restaurants frequented by the press, with waiters bowing and scraping, and well-known editors sauntering up to their table, it made *her* important too. She would never forget their first dinner – both the food and the surroundings had been incredibly exotic, and even the colours were way out: black cabbage instead of green, designer lettuce mottled pink and purple, white anchovies, white chocolate mousse. And soon there would be meals in France as well. He'd told her that once he'd bought his house there, she must come over and christen the bed.

She leaned down and kissed his stomach: a long compensatory kiss, feathering from his navel to his groin.

'Keep on going!' he murmured, settling back to enjoy it.

She did as he asked – she had to make things right. Max might have the power to change her life. He'd read her novel on the plane, and far from dismissing it as schoolgirl drivel, had pronounced it 'raw' and 'raunchy', and said if she could turn out a few pieces with the same attack and verve, there was a good chance he could get them on the woman's page. Apparently the new *Herald* was looking for new journalists. She imagined seeing her name in print, buying up a dozen copies and sending them to her friends, and especially to her father. He wrote to her each month from Melbourne, often joking about his share in her first million, and how he looked forward to being kept in the manner to which he wasn't accustomed. He had always had ambitions for her, but now at last they might materialize.

Hell! She was miles away again. No wonder Max couldn't perform, if her mind was constantly elsewhere. The problem was she just didn't feel like sex tonight. Yet Max was so decent to her, she must do *something* in return.

She crouched between his legs and took Maximus in her mouth again. Their joke-name for his prick had never seemed less apt. She used her lips, her tongue, her teeth, in turn, but with no result whatever. Finally, with a sense of failure, she eased herself up from the uncomfortable position and lay beside him on the bed. 'Look, it doesn't matter, darling. We can always . . .'

'Of course it matters! What d'you think I feel like, letting you down like this?'

You mean letting your*self* down, she thought, retrieving the duvet from the floor. She had been with older men enough to know how crucial sex was to their self-esteem. In fact, the irony was that Max probably needed her just as much as she needed him. A girl two decades younger in his bed proved he was virile and desirable, and gave him greater kudos with his peers.

She lay staring at the ceiling. Her headache was no better and it seemed to make her much more sensitive to the traffic noise outside, and all the sounds within the house: Vince practising his guitar; the wail of one of the Tobin kids echoing up three floors; the Frasers' yappy dog. The low-wattage bedside lamp cast dismal shadows on the walls, and the room smelt grey and stale – Max's sweat and her own tired perfume curdling with a last whiff of chicken. Yet Max always said he liked romantic atmospheres, which meant they shouldn't be at Rainham Road at all, but naked under the waterfall at his health club, or in a four-poster bed at some country house hotel.

Even now, he refused to give up. He was sitting propped against the pillows, rubbing himself with a desperate sort of violence – more self-punishment than stimulation. She almost hoped it wouldn't work. She had no idea of the time; only that it was time for him to go. She was beginning to feel an aversion towards his damp and hairy body. Normally she could ignore his less appealing features, but after hours of fruitless thrashing about, the whole business was becoming a bore.

'Look, why don't I fetch that wine you brought? Then we can cool down with a drink.'

'No, I'm okay now – I think.' He lurched to his feet, still determinedly kneading himself. 'Quick! I want to try something. Lie on your back right at the bottom of the bed.'

She wriggled down the bed and let him arrange her as he wanted. The sooner he was satisfied, the sooner he might leave.

'Lie flat – no, further down, so your bum's just over the edge. Now put your legs right up and out.'

She did as she was told, wondering where he had learnt this new position. Perhaps he had another woman (a decade younger than *her*), or maybe his wife was not quite the superannuated killjoy he'd implied.

He stood between her spreadeagled legs and began pushing into her, semi-stiff at last. All she could see was the bulge of his stomach and his plump and hairy breastlets looming over her. She was pinioned beneath him, unable to move a muscle, while he ground

54

and pounded into her. Despite his grunting efforts, Maximus seemed to be shrinking even further, all but slipping out. If it wasn't *her* fault he was limp, it was probably Elizabeth's – as Max had said three times. He was convinced she'd taken a dislike to him on sight, and was using some weird psychic power to make him impotent. But whatever Elizabeth thought, she didn't want to alienate him – she had far too much to lose. She shut her eyes and saw her name not just in print, but three foot high, in lights; her father by her side as they swept in to the premiere of the Oscar-winning film she'd written.

'Wonderful!' she whispered, feigning a few gasps. Her back ached from his weight and from the strain of holding him in. Keeping her legs so wide apart was terribly uncomfortable, and one of the suspenders was digging into her thigh. She loathed wearing so-called sexy gear in bed, and the tight basque made it difficult to breathe. She pulled irritably at the lacings, tempted to wrench the whole thing off. But a woman's naked body was never quite enough. Men seemed to need the extra titillation of cleavages or G-strings, crotchless tights, stiletto heels, and Max in particular liked her to dress up as a vamp. Yet tonight she'd drawn a blank. It was basically a design fault: if cocks had been made detachable, they could be *permanently* stiff, and be screwed on and off just when they were needed, like the beaters on a Kenwood mixer.

She suppressed a grin as she pictured herself as a pint of cream in a mixing-bowl. With Max the way he was, he would never be able to whip her into peaks. Still, at least he wasn't boastful like Dominic, who delighted in dropping statistics: six times, six hours, sixty women from six continents, six hundred and six positions. If only she could meet a man who didn't need to *prove* anything, and who valued her for herself – a caring, sensitive person who could tell the difference between faked orgasms and real.

Max was on the brink of his own orgasm, judging by the noise he was making. She was surprised he could come at all in such a spineless state, unless he was faking too, in order to save face. She had better pretend to come with him, then she could see him off the premises and crash out in merciful sleep.

Pretending wasn't easy. Every muscle hurt and she was desperate for another pee. (That had been the trouble in the first place. She had dashed out to the bathroom just as Max was warming up, and he claimed the interruption put him off. Then he'd blamed the creaky bed, and finally Elizabeth.)

All at once, Elizabeth was there: no longer disapproving, but pressing close to her in bed. She had slipped off the prim swimsuit to reveal girlish breasts and a fair and downy thatch.

Beattie reached out a hand to touch her – the skin as moth-soft as the voice, and warmer than her own. She let the hand stroke slowly down and up again. Elizabeth was shy, trying to cover her breasts with her arms. Tenderly, Beattie prised the arms away. She had never touched another woman's breasts – the very thought would have horrified her – but it was different with Elizabeth. She knew she must be gentle, though, and show consideration; not grind and grunt like Max. She shut him out behind a high glass wall; let him continue his exertions the other side of it while *she* caressed Elizabeth, softly and erotically. She used the very tips of her fingers to stroke the small pale breasts; tease the nipples stiff. Elizabeth, encouraged, began to touch her in response, gliding a small hand across her stomach. Beattie tensed. Move your hand *down*, she pleaded, without spelling out the words. There wasn't any need for words. Elizabeth understood.

'Fantastic!' Max was crying, somewhere far beyond.

Fantastic, she echoed silently, closing her eyes so she could experience the depth of the sensations – so different from his crude and clumsy gropings. Elizabeth's touch was exquisitely subtle, and so skilful now, she was almost almost coming. If only Max would be quiet and stop telling her she was sensational, she could ignore him altogether and respond only to Elizabeth – her sensational new lover.

8

Beattie forked in a mouthful of pavlova, followed by a gulp of wine. The church clock down the road had just struck twelve, so this was literally a midnight feast. Some feast! She was perched on an old wooden stool in the tiny cluttered kitchen, surrounded by unwashed dishes and the debris of the meal. She pushed her plate away – she'd only get fat if she gorged on meringue and cream. Anyway, she ought to go to bed. Her back was aching terribly and she felt shivery and strange. But she knew she wouldn't sleep. She was far too agitated, worrying about those shameful sexual fantasies. She had never fancied a woman before – the idea was quite grotesque – so what on earth was wrong with her?

She put the wine back in the fridge. All her affairs had been the normal heterosexual kind, beginning at fourteen with a gangly boy in the sixth form. And once she had started work, there had usually been some guy or other around, although none of them had lasted long. Perhaps her lack of any long-term relationship was due not just to bad luck (as she'd always tried to convince herself) but because at some unconscious level she preferred women to men. No, that was quite ridiculous. A few minutes' idle fantasizing about another woman's body didn't turn you into a lesbian.

She drifted into the sitting-room and took down the carved jade elephant from its place of honour on the mantelpiece. Again, she felt touched by the gift. Elizabeth was generous and thoughtful, so it was only natural to be fond of her. That's all it was – affection. Except she was fond of Sal as well, and had never fantasized about *her* breasts; never even noticed them.

She shoved the elephant in a drawer and stood leaning against the bureau. It was probably safest not to see Elizabeth any more. It wasn't just the sexual feelings (alarming enough in themselves), but the way Elizabeth had become so extraordinarily important; continually in her thoughts, as if she was actually in love with her. Max already resented 'that bloody woman', and if she had to choose between them – well, frankly, she needed Max. She would just have to be strong-minded and end a friendship which could turn out to be dangerous.

She moved to the window and pushed aside the curtain. There was not a soul about, not even a passing car. Earlier this evening she had found the noise annoying – now she wished there *was* some noise, to connect her with humanity. But the house seemed fast asleep and the whole of Rainham Road looked shuttered, dark and lonely. She wondered if Elizabeth was asleep as well, and suddenly recalled that earlier midnight feast, when the pair of them had first got to know each other. Except she *didn't* know Elizabeth, not in any depth. If only she'd stayed longer this evening, they could be sitting together now, enjoying a last nightcap. And instead of Elizabeth being always the patient listener, she might have talked more about herself tonight.

She let the curtain fall and mooched despondently back to the bureau. She had just resolved to forget Elizabeth, yet here she was obsessed with her again. Couldn't she *see* how futile it was? Elizabeth had made it pretty clear that she wasn't keen to continue with the friendship – and no wonder when all they had in common was two days at a health farm.

She sat down at the bureau and switched on the computer. The health farm had been on her mind since Max first told her that he liked her novel and suggested she try her hand at some shorter pieces. It might be an idea to write an article about Ashley Grange itself, sending it up as a pretentious place for socialites. She could make the point that no one poor, or black, or pleb – the very sort of people who would benefit most from a health farm – dared venture through its haughty gates. Instead, it was the exclusive preserve of the fat cats, who were in the peak of health already. (That wasn't strictly true, but the truth probably wouldn't matter much to newspapers. In fact, she could put her talent for lying to good use if she took up writing for real. She could even reinvent herself, fabricate a glamorous life, with perhaps a tragic childhood: orphanages, poverty, sexual abuse, the lot.)

She took out a new disk and labelled it grandly 'Journalism', determined to make a start right now. It would stop her thinking about Elizabeth, or worrying about her own sexual peculiarities. And it would prove she was committed – breaking with the Beattie who'd had more than thirty jobs in fourteen years. This was her new *career*, and she would damn well take it seriously.

She went to get her father's photo from the mantelpiece and put it on the bureau to inspire her. She also fetched her dressing-gown; it was chilly in her nightdress, and she was planning a long stint. If she was to make her mark, she'd have to be professional – not fuss about petty things like backache or lost sleep. She typed her by-line at the top in large bold capitals: BEATTIE BANCROFT – LOVE HER OR HATE HER, YOU JUST CAN'T IGNORE HER!

'Right,' she said, glancing at her father and returning his seductive grin. 'This is for you, Dad.'

She paced up and down, trying to ease her back. Professional or not, she couldn't continue writing. The pain had become much worse, despite the aspirins she'd taken. Desperate for a pee again, she stumbled to the bathroom, wincing in the cold-eyed stare of the light. She peered in shock at the contents of the toilet bowl. There was blood in it – not menstrual blood, but the ordinary kind – and quite a lot of it. Surely it couldn't be the cystitis? She'd had attacks throughout her life, and though the pee might burn or sting, there had never been the slightest trace of blood. Christ! This must be something else – some terrifying sexual thing.

She sat shivering on the edge of the bath, all the warnings about using condoms or being faithful to one's partner blaring through her head. Both she and Max had been sleeping around for years. She didn't even know if he had other women now. That trip to France, ostensibly to view a couple of houses – might it have been a cover?

If he'd come straight on from some French girl's bed, it would certainly account for his poor performance tonight.

She flushed the toilet, wishing she could flush away her fears as simply. Panicking wouldn't help, though. The sensible thing would be to get herself to one of those special clinics first thing in the morning. *They* would explain her symptoms: the backache and the blood. Or was it better not to know? Suppose she had something really serious, like hepatitis, or AIDS. The very thought of it made her feel instantly worse – feverish and shaky.

She wandered back to the sitting-room, panicking still further as she remembered Dominic. She had finished with him last May, and he'd had scores of different women before her, and hated condoms as much as Max. Perhaps it had only just caught up with her and she'd risked her health (her life, maybe) for a man she didn't even like.

She picked up her father's photograph – his grin seemed callous now. She was utterly alone: her father half a world away, her mother in her grave, and Max back with his wife on the other side of London. She dared not ring Sal and wake her – she had enough problems of her own. Besides, Sal had always nagged about the condoms, and was bound to think 'I told you so', even if she was too kind to say it.

She returned to the bedroom, trying to blank out all the horrifying statistics: the thousands killed by AIDS; the lingering form of death. No, she mustn't jump to conclusions – it might be something relatively trivial. Besides, *whatever* was wrong, she couldn't do much about it till the morning, so the wisest plan was to get some sleep, or at least rest her aching back. She climbed into bed and pulled the duvet over her. The room still smelt faintly of Max – the last traces of his aftershave. She imagined him in bed, lying next to Michèle. What if Michèle was promiscuous too? If she and Max still slept together (and he'd never actually denied it), there was potentially a whole chain of people who might have infected her.

She inspected herself between the legs, letting out a cry as a pain stabbed through her back, then another, even sharper. She groped her way off the bed. She'd have to phone a doctor – this was really serious. But *who*?

She stopped in the doorway, recalling Elizabeth's words: how unwise it was to have no GP and how easy it was to find one. Not easy, though, in the middle of the night. If only she could phone Elizabeth now, this instant – after all, she'd been *married* to a doctor. But it was half past two in the morning and anyway Elizabeth was *over*. After those wild erotic fantasies, she wouldn't be able to look her in the eye, and it would be even more embarrassing to own up about her promiscuous affairs – and Max's too, for that matter.

She limped to the sofa and tried to lie in a more comfortable position, despite the pains still shooting through her back. Perhaps she ought to phone a hospital, one with a casualty department. But she detested hospitals. They turned you into a case, a number on a computer. And what if they admitted her? She would lose tomorrow's job, and lose Max as well, most likely. He was bound to finish with her if she had caught some ghastly infection. (It wouldn't be *his* fault, of course. He'd just accuse her of sleeping around, then go off with someone else.)

Tears slid down her face. Impatiently she brushed them off and got up again to fetch her elephant from the bottom bureau drawer. It was comforting to hold him in her hands, to imagine Elizabeth picking him out in some elegant antique shop. She hadn't even said a proper thank you. Elizabeth must think her awfully rude. She could ring her now and simply leave a message on the answerphone; tell her how much the present meant, and how she'd always treasure it.

The phone rang on and on. The answerphone must be switched off, or perhaps Elizabeth wasn't there. She might be staying the night at Harriet's – the beloved youngest daughter, who was *allowed* to disturb her mother in the middle of the night. She transferred the receiver to the other hand. Maybe it was just as well there was no reply. Elizabeth would be furious to be woken at this ungodly hour by anyone other than family.

Suddenly the ringing stopped and she heard the familiar, soothing voice – not angry in the slightest, merely worried.

'Hello, hello?' it repeated anxiously.

Beattie burst into tears. She longed to clutch at the voice, haul it up physically from Kent, cling to it for ever, drown in its concern.

'Who is it? What's the matter?'

She couldn't speak for crying. And yet a whole torrent of words was fighting to get out: explanations, apologies, remorse, self-accusations. She scrubbed her eyes, took two deep sobbing breaths. 'Elizabeth . . . it's me. I'm terribly sorry to ring you so late, but I . . . I think I may have AIDS.'

9

'We're almost there,' said Elizabeth, changing gear as they
approached a hump-backed bridge across a stream. 'It's just the
other side of the village.'

'Great,' said Beattie nervously, eyeing the chocolate-box thatched
cottages and chi-chi little shops. With every mile they'd driven out
of London she had grown more apprehensive, and now they were
nearing Elizabeth's house, she could almost hear her stomach beginning to churn. Even the weather seemed uncertain; fitful bursts of
sunshine suddenly swallowed up in cloud; autumn itself prevaricating
between lush greenness and bare brown. The birds were singing with
a lightheartedness she envied, but then they weren't ill, or scared.

They left the village and turned into a narrow winding road. The
houses became larger and more scattered: pretentious mansions
with burglar alarms and smugly perfect gardens. Commuter Kent,
Elizabeth had said, but it looked positively pastoral – fields unfurling
beyond the houses and a huge daunting sky unimpeded by tower
blocks, pylons, hoardings.

'This is us, down here.' Elizabeth was manoeuvring the car along
a rutted lane. The tall trees on either side touched fingers overhead,
and the tangled hedgerows were thick with briars and berries.
Shadows closed them in as they drove through the tree-tunnel; glints
of light freckling Elizabeth's arms. If only they could stop here,
Beattie thought, never actually arrive, but stay for ever in this safely
private shade. But all too soon they reached the end of the lane and
were approaching a pair of gates. Elizabeth rattled through them,
then nosed the car along a gravel drive, pulling up in front of a
rambling whitewashed house.

Beattie peered out of her window at the moss-furred roof with its crowing-cockerel weathervane, the creeper-covered walls. It was nothing like as forbidding as she'd feared. On the contrary, it seemed a friendly house – even reassuringly shabby. The paintwork on some of the windowsills had blistered, and the odd roof-tile was missing. Throughout the long slow journey, Mile End House had magnified in size until it had taken on the proportions of a stately home, no less – swarms of liveried servants touching their forelocks at the door; lakes and landscaped gardens stretching away for miles. The reality was a huge relief: a building on a human scale with no trace of ostentation; the only door-attendant an overweight black cat, and an exuberant front garden where unruly roses and overblown chrysan-themums jostled for pre-eminence. Anyway, even if the house had been on a par with Versailles, it was still a thousand times better to be ill down here with Elizabeth than to be stuck in some anonymous ward in London, with a few overworked nurses for company, and bad-tempered registrars pumping her with drugs.

Elizabeth helped her out of the car and opened the boot to get her case.

'Hello!' called a cheery voice, and Beattie swung round to see a woman in her twenties, with a baby in her arms. She was built on the same small scale as Elizabeth, but had eyes more grey than blue, and a shining bob of pale blond hair.

'You must be Beattie. How *are* you?'

'Okay – I think,' she mumbled, feeling still more pale and tired in contrast to the woman's healthy glow. The baby too looked in the very pink of health, a chubby rosy-cheeked creature, smiling benignly at the world.

Elizabeth made the introductions. 'My eldest daughter, Caroline,' she said, kissing her affectionately, as if to demonstrate their bond. 'And my grandson, Alexander. This is Beattie Bancroft.'

'Nice to meet you,' Beattie said selfconsciously. Caroline's voice was as thoroughbred as her mother's and her English rose com-plexion seemed another mark of her good breeding. She had obvi-ously never stuffed herself with fry-ups or pork pies, but had been fed since early childhood on manna and ambrosia.

'You must be feeling lousy, Beattie. That business with the hospital sounded quite horrendous.'

Beattie was aware that she was blushing. It seemed the most diaboli-cal cheek to have dragged Elizabeth from her bed at half past two in the morning because she was too scared to go to casualty alone.

Elizabeth had refused at first, but she'd sobbed and stormed and pleaded until Elizabeth gave in. Now she felt bitterly ashamed of such emotional blackmail, and had sat in glum silence for most of the journey, responding to Elizabeth's own remarks with the briefest of replies.

'Come in,' urged Caroline, transferring Alexander to his grandma and picking up Beattie's case. 'We've put you in Sarah's room.'

'W . . . won't she mind?'

'Heavens no! She's in Madrid. She works there, lucky thing.'

One daughter less, Beattie reflected gratefully, though there was still Harriet to contend with. Harriet's own illness was one of the reasons Elizabeth had been reluctant to agree to drive to London and leave a feverish daughter all alone. Harriet might (understandably) resent her presence here; regard her as an intruder – another invalid encroaching on her mother's precious time.

Beattie stepped into the hall, which, like the outside of the house, had an air of shabby elegance: well-worn antique furniture, a faded Persian rug. The large gold-framed paintings on the walls might have made it seem oppressive, but the atmosphere was lightened by several homely touches: Dinky toys scattered on the rug, an old duffel coat flung across the banisters, a second cat sitting on the windowsill next to a jam jar of wild flowers.

A small boy rushed out to greet them, but stopped short when he saw Beattie and ducked behind his mother.

'Say hello, Tim,' prompted Caroline. 'This is Beattie. She's come to stay.'

Tim stayed obstinately dumb, despite Beattie's own attempt at a friendly greeting. The silence was uncomfortable; seemed to express the hostility the others felt but were too polite to show.

'Don't worry – he's always shy with strangers,' Caroline explained.

Yes, thought Beattie, that's what I am: a stranger here, out of my depth in this large united family. And there were more introductions to come. An elderly couple were emerging from the sitting-room, gracious smiles in place: the man white-haired and distinguished, with an almost military bearing; the woman small but sprightly. Elizabeth seemed surprised to see them, though she did the honours and introduced her parents: James and Margaret Stanford.

'I'm sorry you're so poorly, my dear,' Mrs Stanford said, shaking Beattie's hand. 'We thought we'd better pop over to see if Elizabeth needed any help.'

64

You mean, to see if I'm causing more mayhem, Beattie corrected silently. Practically the whole extended family appeared to have turned out for the crisis. No doubt they were expecting her to be carried in on a stretcher, after all the fuss she'd made. Okay, so she had a kidney infection, but pyelonephritis (its grand official title) wasn't exactly fatal – the doctor had said it would clear up in a week or two with the right drugs and rest in bed.

'We'd better get you into bed,' Elizabeth was saying, as if tuning in to her thoughts.

'And I'll make some tea,' Mr Stanford offered, looking glad of an excuse to slip away.

'No tea for Beattie,' Elizabeth instructed. 'The hospital said she should stick to lemon barley. Did you get some, darling?' she asked, turning to her daughter.

Caroline nodded. 'I got everything you wanted. And the bed's made up. And I put Mrs Jackson off. She's coming at seven this evening instead. And I've taken all your messages – Janet rang, and Angela, and a Miss Fortescue, who said she'd phone tomorrow. And I'm afraid Tim broke one of your cups, and Robert said he couldn't . . .'

Beattie listened to the litany, feeling still more guilty. She had disrupted a whole day's routine and a host of other people, by the sounds of it. And yet, in the midst of everything, Elizabeth had actually thought of tiny details like lemon barley water.

She followed her upstairs, relieved to leave the others behind. If only she could be alone with her again, like that first night at Ashley Grange: they had sat and talked for hours, as if they were the only two people awake in the whole world.

Elizabeth paused on the landing and pointed out the bathroom: a large and airy room with a profusion of plants and pictures, and a wicker rocking-chair. She moved a pedal car from the top of the stairs, reparking it in a safer place. 'Shall we go and say a quick hello to Harriet? Her room's just along here.'

Beattie nodded dutifully. 'What's wrong with her exactly? I know you said she's ill, but . . .'

'She's got pains in all her joints, and she's lost quite a lot of weight. No one seems to know why. The doctor's mystified. He thinks it may be one of those weird viral things. Normally, she lives in Bristol – she's got her own little flat – but there's no one to look after her there.'

Like me, reflected Beattie. With one big difference: Harriet didn't have to scream and threaten to be given a bed in Elizabeth's nursing home.

Elizabeth stopped outside the half-open door. 'All right if we come in?' she called.

'Yes, fine.'

'How are you, darling?'

'So-so.'

'This is Beattie Bancroft. Beattie – my youngest daughter, Harriet.'

Harriet waved a queenly hand. She *did* look regal, sitting back against her pile of pillows, with her long fair hair scooped up on top. Another blonde, another peaches-and-cream complexion. And, of course, the pedigree voice.

'I'm sorry you've been in the wars! Caroline's told me about it. Kidney things are ghastly.'

'They say I'll live.' Beattie forced a smile, glancing out of the window at the flowerbeds and the apple trees, the fields and hills beyond. A room with a view.

'We'll see you later, darling,' Elizabeth was saying, picking up Harriet's book from the floor.

Beattie squinted at the title: *The Brothers Karamazov.* They were real intellectuals, this family, or at least alarmingly serious readers. She would have to keep her own frivolous magazines strictly out of sight.

Elizabeth led her back along the landing and opened the door into a small but sunny room which also looked out on the garden.

'Right, let's get you settled. You must be dying for a rest.'

Beattie grunted her assent, nervously assessing Sarah's room: Sarah's posters on the walls, Sarah's photos pinned up on a board, Sarah's books on the bookshelves, even Sarah's teddy on the bed. What was she *doing* here, in Sarah's place, masquerading as a daughter when she was nobody and nothing? Why had she phoned Elizabeth at all? She could have stayed with Sal in her familiar basement flat just round the corner, instead of flogging all this way and disrupting everyone.

'Phone for you, Mummy!' Caroline shouted from downstairs.

Beattie winced at the word 'Mummy', which sounded affected and absurd. Yet plain Mum would be equally wrong for Elizabeth. It had been something of a shock to hear Tim calling her Granny – it made her seem suddenly so old, and so inextricably enmeshed in family relationships.

'Excuse me, will you, Beattie? I'll be back as soon as I can. You get into bed and leave the unpacking to me, if you want. You look absolutely exhausted.'

Beattie unpacked the case herself. She *was* exhausted, yes, but she wanted to keep busy, and also to put her own stamp on the room, so it would feel safer and less strange. She placed the photo of her father on the windowsill, where she could see it from the bed, first moving aside some of Sarah's ornaments. She banished the teddy to the wardrobe and put Elizabeth's jade elephant right next to her on the bedside table. By the time she'd hung up her clothes and arranged her toilet things by the basin, the room looked distinctly better – less of Sarah, more of Beattie. Yet she couldn't seem to relax. She kept imagining the family discussing her downstairs – why she'd had to be carted here, instead of going into hospital. The doctor in casualty had, in fact, wanted to keep her in, but she'd refused point blank; all her terror of hospitals surfacing like scum on dirty water. (Her mother had died in hospital, after months and months of vegetating in a side ward. She would never forget those endless visits, sitting hushed and hopeless beside that white hump in the bed.) They had argued the toss for a good ten minutes, the doctor pointing out that if she neglected the infection now, it could affect her kidney function later on in life. He'd also said that she needed more tests and someone to look after her, while *she*'d insisted that she could look after herself. Then Elizabeth had intervened, requesting a private word with him. She must have used her ex-husband's credentials to pull rank, or whatever, because it was eventually agreed that the patient could be nursed in Kent, so long as Elizabeth ensured that she saw a kidney specialist and had all the proper tests.

So here they were – the patient and the nurse, or rather the hysteric and the saint. No one had ever done so much for her before, and she was terrified that Elizabeth might resent her. And even if she didn't, her family most certainly would.

She sat down on the bed, listening to the noises from downstairs: cheerful voices, shouts from Tim, a radio droning to itself. Why was Elizabeth taking so long? Had someone *else* phoned in a crisis? Poor Elizabeth! Her life seemed full of crises. Her patients probably pestered her all day, and, with four children and three grandchildren, there must be continual demands on her time.

She wandered to the window and back, unable to keep still. She ought to make a phone call herself: ring Max and tell him where she was. But she'd need to speak to him in private, which wouldn't be that easy with all these people in the house. Elizabeth had been decent enough to phone her boss at work and explain the situation, but she could hardly expect her to ring Max. Anyway, she owed him an apology – having blamed him for infecting her and all but ordered her coffin. Now, thank God, there was no need for special clinics, though she did feel really ill. Her head and back were aching more than ever, and a sense of total weariness was beginning to creep up on her, as if she hadn't slept for a month. She undressed and got into bed, only at that moment daring to let go, releasing all the tension in her body. She let out a long sighing breath, too tired to worry any more, too tired even to think. She groped out for her elephant, clutched him close against her chest, and allowed herself to sink down into sleep.

She sat up slowly, wondering where she was. It was still light outside the windows, though a reluctant greyish light. The view was totally unfamiliar: an extensive lawn and trees. The bed felt unusually comfortable, the duvet thicker and more luxurious than her own. A noise outside had woken her – a knocking on the door, repeated softly now. 'Come in,' she called, quickly tidying her hair.

'Are you all right? Shall I put the light on? It's a bit gloomy in here.'

A small and shadowy figure; a voice she didn't recognize.

'Yes, do,' she said. 'I'm sorry – I must have fallen asleep.'

'Good! That's what you need. I've brought your pills and a spot of supper. I don't know whether you feel like eating?'

Beattie shook her head, then nodded. She was suddenly close to tears. It was Elizabeth's mother, who had come up with a tray: steamed fish and parsley sauce, and fruit salad in a cut-glass dish. Actually she loathed steamed fish, but that wasn't the point. She was being waited on, being fed manna and ambrosia. And yes, there was her lemon barley in a jug, and six brightly coloured tablets laid out on a saucer.

'Thanks,' she stammered. 'You really shouldn't spoil me. I can come down for my meals.'

'Elizabeth wouldn't hear of it!' Mrs Stanford said, placing the tray on the bedside table. 'She's seeing a patient at the moment, by the way. I thought I'd sit with you while you have your supper – if you don't object, that is. It can get lonely, can't it, being ill?'

'Yes,' agreed Beattie, wondering how she would force the fish down under Mrs Stanford's watchful eyes. They were the same striking blue as Elizabeth's, she noticed, but surrounded by a web of crinkly lines; the skin fragile though fine-textured still; the short grey hair subjected to a corrugated perm. Her movements were graceful and unhurried as she arranged the pillows and helped her to sit up, then placed the tray carefully on the bed, and finally drew up a chair for herself.

'You'd better have your pills last. It says "after meals" on the bottle. And lots to drink, remember.' Mrs Stanford poured some lemon barley and passed Beattie the glass.

'Thanks,' said Beattie again. The word seemed too brief for the gratitude she felt. It was an entirely new experience to have a mother bring her drinks and pills; it had always been the other way round. 'Thanks,' she said, third time, as Mrs Stanford unfolded her napkin for her: a proper linen one, embroidered like the traycloth.

Mrs Stanford laughed. 'You don't have to keep thanking me, my dear. Now come on – eat up before your fish gets cold. I cooked that fish myself. Caroline was making steak and kidney pie, but I thought kidneys might be tactless in the circumstances!'

Now it was Beattie's turn to laugh. She warmed to Mrs Stanford, despite the yawning gulf she felt between them. Elizabeth's mother was so utterly well-bred, her voice outclassing even the rest of her family's: unadulterated top-drawer. And her clothes were so conventional and classic: the soft pink twinset with its single strand of pearls, the tweedy skirt and sensible (expensive) shoes. Beattie realized *she* was wearing an elongated tee-shirt with 'STOP THAT MAN – I WANT TO GET OFF!' printed on the front. It doubled as her nightie, and she had packed in such a rush, she hadn't even thought about how embarrassingly out of place it would look.

She tried to hide the crude slogan with her arm whilst using the other hand to eat her fish. If Mrs Stanford had cooked it for her specially, there was no way she could leave it. She took a tiny morsel on her fork and somehow managed to swallow it. Surprised, she took a larger piece. It tasted quite all right – not fishy as she'd feared, just comfortingly bland. She suddenly registered the fact that she was absolutely ravenous; that she hadn't eaten anything since a mouthful of pavlova at her so-called midnight feast. 'It's good,' she said. 'Thank you, Mrs Stanford.'

'Positively no more thank yous, Beattie! You sit and eat in peace. And do call me Margaret, by the way.'

Beattie settled back. It *was* peaceful in the house now. All the distracting noises had subsided, and her mind was less of a battleground. She sampled some mashed potato, which was buttery and soft – perfect invalid's fare. She pretended she was Tim's age: a pampered little brat with the sort of saintly mother who brought her meals in bed. As a child, she had always been pretending; conjuring up different mothers, different homes. She had dreamed of a country cottage with brothers, sisters, dogs and cats, and now it had almost come true. Cats, if not dogs; two small cutesy brothers; a rural setting with roses round the door, and a placid Grandma smiling by her bedside. She didn't *want* to call her Margaret – it somehow spoilt the fantasy – though she was pleased to be asked, since it must mean she'd been accepted. Strange how none of their names were shortened – *her* parents would have been Jim and Maggie (or more likely, 'you with the face').

'Is the pain any better?' Margaret was asking.

'Yes,' she lied. 'It is.' She wanted to be the perfect patient, in return for the steamed fish – not whinge about her symptoms, but make Margaret really like her. She finished the fish and started the fruit salad: the home-made kind with exotic things like kiwis in it, and some speckly purple fruits she had never seen before. 'Do you live nearby?' she asked, removing a grape-pip from her mouth as delicately as she could.

'Yes, about five miles away. We used to live in Salisbury, right in the Cathedral Close. I have to say, I miss it. We were such a cosy community, and of course the services in the cathedral were wonderful. I'm afraid our village church just can't compare.'

'No,' said Beattie, 'I suppose it wouldn't.' She was venturing into unknown territory. She had rarely set foot inside a church, let alone sat through a whole service. She swallowed the last spoonful of fruit, savouring the sweetness of the juice.

'Don't forget your pills.'

Margaret stood beside her, making sure she swallowed all six. Her nursing duties over, she sat back in the chair, her small gnarled hands folded serenely in her lap. 'Now, tell me a bit about yourself. I hear you met Elizabeth at the health farm?'

'Mm,' said Beattie, on her guard. Ashley Grange was safe enough, but she didn't want to get onto her life history: there would be far too much to censor.

'And what sort of work do you do?'

She hesitated. Temping sounded so dull, and she was desperate to impress this woman, if for no other reason than that she was Elizabeth's mother. 'I'm a . . . journalist,' she said, pulling the covers up to her chin to hide the offending tee-shirt.

'Oh, really? How exciting!'

'Well, to tell the truth, I'm only a beginner. It's not easy to get into. You really need good contacts. But I've just had a piece accepted – my first one, actually.'

'Congratulations. That's marvellous! When are we going to see it?'

'Oh, it'll probably take an age. These things always do – by the time the editor's suggested new angles, and the subs have messed around with it and cut it down to size.' Max's phrases, but they seemed to be making a good impression. Margaret's kind blue eyes were fixed on her attentively.

'In fact, I've got another big job on,' Beattie added airily. It would be even better if she could convince this household that she didn't intend to impose on them too long, but would be out of their way by the end of the week, at the latest. 'And they're screaming for the piece already. Which means I'll have to get back to London pretty quick.'

'But Beattie, my dear, you're *ill!* You can't possibly start work again until this kidney infection's cleared up.'

'Don't worry, I'm quite tough. I'll throw it off in a day or two, you'll see. Anyway, in *my* line of work you can't afford to be ill. It's all rush jobs and deadlines.'

Margaret rose to her feet indignantly. 'I'll jolly well speak to them myself! I mean, you could risk your life, rushing back to work before you're better. If you give me the number of this . . . this editor, or whoever he is, I'll . . .'

She was saved by Elizabeth, who chose that moment to put her head round the door. Beattie was so relieved to be let off the hook, she suddenly collapsed in giggles at the thought of Margaret giving Max his marching orders. The two of them were like completely different species.

'Gracious!' said Elizabeth. 'You *do* sound better, Beattie. The state you were in this morning, I never thought you'd laugh again.'

II

10

'No, you need a hard page-break here,' Beattie said. 'Can you remember how to do it? I'll give you a clue – it's a combination of two keys.'

'Er, is it these two?' Elizabeth's fingers hovered uncertainly over the keyboard, a frown etched deep between her brows.

'Yes, that's right, but hold the control key down while you press return. Good! And now on to the next page. First we'll centre the heading...' Beattie was enjoying herself. She relished being the expert for a change. And she *was* an expert when it came to word-processing, especially with an apprehensive novice sitting beside her.

'Damn!' Elizabeth muttered. 'I've forgotten how you make it go in the middle. Actually, do you mind if we have a break? I can only take so much in.' She stood up and stretched, drifting to the open window to look out at the garden. 'I just can't believe this sun! It's almost unheard-of to have a heatwave in the middle of October.'

'There was one about six years ago. I remember it distinctly.' Beattie recalled the stifling photographer's studio where she'd been posing almost starkers. But naked or not, the heat had been unbearable. She kicked the scene to the bottom of her mind; it didn't belong in Mile End House. For the last few weeks, she had been making a huge effort to be the model guest. No, not guest – she loathed the word – but friend, companion, workhorse. The minute she felt well enough, she had offered to go shopping or run errands, babysit for Caroline, read stories to her wretched child, and generally bend over backwards to earn her Brownie points. She barely recognized herself. It was like playing a new role – one which brought her surprising pleasure, though sometimes she worried that she wouldn't be able to keep it up. The amazing weather had helped her persevere,

75

given her a boost. It was as if October was copying her example, deciding to change its basic character and become sunnier and more benign. She felt in tune with nature, however corny that might sound; sometimes even felt *serene*, for heaven's sake. Perhaps at last she had reached maturity, having failed to make the grade at eighteen or twenty-one, but only now, at thirty.

'We ought to be out in the garden,' Elizabeth observed, still standing by the window and lifting up her face to the warm caress of the sun.

'*You* go, if you like. I want to bash on with your last two chapters. Then I'll have caught up with you, and have everything you've done so far on disk.'

'I just can't thank you enough, Beattie.' Elizabeth fetched her cigarettes from the mantelpiece and subsided on the sofa with them. 'It looks so wonderfully professional – I mean actually printed out and . . .'

'Well, I presume you'll be showing it to a publisher when it's finished, and you couldn't possibly have handed it over the way it was.'

'I suppose I've never quite believed it *would* be published,' Elizabeth reflected, exhaling a curl of smoke. 'I'm only really writing it for myself.'

'But it's good,' insisted Beattie. 'Even *I* find it interesting, and I'm a total ignoramus when it comes to psycho-anything. Mind you, I'm learning a hell of a lot. I never realized how complicated the whole thing was. In fact, I've been dipping into some of your other books.' She waved a hand at the bookshelves, which reached from floor to ceiling, and even spilled over onto the floor. They were working in what had once been Jeremy's study, where there was barely room for the quantities of literature: not only Elizabeth's tomes on psychoanalysis, but the medical books Jeremy had left behind, and rows and rows of novels. 'I feel I ought to mug up on the subject if I'm working as your secretary.'

'Oh, Beattie, don't call yourself that! It makes me sound so grand to have a secretary.'

'You *are* grand. And you *need* a secretary. Once I've finished your book, I'm going to make a start on your correspondence – set up a proper database for your patients' addresses and accounts and . . .'

'Well in that case, I absolutely insist on paying you a proper salary.'

'I've told you, *no*.'

'But Beattie, it's not fair. After all, you're not earning anything else.'

'I get the dole, don't I? And my keep, and marvellous meals? I'd feel insulted if you paid me, on top of everything you've done already. Do you realize, the day after tomorrow, I'll have been here a whole month?'

'Yes, and most of that time you've been working your fingers to the bone. My mother's quite concerned about it. She blames *me*, I'll have you know! She keeps saying I should make you rest.'

'I don't need to rest any more. Anyway, it isn't work – it's therapy, to use your word. Now shut up and let me get on!' She took Elizabeth's practice disk out of the machine and inserted the one she was using for the book text. It was impossible to explain, even to herself, how desperately important it was to be accepted in this household, to find a role she could excel in. The chores and errands didn't count – any fool could do those – but Elizabeth's book was something else entirely. She had transformed a pile of messy, scribbled sheets into a professionally typed manuscript, becoming gradually more skilled at deciphering the untidy writing and spelling the unfamiliar words. It had been intended as a present for her – and not courtesy of Marks & Spencer's this time. She had put her heart and soul into it, determined that the finished pages should be absolutely perfect.

It had helped, of course, to have the new computer. She had started the process on her ancient Amstrad (having returned to London to fetch it, and her car), but Elizabeth had decided that she, too, should own a machine and that Beattie should teach her how to use it. And since Elizabeth knew next to nothing about either hardware or software, the 'expert' had used her contacts to get a really fantastic deal, including a state-of-the-art ink-jet printer she was tempted to smuggle home.

She shaded her eyes against the sun. She was confused about where home *was*. Great to pretend that she had always lived in Mile End House, but the comings and goings of Elizabeth's flesh-and-blood family kept bringing her up with a jolt, reminding her that she was only a casual visitor – and, worse, in danger of outstaying her welcome. She could no longer really claim to be an invalid when the specialist had said that she was definitely on the mend and had cut her pills to two a day. So why the hell didn't she return to her own flat?

She positioned Elizabeth's pages on the copy-holder. *They* were her answer – it would be sloppy and unprofessional to leave the job unfinished. Elizabeth would need her secretary on hand to put the next instalment on disk as soon as it was written. And anyway, there was masses more to teach her. Elizabeth couldn't cope with font changes or with some of the niceties of layout, so she still required a live-in tutor.

She set the page-number for the new chapter and got cracking on the opening paragraph, her fingers flying over the keys. It was high time she stopped worrying and made the most of the fact that she had Elizabeth to herself for once. Harriet was better at last, and had returned to Bristol two days ago; Caroline and family were on holiday in France; Sarah worked abroad in any case, and Emma lived in York with her husband and small daughter. There weren't even any patients coming. In the past, Elizabeth had kept Tuesdays free for charity work at Jeremy's hospital; after his abrupt departure she had given it up, rather than face the painful memories. But she still continued the tradition of keeping one weekday free of patients.

'Get *down*, Boz!' Beattie pushed the hot black body off her lap. 'I can't type with you in the way.' The cat had taken a shine to her right from the beginning, unlike the haughty Tolkien. 'Okay, you can sit on my foot if you insist, but don't you dare disturb me. I'm going to finish these chapters by lunchtime if it kills me.'

'It's finished,' Beattie shouted, bouncing into the kitchen with a pile of newly printed pages.

'Wonderful! Let's celebrate.'

'Not yet. You told me you'd got at least seven more chapters to do, so we're not allowed to celebrate until we've both got to the end.'

'And I suppose you expect me to toss off seven chapters here and now?'

'Of course! I can't be twiddling my thumbs while you swan around waiting for inspiration.'

Elizabeth laughed. 'Will you allow us a break for lunch?'

'Okay. Let's have it in the garden. We can sit on the lawn and pretend we're in St Tropez.'

'It's hotter here than in St Tropez. I heard that on the news this morning.'

'Let's change into our swimsuits then – grab our last chance of getting a tan.'

Elizabeth paused in her cucumber-chopping. 'It seems wrong.'

'What do you mean – wrong?'

'Well, to be lazing on a weekday.'

'Oh, Elizabeth, you're impossible! You *never* laze.'

'You haven't been exactly idle either.'

'Okay. This is our reward for hard labour – a whole afternoon in the garden soaking up the sun. I'll go and put my bikini on.'

'I didn't know you had it here.'

Beattie nodded. On her trip back to the flat to fetch the Amstrad, she had collected a carful of clothes, including a bikini. She had intended using the swimming pool in Sevenoaks, to get some exercise and prevent her getting fat – a definite risk at Mile End House, where she was fed three meals a day (four on Sundays, if Elizabeth's parents came to tea). She hadn't got round to swimming yet, but neither had she put on weight, which seemed miraculous.

She ran upstairs to change, feeling slightly embarrassed walking down again clad in nothing more than two skimpy pieces of polka-dotted nylon. Not that there was anyone to see her except a supercilious Tolkien. Elizabeth was still in her old jeans.

'Aren't you going to change?'

'No. I'm afraid I'm one of those people who have to cover up in the sun rather than strip off. I never seem to go brown, only red and blotchy. Right, take that tray out will you, Beattie, and I'll bring the lasagne.'

'Lasagne? I thought you said we were having a snack lunch.'

'It *is* a snack. And I know you're not keen on sandwiches.'

'Yes, but you mustn't keep cooking for me.'

'I enjoy it, actually.' Elizabeth removed the dish from the oven and sprinkled parsley on top, pausing for a moment as if to marshal her thoughts. 'You see, I've never regarded cooking as a chore, but more of a psychological necessity. I suppose it provides a sort of order – following a recipe and seeing dishes come out right, when that doesn't always happen in life. It was especially important when the children were small and Jeremy was overworking and out a tremendous lot, and the phone never seemed to stop ringing – usually for *him*, of course! And Emma wasn't eating properly and my father was unwell. Sometimes everything seemed so utterly chaotic that I'd use cooking as a means of regaining control. I'd search for some really complicated dish to make, and it seemed to work like a kind of ritual – you know, calming me down and helping me to concentrate on something other than the turmoil all around me.'

Beattie sat in pin-drop silence. At last, Elizabeth was confiding in her, revealing her true self.

'Then later, when I started seeing patients, cooking seemed more helpful still. *Their* lives might not be working, but my lemon soufflé or whatever was absolutely spot on. I bought this ingenious cookbook which had recipes for every day of the year, using only foods in season. I found it rather comforting to follow the instructions to the letter. It was like a confirmation that some things in life were rational and simple, even if the human psyche wasn't. And I got a great sense of achievement when the dish I was making turned out exactly the same as its picture in the book.'

'Like this one?' Beattie asked, pointing to the lasagne. She was surprised – and touched – that Elizabeth had given away so much; let her see that she *too* was vulnerable.

'Oh, I don't need a fancy cookbook for lasagne. And I suppose I no longer need my sense of order, now everything's calmed down. Come on, though – let's eat! The food's getting cold while I stand around philosophizing.'

'I like it when you talk.' Beattie picked up the tray and followed Elizabeth into the garden. 'You hardly ever do – about yourself, I mean.'

'I suppose it's an occupational hazard. As a therapist, you get so used to listening and to keeping yourself absolutely private, it becomes second nature in the end.'

'I'd never make a therapist. I'd tell my patients to bloody well shut up and listen to *me*.'

'You never know, it might even work!' Elizabeth laughed. She unloaded the dishes on to the tartan picnic rug and started serving the food. 'Some patients do get frightfully self-absorbed, and I sometimes wonder if I'm doing them any favours, encouraging them to focus on themselves week after week after week.'

'Well, why not give the whole lot up and become a lady of leisure?'

'Oh, I *couldn't*, Beattie. I'd feel so . . . so . . . purposeless.'

'But you've got your family, and your writing, and all the things you do in the village, and that fund-raising committee you're on. Hell! If *I* had the cash, I'd never work again. I'd loll around all day drinking Alabama Slammers and being massaged by obedient slaves!'

'I thought you were dying to be famous?'

'God! Don't remind me of that.' Beattie waved her fork dramatically. The last thing she wanted to think about was her abortive writing career. It hadn't proved easy to dash off chirpy little pieces – not even in the last few days when she'd been feeling so much better physically. At first, she had blamed the pills and her infection, but now she had nothing left to blame but her own depressing lack of talent. Max had been no help: not only was he peeved that she'd gone rushing down to Kent to stay with a woman he resented, but he was also involved in a major crisis at the paper, which meant he was too preoccupied to see her anyway. In fact, she had never known him so frantic. On top of everything else, his French estate agents had phoned to say they'd found him the ideal house, but urged him to put in a bid immediately, before another buyer snapped it up. That meant a lightning trip to Provence when he hardly had the time to clean his teeth. With such urgent matters on his mind, his offer to launch her into journalism had gone completely by the board. Perhaps it was just as well in the circumstances, since all she had to show him was a few pathetic bits of copy lacking any shape or bite. Oh, to hell with Max! She refused to let him muscle in on this private picnic lunch. If he insisted on working fifteen-hour days in a suffocating London office, good luck to him. *She* intended to put her feet up in St Tropez.

'I'll go and put the kettle on,' Elizabeth said, stacking the dirty plates.

'No, don't.' Beattie stretched out luxuriously on the rug. 'Once you get up you'll start pottering – I *know* you! And you said we'd have a lazy afternoon. It's so glorious out here.' She gazed around at the lushness of the garden: scarlet roses still in bloom, purple daisies, golden rod. The branches of the apple trees were bowed beneath their weight of fruit; the odd bloated wasp blundering around them in drunken figures of eight. She breathed in all the smells: ripe and rotting windfalls, honeysuckle, roses, smoke from next-door's bonfire. The hedge itself was aflame with orange berries, red and yellow leaves. And yet the sky was that deep summer-blue found only on schmaltzy calendar-scenes; the slightest blemish airbrushed from the clouds.

'Jeremy wouldn't think it was so glorious.' Elizabeth settled back in the shade of the mulberry tree. 'He used to insist on regimentation in the garden. I think he expected the plants to stand to attention,

81

like the nurses at his hospital. And I suppose, being a surgeon, it was in his nature to be a bit of a hacker and slasher. Anything too tall or out of line was instantly cut down. He'd be appalled to see this jungle,'

'It's *not* a jungle,' Beattie objected, feeling a sudden violent loathing for the man. He had cut his wife down, too: taken everything she'd given him – lemon soufflés, decades of devotion – then dumped her for someone else. This was the first time Elizabeth had talked about him with anything bordering on resentment. On the rare occasions she mentioned him at all, it was always in an impassive way, betraying neither approval nor hostility.

'Beattie . . .'

'What?'

'I've been feeling rather guilty about those articles you were meant to write. You've been so busy with *my* work, you probably haven't had a chance to do them.'

Beattie sat up sharply. 'I *have*. It's not time I need, it's talent. I'm obviously not cut out to be a writer.'

'But you *are*, my love. I mean, that marvellous poem you wrote about the elephant. I found it really moving.'

'Oh, poems don't count. I'd hardly get my name in the *Herald* with *that*!'

'You're always putting yourself down, Beattie. I should imagine poetry's the most difficult thing to write of all.'

'It's not poetry, it's doggerel.'

'There you go again! You have lots of different talents, but you're for ever telling yourself – and me – how you're no good at this and no good at that. I mean, take Tim as a minor example. You keep saying you're useless with children, yet Caroline told me just the other day that you've really made a hit with him. Apparently he was asking her when you'd be babysitting again.'

Beattie shrugged. She had only *pretended* to like the little monster, so all that Caroline's remarks proved was she was a master of deception. Her poem, though, was infinitely more important. She had begun it as a brief thank-you to Elizabeth and it had turned out long – and serious. She brushed an insect off her leg and remained studiously looking down. 'Did . . . did you really like my poem?'

'You know I did. I told you.'

'Yes, but I thought you were just being kind.'

'Beattie, you know me better than that. Anyway it would hardly be kind to encourage you in a line of work if you had no aptitude for it.'

Beattie struggled with a conflict of emotions. She was elated by the praise, but also worried that it might perhaps be some subtle ruse to dispatch her back to London. Elizabeth was far too tactful to tell her straight that it was time for her to leave, but that phrase 'a line of work' could be interpreted to mean that her duties here were over.

She flopped miserably onto her stomach. If she returned to Westbourne Grove and failed to make it as a writer, she'd be back to soulless temping. There was no sense of belonging in the temp world. The assignments were usually short, so as soon as she'd sorted out the names and faces in one job, she would move on to the next. It was permanence she craved – the solid permanence of this house, where Elizabeth had lived for more than twenty years. At least she had a key now, which made her almost family. She guarded it with her life, feeling a surge of pride and pleasure each time she unlocked the door. But if she returned to London, she would be expected to give it back. Perhaps she could take a job as Tim's nanny – after all, he *had* been singing her praises. Except that was Caroline's role. And anyway, babysitting now and then wasn't the same thing. If she had to cope with the wretched kid full-time, she'd probably bash his precocious brains in.

'What's wrong?' Elizabeth asked.

'Nothing. Why?'

'You look sort of . . . defeated.'

'No. I'm fine. Just making sure I don't end up with a brown tummy and a white back.'

'Your back's caught the sun already. You do tan well! I envy you.'

'Yes, but look at my thighs. They're disgustingly fat.'

'They're *not*, Beattie. When are you going to accept that you're actually very slim?'

'Never!'

'Well, promise me one thing? You won't run yourself down any more today. It's going to be Wonderwoman Beattie, at least till the stroke of midnight.'

Beattie laughed. 'Okay. Let's both be Wonderwomen – breathtakingly beautiful, filthy rich, frighteningly intelligent and . . .'

'Pursued by suitors young and old,' Elizabeth interjected. 'Damn,' she added, getting up as the phone shrilled from the open window. 'There's one of them pestering me right now.'

'Don't answer it.'

'I must. You never know, it may be the Aga Khan.'

'Well, don't let him keep you too long. You can do better than a mere billionaire, and a pretty ancient one at that.'

Elizabeth ran into the house, still laughing, while Beattie continued toasting her back. The most stunning back in the world – the slimmest and most gorgeous thighs. Yes, she *would* be Wonderwoman, and there would be absolutely no question of leaving Mile End House. On the contrary, Elizabeth would insist she stayed for ever and bar the door to everyone else.

She closed her eyes, savouring the sensation of the warm sun on her skin. Her breasts were squashed against the rug. Its rough texture was a turn-on, arousing in her the feelings she had been trying to suppress all month. She slipped the bikini straps off her shoulders, pushed the top right down and let her hand stroke across the nipples. The casual touch produced an instant reaction: her whole body seemed to kick-start into a fury of excitement, as if demanding recompense for its four weeks of frustration. She knew her wild explosive side had no place at Mile End House. Perhaps that was why she had kept herself so busy – trying to turn herself into someone safer and tamer: the perfect daughter, like Harriet or Caroline, who hadn't gone through thirty men in half as many years.

She rubbed her breasts against the prickly rug, back and forth, back and forth. They were crying out for more – a mouth on them, a tongue on them, teeth grazing to that point of almost pain. She pinched her nipples hard, as if to punish them. Okay, so she was missing sex. Well, all she had to do was return to London and ring Max. He might be up to his eyes, but he wasn't working nights.

Boz strolled across the lawn and parked himself beside her on the rug. 'Have you come to help me out?' she grinned, shifting her position so she could lie with her breasts against his fur. It was warm and soft, and tickled, and the cat appeared to be enjoying it as well. His eyes were closed and he was lying with his legs stretched out in a shamelessly abandoned way; a steady purr rumbling in his throat. She copied the noise as she brushed her breasts against him, moving them slowly, slowly down from his nape to his long tail. She glanced surreptitiously around, then groped a hand inside her bikini bottom, scratching her nails through the coarse hair. Why couldn't she have *fur* there – soft, luxurious jet-black fur like Boz's – instead of her own boring-brown wire wool? She tried to imagine Elizabeth's thatch: short and dense and creamy-pale like Tolkien, or maybe dark and wild and sprouting in profusion – an amazing contrast to her restrained and tranquil temperament. She longed to see Elizabeth with nothing on at all, to be allowed to study her quite freely, even her most secret places.

Angrily, she pulled her hand out, fastened her bikini top and turned over on her back. Elizabeth was her hostess and her pupil. Things had only worked out so well between them because of her non-stop efforts to be dutiful and professional. It would all blow up in her face if she relaxed her hold on those alarmingly sexual feelings. Even with them bottled up, her obsession with Elizabeth still seemed overpowering. However many other people might be in the house – charming daughters, distracting kids, brainy grandfathers, well-meaning friends and neighbours – it was Elizabeth who magnetized her, like a tiny moon tugging at the tides.

She sat up on the rug and peered through the french windows. She constantly needed to know what Elizabeth was doing, where she was, *how* she was. Nights were hardest of all. It was awful having to shut her bedroom door and imagine Elizabeth behind her own door, sleeping all alone. At least she was lucky enough to be with her most of the daytime, and had seen her now in a score of different roles, dressed in anything from an apron to a sundress. Yet still it wasn't enough. Secretly and desperately she wanted to lie close to her, even crawl inside her body, for God's sake.

She jumped up from the rug, startling Boz who gave a mew of protest. If the warm seductive weather was having this effect on her, then she would be better off inside. Anyway, she wanted to find Elizabeth. She'd been gone for ages, so she'd probably finished on the phone by now and got diverted onto some job or other.

'Come on, Boz, let's go and see what she's up to.' The cat followed her into the kitchen, but Elizabeth wasn't there, and she'd learned never to yell out for her in case she was talking to a patient on the phone. She edged into the hall; heard the murmur of Elizabeth's voice coming from the consulting room. So it *was* a sodding patient, or a shrink, maybe, trying to persuade her to take on another case.

She trailed into the drawing-room and sank disconsolately into an armchair. This room always aroused in her a mixture of envy and resentment. Even its name sounded pretentious, as if it were giving itself airs. In her childhood home, they'd had a 'front room', and no one sat there anyway. It was kept for visitors – who never came. She glanced from the grand piano, with the Bach sonata open on it, to the portraits of the daughters on the walls. She had never learned music – there hadn't been the cash for lessons, let alone an instrument – and as for having her portrait painted when she was barely out of nursery school, the very idea made her hoot. Her parents had a few snapshots of her jumbled in a drawer, but nothing on display, whereas here family photographs were almost part of the furnishings, and all graced with silver frames. They showed the girls at every age and stage, posing in their school uniforms, or with various doting relatives and a whole succession of pets: cats, dogs, hamsters, a tortoise and an angora rabbit. But her favourite photo was the one of Elizabeth standing on her own, looking achingly young and frail, and with the same fair hair as her daughters. She went over to the mantelpiece to study it again, touching a finger to Elizabeth's open lips. She must have been speaking as the picture was taken, probably saying 'Get a move on!' or 'The sun's in my eyes.'

No – saying, 'I love you, Beattie, I need you, Beattie, I've enjoyed this month with you, Beattie, more than any time in my life.'

'Stupid cow!' she reproved herself, moving back to the piano to take another look at Jeremy. There was only one photo of him in the house. The others had presumably been removed, and this one permitted only because he was more or less eclipsed by one of the daughters (in a tutu) and a large shaggy-coated dog.

She stood staring at his stern fastidious profile, trying to picture man and wife together; once (presumably) a loving couple. Then she slipped out to the hall again, to see if Elizabeth was still on the phone. Yes, worse luck. Her voice sounded louder now – even rather vehement – though the words were indecipherable. How dare these bloody patients monopolize Elizabeth – not only take up her time, but upset her into the bargain. She resented the whole pack of them: doctors, patients, shrinks. Christ! She wasn't even allowed to set foot in Elizabeth's consulting room. It was like some holy shrine, barred to outsiders. But she *wasn't* an outsider – she was typing Elizabeth's book. One of the reasons she had offered to do it in the first place was to find out more about the world of psychotherapy. Okay, now that she *did* know more, it struck her as a most peculiar world, but at least she was beginning to understand what made therapists tick, their unpronounceable jargon, the mind-boggling things they argued about.

She strode into the kitchen and sat down at the end of the table in what had once been Jeremy's place. That was out of bounds as well. She had sat there at a meal once, and Tim had instantly told her off. 'That's *Grandpa's* chair,' he'd protested. 'And you're not allowed to sit in it.' Everyone had looked embarrassed and she'd jumped up like a scalded cat. She had vaguely noticed the vacant seat, but hadn't realized it was left empty on purpose – as another sort of shrine, almost. Were they keeping it free for him in the hope that he'd come back? Not much chance of that at present. He'd decided to take a sabbatical year and had gone to live in Geneva with wife Mark Two, a safe distance from his discarded family.

She placed her hands defiantly on the wooden arms of the chair. It was the only one with arms: the man's chair, the special chair. If she sat in it, then *she* was special: Elizabeth's mate Mark Two – bed-mate, soul-mate, everything. She closed her eyes and imagined the pair of them starting out together. No intrusive children or egoistic patients, just Elizabeth and her; committed, married, joined.

Suddenly she heard a noise: the door-handle being turned. She leapt to her feet – too late – stared at Elizabeth's face. She was crying, for heaven's sake!

'I'm sorry,' she stuttered, hardly able to believe that Elizabeth could mind so much about some footling chair. She ran towards her, clutched her arm, words spilling incoherently. 'Look, please don't cry. I'm sorry. I didn't know it would upset you like this. I'll never sit there again, I promise.'

Elizabeth looked at her blankly, struggling to restrain her tears. 'Beattie, I . . . I . . . don't know what you're talking about.'

'Well, Jeremy's chair. Tim told me not to sit in it. I'm really really sorry. It was stupid of me – tactless . . .'

Elizabeth started laughing, a hysterical, uncertain laugh which was almost worse than the tears. 'I'm . . . I'm not upset about Jeremy's *chair*. I'm upset about his . . . his son.'

'What?'

'Loretta's just given birth. A boy. Eight pounds. Mother and child both doing well.' Elizabeth's voice was distorted, out of control.

Beattie led her to the table, sat her down and laid a tentative hand on her shoulder. Tears began to prick at her own eyes, but she blinked them furiously away. She'd be no earthly use to Elizabeth if she started crying too. She must remain strong and calm and sensible.

'I . . . I'm sorry, Beattie. This is nothing to do with you. I don't even know why I mind so much. Look, I'd better go upstairs.'

'No.' Beattie put an arm round her, part comfort and part anchor. 'Of *course* you mind. Anybody would. He was your *husband*, wasn't he, all those years? You're bound to feel upset.'

'I think it's worse because it's a boy. Jeremy was desperate for a son and I always felt I'd let him down, producing a string of girls. And now . . . now Loretta's done it, first go.'

'The *bitch*!' said Beattie. 'I'll kill her!'

Elizabeth squeezed her hand. 'Oh, Beattie, you are a dear.'

'Well I *will* kill her. I'll kill anyone that hurts you. Including that rotten shitty Jeremy. Why the hell did he have to tell you anyway?'

'Oh, it wasn't Jeremy. It was a friend of ours – Evelyn Sanderson. She said we had to know. And I suppose she's right. We do. I mean, apart from anything else, Harriet's planning to stay with them next month. We talked about it when she was here. She misses him more than the others – she's the youngest, you see, and she hasn't got a partner. She'd be devastated if she turned up in Geneva and found a baby had arrived out of the blue. That's why Jeremy asked Evelyn to phone and break the news.'

'You mean you didn't even know Loretta was pregnant?'

'Well, no, I didn't – none of us did. I'm pretty sure he decided to take a sabbatical and take it in Geneva precisely to get away from the family and avoid any awkward scenes. Actually, it's not a good career move, but I suppose once the year's over, he'll return to surgery and pick up where he left off, but complete with new wife and baby.'

Beattie sat down beside Elizabeth. 'But Geneva isn't far,' she said. 'I'd have thought one of the girls would have visited him *before* this and realized Loretta was expecting.'

'No, he always had some excuse to put them off. He did see them once or twice on his own – in odd hotels and things – but he'd say he hadn't found a house yet, or Loretta wasn't well or something. I suppose he didn't want them to know. You see, they've only been married six months and he was probably a bit embarrassed about the girls working out the dates.' Elizabeth gave a bitter laugh. 'I mean, *he* was the one who used to lecture them about "being careful" with their boyfriends. And Loretta's not much older than they are, which makes it still more tricky.' Elizabeth caught her breath, as if the name Loretta was painful to pronounce. 'So he leaves *me* to tell them. Like he left me to tell them he was leaving. They were terribly upset of course, but he was so besotted with his new love, no one else existed – not me, or his family, not even his precious work.' She broke off to light a cigarette, her hand trembling as it struck the match. 'I'm sorry, Beattie. I shouldn't be telling you all this.'

'Don't be silly, of course you should. It's no good bottling it up. You're such a saint as a rule, I sometimes feel . . .'

'Beattie, I'm *not* a saint. Far from it! When I first heard about Loretta I was so full of rage and jealousy I could have murdered her in cold blood. They say time's a great healer, and I hoped and prayed that was true. As the months went by, I kept telling myself I'd recovered – you know, accepted the situation and made a new life on my own, but I have to admit it hasn't worked out that well. I mean, I'm so thrown by this one phone call, I feel I'm practically back to square one. Oh, I know that sounds ridiculous and I'm probably overreacting, but when Evelyn said a boy, I . . . I . . .' She swallowed, tears sliding down her face again. 'And they've called him Jeremy, of course. If only we'd *known* that she was pregnant, it wouldn't have been such a shock.'

Beattie got up to put the kettle on. Shock required hot sweet tea. Or maybe brandy. She wondered if there was any in the house. None of the family seemed to drink much (and she too had been unusually abstemious), but now she needed a shot of Dutch courage as much as Elizabeth did. She had somehow become the therapist and Elizabeth the patient, and the responsibility scared her out of her wits. The fact that she was wearing a bikini only seemed to emphasize her professional nakedness. She had no training or experience, yet whatever happened, she must handle this crisis right. She went to ransack the sideboard in the dining-room, found half a bottle of Martell and poured a slug for each of them.

'Here, drink this,' she urged, returning to the kitchen with the glasses. 'Dr Bancroft's orders!'

'Oh, no, really. I'm okay now.' Elizabeth stood up. 'I'll just go upstairs and . . .'

'Elizabeth . . .'

'What?'

'Please don't keep running away. I want to help. I mean, *really* help.'

'I know you do, Beattie dear, but I can't talk any more. I'm completely drained.'

'Well, you need time to recover, like you're always telling me. Why not go and sit in the garden? Then I can keep an eye on you and make sure you're not murdering anyone in cold blood!'

Elizabeth managed a smile. 'Oh, Beattie, I'm so glad you were here.'

'Honestly?'

'Yes, honestly. If I'd been on my own, I think I'd have put my head in the gas oven.'

'You're joking, I hope?' Beattie asked in alarm.

'Oh yes. One of the things about having children – and grand-children – is that you're honour bound to be there for them.'

A pity *Jeremy* wasn't so honourable, Beattie thought bitterly, going to check on the kettle. It would be tea as well as brandy, and every-thing set out beautifully: the silver teapot and best bone china cups, milk in a jug, not the bottle plonked on the table (as it was in Rainham Road). She placed the tea-strainer beside Elizabeth, noting with approval that she was already sipping her brandy.

'Knock that back and I'll go and get you a top-up.'

'Beattie, I *never* drink in the afternoon. You're leading me off the straight and narrow!'

'Yes, but this is exceptional circumstances.' Beattie took a gulp from her own glass. 'Anyway, you were saying earlier on that we ought to celebrate – you know, because I'd finished typing the book. Well . . .' she raised her glass '. . . this is for shock *and* celebration.' She looked anxiously at Elizabeth, hoping it hadn't sounded insensi-tive. She was only trying to distract her from Loretta and the brat.

'Okay, cheers!' Elizabeth clinked her glass to Beattie's, then took another sip. She was already looking less pale and fraught, thank God.

'Let's drink to your book,' urged Beattie. 'That it's a huge success and outsells Jeffrey Archer!'

'Heavens! I hope not. My colleagues already think I'm being dis-loyal in writing it at all – those I've dared to tell.'

'I can't see why.' Beattie ran to make the tea; the kettle was just coming to the boil.

'Well, they say I'm washing dirty linen in public. But there *are* a lot of abuses and I feel it's only right to . . .' Elizabeth paused in mid-sentence and took a long slow draught of brandy, as if to plug her mouth. 'No, I mustn't start on that subject. I really do feel whacked. Let's take our tea into the garden. It was a good idea of yours. It's so peaceful out there and we can shut the door on Jeremy.'

'Great!' said Beattie. She transferred the tea things from the table to a tray, adding the glasses and the brandy bottle. She – or Elizabeth – might need another shot of courage.

'Oh, look,' said Elizabeth, as Beattie stepped into the garden. 'Boz is coming too. It's amazing the way he follows you. I've never known him become so attached to anyone before. He's always been a friendly chap, but this is the first time he's ever been besotted!'

Beattie walked out onto the lawn and set the tray down carefully. Lovingly she fondled Boz's head. If only Elizabeth would follow his example: shadow her wherever she went, attach herself in every sense, become – heavenly word! – besotted. She suppressed a stupid grin. Okay, so it wasn't very likely, but at least the two of them were closer now than they'd ever been since they met.

11

'It's getting rather chilly now the sun's gone down.' Elizabeth sat up in her deck chair and gave a mock-shiver. 'You must be freezing in that bikini.'

'Don't worry – I've got my love to keep me warm!' Beattie stroked the sleeping Boz, curled up on her stomach. 'Not to mention the brandy.' She reached out for her glass, drained the last few drops.

'We really ought to have some food, you know, to soak it up. I'll go and put the supper on.'

'No, stop being so dutiful. We can have walnut whips for supper – the two you bought for Tim.'

'I thought you were worried about getting fat?'

'Oh, no, I'm Wonderwoman. And *I'll* get the supper tonight – walnut whips on toast.'

'I can't wait!'

Beattie scrambled up from the rug, capsizing Boz. 'I tell you what. Let's get into our dressing-gowns and pretend we're at Ashley Grange. Stop it, Boz! I'm not your slave you know.' She ran a hand along the curve of his back and was rewarded with the familiar purr. 'We ought to send *him* to a health farm. He's obviously a massage freak.'

'Yes, but he wouldn't like the meals.'

'I bet he jolly well would! They were always serving fish. All those dainty little bits of sole and turbot, decorated with star-fruits and what-have-you. You know, one thing I could never quite get used to was sitting in that great posh dining-room with some work of art on my plate, and being expected to eat it in my grotty old dressing-gown. It seemed so weird. And the people who built the house would've had a fit. *They*'d have eaten their meals dressed in crinolines or tiaras or something.'

'It suited *me*,' said Elizabeth, stacking the tea things on the tray. 'I loathe dressing up. In fact one of the few good things about Jeremy leaving was that I no longer had to look the part of surgeon's wife. I really hated attending all those functions dolled up in my glad rags. Now I've stopped going to the hairdresser's and I bought my first pair of jeans just six months ago. Sheer bliss!'

'Well, it's casual dress this evening.' Beattie followed her into the house, Boz bringing up the rear. 'I'll go and put my dressing-gown on. But you've got to promise not to do the washing up or start cooking some exotic meal.'

'I won't lift a finger till dinner is served. Where are we having it, by the way? The kitchen or the dining-room?'

'The dining-room, of course. This is Ashley Grange, remember, so it's chandeliers, swanky waiters – the lot. Oh, and you'd better turn the answerphone on. Guests aren't allowed to take calls during meals.'

'Right. I'll do it while you change.'

Beattie flounced upstairs, disappointed that Elizabeth didn't intend to enter into the spirit of things and change as well. If they were both in dressing-gowns, it would be much more intimate. She tried to imagine her as the conventional surgeon's wife – dressed more like Margaret, maybe, in tailored blouses, tweedy skirts, and with her hair crimped in a perm. No, the image was completely wrong. She had come to love Elizabeth just the way she was: untidy hair, faded jeans, face bare of any make-up.

She sat down at the dressing-table and studied her own face in the mirror. Her eyes looked very dark and very bright, and her new even-more-spiky haircut (a treat from Elizabeth on a recent trip to Sevenoaks) gave her a dramatic air. Yes, Wonderwoman, definitely. And not even all that fat. She stripped off her bikini, sprayed herself with scent and buttoned her dressing-gown over her naked skin. She left the top three buttons undone, slipped a hand inside and stroked her breasts. It felt dangerously exciting, as if the sun, the brandy and Boz's fur had all been working on her, weakening her defences. She must be bloody careful. In the last few hours Elizabeth had talked to her more freely than ever before. It would be crazy to ruin everything, risk the shutters going up again.

She walked slowly and deliberately downstairs, though her natural inclination was to gallop. She found Elizabeth in the kitchen, keeping her promise of doing nothing: leaning on her elbows at the table, blowing out a lazy puff of smoke.

'Beattie, let's stay put. I'm not that keen on chandeliers, and anyway it's warmer in here.'

'Okay.' Beattie was happy in the kitchen, a big homely room with a scrubbed pine table, a proper walk-in larder, and a marvellous old oak settle heaped with patchwork cushions (Boz curled up in the midst of them). Even here, there were pictures on the walls: great vivid splashy sunflower prints in oranges and yellows. 'I'll go and mix the drinks,' she said, giving Boz a stroke as she passed.

'What drinks?'

'Well, I thought we should have an aperitif, as we're dining gracious-style. I saw some vodka in the sideboard.'

'Absolutely not, Beattie. We've drunk quite enough for today and anyway you've got to look after your health. What would Lofty say?'

Beattie made a face. She still found it very odd referring to a top-drawer kidney specialist by his nickname. But then never before had she had a doctor's appointment in a palatial Queen Anne residence, rather than some grotty little surgery rife with germs and screaming kids. After her consultation, Mr Clarence Lofthouse (less intimidating than his pompous name and half-moon specs had led her to expect) had actually shaken her by the hand and invited her into the garden; talked about his dahlias and asked if she liked gardening – treated her as a friend, in short. Just one of the many perks of Mile End House.

Elizabeth stubbed out her cigarette and relaxed back in her chair. 'If we're going to eat Tim's walnut whips, why don't we go the whole hog and steal some of his Bongo Tropical juice? Can you rustle up a Bongo tropical cocktail?'

'Well, I could if I had some gin.'

'We'll *imagine* the gin.'

'All right, I'll serve it in champagne glasses with ice and bits of fruit.'

'I'm afraid we'll have to imagine the champagne glasses too. We had some when we first married, but they got broken over the years.'

'No problem. We'll have it in tumblers. With straws, if you like.'

'Yes, straws I have got. Tim's again. They're somewhere in the larder, with his Pop Tarts.'

Beattie went to look. The wretched kid didn't even live here, yet his indulgent grandma stocked up with all his favourite things. And not just for Tim. The larder was fairly groaning with goodies for the family: herbal teas for Margaret, the home-made shortbread James adored, Harriet's no-longer-needed invalid foods, and even jars of baby food to spare Caroline the chore of bringing her own.

She found the packet of stripey straws – posh ones, naturally – and went to make the drinks. Then she unwrapped the walnut whips and placed each one on a dinner plate, which she set down with a flourish on the table. 'Your dinner, *madame*, with the compliments of the chef. He's spent all day creating this magnificent new delicacy, which tastes exactly like a walnut whip but has fewer calories than a lettuce leaf and doesn't rot your teeth.'

'Wonderful! I'll order a crate.'

'Certainly, *madame*. Will that be cash or account?'

'Oh, account. It's so vulgar to pay cash.'

Beattie sat down opposite Elizabeth and watched her as she went to work with a teaspoon. She had sliced the top off her walnut whip and was scooping out the creamy contents as if it were a soft-boiled egg. Ashley Grange finesse, maybe, but that wasn't actually the way to go about it. She picked up hers in her fingers, bit off the nut and crunched it in her teeth, then began licking at the chocolate cone. 'Mm, delicious. I haven't had one of these for yonks.'

'Tim eats far too many. I really shouldn't keep buying them for him. I'm trying to wean him on to nuts and raisins.'

Beattie gave a non-committal grunt. She had no desire to discuss Tim's dietary habits. Her mind was on Elizabeth – Elizabeth's chocolate breast. She swirled her tongue round and round the nipple, relishing the sensation of Elizabeth succumbing – liquefying, melting, opening to her everywhere.

'I'm afraid it's too sickly for my taste.' Elizabeth put her spoon down. 'It's funny, you know – I used to have a passion for sweet things, but once I took up smoking, I lost it completely.'

'I thought you'd always smoked?'

'Oh, no. Well, I did when I was very young, but probably only to defy my parents. They seemed frightfully staid at the time. They strongly disapproved of smoking, drinking and gambling. And that was in the sixties when everyone else was going wild. Mind you, it felt pretty wild accepting my first cigarette. I was all of seventeen and had just left home and gone to work in a rather chichi art gallery in Cheltenham. There was this chap I worshipped from afar – Hugo he

95

was called, the son of the gallery owner. Although he was only my age, he seemed fearfully sophisticated, and when he offered me a du Maurier in that natty red and silver packet, I'm afraid I instantly succumbed.'

'But didn't you go to university?' Beattie interrupted, less interested in the smoking details than in gleaning further precious nuggets from Elizabeth's past.

'No, actually I didn't. In fact, that's always been a bit of a sore point. My father was terribly disappointed. I mean, being an academic himself, he always hoped I'd follow him to Cambridge. But I simply wasn't bright enough.'

Beattie stared. Elizabeth seemed incredibly bright. And the words she used in her book were so damned complicated, most ordinary people would never have *heard* of them, for God's sake. She'd had to resort to a dictionary herself, and even then she was often at a loss. She'd assumed Elizabeth had a whole string of degrees – the perfect match to her brilliant surgeon-husband. 'But how did you get to be a therapist?' she asked. 'I thought you *had* to have a degree?'

'Far from it! That's one of the abuses in my profession, I'm afraid. Some of them are charlatans and totally untrained.' Elizabeth paused to sip her cocktail: a gaudy orange concoction with chunks of pear and apple in it. 'But the training *I* did required a "degree or equivalent", as they put it. They stretched a point in my case – you know, because I'd been a magistrate and served on lots of worthy committees and suchlike. And I'm sure it helped being married to Jeremy. To tell the truth, I've always felt a bit of a fraud. I suspect I was accepted on his merits rather than my own and given preferential treatment, which wasn't really fair. But you see I was already thirty-five and I couldn't face starting from scratch with a degree course before I even embarked on the training, and with four children into the bargain.'

Beattie pushed her walnut whip away. This was quite a different Elizabeth from the one she thought she knew – a new, sub-standard Elizabeth who had let her father down and who actually felt a fraud (as she did so often herself). They were definitely drawing closer; Elizabeth leaving school at seventeen and working in some gallery rather than cramming for her entrance exams to a toffee-nosed university. 'What sort of work did you do at the gallery?' she asked, determined to learn more of Elizabeth's curriculum vitae. They had got sidetracked from her original story and jumped ahead nearly twenty years.

'Oh, I was only a glorified receptionist. And even that was arranged through my father. He was a friend of Hugo's parents, you see, so it was a matter of pulling strings again.'

'And did you and Hugo hit it off? I mean, after that first cigarette, did he sweep you into his arms or carry you off to the woods or something?'

'Oh lord, no! I was a shy retiring violet and he was always out with glamour-girls. He married one, eventually.'

Elizabeth looked wistful, Beattie noticed with a pang of jealousy. How could she not be jealous of someone Elizabeth 'worshipped from afar'?

'Anyway, I was married myself by then. That's why I had to stop smoking. Jeremy was still only a student, but he'd seen smokers' lungs in the lab – pickled in a jar and coated with ghastly tarry stuff. I never touched another till he left.' She laughed and took a sip of her drink, both hands cupped around her tumbler. 'In fact, it's quite a funny story.'

Beattie willed her to continue, relieved to see her so relaxed and talkative. The brandy must have loosened her up, but she too had played a part in the process; changed her tears and wretchedness to a surprisingly cheerful state. Not bad for a once-off therapist who'd never had a day's training in her life.

'Whoops!' Elizabeth made a gurgle through her straw. 'They wouldn't like *that* at Ashley Grange! Yes, the only reason I took up smoking again was that I was so upset by the whole Jeremy business I went to see an analyst myself – one I didn't know, but who'd been highly recommended. In the introductory session he offered me a cigarette. I refused of course, and he said did I mind if *he* smoked. I must admit I was a bit surprised, but I had so much else to mind about, it seemed neither here nor there. Then, while we were talking about Jeremy, Jeremy, Jeremy, I suddenly had this intense desire to smoke. I suspect it was a rebellion thing again. Not against my parents this time, but my sanctimonious husband. He'd always imposed such a strict moral code on the rest of us, yet here he was flouting it himself, becoming a different person, almost.' She picked out a piece of apple from her glass and nibbled it reflectively.

'I remember stopping in mid-sentence and asking Dr Grübinger if I could change my mind and have a cigarette. Well, I coughed a bit and my eyes began to water, just like that first time when I was only seventeen. Then, as I blew the smoke out, I felt this really violent anger. It was actually quite terrifying. You see, up to then I'd been sort of numb with misery and hadn't even realized I was angry. I sat there in silence, probably looking reasonably calm, but inwardly I was exploding, screaming out: "I *will* smoke! I *will* scream! I *will* get even with his bloody woman!" '

Beattie gripped the edge of the table. Elizabeth had never, ever, sworn before, and her voice had become much louder; the echo of her furious words seeming to reverberate round the room. She gulped her drink, wishing it was stronger. 'I . . . I thought you said it was a funny story?'

'Well *don't* you think it's funny, Beattie? I mean, going to a therapist to try to get over one problem and coming away with another? The last thing I wanted was to take up smoking again. It's a dreadful waste of money, and it's already given me two bad bouts of bronchitis. Besides being terribly bad for my children and grandchildren to have to inhale my smoke – bad for you as well, my love.'

Beattie leaned across and squeezed her hand. 'I don't care. I only mind about *you* – I mean, being so upset and getting rotten bronchitis, on top of everything else. Wasn't Dr Whatsit any bloody use then, apart from ruining your lungs?'

Elizabeth picked up her cigarette packet and put it down again. 'Well, no, he wasn't, really. In fact that's what made me much more critical of therapy. It's not that he lacked the skills – far from it – he was extremely sensitive and perceptive. But all that probing into my childhood somehow seemed irrelevant. I'd already raked it over ad infinitum when I was going through my training analysis and I just couldn't face it again. And then the jargon, and the silences, and the professional detachment, when I suppose what I wanted was to weep in his arms and have him stroke my hair and say "There, there! Don't cry, Elizabeth." But of course that was strictly forbidden. We don't use people's names. It's all part of the training – or at least my strict Freudian one – not to get too close, not to show any genuine human warmth.'

Elizabeth was now fiddling with her lighter, snapping it on and off, wincing slightly at each tiny burst of flame. 'And even my grief and anger seemed to be analysed to death – made frightfully involved and complicated when feelings like that are just a natural reaction. I've come to think since then that perhaps depression should be . . .

honoured, almost, as courageous and appropriate and . . . Oh look! Tolkien's come to join us.'

Beattie resented the intrusion, which had stopped Elizabeth in full flow. The cat was meowing loudly, winding its aristocratically bony body (part Siamese, part Abyssinian) in and out of Elizabeth's chair-legs.

Elizabeth got up automatically, responding to his shrill demands. 'I suppose he wants his supper.'

'Fusspot! Let him wait.'

'Oh Beattie, don't be unkind.'

'Okay, I'll feed his majesty. I'm chef tonight, remember.'

'Thanks. Don't give him a walnut whip, though!'

'He can have Whiskas and be grateful.'

'He's never grateful. Cats aren't. I suppose they're a bit like analysts in that respect – aloof, and undemonstrative, and refusing to give you love.'

'Boz loves you to death.'

'He loves *you* to death, you mean! Anyway, Boz isn't typical. With a lot of cats you just have to accept that you give more love than you get.'

Like grandchildren, thought Beattie, getting up to open the tin. And men. And most relationships. She was beginning to feel depressed. The evening wasn't going according to plan. They were meant to be relaxing at Ashley Grange, getting closer physically, not just mentally. She spooned jellied chicken and rabbit onto two plastic plates. Boz had arrived as well now and was also singing for his supper.

'Hey, Elizabeth, I've got an idea.' She chucked the empty can into the waste-bin. 'Why don't we give each other a face pack? I've got some cucumber masque upstairs. It says on the tube it works like an instant face lift.'

'My face needs more than a lift, Beattie – complete restructuring, I'd say.'

'Now *you*'re running yourself down, like you're always telling me not to.'

'It's different for me. I'm fifty.'

'So? Jane Fonda's fifty-six. I know, let's do a Jane Fonda work-out too. I've got the video with me.'

'God forbid!' Elizabeth shuddered. 'I'll settle for the mask, thanks.'

'Honestly?'

'Yes. Why not? If this is our day off, we'd better make the most of it. My schedule's awfully full tomorrow.'

'Forget tomorrow. We're at Ashley Grange, remember, so we've nothing to do but laze around and have massages and facials. Right, if *madame* would like to come upstairs either to the Bluebell Room or the Daffodil Room . . .'

'Can't we do it down here, in the Sunflower Room? I'm feeling too lazy to move.'

'Oh no. I've got all the gear in my room – turbans to protect your hair and those cooling pads for your eyes and . . .'

'Gracious! It *does* sound complicated.'

'But of course. Our amazing new beautician, Beattie Bancroft, has just been flown first-class from Paris to give Madame Hargreaves the whole shebang. *No*, Boz, not you! You don't want cucumber gunge on your fur.'

'Elizabeth, you're not to speak. The mask will crack and undo all the good.'

'*You*'ve been talking non-stop.'

'I know. And look at mine!' Beattie peered in the mirror, grinning at herself. 'There's hardly any left around my mouth.'

'D'you want me to put some more on?'

'No, you lie still. You're meant to be relaxing on your couch.' Beattie turned the main light off and left just the bedside lamp on. She wanted the atmosphere to be intimate and restful. Actually, it had taken some persuasion to get Elizabeth to lie down, but there was only one chair in the room so she'd insisted that she have the bed. It was quite a triumph to have coaxed Elizabeth in here at all. She very rarely set foot in the room, presumably concerned about her guest's need for privacy. 'I don't *want* privacy,' she often longed to shout. 'And I'm not a guest – I'm your partner and your soul-mate.' Elizabeth, though, seemed to value her own seclusion: her bedroom was as much forbidden territory as was her consulting room. Beattie had peeked in several times (when she was safely alone in the house) and stared at the double bed, imagining Jeremy lying there, seeding those four daughters. And she had felt almost lump-in-the-throatish at the sight of the toy giraffe propped up against the pillows – Elizabeth's sole bed-mate now. There were the usual photographs, of course: the girls again, mostly as young babies, cooing and gurgling all over the place. She had longed to creep in and study them, study everything in detail: Elizabeth's books, clothes, face-creams, underwear. Yet a sense of loyalty had stopped her, combined with twinges of conscience.

She stretched luxuriously in her chair. At least this was the next best thing: having Elizabeth in *her* room, wearing a dressing-gown, at last, and actually lying on her bed. If only they could lie together, forget their separate boundaries and merge into each other. Her gaze strayed back to Elizabeth's green face – the closed eyes beneath the cooling pads, the small neat hands clasped across her stomach. It had been fantastic putting on the mask, having an excuse to lean right over her, being allowed to touch her skin. It was so soft, that skin, and alarmingly fragile, as if a clumsy hand might snag it. She had made her fingers like velvet, stroking them slowly down from forehead to throat and back again. When Elizabeth said how soothing it was, she had responded with a silly joke about her Paris training; hiding her true feelings. It was becoming quite a strain, having to be bright and breezy when she felt so strangely moved and ached to say things to Elizabeth which she knew would sound excessive.

'Right, *madame*. It's time to wash that off now.'

'Do you want me to get up?'

'No, stay where you are. I'll bring some water in a dish.' Beattie ran the water in the basin until it was comfortably warm, looped two towels over her arm and walked back to the bed. At the beginning of the treatment she had pushed aside the lapels of Elizabeth's dressing-gown to prevent it getting messy; exposing her neck and throat. Now, before taking off the eyepads, she glanced surreptitiously at that tantalizing V of pale bare flesh. She could see just a glimpse of breast, the beginnings of a curve, which made her feel both protective and aroused. Many women in their fifties had ghastly scraggy boobs, or great revolting floppy things, or those high-shelf bosoms like the prow of a ship. Elizabeth's were perfect – the frustratingly little she could see of them. She forced her eyes away. It still scared her stiff to have these feelings for a woman, and she was no closer to understanding them. It wasn't that she had gone off men. Some guy had called last week to mend the dishwasher and she had admired his muscly body under the overalls; even imagined having it off with him there and then on the kitchen floor. And she sometimes found herself thinking of Max, despite her resolve to leave him stewing in his London office. Only yesterday she had been remembering his 'tail' – the little tuft of dark coarse hair at the bottom of his spine – and the thought had turned her on. So why was she standing here half-paralysed by this intense desire to stroke Elizabeth's breasts? They were so close to her, so accessible, almost begging to be touched. She had only to slip that dressing-gown a little further down, then cup her hands around their naked warmth. Maybe Elizabeth would like it. She could well be frustrated now that she was living on her own. But they had never once discussed sex, so she had no idea whether Elizabeth missed her man in bed, or whether she had also had these feelings for a woman – overwhelming feelings which . . .

'What's wrong?' Elizabeth asked, fidgeting on the bed. Fortunately she was blinkered by her eyepads, but she was clearly wondering at the delay.

'Nothing. I . . . I'm just giving your mask another couple of minutes. It has to set really hard before I take it off. Yes, it's okay now.' As she removed the eyepads, Elizabeth's blue eyes gazed startled into her own.

'Gracious! I'd forgotten you had your mask on too. Oh Beattie, you do look funny!'

'Well so do you.'

'A couple of ghouls.'

Beattie dipped the flannel into the water, relieved on this occasion that they were back to harmless banter. 'Wouldn't it be awful if there was a fire or something and we were found like this by the fire brigade.'

'They'd take to their heels and run.'

And our charred bodies would be discovered side by side, thought Beattie, relishing the macabre scene: she and Elizabeth together at last, if only in death. She tried to concentrate on what she was doing, lapping at the hardened mask with the flannel. 'Your skin does look good, you know,' she said. 'It's gone all sort of glowy. No, don't move. I'm going to put some Emulsion '99 on.'

'Some *what?*'

'I bought it at Ashley Grange. It's meant to be a scientific breakthrough – a new wonder-cream to stop you ageing.'

'Oh, Beattie, you don't believe that, do you?'

'Yes and no. It's a bit like God or Father Christmas. I *want* to believe in them, so I sort of kid myself I do. Anyway, I can't bear the thought of wrinkles, so Emulsion '99 just *has* to work!'

'I can't understand why you're so worried about ageing. Compared with me you're barely out of nappies.'

'It's weird, though. I've never really *felt* young. Even as a kid I was always worrying about death and stuff.'

'I expect that's because your mother was ill. It makes a huge difference to a child.' Elizabeth put a finger to her cheek, testing the effect of the wonder-cream. 'Mind you, I didn't feel young either, and *my* mother was in the pink of health.'

Beattie spread more cream on Elizabeth's face, just for the pleasure of rubbing it in. 'I always imagined you had an idyllic childhood. I mean, your parents seem so devoted, and you had money, didn't you?'

'Well, yes. It was fairly calm and comfortable on the whole, but I suppose I felt overprotected. My mother regarded everything as dangerous – riding, skating, swimming, even climbing trees. It was a major calamity if I grazed my knee or caught a verruca at the swimming baths, so I was practically wrapped in cotton wool. And I always seemed to be with grown-ups. My parents had such high standards, you see, they were terribly fussy about who I played with – and where. So most of the time I didn't play with anyone, at least not at home or in the holidays.'

'It was like that for me as well, but for completely different reasons. I never invited my friends round because Mum was stuck in bed and Dad was usually staying in digs at the other end of the country.' Beattie glanced at her father's photo on the windowsill. She loved his smile, which was both vulnerable and seductive at once, as if he was flirting with her while begging to be cared for. She had inherited his Latin eyes and dark rebellious hair; was always secretly glad that she didn't take after her mother (who'd had mouse-coloured hair and weak blue eyes more often closed than not). 'I used to hope against hope that he wouldn't have to go away all the time, but there are so few parts in London, except for really established actors. So he had to do long summer seasons in places like Blackpool or Scarborough, or Christmas panto in the back of beyond. Mind you, it all seemed terribly glamorous at the time – my father a real live actor! I idolized him. I still do. When he *was* at home, I didn't want my friends around. We'd go out together – just him and me – and I felt I couldn't get enough of him. But then he'd push off yet again and it was back to me and Mum. Or just *me*, it felt like sometimes, when she was asleep upstairs all day. Damn!' She clapped her hands to her face. 'This stuff keeps flaking all over the place. I'll have to wash it off. Don't move though, will you? I want to give you a face-massage.'

'But what about you? I'm getting all the pampering.'

'You deserve it. Anyway, I'm enjoying myself. Hold on a sec while I make myself more human.' Beattie leaned over the basin and splashed water on her face, then rubbed it with the flannel. She stood up, still dripping, and mopped herself with a towel. 'D'you know, I've never told anyone else about my mother. I suppose I've always been too ashamed, especially as a kid. That's why I didn't want my friends round. I was scared they'd tell the whole damned class that Betty Cook's mother was some kind of freak.'

Elizabeth smiled in sympathy. 'I'd forgotten you were called Betty. It's funny, isn't it, I longed to have a nickname – to be Lizzie, or Beth, or Betty, instead of a great formal mouthful like Elizabeth.'

Beattie peered in the mirror and removed a last green streak from her neck. 'I suppose neither of us had a proper childhood.'

'Oh, I wouldn't go as far as that. I was very lucky really. My parents were always *there*, and they doted on me, and . . .'

'Yes, but it must have been awfully stifling, stuck in that cathedral close with all those stuffy people. And you never had a chance to break out. I mean, you were married by nineteen, weren't you, and supporting Jeremy through medical school.'

'I've broken out *now*.'

'Oh Elizabeth, you haven't! You're still as dutiful as ever.'

'I'm not. You keep calling me a saint, Beattie, but some of my friends see me more as a sinner, or a black sheep, at least.'

'God, they ought to meet *my* crowd!'

Elizabeth laughed. 'I doubt if they could cope. They think *I'm* bad enough – I mean, a middle-aged single parent who suddenly takes up smoking and wears clothes from Oxfam shops and no longer bothers to give dinner parties or go to church on Sundays.' She sat up on the bed, pulling at her turban. 'And my analyst friends are shocked for different reasons – because I've started breaking the rules. After my experience with Dr Grübinger, I began to rethink my own way of working. Now, I'll hold a patient's hand if I think that's what they need, or make them a cup of tea, or extend their time beyond that rigid fifty minutes.'

'Well none of *that* sounds exactly revolutionary.'

'You'd be surprised. I once visited a patient at home because she was too anxious to come out herself. One of my colleagues got to hear of it and was deeply disapproving.'

'They're bonkers if you ask me – the shrinks, I mean, not the patients. Well, all except you, maybe.'

'Thank you kindly!'

'Hey, don't take your turban off. I'm only halfway through your facial.' Beattie threw the towel on the wash-basin and coaxed Elizabeth back on the bed. 'I know – let's pretend we're students at Cambridge. This is our very first term and we're getting ready to go out to a May Ball.'

'What, in October?'

'Yes. We've got a date with two super-gorgeous princes. And they're both absolutely loaded.'

'Am I allowed to wear my jeans?'

'Certainly not! Jean-Paul Gaultier is just putting the last touches to our outfits.'

'Who's he?'

'Elizabeth, *honestly*, I despair of you! He makes Madonna's clothes. And don't say "Who's Madonna?"'

'I won't say anything. I'll just lie back and enjoy this marvellous massage.'

Beattie determined to *make* it marvellous – and sensuous, of course. She stroked her little fingers along Elizabeth's eyelids, feeling the curve of the eyeball, the fluttering of the lashes. It was so delicate, that area: the soft fair brows and gentle arc of the brow-bone, the faint blue veins on the lids. She regarded it as a privilege, this freedom to examine the texture of Elizabeth's skin; explore every tiny follicle and pore. And Elizabeth trusted her now, relaxing completely and submitting to her touch. Although it was getting on for nine o'clock, she seemed in no hurry to go. Ordinarily, she would have pleaded the pressure of work: phone calls to make or urgent reports to write. This evening was a milestone – a progression from wary friendship to something much more intimate.

She let her hands glide down to Elizabeth's mouth, outlining its shape, one unhurried finger brushing across the lips. The lips opened and relaxed, and it took a great effort of will not to lean over and kiss them. To regain her self-control, she fixed her eyes instead on the River Phoenix poster tacked up above the basin. She had imposed her own disorder on Sarah's small domain, and now it *did* resemble a student's room, with its clutch of dirty coffee mugs on the floor and the books she'd borrowed from downstairs piled on every surface.

'Elizabeth . . .'

'Mm?'

'You know, we ought to break out *together*. I mean, neither of us had any frivolous student days, so we should grab the chance before it's too late. Students have it made, with those great long holidays they get. They're free to go where they please – hitch-hike round the world or back-pack to Tibet or whatever.'

'So you want me to give up all my patients and back-pack to Tibet?'

'Well, maybe not Tibet. But we could do something exciting nearer home – hot air ballooning, or parachuting, or . . .'

'I'd be absolutely terrified!'

'No you wouldn't. Not with me.'

'Well, if you *want* me to die of fright . . .'

'Okay, *you* suggest something then, to get us out of the rut we're in – something to shake us up a bit.'

Elizabeth considered for a moment, then half sat up. 'Actually there *is* one thing I've always wanted to do and that's go horse-racing.'

'Haven't you ever been?'

'No, never. My parents were so opposed to gambling, I suppose I've always thought it might start me on the slippery slope to bankruptcy and ruin.'

'It might! Though it's nothing like as hair-raising as what I had in mind. I wanted us to go really wild – bungee-jumping, or white-water canoeing, or riding bucking broncos.'

'It's quite hair-raising enough for me, thanks, to risk losing my shirt on a horse, without riding the things as well.'

'Mightn't your parents still object, though?' Beattie was reluctant to offend them. She had become very fond of Margaret, despite her starchy ways. And James was trying to teach her the rudiments of Greek.

'Oh no. They've mellowed now they're in their eighties. Daddy's even rather partial to sherry, whereas in his younger days drink was Evil Number One.'

'And gambling Evil Number Two, I suppose. Hell, our fathers couldn't have been more different. *My* dad was a betting man and I hardly ever saw him without a cigar in one hand and a glass of something in the other – and I don't mean Bongo juice! He used to take me to the races, the rare times he was home. Sandown was his favourite course. It was the nearest to us then. Tell you what, I'll take you there myself.'

'Oh, I'd really love that, Beattie. I've always had a passion for horses. Occasionally I watch the racing on television, but it's not the same.'

'No, you miss all the atmosphere and the noise and smells and everything. What I'll do is get hold of a racing diary and find out when the next meeting's on, and we'll make a day of it. We can have lunch first in the restaurant, and then dinner out in Esher afterwards. There are loads of decent places near the course.'

'Do make sure it's a weekend, though. You know I can never cancel patients.'

'There you go, Elizabeth – dutiful again! The whole point of this exercise is that you're going to stop being so damned *good*.'

'It's not a matter of being good, my love. It's a matter of being professional.'

'Well, I don't want you to be either, at least for a few weeks.'

'Okay. I'll mortgage the house, sell the car, and blue the whole lot on – what's his name? – Arkle.'

'Fantastic! Except Arkle happens to be dead. He died over twenty years ago.'

'Whatever horse you suggest, then. Just make sure it's still alive.'

'Okay, you're on! Now lie back and be quiet. This is your pre-Sandown facial, and your beautician needs to concentrate.'

12

'That's our horse!' cried Beattie, pointing to the far side of the parade ring. 'The chestnut with the white blaze. God, he's sweating up a bit.'

'Is that bad?' Elizabeth asked anxiously, pressing closer to the rail.

'Yes and no. He could simply be keen. But it's more likely to mean he's nervous. He's swishing his tail as well, you see, and that's often a bad sign.'

'I know just how he feels. I'd no idea how nerve-racking it would be.'

'Just wait till they're off! I'll be biting my nails to the quick then.' Beattie consulted her watch. 'Only fifteen minutes to go. Oh, look at Star Attraction! He moves so well, maybe we should have backed *him.* There's a prize, by the way, for the best turned out horse in the ring. I wouldn't be surprised if Star Attraction won. He looks gorgeous, doesn't he?'

'Well, *you*'d certainly win the prize for the best turned out racegoer.'

Beattie flushed with pleasure. It was rare for Elizabeth to comment on anyone's appearance – she tended not to notice trivial things like clothes. Her entire outfit was brand new, bought specially for the occasion: a navy trouser-suit with a scarlet polo-neck, a red and navy cloak, and horrendously expensive knee-length boots. All paid for on the Barclaycard, of course, along with their tickets for the Members' Enclosure and lavish champagne lunch. She had been forced to return to London and take a fortnight's temp work, but even so, her credit was stretched to the limit. She was praying for good luck today, then she could use her winnings to get back into the black. Elizabeth had kept trying to pay her share – whipping out her purse at the entrance to the course and her cheque-book during lunch – but she had refused to take a penny. This outing was *her* treat.

'And you really look the part,' Elizabeth was saying, 'with those binoculars round your neck and the *Racing Post* under your arm.'

'Well, we have to study form, you know, if we're going to make a habit of racing. We must look out for things today that'll help us pick the winners at the *next* meeting we go to.'

'Beattie, you're so knowledgeable! I feel an utter ignoramus in comparison.'

Beattie gave a modest shrug. She was very much an amateur, in fact, but she knew where to go for help: she had mugged up all the sporting papers and phoned a few old racing contacts. Thank God for Tony, who had given her some tips. They'd arranged to meet after the first race and she was keyed up about that too. It was five years since they'd last seen each other and he might think she hadn't worn too well. One thing was for sure: he'd be surprised to find her dolled up to the nines like this, when he was more used to seeing her stripped to the buff.

'Here's ours,' she said, nudging Elizabeth's arm. Jumping Jack frisked past right in front of them, tossing his head so wildly that the stable lad could barely keep control of him. 'Hell! He *is* in a lather. And he's a bit on the small side, don't you think?'

'Better a good little 'un than a bad big 'un,' a voice piped up behind them. Beattie turned to see a gnarled old man, pretty small himself, dressed in a once-smart suit and a trilby.

'And that's a damn good jockey he's got,' the old chap continued, obviously glad of a chance to talk.

'Yeah, I know,' said Beattie. 'He's had a lot of winners lately. Oh, look,' she said, turning back to the ring. 'Here come the jockeys now. Watch this, Elizabeth. They're introduced to the owners first, then given instructions by the trainers. Apparently Jumping Jack's trainer's come all the way from Yorkshire. He must think it's worth his while. Anyway, let's keep our fingers crossed.'

'What's that bell for?' Elizabeth asked.

'That's the signal for the jockeys to mount. Quick! Let's go and get a good place in the stand and watch them cantering down to the start.'

She pushed through the crowd and bounded up the steps, Elizabeth close behind. It gave her a real kick to be in the Members'

Enclosure, when she and her father had always slummed it in the cheapest ring. But only the best would do for Elizabeth: best food and wine, best vantage point. Even the weather was remarkably good for the first week of November – cold, but bright and sunny; the sky a confident blue.

They emerged on to the stands and chose good seats in the second row, right opposite the winning post. Some of the runners were just galloping past, showing off their paces to the crowd.

'Keep an eye out for ours, Elizabeth. Even the way they go down to the start can tell you quite a bit – whether they're sluggish or dead keen or nervous or whatever.'

Elizabeth looked in bemusement at the passing group of horses. 'I can't tell one from the other. At least three of them are chestnut.'

'Yes, but ours has a sheepskin noseband, and the jockey's colours are bright purple and green with hooped sleeves and a quartered cap. He should be easy enough to pick out. Ah, there he is, going like the clappers. Let's hope he doesn't exhaust himself before they've even started.'

'Only three minutes to go now.' Elizabeth's excitement was written all over her face. Beattie felt enormously relieved. She had put so much effort into organizing this jaunt, she was desperate for it to be a big success. But as the day drew nearer she had begun to worry that it could prove a disappointment – Elizabeth might get bored or simply tired. She knew *she* wouldn't flag, despite getting up at the crack of dawn this morning. She had been at the newsagent's the minute it opened, so she could study the racing papers for a good couple of hours before driving to the betting shop in Sevenoaks. She had decided on a treble: two horses favoured by Tony and her own choice, By George, who was running in the fourth race. Then she'd put single bets on all three as well, paying by cheque this time (credit cards weren't accepted, alas), and refusing to consider how much it was all costing. With Elizabeth to impress, she couldn't stint on anything.

She trained her binoculars on the start and listened to the commentary, shaking her head in dismay as Jumping Jack was reported to be highly nervous and to have turned round at the start. 'Oh God!' she wailed, 'now he's reared and thrown his jockey. Bloody hell – trust me to back a rebel!'

'I'm afraid there'll be a delay,' the commentator continued in his maddeningly cool tone. 'Jumping Jack is loose and running down the course. He's heading for the first hurdle. No – he's just veered to the right.'

Beattie sank back in her seat despairingly. 'Just our luck,' she whispered to Elizabeth, 'if they decide to go without him.'

'*Would* they do that?' Elizabeth whispered back, lighting a cigarette to calm her nerves.

'They might if he plays up too long. They can't delay the start for ever. No, I think we're saved, thank Christ! He's just been caught.'

The commentator confirmed it. 'Jumping Jack is being led back to the start. His rider's unhurt. He's remounted and all looks well. Now they're coming into line again. They're under starter's orders and they're *off*!'

It was so sudden, Beattie jumped, peering through her binoculars at the swarm of bobbing heads and trying to make out the distinctive green and purple. 'Great!' she murmured to Elizabeth. 'He's up with the leaders and going really well.' Shut up, she told herself, and listen to the commentary.

'And Hereward is still in the lead as they come to the first flight, with Jumping Jack on the far side and Irish Mist in third.'

She shivered with excitement as Jumping Jack flew over the first hurdle, taking off so eagerly he left a fair bit of daylight between himself and the jump.

'Jumping Jack comes upsides with Hereward . . . Irish Mist in third, and Pole Star making ground on the inside.'

'Oh shit,' she muttered under her breath, 'I've lost him. I can't see him anywhere.' She looked in desperation for the colours. Blue and white, black and gold, turquoise and maroon – everything but hers.

'And coming up to the fourth now – it's Hereward, with Irish Mist and Pole Star, and Jumping Jack lying fifth.'

Beattie gritted her teeth. At least he was still running, but losing ground already. 'Oh God,' she hissed to Elizabeth. 'I can hardly bear to watch.'

'Hereward is a faller there, and also Star Attraction. And Pole Star's been brought down. That leaves Irish Mist in front, then Money Mad, a length ahead of Jumping Jack, who's making ground on the inner.'

She gave a triumphant grin as Jumping Jack moved into second place once more and took the fifth hurdle in great style.

'And it's still Irish Mist in the lead, but Jumping Jack is going well enough in second. Then there's quite a gap to Money Mad and Pole Star. Connemara's been pulled up, so just seven left in the race. And it's still Irish Mist as they approach the second last. But Jumping Jack is coming back at him . . . They're both over that one safely and racing to the last together.'

The commentator's voice was rising to a crescendo and, as if on cue, the crowd suddenly came alive – roaring, cheering, all but raising the roof.

'Come on, boy!' Beattie yelled. 'Come on, come on, come *on*!' She could hear Elizabeth shouting next to her, caught up in the excitement. The noise was surging all around them – a roar of hope and exhilaration; a few of the spectators jumping up from their seats to urge on the two contenders. Beattie grabbed Elizabeth's arm as Irish Mist and Jumping Jack cleared the last hurdle at exactly the same moment, then thundered down towards the winning post. The commentary was frenetic, a paroxysm of urgent words to suit the race's climax.

'They're neck and neck! Irish Mist and Jumping Jack, they're battling to the line. Jumping Jack and Irish Mist! Yes, it's Jumping Jack!' – an orgasmic yelp – 'It's Jumping Jack by half a length.' The voice slowing to a smug post-coital drawl. 'Jumping Jack the winner.'

'Brilliant!' Beattie exulted. 'We've won, we've won, we've won!'

'Made your fortune, have you?' grinned the lanky man beside her.

'Well, it's a start.' Beattie returned his cheerful grin. One of the reasons she loved racing was that people were so friendly – a good-tempered crowd determined to enjoy themselves and always ready to share your triumphs. Her neighbour was still eyeing her admiringly. She knew she looked her best today. It was mainly for Elizabeth, of course, but also partly for Tony. If they were going to take up racing in a big way, then a close relationship with a trainer couldn't fail to help.

She took Elizabeth's arm and steered her into the throng of people making for the unsaddling enclosure. They jostled for a place right next to the fence and watched their horse being led into the winners' circle, his flanks flecked with frothy sweat.

'His trainer looks like the cat that got the cream.'

'So do you,' smiled Elizabeth. 'How much have we won?'

'Only thirty quid. But it goes on our next horse, you see, and if that one wins as well, then . . .'

'I think it's marvellous to have won at all. Though for goodness sake don't get too technical. I still can't make head or tail of the betting.'

'Never mind – I'll explain it over dinner this evening. I'll go through all the different odds and write them down for you. Gosh, Jumping Jack is still on his toes. What a goer! You'd almost think he wanted to run again. Hold on a sec – I'd better mark my race-card.' She pencilled 1, 2 and 3 against the winner and the placed horses, and scribbled down their odds. 'Only the first three are allowed in this enclosure,' she told Elizabeth. 'The rest are unsaddled at the stables.'

'I'm surprised we can get so close,' Elizabeth observed, putting her hand out over the rail. 'I can almost touch Irish Mist from here.' She gazed in delight at the large bay mare, who seemed to be putting on a show especially to impress her: flanks heaving, nostrils flaring, one foot pawing the ground. 'And those flowers are really beautiful. Everything looks lovely, doesn't it? I don't quite know what I expected – something much more tatty, I suppose. I'd no idea a racecourse could be so attractive.'

Beattie accepted the compliment as if she personally had planted the purple heathers and shaggy bronze chrysanthemums; manicured the grass; watered the course itself. Elizabeth was right – everything *did* look great: the trees burnished gold and yellow, the autumn air crisply cool and clean, the horses gleaming with health. But that was how it *had* to be for Elizabeth's big day out.

'D'you know, I remember being here, in this very spot, when I was a kid. I suppose I must have been seven or eight, and Dad brought me to the Whitbread Gold Cup as a treat. The Queen Mother presented the prizes. I can see it as if it were yesterday. She stood just there in the winners' circle, on a sort of platform thing. She was wearing a blue lace dress and a big blue feathered hat.' Beattie raised her hands two feet clear of her head each side, to indicate its extravagant dimensions. 'The winning jockey came up to her and gave an awkward sort of bow. He must have been terribly shy because I remember him blushing to the roots of his hair. I was sitting on Dad's shoulders so I could see better than anyone, and I felt I'd *burst* with excitement – I mean, out with my famous dad, and seeing my first Royal and . . .'

She broke off as another, darker memory overshadowed the first – something that had happened earlier in the race. One of the horses had fallen really heavily. It managed to stagger back to its feet, but stood panicking on three legs, its broken foreleg dangling. A couple of men had rushed onto the course, carrying canvas screens. Then the vet appeared – followed by the knacker's van. 'A shining mass of flesh and bone, reduced to dog-meat,' her father had said quietly. She would never forget his face: the pain on it, the sadness. But no way would she mention it to Elizabeth – nothing must spoil the happy atmosphere. 'Come on,' she said briskly. 'It's time for our drink with Tony.'

They were meeting him in the Owners' and Trainers' Bar, which was invitation-only, and only a step or two away. She was dying to write and tell her father that she had been drinking with the nobs. Maybe she and Elizabeth would win so much today that they'd be able to join Sandown as annual club members – better still, *life* members (if such a thing existed), which would tie them together for years. And since she would need a lot more tips, perhaps she and Tony should take up where they'd left off. It seemed a fair enough arrangement: inside information in exchange for a bit of sex, and Max need never know. She had seen Max just last week, when she'd been in London temping. He had bought his house in France at last, and got it at a knock-down price, so he should have been over the moon. Instead he was bleary-eyed and grouchy, annoyed with her for being away so long, and still in a hell of a state about the ever-increasing problems at the office. The sex had been a let-down – partly her own fault, of course. She had found it difficult to respond to him, when she was seeing him through Elizabeth's eyes as chauvinistic and graceless; sometimes downright rude. Then later, over dinner, she had mentioned writing a satirical piece on life in commuter Kent. He'd pooh-poohed the idea – it had been done a million times before and had no chance of being accepted. So her journalistic career was obviously on hold – perhaps just as well when she was so involved with Elizabeth.

They had now reached the entrance to the bar: white pillars, a veranda, and a notice saying 'Reserved for Owners and Trainers'.

'Are you sure we're allowed in?' Elizabeth asked nervously as Beattie swept past a clutch of security men.

'Yes, 'course,' said Beattie. 'Tony's expecting us.' She felt less confident than she sounded, and stood dithering on the veranda, peering through the glass. The bar was small but packed; a sea of strangers watching her, judging her an interloper. Well, she'd damn well have to act the part, pretend she owned a dozen Arab thoroughbreds and could swan into this sanctum with as much right as Sheikh Mohammed.

Ah, there was Tony, thank God, sitting at a table near the back, with a bottle of Veuve Clicquot in an ice-bucket. The champagne must be for *her*, not to celebrate a winner, since he hadn't had a runner in the first race. She was touched by the gesture, and experiencing the frisson of meeting an ex-lover: appraising his body, picturing it naked; recalling the secret things they'd done together. He hadn't spotted her yet, so she stopped where she was and pointed him out to Elizabeth, proud of his smart appearance. He was wearing a natty suit in a fine grey check, a plain cream shirt and highly polished brogues, with a brown trilby on the seat beside him. Suddenly he glanced in her direction, his whole face lighting up. He held her gaze for several seconds, then let his eyes move slowly down her body, just long enough to undress her – as she had done with him. Then he sprang to his feet and made his way towards them. Once she'd introduced Elizabeth and he'd shaken hands and made a few polite noises, he turned to *her* with an air of mingled hesitancy and eagerness. She gave him the green light, opening her arms and pressing herself against him as a sign that things weren't over, necessarily.

He shepherded them back to his table and settled Elizabeth into a chair. 'I thought champagne would be in order,' he murmured with a suggestive smile at Beattie, as he motioned her to the seat beside him. 'And Alistair's promised to join us. Yes, there he is now.' He waved to the slim dark figure just striding through the door.

'Alistair's the owner,' she explained to Elizabeth. 'His horse is the one we've backed in the third race – Mine's A Pint. He called her that because she's partial to the booze.'

'You mean, horses *drink*?' Elizabeth asked in amazement.

'Some do,' Tony said. 'I know Arkle was fond of Guinness. And when Mandarin retired, he had two bottles of Mackeson every single day, courtesy of the local pub in Lambourn. Mine's A Pint prefers Newcastle Brown, and she's not averse to sweet things either. She filched a piece of cake off me last week.'

Beattie laughed, one eye on Alistair, who had stopped to greet a friend. She hadn't met him before, but had heard a good deal about him when she and Tony were going out. (Or staying in, more accurately. They'd never had time to go out – Tony was too busy with his horses – so they would get together between the sheets once a month or less.) She watched Alistair saunter towards them: a handsome man, in his latish fifties she'd guess; his black hair shot with silver, his suit exquisitely tailored under an expensive-looking coat – cashmere possibly. She was glad that Elizabeth had made an effort with her clothes. If they weren't exactly fashionable, at least they were a vast improvement on her jeans. She had even dug out a hat – a jaunty little number with a speckled feather in it, which helped to redeem her rather boring suit (sludgy green and a most unflattering length).

Tony made the introductions, then poured four foaming glasses of champagne.

'Cheers!' said Beattie, hoping her accent measured up to her surroundings. Actually, she was finding it much easier to talk 'posh', with the benefit of Elizabeth's example over the past few weeks. Alistair sounded every bit as pukka as the whole Hargreaves family put together, and his face had those haughty cheekbones you never saw on plebs. Tony was less top-drawer. He'd been a jockey in his younger days and, after years of near-starvation (not to mention laxatives and saunas) had now put on flesh, especially round his middle. But he had an attractive face, well tanned from sun and wind, and the sort of eyes that looked as if they were enjoying a permanent (probably risqué) joke.

'Well, at least the first leg of our treble has come up,' she said, meeting those blue eyes again and winking in response.

'Did you back them separately as well?' asked Tony.

'Yes, though I didn't plan to originally. I rather like those all-or-nothing bets. I know they're risky, but that makes them more exciting.'

'Exciting maybe, but crazy,' Alistair remarked, producing a silver cigarette case and offering it around. 'I mean, you're lucky to get *one* winner, let alone three in a row. Who did you pick as your third?'

'By George.'

Tony made a grimace. 'You should have stuck to the two I suggested. I have my doubts about By George. He pulled up lame last time, and fell the time before. And I don't entirely trust his trainer.'

'Yes, but he came second on this course last year, and he was doing jolly well when he last ran at Newbury, until he was brought down.' She didn't add that she'd been influenced by his name. She knew it was the height of folly to back horses on such illogical grounds, but in By George's case there were two names to attract her: George itself – her father's pet name for her – and the trainer's name, Scotty

McGuire. Her dad's own nickname had been Scotty, at least among his actor-friends (following a part he'd played dressed in kilt and tam-o'-shanter). It seemed a wonderfully good omen that both names had cropped up, linked with one another, and both connected with her father. She had a feeling he was with her here in spirit, as if he knew instinctively that she was revisiting their former haunt and had come to share the occasion. And anyway, whatever Tony's opinion, By George's form wasn't bad. You could hardly blame a horse for being struck into or brought down.

'Well, I only hope *our* horse doesn't spoil your luck,' Tony said, breaking off to explain to Alistair that Mine's A Pint was the second leg of Beattie's treble.

'What do you think her chances are?' Elizabeth asked, obviously feeling it was time to contribute something to the conversation.

'She's been doing jolly well on the gallops,' Tony replied enthusiastically. 'And she seems to cope with the ground.'

'Yes, the going will certainly suit her,' Alistair chipped in. 'It was far too firm last time. She prefers a bit of cut – likes to dig her toes in! On the whole, I'd say we're very hopeful, barring accidents, of course. The most important thing is that she comes back in one piece.'

He topped up all four glasses, then turned to Elizabeth, perhaps sensing that she was out of her depth with so much racing talk. He began asking her a few bread-and-butter questions, such as where she lived and what she did, and had she been to Sandown before? Beattie glanced at them with a flicker of anxiety. The smoke from their two cigarettes was merging together in a way she found disquieting. The last thing she wanted was for Elizabeth to be chatted up by some wealthy Mr Swish and whisked off to a new life in the fast lane. No, that was hardly likely. The tall blonde in the corner would probably be more Alistair's type: a gorgeous creature with black-stockinged legs and hair down to her waist. There were several other glamorous females in the room, and a suspicious-looking character wearing dark glasses and a scowl, and a marvellous silver-haired chap who seemed to have sprung from the Victorian age, complete with sideburns and gold watch-chain. She imprinted all the details on her mind, so she could relay them to her father later on; write him a full report on the day. Pity she hadn't brought her camera, then she could have sent him some photographs as well – proof she'd actually been hobnobbing with the owners; that it wasn't just a pipe dream.

She sipped her champagne slowly, savouring each mouthful. She wasn't exactly a wine buff, but guessed it would be vintage. She watched the waitresses gliding between the tables, dapper in their black and white, with pink bow ties and accents almost as high-class as their customers'.

The talk at their own table had returned inevitably to racing: how worried Alistair had been by Jumping Jack's wild antics at the start. He too had backed the horse after talking to his stable-lad, who'd seemed highly optimistic about his chances.

'That horse is either brilliant or a nightmare!' Tony put in with a grin. 'But he particularly likes this course, so I felt he'd pull it off today.'

'And he *did*,' said Beattie, patting Tony's arm. 'Thank you, wonderful man!' She flashed him a brief smile, implying that her words of praise had a wider application than the racecourse.

Alistair put his glass down and gave a quick glance at his watch. 'If you'll all excuse me,' he murmured, 'I must dash off and put something on the next race.'

'Who's he going to back d'you think?' Beattie asked, once he was safely out of earshot.

Tony's face gave nothing away. 'That would be telling, wouldn't it?'

'Oh, go on, Tony, give us a hint. We've got nothing on this race, but there's still time for us to nip down to the bookies and maybe win a bit extra.'

'Well, let's put it this way – I wouldn't be surprised if my black-haired friend fancied a horse with that colour in its name.'

'In The Black!' Beattie carolled. 'That sounds the perfect horse for me. Thanks a million, Tony. Any chance of seeing you later?'

'Sure. Why not come and meet us here after the last race – if you're not in any hurry to get home, that is.'

Beattie turned to Elizabeth. 'How do *you* feel?' she asked. This was Elizabeth's day, after all.

'Yes, that's fine. I'd love to.'

'Okay. And if our treble comes up, Tony, it'll be drinks on *us* this time.'

'Right, off to collect our winnings!' Beattie said, steering Elizabeth through the crowds towards their bookie.

'*Your* winnings, you mean. My horse came in last.'

'Well, I told you not to go by their names. Lightweight, for heaven's sake! It was bound to lose with a name like that.'

'But I *feel* lightweight today, Beattie – freed from all my usual responsibilities. I didn't want some miserable-sounding name. And there wasn't a lot of choice.'

'Anyway,' said Beattie, 'everything we win today, we share. I'm putting on all the bets for you as well as me. Including the treble, of course.'

'But that's not fair. I mean I . . .'

'Of course it is,' Beattie interrupted. 'Be careful! That idiot's not looking where he's going.' She pushed Elizabeth out of the path of a lurching red-faced yobbo, obviously the worse for wear – another winner perhaps.

'Gosh, it's so exciting, isn't it? I just love the atmosphere.'

Beattie nodded. 'It's the smells I remember best – fried onions and hot doughnuts and a few new ones since I was here as a kid.' She sniffed the air, wrinkling her nose in distaste. 'What on earth are they selling over there?'

'Curried seafood,' Elizabeth said, peering at the notice on the stall.

'D'you fancy some? Or jellied eels? Or cockles?'

'No thanks. Not after salmon *en croûte*!'

Beattie didn't tell her that she and her father used to feast on fish and chips at the races (out of the paper, of course), followed by Mr Whippys. They must have looked a couple of tramps, licking their greasy fingers and then attacking their ice-cream cornets, laughing as it dripped on their clothes. The bookies' ring was a world away from the Members' Enclosure. No cashmere coats or suits and trilbies here, only tatty anoraks and faded jeans and trainers. A lot of people were snacking on the hoof, as she and her dad had done: dipping into bags of chips, or with ketchup dribbling down their chins from burgers or hot dogs. And there were a few undeniably rough types with drinkers' bulbous noses, or mean and brutish faces, she wouldn't care to meet on a dark night.

She caught sight of a gipsy woman accosting passers-by, peddling sprigs of lucky heather to the punters. 'We must have some of *that*,' she exclaimed, pulling out her purse.

'Beattie, you're so superstitious!'

'Of course. All writers are,' she said airily. (Max had told her that.)

'Do you plan to write some articles on racing? I'm sure you'd do them marvellously well.'

'Maybe.' Beattie changed the subject swiftly, remarking on one of the bookies: an old stalwart by the looks of him, with mutton-chop whiskers and an ancient bowler hat. 'By the way,' she asked, studiously off-hand. 'Did you fancy Alistair?'

'Who?'

'Oh, Elizabeth, you're impossible! Mine's A Pint's owner – the one who joined us in the bar. You obviously *didn't* fancy him if you can't even remember his name.'

'Oh, *that* Alistair. I thought you were talking about a horse.'

'Well, did you?'

'Did I what?'

Beattie groaned. 'I'm sure that champagne's affected your brain.'

'Well, I must admit it rather went to my head.'

'Good though, wasn't it?'

'Superb.'

Yes, thought Beattie, superb that Elizabeth had loosened up and was obviously enjoying herself so much. There was just the little matter of Alistair to get straight. '*I* thought he was rather dishy,' she persisted. 'Just the right age for you. And a fellow smoker and everything.'

'Are you trying to marry me off again?' Elizabeth asked, laughing.

'You could do worse. I mean, he's tall, dark and handsome. *And* rich.'

Elizabeth's face became serious. 'No,' she said, shaking her head. 'I'll never marry again. I decided that on the day of the divorce, and I've found no reason to change my mind.'

Beattie gave her a brief impulsive hug, prompted partly by the sadness in her voice, but also by enormous relief. It was bad enough having to share her with parents, children, grandchildren, neighbours, friends and patients. But the thought of someone else taking her away – someone even closer than all that lot put together – was too awful to consider.

'I suppose it's rather selfish,' Elizabeth mused anxiously, straightening her hat, which had been knocked askew in the hug.

'*Selfish!* Elizabeth, you're the most unselfish person I've ever met.'

'I'm not, Beattie. You're idealizing me again. Living alone *can* make you very selfish. When you're married, there's always someone else to consider – their work and moods and everything. And Jeremy's work was so demanding, it affected the whole family. Often he wouldn't come home till very late, or he'd be frightfully tense and snap at us all. And he was a tremendously tidy person – he expected the house to be immaculate and everything in its place. That's not easy with four children, I can tell you. Now I'm on my own, I can let things go – not worry if the drawing-room's untidy, or my hair's a mess, or I've scheduled a patient in the dinner-hour.'

'If you ask me, *he*'s the one who's selfish,' Beattie said, squashing a paper cup underfoot and imagining it was Jeremy.

'No – just under a lot of pressure. But let's not talk about him. I feel it's terribly disloyal. And anyway, I'm having such a lovely day, I don't want to spoil it.'

Beattie took her arm and squeezed it. She would make bloody sure there were *lots* of lovely days, to compensate for that foul-tempered pernickety man.

They continued arm in arm through the crowds, making for the Charles James pitch. 'Right, here we are,' said Beattie, gesturing to the brilliant yellow board with its two plastic Union Jacks fluttering on top. 'And there's quite a queue, as usual. Even when I was a kid he seemed to be one of the most popular bookies.'

'Did you always use him?'

'Oh yes! Dad was a great friend of his. Charles James Woolgar was his full name, although he was always known as Sonny, for some reason. He died almost twenty years ago and Roy took over from him. If you don't inherit your pitches from a relative, you can wait years to get a foot in. God! It was quite a shock seeing Roy again. Mind you, he looks just the same, apart from having a bit less hair.'

Roy caught her eye and waved. 'Won't be long,' he mouthed, handing over a wad of notes to a mountain of a woman in a scarlet pompommed hat.

'There don't seem to be any *female* bookies,' Elizabeth observed, glancing around at all the different boards. 'Steve Gibbs, Fred Button, Jolly Joe – but no Jolly Josephine.'

'No, it's still very much a man's world,' Beattie told her. 'And terribly stressful – as frantic as the Stock Exchange, by all accounts. Old Mr Woolgar died of a stroke, brought on by stress apparently. Although he never seemed uptight. He was a real extrovert – a showman with a marvellous patter, and always impeccably turned out: hand-made shirt, bowler hat, the lot.'

'Roy looks pretty smart himself.'

'Oh, yes. He wouldn't let Sonny down.' It struck her only now that Roy had probably idolized his father as much as she did hers. As a child, she hadn't been aware of what a struggle her dad's life was – the walk-on parts in second-rate shows, the endless money worries, offset by the eternal hope of winning at the races. For her, he had held the charisma of all the great actors he talked about – Gielgud, Wolfit, Olivier – and she'd had no idea that his fortunes and experience were so utterly remote from theirs.

'Hi, Roy – again!' she said as they moved up to the head of the queue. 'I bet your ears are burning.'

'Why? I hope you're not telling your friend all my vices?'

'No, all your virtues. And I do apologize for winning.'

'That's okay. It's a real pleasure paying *you*, George. It brings back such happy memories. I only wish our two fathers could see us here together again, after all these years.'

'Why does he call you George?' Elizabeth enquired as they ambled off through the crowds, Beattie's winnings stowed safely in her purse.

'Because my dad always did.'

'Oh yes, I remember now – you told me. But you never explained why.'

Beattie chewed her thumb. It was another sad story, like the death of the injured horse, which would only cast a shadow on the day. 'Oh . . . it's a bit too long for now,' she hedged. 'And we don't want to be late for the next race.' She kicked a Kentucky Fried Chicken carton out of the way. The ground was strewn with litter: discarded tickets, doughnut boxes, crumpled paper serviettes. 'You know, I doubt if Roy ever knew my real name. He probably thought it was Georgina.'

'George suits you, actually. It's just your sort of name.'

'Yeah. I like it too. Hey, shall I be George again – adopt it as my racing name?'

'Why not?' Elizabeth laughed, still a little high from the champagne. 'Nice to meet you, George.'

'And nice to meet you, Sophie.'

'Sophie?'

'It's the horse you fancied in the fourth race, remember? Countess Sophie.'

'Oh yes. I liked the Countess bit. I've got a second cousin twice removed who claims to be a countess – although I think it's only delusions of grandeur.'

'Well, second cousin or no, don't you *dare* put money on her! She's a rank outsider – twenty-five to one. You'll be throwing it down the drain. Shit! It's less than five minutes to the next race. We're too late to go to the paddock now, or we won't get a decent place on the stands. No, let's watch this one from the rails, right near the last fence. It's exciting standing so close and watching them fly over.'

'Well I only hope they don't all fall on top of each other, like they did in the first race. I've no desire to see *that* sight at close quarters.'

'Yes, and it's a steeplechase this time, not a hurdle, so the jumps will be much stiffer. Just pray Mine's A Pint does her stuff. She's *got* to win, or we can kiss goodbye to our treble. Do you understand that, Countess Sophie?'

'Yes, Count George, I do.'

13

'More champagne?' asked Beattie, trying to catch the waitress's eye.

'No, Beattie — sorry, *George* – I really couldn't. I'll disgrace myself if I drink any more!'

'More tea then?'

'Yes, just half a cup please. And by the way, I absolutely insist on paying the bill this time.'

'Sorry – out of the question. It's all paid for in advance.'

'George, honestly, you'll bankrupt yourself.'

'Look, we've just *won*, for heaven's sake!'

'But not that much, I thought you said.'

'Well, no. Mine's A Pint was only five to two. But remember it goes on our last horse. So if *he* wins, we could make a thousand or more.'

'A *thousand?*' Elizabeth's teacup froze halfway to her mouth. 'I can't believe it!'

'Well, it's true. I keep trying to explain it to you. "Multiplied odds", it's called, and what happens is that the money you put on . . .'

'It's no good, George. I just can't take it in. My brain's addled by excitement and champagne.'

'I expect Alistair feels much the same. Did you see his face when everyone applauded Mine's A Pint?'

'No. When d'you mean?'

'In the winners' enclosure. I was expecting him to lead her in himself – the owners often do. I think it was rather nice of him to let the stable-lass do it.' She could afford to be magnanimous towards Alistair, now that Elizabeth had made it clear that he wasn't in the running for her affections. 'Mind you, I thought she went a bit over the top, slobbering over the horse like that, and then bursting into tears. Still, I suppose horses are her whole life.' And Tony's too, she

124

reflected, recalling his ecstatic smile as he stood proudly by the 'FIRST' sign, patting the winner's neck. 'God! I only hope By George can pull it off too.'

'What shall we do with the money if he does win?'

'Don't *say* that! It's bad luck.'

'Why?'

'I don't know. It just is. Listen, what do you reckon, shall we stand by the last fence again, or near the winning post this time? I think I favour the fence. I mean, if it was lucky once, it may be again.'

'If you don't mind, Beattie, I'd rather we sat in comfort in the stands. I don't think my nerves are up to standing by the rails a second time. I still feel rather shaky from seeing that ghastly fall.'

Beattie shrugged. 'It wasn't really ghastly. The horse is quite okay – it got up and walked off. And it's terribly exciting, watching them whoosh over under your nose.'

'*Too* exciting for me! I had to keep covering my eyes. Then when that jockey fell off right in front of us, my heart was really in my mouth. I thought he was concussed at first. Thank goodness he managed to duck under the fence.'

'That was the safest thing for him to do, so long as there weren't any others coming up behind. Otherwise he *might* have been concussed. They're frightfully brave, the jump-jockeys. I mean, some of them have broken practically every bone in their body. I remember my dad telling me about one he knew who'd broken an arm and a leg twice each, and his collarbone four times. That must be a record! And a lot of them have false teeth, you know, even the really young ones.'

Elizabeth looked incredulous, and put her hand up to her mouth, as if her own teeth might be in danger.

'Honestly, it's true. They take their teeth out before they ride. Sometimes you can see them smiling toothlessly as they leave the paddock to canter down to the start.'

'I just don't know where they find the courage to ride a race at all, Beattie.'

'*George!*'

'What?'

'My name's George today, remember.'

'Yes, so it is. I'm sorry. Another pastry, George?' Elizabeth passed the plate.

'Yes, why not?' She took an apricot tart. Since she'd been staying with Elizabeth, she had got into the habit of eating much more than normal, yet she still hadn't put on weight. Obviously part of Elizabeth's magic. And anyway, it seemed a crime to waste this slap-up tea. There were tiny crustless sandwiches (smoked salmon and egg-and-prawn) and every kind of cake from a squidgy chocolate gâteau oozing cream and brandy to the classiest of fruit-cakes with more fruit in it than flour. The Members' Restaurant had certainly excelled itself – at lunch as well as tea. All around them seriously rich people were pigging themselves, or knocking back the booze, or smoking ostentatious cigars – the sort of fat-cat breed who didn't give a toss about their bank statements if they wanted to snap their fingers and order another magnum of champagne. She watched the noisy group at the next table – expense-account businessmen, most likely – sprawled back in their chairs and all ragging each other and guf-fawing, glasses in their hands. They had doubtless been drinking since well before lunchtime, watching the races on television or keeping an eye on the proceedings below. She had specially requested a table overlooking the parade ring, to ensure Elizabeth had the best view in the restaurant.

She swivelled round in her chair to survey the row of television screens. 'Oh *no*! By George's odds are lengthening. That's a very bad sign. And, God! I don't believe it – Countess Sophie's have shortened.'

'I'd better back her then,' Elizabeth said, forking in the last knob of her chocolate éclair.

'Over my dead body! If you want an extra flutter in this race, I should go for Big Jemima.'

'Oh, no. I had an aunt called Jemima, and she *was* big – sixteen stone. I couldn't stand her as a child.'

'You've got too many relatives,' Beattie muttered darkly. 'Anyway, I keep telling you, you mustn't go by the names.'

'What else can I go by?'

'Well, your race-card for a start!' Beattie picked up her own and waved it at Elizabeth. 'Listen to what it says about the horse you backed last time: "Alexander II is out of his depth in this grade. Definitely one to leave alone."'

'Yes, but he's my grandson's namesake. I put the money on for *him.*'

'Chucked it away, you mean.'

'Anyway, I don't *need* to study form, when you're the expert.'

'Don't speak too soon, for heaven's sake. By George's odds have just lengthened again. He's out to ten to one. I don't know how I'll be able to watch this race.'

'Perhaps we should stay here, then – carry on with our tea and pretend it isn't happening?'

'Oh, no.' Beattie's eyes were still on the screen. 'That would be even worse.' Besides, she thought, you could hardly ignore a race when six separate televisions would be relaying every second of it. She pushed her plate away; the cake had suddenly become tasteless. If she lost on the treble – which looked increasingly likely – it would be impossible to pay her bills. Worse than that, she would lose Elizabeth's respect; would no longer be considered 'brilliant', 'expert', 'knowledgeable', but a reckless little fool. All day she'd been saying how stupid it was to go by horses' names, yet that was just what she had done herself, to some extent at least. It was so easy to get carried away by some irrational hunch. Elizabeth had already made a comment about how addictive gambling could be – they'd been standing by the Tote before the second race, watching the swarms of punters queuing at the rows of little windows and sliding their money across. 'Gosh, it's so quick and easy, isn't it?' Elizabeth had said. 'No wonder people lose so much.' Perhaps some of her patients were gamblers – manic or obsessional types she might classify as genuinely sick. And supposing . . .

'What's wrong?' Elizabeth asked, perceptive as ever to her slightest change of mood.

'Nothing.' She turned back from the screen with a determinedly cheerful expression. If they *did* lose, she must make light of it, pretend her recent London earnings would easily cover everything. And she could always say that the bets themselves had cost her only peanuts – Elizabeth would never know. If she gave any hint of her money worries, Elizabeth would refuse to go racing again – and whatever happened, they must continue going. It was their escape, their student spree, which would not only draw them closer by giving them a mutual interest, but also get them out of the house in Kent, away from Elizabeth's hangers-on and her demanding family.

'Oh, look,' Elizabeth said, peering out through the huge expanse of glass. 'Some of the horses are just coming into the parade ring.'

Beattie seized the binoculars and moved closer to the window. 'And By George is first – how odd!' Could that be a good omen, she wondered, or was she clutching at straws? He certainly looked fit, and was walking in a relaxed and confident way. He was also extremely well turned out: groomed in chequerboard-style and with his mane elaborately plaited. He was followed by the favourite: Morning After, a strawberry roan with a dramatic near-black tail. Beattie trained her binoculars on him, noticing his huge black dangling cock. She knew from talking to Tony that most jumping horses were gelded – Morning After anything but. Apparently an erection was often a bad sign: the horse's mind on the fillies rather than the race. Well, if it spoiled the favourite's chances, so much the better. She was beginning to wish, uncharitably, that every other runner in this race would be withdrawn or pulled up lame.

She kept her glasses fixed on the horse, fascinated, despite herself. Winning stallions could earn *thousands*, just for a single session. If only *she* were a famous racehorse and could charge Max a cool seventy grand a time, all her money problems would be solved in one night.

Grinning, she pulled Elizabeth to her feet. 'Come on, we've gotta run. We ought to be down there, taking a closer look at By George. His odds haven't shortened, so we'll have to pray for a miracle!'

'And Morning After is still leading, with Merlin on the outside and Hiawatha making ground on the inside. Big Jemima is lying a long way fourth, followed by Midshipman and By George. By George's jockey looks to have lost an iron. He seems to be in difficulties.'

Beattie groaned out loud. That stupid bloody commentator – did he *have* to sound so gloating when their horse was in dead trouble? The race was halfway through, and By George had failed to distinguish himself so far. And for his jockey to lose a stirrup seemed the kiss of death.

'Hiawatha's on the inside, looking for room. He's still behind, but Big Jemima comes off the rails and . . .'

'But what about By *George*?' Beattie muttered, trying to pick him out on the far side of the course.

As if in answer, the commentator resumed. 'And By George is catching up now, coming through the pack. His jockey's got his iron back all right, and he's making a bit of speed . . .'

It's too *late*, she thought. He just can't do it in the time, not with five in front of him. She began to pray, desperately and soundlessly: 'Dear God, Dear Anyone, let By George win and I'll give up lying. I'll really try to change. I'll become a better person, more unselfish, more . . .'

'And now they're coming round the bend, approaching the fourth last. Morning After's been hampered there. Merlin stumbled in front of him and he's lost all impetus. And Big Jemima has just pulled up.'

Beattie listened in amazement. The favourite hampered, and two other well-backed horses out of the running? Her prayers must have worked already. Perhaps there *was* some Power protecting her, wanting her to become a better person. She turned her attention back to the race, peering through her binoculars to pick out her jockey's blue and gold.

'And now By George is making late headway towards the leading trio, with Hiawatha still in the lead, followed by Morning After.'

She leaned forward in her seat. They were sitting in the front row of the stands; even so, certain stretches of the course were still difficult to see in any detail. But there were only three more fences left; the horses pounding nearer all the time.

'And now they're coming up to the pond fence. Hiawatha just brushed through the top of that one, leading By George in second place, with Morning After lying third. The rest of the field are safely over.'

Beattie was sitting so stiffly, her whole body ached from tension. Her palms were sweaty, her face screwed up.

'And now, approaching the last fence, it's still Hiawatha from By George. They're both in the air together . . . By George jumped slightly left and they may have come together there. They're neck and neck now on the climb to the finish.'

Beattie let her binoculars fall and fixed her eyes on the two horses thundering towards her, though her overwhelming instinct was *not* to look, to turn her back, hide her face.

'By George is drawing away, but it's very very close! You can forget the others. By George's stamina is beginning to tell and he's . . .'

Beattie clenched her fists. Sweat was beading on her forehead, snailing down between her breasts. She felt feverish, almost ill. Never in her life had she screwed herself into such a state over the outcome of one race.

'And there's nothing to choose between them now! Hiawatha is coming back with every stride. This is a tremendous finish!'

The commentator's frenetic tone only increased her agitation, and the roar of the crowd had risen to a riotous crescendo. Even Elizabeth was on her feet, shouting for By George, and behind her raucous voices were urging Hiawatha on. But she herself sat dumb.

Her mouth wouldn't seem to function, although her heart was working overtime, thumping uncontrollably in her chest.

'By George is coming away by a couple of lengths. Yes, it's By George the winner, from Hiawatha second, and Morning After a long way back in third.'

Beattie let her breath out in a long and shuddering sigh. She still felt hot and sweaty, but gloriously so. A few people were groaning over Hiawatha's defeat, but they were only paper cut-outs. Elizabeth alone was real: darling solid Elizabeth, reaching out to clasp her hand and grinning from ear to ear. Beattie fell upon her – hugged her, kissed her, whirled her round and round.

'Oh Elizabeth, we've *done* it. Let's go back to the restaurant and order . . .'

'Stewards' enquiry!' barked the tannoy.

Beattie stood stock still, her euphoria punctured like a burst balloon.

'What's happening?' Elizabeth asked, as a jabber of consternation broke out all around them.

Beattie slumped back in her seat without a word.

Elizabeth touched her arm. 'Look, *please* explain what's going on.'

'What they just said,' she snapped. 'A stewards' enquiry.'

'But why?'

Beattie glanced at Elizabeth's face and felt instantly ashamed. It was unfair to take it out on her, or expect her to know all the ins and outs of racing. The least she could do was explain. 'It must have been at the final fence when the two horses came so close. If By George hampered Hiawatha, then he might not be the winner after all. The stewards get together with the two jockeys and thrash it out between them – study the film and try to decide what happened. It could take a good ten minutes.' She dragged herself to her feet, noticing her scuffed and muddied boots – no longer gleaming-new. 'Let's go to the bar,' she said despondently. 'I need a stiff drink.'

'But he *may* still have won,' Elizabeth insisted, clearly determined to cheer her up.

'Yeah, I'd say he did,' the man beside them butted in. 'It wasn't his fault – you could see that. And anyway it was only very slight.'

'I wouldn't be so certain,' the guy behind chimed in. 'If you ask me, it's only an even-money chance. And you can never be sure what the stewards are going to say. They're damned strict these days – they have to be.'

'Well, they'll be betting on it in the ring,' the first man said, mooching off with a shrug.

Instantly Beattie came to life again. 'Wait here,' she ordered Elizabeth. 'Don't move or we'll lose each other.'

'Where are you going?'

'To . . . er . . . have a pee.'

'I'll come with you. I need one too, after all that tea!'

'*No.*' Beattie was already elbowing her way through the crowd, careering down the steps towards the bookies' ring. She didn't bother going all the way to Roy's pitch, way down at the back, but stopped at the first bookie's board she came to. 'What odds are you giving on By George getting the race?'

'Two to one on.'

She hesitated. Odds like that were hardly worth betting on at all. She totted up the contents of her purse, down to the last small coin: fifty pounds seven pence. If she blued the lot on By George, it would be a sign of her faith in the horse, and, if he won, she'd have an extra twenty-five pounds in hand. She could do with some ready cash – the betting shop in Sevenoaks didn't open till Monday morning. But suppose he *didn't* get the race and Hiawatha was declared the winner instead? Surely it would be far more sensible to hedge her bets and back Hiawatha anyway? She was already in danger of losing hugely on By George, so it was downright stupid to throw good money after bad.

She turned back to the bookie. 'And what are the odds for Hiawatha?'

'Five to one.' The same sullen drawl – he didn't seem to *want* her bloody cash.

She stood dithering again. She could win two hundred and fifty quid on Hiawatha. That would impress Elizabeth and also soften the blow of losing on the treble. Impulsively she tipped her stash of notes and coins into the bookie's hand. 'Fifty pounds on Hiawatha, please.'

He began counting the money, his face suspicious now as well as surly – none of Roy's easygoing banter.

'No, wait,' she said, flustered. 'I didn't mean Hiawatha.'

'What *did* you mean?' he asked with a scowl.

'By George!' She made his name a clarion call. Of course he'd get the race. He was meant to win and he *had* won. Her prayers had been answered, hadn't they? Anyway the horse was very special – connected with her father and her childhood. She simply had to put her trust in him, not let anyone or anything undermine her confidence.

The bookie gave her a ticket, and she made her way back to the stands, passing little huddles of punters with expectant anxious faces. The whole atmosphere was tense: people with serious money at stake hanging restlessly around, not knowing whether they'd won or lost; the course itself suspended in a limbo until the stewards reached their verdict.

She consulted her watch. Seven minutes had passed. In another three or four, their fate would be decided.

She ran up the last few steps towards the stands. Elizabeth was sitting alone in the front row, looking small and rather lost, and smoking the inevitable cigarette. She stopped in her tracks, still a yard or two away from her, suddenly aware that their whole friendship was in the balance. A thought had flashed to her from nowhere that if By George was confirmed as the winner, then the relationship would last, would develop into love; if not, then . . .

Don't be so *stupid*, she told the superstitious voice. It was utter nonsense – just another irrational impulse which would only make her still more wretched. Yet now the idea had lodged in her head, she couldn't seem to shift it. Something seemed to be telling her that it wasn't just her cash she could lose, but Elizabeth herself – their bond, their future, everything.

She went up to Elizabeth and touched her on the shoulder. 'Listen,' she stammered, humiliatingly close to tears. 'You do know I'm . . . I'm very fond of you.'

Elizabeth smiled and squeezed her hand. 'And I'm very fond of *you*, George. Look, don't be too upset about the race. If By George doesn't win – well, it's not the end of the world.'

'But it *is*,' she countered frantically. 'You don't understand.'

Elizabeth stubbed her cigarette out and fumbled in her handbag. 'If you're worried about the money side, let's settle up here and now. I've been trying to do that all along. It really isn't fair, you paying for everything.'

'No. I refuse to take a penny. Anyway I'm *not* worried. I earned so much at that job in Hammersmith, I'm out of the wood, thank heavens! In fact I'm going to buy us both a drink. These bloody stewards seem to be taking for ever to make up their minds.'

She grabbed Elizabeth's arm and marched her off to the nearest bar. 'You sit here,' she said, pouncing on the one remaining chair.

'And I'll do my best to get served.' She joined the crush at the bar, and was immediately engulfed in a hubbub of speculation and argument; stranger talking to stranger, self-confessed experts broadcasting their opinions to anyone who'd listen.

'It was an extraordinary race, whatever happens,' declared a woman in a fun-fur. 'By George didn't look as if he had it in him. And I wouldn't have given much for his chances five out. Then to suddenly accelerate like that . . .'

'I was furious,' her friend put in, waving a twenty-pound note at the barman. '*I* had all my money on Morning After.'

'The whole thing was so unpredictable,' the guy behind them remarked. 'I mean, even Morning After wasn't anywhere near the lead until almost halfway through. But that often happens, doesn't it? I've been racing for more than thirty years and I've seen real turn-arounds in my time. I guess that's the fascination of it.'

'Yeah, I remember back in 1974 – there was a complete reversal when . . .'

Shut up! Beattie didn't say it, just gritted her teeth instead. She couldn't stand this babble, these maddening know-alls who didn't have as much to lose as she did. She checked her watch again. A good fifteen minutes had passed. What in God's name were those stewards *doing*, keeping everyone on tenterhooks?

At last it was her turn to be served. She ordered two double brandies and got out her purse to pay for them; staring in horror at the two remaining coins – a 2p and a 5. How on earth could she have forgotten, for Christ's sake? She'd just unloaded all her money on the bookie. She tried to hide her face as tears began sliding down her cheeks. People would think she was crying because her horse had lost. But it was worse than that – far worse. How could she go back and ask Elizabeth for money when she'd waved it away so imperiously just a moment ago? Elizabeth would *know* she had been lying and might never trust her again.

'Five pounds fifty,' the barman repeated tetchily.

'I . . . I'm sorry, I . . . seem to have mislaid my . . .' She turned and fled towards the door, refusing to be seen in tears. She knew she was over-reacting, but the prospect of losing seemed utterly unbearable. It wasn't just the money – somehow she could make more money, with Max's help, with overtime, with more tips from Tony, even. But if she lost Elizabeth, there was simply no one to replace her, no one in her league.

A man standing by the door lurched forward, accidentally slopping his drink on her expensive navy suit.

'Can't you bloody well look where you're going?' she stormed. 'I've a good mind to . . .'

The tannoy cut across her voice. She whirled round in frustration. She hadn't heard; had missed the crucial announcement.

'What did it say? What did it say?' she implored the man she'd just berated.

'You've changed your tune, darling, I must say! It was "bloody well" a moment ago.'

She grabbed his lapel. 'Look, tell me who's won, for Christ's sake, and I'll go down on my knees and kiss your feet.'

He grinned and took a gulp of beer. 'The placings remain unaltered, so By George is still the winner – damn him!'

Beattie fell to her knees and kissed the man's muddy shoes – kissed them with total passion and abandon, the way she would kiss Elizabeth tonight.

14

'Which bed do you prefer, Sophie?'

'I don't mind,' Elizabeth said, slipping off her coat in the overheated hotel room. '*You* choose.'

'Okay, I'll have the one by the window, then I can look out at the garden.'

'Well, you'll have to wait till the morning for that. You won't see much in the dark.'

Beattie felt a stab of fear. Never in her life had she slept without a nightlight. But what was she to do, sharing a room with Elizabeth? It was easy enough in Kent – she just left the bedside lamp on all night – but Elizabeth might object to that, or find it difficult to sleep. She had no intention of confessing that she was frightened of the dark. It would make her sound a wimp, or like a pathetic child of two. Well – she shrugged and heaved her case up on the bed – that was a problem to be dealt with later on. Like the other little problems, such as where and when they got undressed (together or apart), and whether they should share the bathroom or use it separately. If only they could share *every*thing: double bed, long luxurious bath, towel, flannel, toothbrush, comb; become so as one they even shared each other's secret fears.

'I'll have these drawers shall I, George? And you have those by your bed.'

'Okay.' She stifled a grin. Clearly it wasn't going to be easy. How could they become as one if their clothes were so rigidly separated? She preferred the thought of her pyjamas nestling close to Elizabeth's nightie, their tights rolled up together, their bras and pants entwined. But Elizabeth was already arranging her underclothes singly and apart, then shutting the drawers to prevent any chance of an intimate encounter.

She stuffed her own things in the largest bedside drawer without bothering to sort them out, reluctant to waste precious time unpacking. She had Elizabeth to herself for a glorious two days – and truly to herself this time. Family and patients were hardly likely to pursue them a hundred-odd miles to Cheltenham. She could still barely believe her luck in coaxing Elizabeth away at all, especially at such short notice. She had managed to deflect the tidal wave of objections, stressing to Elizabeth that they were obviously on a winning streak which it would be criminal to ignore, and that they couldn't miss such an important event as the Mackeson Gold Cup. She blessed her good fortune that the venue was Cheltenham – Elizabeth's old haunt. She was sure *that* was as much an attraction for her as another day of racing: the desire to see the gallery she had worked in as a naïve eighteen-year-old, or the tiny bedsit she had furnished proudly with sixties bric-à-brac. So they'd agreed that Saturday would be racecourse day and Sunday Memory Lane.

'Shall we go and have a drink?' she suggested. 'The bar looked super – olde-worlde beams and things, and an enormous log fire.'

'Don't you think it's a bit late for drinks?' Elizabeth demurred. She looked pale and rather tired: not surprising, when she'd had patients all day. If only she had cancelled the last two, they could have got away much earlier and enjoyed a leisurely dinner here at the hotel, instead of stopping for a rushed meal en route.

'It's only five to ten,' Beattie pleaded. 'We did the journey in record time.'

'You're telling me! I've never known my poor old car go at such a lick! I was trying not to look at the speedometer.'

'I'm sure I never went a fraction over fifty.' Beattie grinned and slammed her case shut – the rest could wait till later. 'Come on, just a quick one.'

'Listen, George, my love. I don't want to sound like a spoilsport, but I'm a bit worried about this drinking. I mean, all that champagne we had last Saturday and . . .'

'But Saturday was special. We won the treble, for heaven's sake! We *had* to celebrate.'

'I know, but I'm concerned about your kidneys. You know what Lofty said.'

'Okay, I promise I'll cut down from Monday. This is our weekend off, remember, and judging by your diary there won't be any more this side of Christmas, so we've got to make the most of it. And anyway, we're supposed to be students, and I've never known *them* be particularly abstemious!'

Elizabeth laughed. 'You're wonderfully persuasive, Beattie.'

'*George!*'

'George. D'you know, Mummy heard me call you George and she was quite upset. She thinks Beattie's bad enough. She found out you were christened Elizabeth, so if she had her way, Elizabeth you'd be.'

'But it would be rather muddling wouldn't it – *both* of us Elizabeth? Tell you what, once I get back to London, I'll be teetotal Elizabeth – nose to the grindstone and all that. But this is only Friday evening, and George and Sophie have just met on their first day at university, and they've decided to go out together for one harmless little drink.'

'Hey, listen, Sophie – why don't we come back here for Christmas? They're doing a special package deal with everything thrown in: carol singers, a dinner dance, a mystery tour on Boxing Day . . .'

Elizabeth glanced at the leaflet Beattie had picked up in reception. 'It's a lovely idea, but I'm afraid I'd be hung, drawn and quartered if I didn't lay on my usual Christmas at home. It's a family tradition, you see, and everyone comes en masse.'

'You can always break traditions.'

'To be honest, Beattie, I don't think I'd want to. And *they*'d all be upset. Last year was very difficult, of course – the first Christmas without Jeremy. Caroline offered to have it at her house instead, but she really hasn't the room. And it was good for me in the end: I was kept too busy to mope.'

I bet you were, thought Beattie, crumpling up the leaflet and tossing it into the fire. 'Last year was weird for me as well. I spent Christmas with a friend of mine called Sal and we pretended we were Muslims so we could ignore the whole caboodle.' She sipped her Southern Comfort, wincing at the memory. The two Muslims had got disgustingly drunk on days one, two, three and four, and finally quarrelled hammer and tongs. 'Actually, I should have gone to Melbourne. My father invited me over – but there was just the little problem of the fare. He promised to pay most of it, but in the end he couldn't get the money together. He's asked me again this year, but I expect the same thing will happen.'

'But, George, *you*'ve got the money this time!'

Beattie diverted Elizabeth's attention by pointing out the flirtation in progress between the barman and a startlingly blond female dressed to kill. They had already argued quite enough about what they did with last week's winnings. Elizabeth had wanted her to invest the cash, as security for the future. *She*, however, was adamant that the money was not hers but *theirs*, and to be used for further jaunts like this, not put in some boring building society. Besides, by the time she'd paid her Barclaycard bill, the sum had dwindled alarmingly, and then she'd bought a present for Elizabeth (which she planned to give her shortly), and a huge bouquet of flowers for Margaret, and some expensive books for James, and . . .

'Would you *like* to go to Melbourne?' Elizabeth asked, cupping her hands around her glass.

Beattie sat considering, staring into the fire. 'Well, I'd love to see the country, of course, and it would be great to spend Christmas Day in the sun. But I suppose I'd be pretty nervous, too.'

'Of travelling on your own, you mean?'

'Oh no, not that. It's more to do with Dad. I haven't seen him for a while, you see – five and a half years, in fact. And the last time we spent Christmas together – which was in Potters Bar, not Melbourne – I'm afraid it wasn't a wild success.'

'What happened?'

'Not a lot. He kept . . . disappearing. I wasn't sure if he had a woman tucked away in the next street, or if he was nipping off for a drink, or *what*. But it made me very tense.' She broke off, feeling guilty – she had no right to run her father down. Yet that Christmas *had* been ghastly, lonely and disorienting, and she was worried by the last photograph he'd sent. It was only a blurred snapshot, but he looked distinctly older, and also sort of jowly, as if he'd run to fat. She guessed he was still drinking, and perhaps it had caught up with him at last. He was almost sixty, after all – no longer the dishy young father she revered on her bedroom windowsill (now honoured with a silver frame).

'Listen, George, why not come to *us* for Christmas? I hate the thought of you being left alone, whether you're in Westbourne Grove or Melbourne.'

Beattie fiddled with her string of beads – another purchase from the winnings. 'You'll have more than enough guests by the sounds of it.'

'You're not a guest. You're family.'

Too choked to speak, Beattie took refuge in her glass. She had achieved two important ambitions at one stroke: finding a solution to the thorny problem of Christmas, and being accepted by Elizabeth as part of her own circle, as close to her as a daughter or a husband. She felt a heady glow of pleasure which was nothing to do with alcohol. The weekend had got off to a perfect start, and who knew what might happen later on? As soon as they had finished their drinks, they were going up to bed together, sharing a room like man and wife. (She had actually told Elizabeth that she'd tried to get single rooms, but that bookings were so heavy the hotel had only twins left. Okay, it was a lie, and she had promised to stop lying, but she couldn't reform her character overnight. It was Elizabeth who would help her change, and the process was about to start.)

'I'd *love* to come for Christmas,' she said, realizing that she hadn't yet responded to the suggestion. 'But are you really sure I won't be in the way?'

'Of course not. It may be a bit of a squash, but as Daddy always says, the more the merrier! Anyway, it'll be nice for me to have you there.'

Beattie all but kissed her. Instead, she opened her handbag and drew out a small package wrapped in By George's colours: shiny gold paper with a blue rosette on top. 'Happy Cheltenham,' she murmured, passing it across.

'What's this?'

'Just a weenie present.'

'Beattie, *no*! You mustn't buy me any more presents.'

'*You* bought me the elephant. And he's upstairs, by the way. I've become so fond of him I couldn't bear to leave him behind.'

'That was rather different – I came to dinner with you.'

'Well, you've come away with me.'

'But I haven't bought you a present.'

You *have*, Beattie longed to say: the present of yourself – a whole amazing forty-eight hours of you, with no one else to nab you. But Elizabeth was looking disconcerted, as if she *did* object to the gift. Having a shrink for a friend could make things awfully complicated. She had read enough of Elizabeth's books to know what the interpretation would be: that she was using the presents to buy Elizabeth's affection (as apparently some patients tried to do – sometimes quite unconsciously – to create a bond or a sense of indebtedness). But she *wasn't* a patient and that *wasn't* her intention. Elizabeth had just told her she was family, and members of a family gave each other gifts as a matter of course. 'Well, aren't you going to open it?' she asked.

Elizabeth removed the rosette and slowly unwrapped the paper, revealing the padded velvet box. Beattie wished she'd show more enthusiasm. If Elizabeth had given *her* a real gold bracelet with her name on, she'd be jumping for joy. But Elizabeth's expression remained rather apprehensive, even when she'd opened the box.

'Oh, Beattie, dear, this is *much* too extravagant!'

'No, it's not. I got it cheap,' she lied. 'And I had it engraved with "Sophie". See? – on that medallion there. It's a little memento of Sandown.'

Elizabeth's thanks sounded forced and somehow hollow – no spontaneous cries of delight, no rush to try the bracelet on and admire it. Perhaps she didn't like it? Frankly, it *did* look a bit vulgar now, and too chunky for a delicate wrist. Maybe jewellery wasn't a good choice at all when Elizabeth hardly ever wore any. But bracelets were symbolic – the next best thing to rings. And what she had hoped was that Elizabeth would be inspired to go out and buy a bracelet engraved with 'George'. Then they would wear their matching love-tokens day and night; never take them off.

'You do like it, don't you?' she pressed, picking up the box and stroking its plush lining.

'Of course I do. It's . . . beautiful. And *very* generous of you. I don't know how to thank you.'

Well, you could sound as if you *meant* it, for a start, Beattie thought dejectedly, or put your arms around me and give me a big hug. But Elizabeth was still looking slightly strained and she'd still made no move to put the bracelet on. Perhaps she was simply tired – exhausted by the journey and her patients.

'Shall we have an early night?' Beattie suggested. 'We'll need all our energy for tomorrow. Gold Cup Day's really hectic.'

'Yes, that's a good idea,' Elizabeth said, shutting the bracelet back in its box and rising to her feet. 'I hope you've picked some winners for us.'

'I'm working on it, don't worry. And I've ordered the racing papers for the morning, so I can study them first thing.'

'Well, I'm expecting another thousand at least!'

'No problem. I'm hoping to make it *ten* thousand.' She picked up Elizabeth's glass. 'Aren't you going to finish your drink?'

'I won't, if you don't mind. I find Southern Comfort a little too sweet for my taste.'

'I'm sorry – it was me who talked you into it.'

'That's okay. I'll try anything once.'

Oh, *will* you? Beattie thought, draining the glass herself. If Elizabeth's words were true, she'd *need* a second drink.

Beattie tissued off her lipstick and sat on the edge of the bath, admiring her surroundings, so different from most clinical hotel bathrooms with their standard fitments and neon glare. Here, there were soft pink lights and Laura Ashley curtains and a marvellously old-fashioned bath mounted on four lion's feet. Her long search for the right hotel had paid off in the end. She had wanted something luxurious, but less grand than Ashley Grange. This sixteenth-century manor house was the perfect compromise – not too big or opulent, but full of charm and character. There was a minstrels' gallery downstairs and the dining-room looked out across a trout lake. And she loved the little personal touches: the bowls of pot pourri on every landing, the hand-embroidered pillow-cases and basket of fruit in the bedroom.

She crept to the door and listened for a moment to see if Elizabeth had finished on the phone. She hoped to God she wasn't counselling some patient in a crisis – if the crisis was too dire, it might put a kibosh on the whole weekend. Or maybe Harriet was ill again and demanding to be nursed at home – instantly, tonight. There was no sound of a voice now, so she put her head round the door. 'Everything all right?'

'Yes, fine.' Elizabeth was still sitting by the phone, scribbling something on a notepad.

'I thought I'd have a bath. Do you want one first?'

'No, I think I'll leave mine till the morning. I prefer a shower in any case – nice and brisk to wake me up.'

'I'm the opposite. I like a good old wallow in the hottest of hot water, with some lovely relaxing bath oil. Can't I tempt you, Countess Sophie?'

Elizabeth smiled and shook her head. She still had on her navy skirt and sweater, with her hair tied back severely the way she wore it for her patients.

'Well, why not come and talk to me while *I* soak?'

'I'm afraid I've got to make another call.'

'Elizabeth, you promised to leave work behind.'

'It isn't work, my love.'

What is it then? Beattie bit back the retort. It made her really livid that Elizabeth couldn't go away for a day or two without ringing all her daughters to say goodnight, or tucking up her grandchildren long-distance. No, that wasn't fair. For all she knew, Elizabeth might be phoning a friend in trouble. She had a lot of those, unfortunately.

She went to run her bath, turning both taps on full and pouring in a great whoosh of foaming oil. Elizabeth was obviously on edge tonight, so best to leave her be. Tomorrow evening would be different. By then she'd have had a whole night and a day to relax, and if they did well at the races, she'd be as excited as she had been after Sandown, and ready to celebrate. She must stop trying to force the pace. It was enough that they were away together – a huge triumph, actually – and if she went too far too fast, she'd only scare Elizabeth off. Anyway, she was still alarmed by her own feelings. Why should she *want* to share her bath with a woman: see her naked body, stroke her breasts, kiss her on the mouth? It wasn't simply *any* woman – the thought of doing such things with her other female friends left her completely cold, if not repelled. So what was different about Elizabeth?

She slipped off her dressing-gown and climbed into the bath. It was time she stopped agonizing and just enjoyed the weekend for what it was, accepting whatever happened (or *didn't* happen): wins or losses, responsiveness or rebuffs. The main thing was they were *here,* and she was no longer even in debt, and, best of all, Elizabeth had called her a genius (at least as far as betting was concerned). She was determined to live up to the description, and had already subjected Tony to an in-depth interrogation, winkling out the best tips for tomorrow in return for a definite promise to resume their in-depth relationship.

She lay back in the bath, only her nipples showing; closed her eyes and imagined herself in bed with him again. He had always made love in silence, but an intense and eager silence, as if words would only detract from his performance. She remembered the way he used to look at her: possessively and greedily, like a dog with a huge marrowbone. And after they'd both come, he loved it if she touched herself and came five or six times more. He said he'd never met a woman quite so avid, and she'd tell him that it took an avid man to turn her on. Just the thought of it was beginning to arouse her. She pretended they were in her flat, the springs on the bed creaking rhythmically and wildly, then Tony's sudden triumphant cry: 'Oh, Beattie, no, no, *no*!' That always made her giggle – a guy who shouted *no* when he was coming; no when he meant yes. But then men were pretty weird: she had never known two of them make love in the same way.

She groped a hand down between her legs. Now Tony had come, she had to please him further; put on her little show. Sometimes it *had* been a bit of a show, because she wanted him to admire her, to regard her as outrageously sexy, a woman he would never forget. (It seemed one small way of *achieving* something, to be remembered for ever by her lovers.) But this evening she was genuinely aroused. The steamy room and hot pine-scented water, the sense of excitement and escape (and even apprehension) were all working on her, electrifying her body. She watched her nipples stiffening: two pink points amid the soupy green. She stroked them with her left hand while the right continued gratifying Tony – almost *shocking* him tonight, because she was so frantic, so greedy.

Suddenly she heard a noise: the door-handle being turned. She looked up in surprise. Not Elizabeth surely – she wouldn't come in without knocking. Yet there she was, peering round the door. She had taken off her skirt and jumper and changed into an old-fashioned white lawn nightgown: ankle-length with a prudishly high neck. Beattie didn't stop what she was doing, though she was well aware that Elizabeth was watching her. 'Are you going to have a bath after all?' she whispered teasingly. 'You can share mine if you like. It's lovely and warm.'

Elizabeth shook her head. She was obviously embarrassed, yet seemed fascinated too by the swirl of water churned up by that restless hand. Beattie closed her eyes. She had reached that point where it was impossible to stop; where nothing else existed but the thrill and squall and seethe between her legs; when she *had* to come, and had to involve Elizabeth – shout out loud like Tony: 'Oh, Sophie, no, no, *no*!'

And suddenly Elizabeth was at the door – the real flesh-and-blood Elizabeth, fully dressed and looking not intrigued but thoroughly alarmed.

'Beattie, what's the matter? Are you *hurt*?'

15

Beattie opened her eyes to darkness, choking, smothering darkness. She groped out her hands in panic, about to scream hysterically, then all at once remembered where she was. She turned on her side towards the other bed and, although it was too dark to see, she knew Elizabeth was there, protecting her, warding off the nightmares and the ghosts. She could hear her steady breathing, that rhythmic reassuring sound which had kept her safe all night – so safe she'd managed to sleep without a nightlight. It was a huge achievement, akin to climbing Everest. At first she'd doubted whether she'd have the courage. As Elizabeth switched the light off, she had felt the heavy corpse of darkness pressing down on her face, filling the hollows of her eyes and mouth. She had fought the terror, determined not to cry out again and scare Elizabeth a second time. So she lay there trembling and sweating until eventually, incredibly, she realized that the fear was going – that Elizabeth could *make* it go, just by being in the room. And gradually, as her eyes grew more accustomed to it, the darkness no longer seemed so dense, and she was able to make out shapes in the gloom, regain her sense of boundaries.

And, finally, she had slept – slept peacefully and deeply – only waking at this moment to a different sort of darkness, less stifling and impenetrable. Maybe dawn was not far off. She leaned over to the window and lifted the bottom of the curtain. Outside, black was smudging into blue, the first birds twittering unmelodiously. She squinted at her watch – yes, truly morning, and later than she'd thought: already seven o'clock. She worked her feet loose from the duvet and swung her legs out over the side of the bed, fixing her whole attention on Elizabeth, willing her to open her eyes. But the breathing continued steadily and deeply, its rhythm undisturbed.

Anyway, it wasn't fair to wake her when they hadn't got to bed till well past midnight. Her attempts to explain why she'd cried out in the bathroom had increased Elizabeth's anxiety, rather than allaying it. She'd pretended that she'd nodded off, but been woken by a ghastly dream: the two of them were imprisoned in a cell together, then a strange man had turned up and tried to drag Elizabeth away, so she'd clung to her and screamed to stop her going.

'Do you often have nightmares?' Elizabeth had asked.

'Yes,' she said, and this time she wasn't lying. 'Terrifying ones. I wake up drenched in sweat.' And that had started them talking about deep important things – dreams, divorce, fathers, God – though she'd been far too embarrassed by what had happened in the bathroom to bring *that* up for discussion. And when at last they went to bed, she'd still felt hopelessly confused; torn between her longing to give Elizabeth a goodnight kiss and her fear of being some kind of freak.

And now the sight of Elizabeth lying there asleep brought all the erotic feelings surging back. Her nightdress *wasn't* prim and proper, but a girlish gingham one which came just below her knees and had ruching round the bodice, emphasizing her breasts. Not that she could see the details; with the heavy curtains drawn, Elizabeth's body was no more than a vague hump. But gazing at that shadowy hump, it felt as if their roles had reversed: Elizabeth the vulnerable one and *she* the brave protector. For the first time it came home to her what divorce had meant for Elizabeth. After thirty years of sharing a bed, it must be devastating to sleep alone – no one there on tap, to cherish and support you, no late-night conversations, no cuddles in the early hours. If only *she* could act as Jeremy's replacement and give Elizabeth back some of what she had lost. For her it would be a completely new experience. Despite her succession of lovers, she had never actually shared her life with anyone. All her men had belonged to someone else, like Max or Pete or Dominic; or had lived miles away, like Tony, and just came up for the evening; or had been one-night stands or fly-by-nights. It hadn't really bothered her before. She hadn't known what she was missing – how comforting it was to be able to reach out in the dark and have someone *there*, to respond.

She got up from her own bed and moved closer to Elizabeth's, squatting down on the carpet, level with her head. She longed to slip in beside her, to feel her sleepy warmth, slide her hand beneath the nightie and stroke her thighs, her breasts. Instead, she stroked the duvet, her hand inching towards the mass of hair, tousled on the pillow. The desire to touch it was so strong, she feared she would explode. She'd better get out before she went too far. Elizabeth needed to catch up on her sleep and *she* needed some diversion. She would take herself for an early morning walk and leave Elizabeth in peace.

She crept to the wardrobe to get her coat and shoes, and tiptoed out of the room. Once outside, she buttoned her coat over her pyjamas (an ivory-coloured silk pair bought specially for the weekend), slipped on her shoes and stole along the passage. The hotel was hot and hushed, and as she walked downstairs the faint scent of flowers and pot pourri gave way to stronger smells: coffee brewing, bacon frying. Despite the breakfast preparations, no other guests seemed to be about, and, stepping into the garden, she felt a sense of real elation, as if she'd just hatched from her shell on the first morning of the world. And it was a wonderfully mysterious morning – hazy blue with blurred shapes slowly emerging through the mist like photos from dark negatives.

She shivered as she set off along the path. The bedroom had been fuggy, and this sudden jolting coldness was like diving into a plunge-pool after sweltering in a sauna – a pool of gauzy blue. All other colour had drained from the garden or migrated to some gaudier world where the sun stayed up all night. The dark branches of the cedar tree carved a geometric pattern on the sky. The beeches were less distinct, just a faint blue tracery of twigs, fading into cloud. She marvelled at the silence. London always had its traffic, and even Kent could be rackety, with crowing cocks, or tractors, or early-morning delivery vans. But here the quiet was three feet deep. Even the birds were cheeping only tentatively, as if they'd been told to keep the noise down. The hotel advertised its peaceful setting as one of its attractions. It was set well back from the road, on the outskirts of a village five miles out of Cheltenham. And perhaps it had devised a rule that all traffic had to muffle its wheels, all planes fly over silently. She glanced up overhead. Yes, an obediently noiseless plane had left a long white furrowed vapour-trail. She remembered as a child thinking planes must get ticked off for messing up the sky like that, the same way as *she* would get an earful from her mother for making a stain on the carpet.

She wandered onto the lawn, looking back at her footsteps on the grass: a chain of silver on wet blue. Everything was so beautiful, she was beginning to feel poetic – similes and metaphors sprouting in her mind; words arranging themselves into rhymes. She picked up a dead rocket lying on the grass, a relic of Guy Fawkes night. Normally she loathed November – a bleak bad-tempered month, which replaced natural light and sunshine with fairy-lights and tinsel as the con of Christmas took hold and good cheer was sprayed on everything like lacquer. But this year was miraculously different. Not only would Christmas have some *real* cheer for a change, but even November had been extraordinarily mild, as if Elizabeth had been giving it some therapy and turned it from a depressive into a reformed and sunny month.

She stood under a copper beech, examining its smooth grey bark, touching its cool leaves. She wanted to be aware of every detail, to treasure this moment, seize it with both hands. It was *her* tree, *her* sky, *her* morning – presents from Elizabeth, wrapped in blue and silver. So often she found herself looking back: to her childhood or her father or the dreary years following her mother's death; or looking forward to some dream or hope or fantasy. But now she had *attained* a dream: she and Elizabeth were actually away together, with the whole day stretching ahead of them, and it might prove to be the best day of her life. It was time to break with the past: toss it onto the compost heap, burn it with the autumn leaves. And the future she would leave to itself. If she built 'now' after 'now' with Elizabeth, that would be her future, and they would be spending it together.

Exhilarated, she ran down to the lake, which looked glassy in the murky light. Clumps of willows were hunched over it and she noticed an ancient wooden skiff moored beside a boat shed. The ducks scattered at her approach, protesting with indignant quacks and squawks. They had been sleeping on the bank and she'd been far less worried about waking them than about waking Elizabeth. Most were the common or garden kind, but there were a couple of more unusual birds amongst them: an exotic black and white thing with a scarlet beak and crest, and a much smaller greenish duck, drab except for its long and speckly tail feathers. The two appeared to be mates, despite the difference in their size and breed, cuddling up to each other and rubbing beaks. George and Sophie, thought Beattie with a grin: George in her new gear with scarlet lipstick and hennaed hair, and Sophie more restrained but with a jaunty speckled feather in her hat. While the other ducks plonked into the water and set about the business of the day, these two stayed on the bank, still nuzzling and canoodling.

She managed to get right up close to them, surprised how tame they were. Perhaps they were used to being fed by the hotel guests. 'Sorry I haven't any bread for you,' she murmured, crouching down at their level and hitching her coat free of the mud. She watched George smooth Sophie's plumage with his beak, wondering why differences had to matter so much. If two people really cared for one another, all the rest was superficial. She stroked each bird in turn, sending up a silent plea that the two would stay together; remain a pair till death.

Sophie gave a solemn 'Quark', which sounded like an 'Amen'. Laughing, Beattie stood up and walked slowly back to the house. The sky had lightened to a pale and pearly grey and the colours in the garden were beginning to return: the pink shout of a rose, the sad mauve of fading Michaelmas daisies. Another poem was stirring in her head: a comic one inspired by the ducks. She would compose it for Elizabeth, like her famous elephant poem, and put a secret message in it about pairing and devotion.

Her high thoughts took a nose-dive as her stomach rumbled loudly, reminding her how hungry she was. She peered in at the dining-room window; a lavish buffet breakfast was laid out on the table: every sort of cereal and fruit, croissants, brioches, crusty rolls, even Danish pastries. A further array of dishes were clustered on a hot-plate: bacon, eggs, and sausages, kedgeree and kippers. She started planning what she'd have: Sugar Puffs, then eggs, then fish, then croissants, toast and fruit. And she wouldn't give a toss about her weight. Her struggle with endless tedious diets belonged to the past, and the past was over and done with. The final course of her breakfast would be a great big bowl of porridge. They *had* to have porridge – it was their special food, which had first bonded them at Ashley Grange. She'd drench it with cream and sugar, then they'd eat it from the one shared dish, taking turns with the same spoon.

She ran in through the side door, wiped her wet feet and finger-combed her hair. Before she gorged herself on breakfast she must study the racing papers and decide what bets to place. Today she had a hunch they'd make their fortune – win so much they could buy a brand new car, and a cottage in the country, and perhaps a racehorse into the bargain, so they could swan into the Owners' Bar without needing an invitation.

She bounded into reception to see if the papers had arrived, feeling a shade embarrassed by her gear: mud-encrusted pyjama hems, sodden slingback shoes and a dramatic winter coat on top, striped stinging-green and purple. Little clusters of guests were emerging from the lift, or making their way to the dining-room. They all looked very conventional – the men in sober suits, the women in mimsy dresses or dreary pastel jumpers, their hair immaculately coiffed. And they were all miles older than her: blue-rinsed matrons with doddery husbands, or white-haired wrinklies who'd probably long since buried their men. At Ashley Grange she'd been feeling old and past it; today she was newborn.

She swept up to the desk, flinging a confident smile at the receptionist. She had no need to apologize for wet shoes or tousled hair. She was Wonderwoman this weekend: a genius at picking winners; a poet to rival Keats; a lionheart braving the dark without a nightlight, and so stunningly slim and exquisite, *Vogue* had just snapped her up for six successive covers. But best of all, she and Elizabeth were about to have a humdinger of a day, followed by a superincredible night, curling up together like that pair of devoted ducks.

16

It is indeed right
it is our duty and our joy
at all times and in all places
to give you thanks and praise
holy Father, heavenly King,
almighty and eternal God.

Amen, said Beattie silently. She wasn't sure about the existence of an almighty and eternal God, but she wanted to give thanks to *some-one* for the way the weekend was going. She coughed to stifle a laugh. She could hardly believe that after all her hopes and fantasies about spending Sunday morning naked in bed with Elizabeth, she was actually kneeling next to her in church. And it was *she* who'd suggested it, to Elizabeth's undisguised astonishment.

She glanced triumphantly around at the stone arches and carved choir screen, the white-clothed altar with its gleaming golden candle-sticks and elaborate flower arrangements. She was now an official churchgoer – another new achievement. She had always scorned religious people as boring and po-faced, but Elizabeth's view of God was so interesting and original, it had stopped her in her tracks. Elizabeth was always doing that: introducing her to new ideas; authors she'd never heard of; music she'd labelled 'difficult'; art she'd shied away from as 'modern' or peculiar. And last night, when they were talking well into the early hours, Elizabeth had tried to describe her God – not a Father or a Judge or a spoilsport or a wimp, but a much more abstract and mysterious Being (and quite beyond her, if she was honest).

'So why,' she had asked, 'do you go to a church that has such a *different* kind of God?'

'Well, actually I *don't* go much these days. But when I did, it was more because of the ritual. And as I get older, I realize that perhaps it doesn't really matter whether you believe or not. Ritual's important in itself. And anyway, I'm sure it's good for the soul to sit in beautiful surroundings, listening to poetic language and soaking up history and tradition.'

So here they were, nurturing their souls together, having first stuffed their stomachs with a delicious four-course breakfast. Unfortunately no porridge, though. ('I'm sorry, madam, but I'm afraid we have no call for it.')

A gentle nudge from Elizabeth prompted her to her knees. She was so unfamiliar with church services, she kept finding she was standing when everyone else was sitting, or thinking about porridge (or her poem, or the racecourse, or Elizabeth's naked body) when she was meant to be kneeling for some prayer.

'Our Father, who art in heaven . . .'

Well, at least she knew *that* one, and could join in fairly confidently. Her own father would hardly recognize her. The nearest *he* had ever got to church was playing comic vicars in duff plays. Sadly, he wouldn't really understand the attraction it held for her. In fact, she was surprised herself to find how inspiring it was to be kneeling in a church old enough to be mentioned in the Domesday Book; to feel a bond with all the people who had sat here over the centuries, repeating the same ceremonies. And she liked the words she'd heard – poetic language, as Elizabeth had said, which she might work into her own poems: Hosanna in the highest; God from God, Light from Light; the kingdom, the power and the glory. And the organ was terrific – jubilant yet solemn, just the sort of music to accompany good sex. No, she mustn't think of sex again. Most of the people around her looked as if they never indulged in it: women in sensible shoes and horsy-patterned headscarves, now clomping up to take Communion, and the odd token worthy man.

She smiled at a wooden angel carved above the pulpit. She might not believe in God, but she did believe in angels: Angels of Mercy who had persuaded Elizabeth to tell her that yesterday had been 'absolutely perfect', despite the fact that they hadn't won on a single race. Strangely, she wasn't that despondent about losing. Admittedly they had chucked away fifty pounds between them, but mainly through bad luck rather than bad judgement. One of their horses had been kicked at the start, another brought down at the water-jump, and their last remaining hope came in a lousy second when they had only backed it to win. But they'd still had a fantastic time, and when they'd finally got back to the hotel, Elizabeth seemed wonderfully relaxed. It was obvious that she *needed* trips away; she was stuck at home far too much, ministering to her patients or her family. It must be *her* responsibility to see she didn't work too hard in future and took regular breaks every month or so. And that had made her relax in turn. If they had other weekends to look forward to, then she didn't have to fret so much about *this* one, but just let things take their natural course. Once Elizabeth felt totally at ease with her, the friendship would develop along the lines she wanted. It would take time and patience, that's all – and a few more dates in the diary.

She stood up guiltily, again several seconds behind the clockwork congregation, who also had their hymn-books open. She fumbled to find the right page, but Elizabeth forestalled her, jabbing her finger under hymn number fifty-five and smiling in encouragement.

> Zion hears the voice that singeth,
> With sudden joy her glad heart springeth,
> At once she wakes, she stands arrayed:
> Her Light is come . . .

She tried her best to follow the tune. The hymn was marvellously rousing and she certainly shared its sentiments. Her heart *did* springeth with sudden joy, and Elizabeth her Light *had* come. For a second night she had slept without a nightlight, and now felt brave enough to dispense with it altogether, even when Elizabeth wasn't there. She realized she was growing; leaving her childish fears behind and becoming more mature at last, and also growing intellectually and spiritually. Elizabeth was mother, teacher, guru. Without lecturing or preaching or ever talking down, she was constantly giving her new slants on things, and had opened up a much wider world. If they carried on like this, Beattie Bancroft would soon be a full-blown culture vulture and a pillar of the church.

She let her voice swell out in the last verse of the hymn, and sat down at exactly the right moment. Better and better! Except everyone else was suddenly kneeling again. She quickly did the same, wondering just how long it took to get used to all this upping and downing.

'...and the blessing of God Almighty, the Father, Son, and the Holy Spirit be among you and remain with you always. Amen.'

'Amen,' she echoed, loudly. She loved the thought of being blessed as she knelt beside Elizabeth: their weekend blessed, their union. Secretly, she would regard this as their marriage service – that all-important ritual Elizabeth had mentioned, binding them for ever. She wondered how many weddings had taken place in this church; hundreds of thousands of couples exchanging vows and rings. She longed to repeat those vows to Elizabeth; to promise to love, serve, honour and protect her, till death did them part.

Reluctantly she rose to her feet. The service was over and people were making their way down the aisle or already standing chatting in the porch. She and Elizabeth were included in the friendly greetings, as if they'd lived here all their lives. Perhaps they should move to Cheltenham, buy their country cottage *here*, far away from Elizabeth's dutiful life in Kent.

'Shall we go for a walk round the village?' she suggested as they turned out of the lychgate. 'We can look at all the properties and see which ones we fancy.'

'I thought you said you wanted to feed the ducks?'

'Oh yes, so I did. I've just *got* to show you George and Sophie! And then we'll drive into Cheltenham and find your gallery.'

'It may not be there any more.'

'Never mind. There's still masses else to see. We really need much longer here. I know – how about cancelling all your patients and playing truant for a week?'

'Good idea! I'll phone them right away.'

Beattie laughed and took her arm. 'Sophie ...'

'What?'

'You mustn't forget your book, you know. You haven't written anything for ages. I'm still waiting to type the last chunk, so you can send it off to a publisher.'

Elizabeth stopped, frowning to herself. 'It's funny, but since you've been staying, it hasn't seemed so important. I think I was probably using writing as a crutch, to stop myself falling apart. And actually you've helped me more than any book.'

Beattie could barely speak. '*H* ... *have* I, Sophie, really?'

Elizabeth nodded. 'I suppose I tend to take life a bit too seriously and you've helped me lighten up.'

Beattie didn't answer. What did Elizabeth mean? That she was some sort of clown, with no depth to her, no intellect? No. She'd spoken with real affection. It was not a put-down but a compliment.

'You're one of the few people I know who really make me laugh. You're so deliciously irreverent, George! Some of my friends do tend to be rather humourless – I mean, frightfully worthy mortals and all that, but they can't take a joke against themselves. And also you're very honest, which is rare.'

'*Honest?*' Beattie thought with horror of the countless lies she'd told.

'Yes. You say what you mean and that's refreshing. And you never spout opinions just because they're fashionable or acceptable or safe or whatever. So many people are taken in by superficialities, but you see through all that. And another thing – I always feel much younger when I'm with you, as if we really are students.'

'We *are*!' Beattie seized her hand and towed her jubilantly along, down the winding lane to the hotel. 'No, we're not – we're five-year-old kids, off to feed the ducks!'

'You mean you've *never* had an affair?' Beattie asked in astonishment.

Elizabeth shook her head.

'But what about before you were married? You must have slept with *some*one other than Jeremy?'

'No.' Elizabeth sat back on the bench, crumpling the paper napkin which had held the bread for the ducks.

'But how can you be a therapist and understand people like me – people you'd call promiscuous?'

'Well, actually, I wouldn't use that word. I find it too judgemental. And anyway labels never help. People have affairs for all sorts of different reasons. It could be a sort of addiction or compulsion, or they may be seeking approval or security.'

'Huh! You don't get much of either – not in my experience, anyway.'

Elizabeth squeezed her arm. 'How are things with Max, by the way? You haven't mentioned him for a while.'

Beattie shrugged. 'I suppose really I should stop seeing him. I mean the relationship isn't going anywhere, and he's always so uptight about his work. And anyway, he's married. Of course, he *says* the marriage means nothing to him. But then all married men say that – until you bump into them with the wife, and they're billing and cooing like a pair of bloody lovebirds. The problem is, I *need* Max. I'll never make it as a journalist without him.'

'But how d'you know that, Beattie? You haven't even tried yet. Surely if they're good enough, you can get your pieces accepted on their own merits.'

'Oh, it's not as easy as that. You need influence, and contacts. And anyway, I should have started years ago – got a job on a local paper and worked my way up. Without that sort of background, I haven't got much hope – except through Max.'

'Well, maybe so, but it's still not a frightfully good idea to sleep with a man who doesn't treat you well.'

'He doesn't treat me *that* badly.'

'You said he did. You told me he swore at you and shouted.'

'Well, I shout back. *And* swear.'

Elizabeth laughed. 'It sounds like the perfect relationship!'

Beattie brushed the crumbs off her coat, wishing she had filched more bread from breakfast. The hungry ducks were still clamouring around them. There was no sign of George and Sophie, though. *They* were probably tucked up in bed together, like Max and his rotten wife. Bugger Max! She didn't want him spoiling the weekend. Besides, she could hardly admit to Elizabeth the *other* reason she needed him – it would make her sound heartless and hard-boiled. Yet Max's power was like adrenalin, and she still craved her weekly shot. It always boosted her flagging confidence to be seen with him at important press dinners or Soho publishing parties, and to be treated as an equal by the glitzy people they met. However fond she was of Elizabeth, when they walked into the hotel together they were just two nondescript women or, worse, a pair of spinsters who had failed to hook a man. But when she swept into some night-spot with Max, she was envied and respected as the mistress of a big shot. That was hard to give up.

But it was all such a dreadful muddle. How could she sleep with Max, fantasize about Tony (and *other* men as well – the head waiter in the hotel, for instance, a ravishing young Greek), yet also want Elizabeth, want her more than anyone?

She jumped up from the bench. 'Let's go in. It's getting cold.'

'It's still lovely and bright, though, isn't it? I think you must have a direct line to the Great Weatherman in the Sky, George. Whenever we're out together, we seem to attract the sun.'

'All part of the service, ma'am,' grinned Beattie.

'It's funny,' Elizabeth mused as they wandered back to the hotel. 'When I was going through my divorce, it changed my whole perception of things, even the different seasons. Spring felt terribly fragile, as if the blossom might be blown away and the new shoots killed by frost. And summer seemed too . . . heavy. The trees were crushed by their weight of leaves, and it was so dry and dusty, it was difficult to breathe. Only winter was kind – everything pared down to the bone.'

Beattie stared at her in surprise. Elizabeth rarely gave so much away, and it was not her style to wax lyrical, as if she was about to launch into a poem herself. Maybe they were growing genuinely more alike, taking on each other's characteristics. She found the thought appealing and was also touched by Elizabeth's honesty – the way she had revealed her vulnerability. It made her feel more guilty, though, about her own deceptions, her constant need to paint herself in a more favourable light. Last night, they'd been discussing lies and Elizabeth had said that she never told them on principle, not because she was 'good', but because lies made life too complicated and undermined the basic trust between people. She had pretended to agree, so how could she admit now that she *had* undermined that trust? Anyway, there were loads of things she just didn't want Elizabeth to know: the fact that she couldn't cook and didn't intend to learn; her often hostile feelings towards Caroline's precious baby, and especially all the tacky details of her past affairs, including two grisly late abortions. She had learned as early as sixteen that if your life was a mess, you *had* to lie, otherwise no one would accept you.

'Oh, look!' she exclaimed, distracted from her gloomy thoughts by the sight of George and Sophie waddling towards them across the lawn. 'Those are the ducks I told you about. They must have known we were looking for them.'

'Gosh! Aren't they tame?' Elizabeth remarked, as Beattie bent down to stroke them. 'Or perhaps you've got a way with ducks, like you have with Boz.'

Beattie laughed. 'No. They're obviously spoiled rotten by the visitors and have just got used to being petted.'

'Which is which?' Elizabeth asked.

'Can't you tell?'

'Well, I suppose the little green one's Sophie.'

'Yes. See the feather in her hat? And she's a nicer character than George. I saw them earlier on this morning when I went out for my walk, and Sophie was the model of unselfishness. A man was throwing them some bread and she let George have the lion's share, hardly took a mouthful for herself.'

'They certainly seem fond of each other.' Elizabeth watched them bill and coo; George rubbing his red beak against Sophie's smaller brown one.

Beattie longed to follow suit, to touch her lips to Elizabeth's, to stroke and smooth her hair (as the ducks preened each other's feathers), to accompany her everywhere, bed down with her at night. For the moment, though, she contented herself with taking her friend's arm and steering her gently back towards the hotel. If they didn't set off for Cheltenham soon, there wouldn't be time for all they planned to do there.

Hearing a familiar 'quark' behind her, she swung round to see the pair of ducks trundling along in pursuit. 'Oh, they're *following* us!' she laughed, secretly delighted. It seemed somehow a good omen; a sign that she and Elizabeth would become as close, as loving.

The ducks continued to chug after them right up to the hotel entrance, then George turned tail and dived into the shrubbery; Sophie scurrying after him as if she couldn't bear to be parted from him, even for a moment. Beattie watched them go, then turned back to Elizabeth, who was waiting by the door. 'Do you want to leave straight away,' she asked, 'or shall we stop for a quick coffee in the lounge first?'

'No, let's have coffee in town. There are lots of super little cafés in Cheltenham – or there were in my time, anyway.'

'Okay,' said Beattie, fumbling in her handbag for the car keys. 'Let's get going then. Are you ready for your trip down Memory Lane?'

Elizabeth looked suddenly apprehensive. 'I know it sounds ridiculous, but I'm actually quite nervous about it.'

'Why?' asked Beattie, opening the car door and tossing her scarf and bag in the back. 'Are you frightened everything will have changed, or disappeared?'

'No. I think I'm more concerned that *I'll* have disappeared. The person I was then, I mean – the *real* me.'

* * *

'It's still *here*!' Elizabeth cried, running excitedly towards the gallery. 'And it looks exactly the same! Even the door's the same colour.'

'Fancy you remembering,' Beattie said, panting up behind her. 'It's as much as I can do to remember the colour of my front door *now*, let alone some place I worked in thirty years ago.'

'Well, it's hardly the same for you, my love. Thirty years ago you were only a babe in arms. Remember, your birthday and my wedding day were only two days apart.'

'That always makes me feel a bit . . . weird.'

'It makes *me* feel positively ancient! Gosh, I wish we could go in. I was forgetting it was Sunday. It looks a really interesting show.'

Beattie scrutinized the poster on the door: 'New Perspectives – Paintings and Drawings of the Twentieth Century', followed by a list of names which meant absolutely nothing to her. They obviously meant something to Elizabeth, because she was exclaiming over one of the pictures in the window. To *her* it was simply a series of rather crudely daubed red blobs. She wished she could let fall some casual but brilliant remark, to astound Elizabeth with her shrewd artistic judgement. Probably safer to keep quiet, though, in case she made a boob. The other picture in the window looked slightly less daunting. At least it showed a person – a man without his clothes, though she had to say he didn't turn her on. She pressed her nose against the glass, to try to see the inside of the gallery. It was certainly impressive: an elegant high-ceilinged room with a sea-green carpet and a bowl of hothouse flowers standing to attention on the swanky antique desk. And of course works of art crowding every wall.

'Mr Clayton-Brown always liked Keith Vaughan,' Elizabeth observed, as she too peered in at the interior of the gallery.

Beattie said nothing. Both names were unfamiliar, and anyway Elizabeth appeared to be talking to herself.

'Surely he can't be still alive, though? He'd be about a hundred by now. He married very late, you see, and had Hugo in his forties.'

Beattie stepped back from the window. Hugo did ring a bell – that sophisticated guy Elizabeth had worshipped from afar and who'd offered her her first cigarette. (What *else* might he have offered her, she wondered?)

'I suppose Hugo must have taken over. The gallery's still called Clayton-Brown, and he was the only child – spoilt rotten by his mother, I always used to think.'

'Lucky Hugo.'

'Perhaps we could go and ask in the pub?' Elizabeth reflected, already crossing the road towards the Fox and Hounds, a half-timbered building three or four doors down. '*That* looks just the same, as well. We used to go there for lunch. Believe it or not, I'd never set foot in a pub before and it felt unbelievably decadent! There was this barman called . . . What was it now? Arthur? Angus? I don't know. Anyway, he was tall, dark and handsome, and he used to tease me unmercifully. It made me blush to the roots of my hair.'

'There he is!' Beattie whispered, as they approached the small, fair and decidedly plain man behind the bar.

Elizabeth hid a smile. 'These drinks are on me,' she insisted. 'What do you want?'

'Well, since this is Nostalgia Day, I'll have a Tia Maria and Coke. That was the first drink I ever had – aged thirteen and a half.'

'In that case, I'd better have a Babycham – the first drink *I* ever had, aged eighteen and a half.' Elizabeth gave their order to the barman, then enquired about the gallery, explaining that she had worked there once for old Mr Clayton-Brown.

'Yeah, he died about five years ago. He was nearly ninety-three, you know, but he still dropped in here every day for his lunchtime tot of whisky. His son runs the gallery now, with a couple of assistants. They usually come in for lunch.'

'You mean Hugo?' Elizabeth asked, looking round, as if he might suddenly materialize. But the pub was practically empty, tucked away in a side-street some way from the town centre, and probably only busy during the week.

'Yeah. He'd remarried a year or so before the old man died, and moved back to the area. The new wife's arty herself.'

Elizabeth leaned forward on the bar, all ears. 'Do they still live nearby?'

'Not far. Winchcombe way.'

'Why don't we go and look them up?' Beattie said, drawing up two stools. She knew it would please Elizabeth, who was already delighted about finding the place where she'd lived in the sixties still more or less unchanged. It would be an extra bonus if she could also meet her old flame again. Hugo hardly posed a threat now – not with a new artistic wife. He might even invite them to the gallery and give them a private tour, then Elizabeth would go home really happy and pronounce the weekend a total success.

'Oh no, we couldn't possibly barge in on them! I doubt if he'd even remember me. Besides, they'll be in the middle of Sunday lunch.'

'No they won't,' the barman put in with a grin. 'They'll be playing golf. They're fanatics, both of them – never miss a Sunday. They bought a house right next to the course.'

Elizabeth looked at him in surprise. 'I can't imagine Hugo playing golf,' she remarked to Beattie, slowly shaking her head. 'It makes him sound so . . . staid. The Hugo I knew would have been more likely to go bungee-jumping!'

Beattie watched her gaze around again, as if she were gathering up old memories. The pub was rather oppressive inside, with walls panelled in dark wood and a shabby carpet the colour of dried blood. But judging by the expression on her face, Elizabeth was peopling it with figures from her past; viewing it as magical, not gloomy.

'I must admit,' she confided, 'I'd love to see him again. I do find it fascinating, the way people change.'

'Well, let's go and suss him out then,' Beattie said. 'Where *is* the golf course?' she asked the barman.

'About two miles this side of Winchcombe. Claybridge Heath, it's called.'

'Beattie, no! We can't interrupt them in the middle of a game.'

'It's almost half past twelve, so they'll probably be finishing quite soon. If we're quick, we might catch them in the clubhouse.'

'But we can't just wander into a private club.'

'Why not? We'll simply say we're looking for an old friend. Anyway, I'd like to go to Winchcombe. The hotel porter was telling me there's a really super restaurant there, so if we don't manage to track Hugo down, we can pig ourselves instead. Come on! Knock back that decadent Babycham and let's go and find your Romeo.'

'Look, I honestly don't think we ought to . . .'

'Come *on*!' Beattie marched Elizabeth firmly along the passage and into the golf club bar. 'No one's given us a second glance. You look just the part in your tweedy skirt. You know, we *could* actually take it up – join a club in Kent and play every Sunday ourselves.' Pete had been a golfer, so she knew how long the average game could take and how addictive the sport was. It would give her and Elizabeth masses more time together and a new joint passion in life. 'Any sign of Hugo?' she asked, leading the way to a table in an inconspicuous corner.

'I'm not sure I'd even recognize him. He used to have this wonderful fair hair – wasted on a man, really – but he's probably gone grey by now. Though who am I to talk?'

Beattie looked at the spate of grey heads all around her. Any one of them might be Hugo: middle-aged, middle-class, well-spoken and well-heeled. 'What's he like? Fat or thin? Short or tall?'

'Oh, *tall*! Six foot. And slim.'

She scanned the room again. No slim six-footers here. Maybe he *was* still out on the course, or had already gone home for lunch. 'We could always ask,' she said. 'Someone's bound to know him.'

'I'd rather you didn't, Beattie. I still feel we're trespassing. I'll tell you what, let's . . . Oh, look! That chap who's just come in – that's *him*, I know it is!'

Beattie swivelled round in her chair. The man was certainly tall and reasonably slim, but if he hadn't been Elizabeth's teenage heart-throb she wouldn't have spared him a second glance. The once-fair hair was not so much grey as mouse, and was receding at the temples and thinning on top. Deep lines were etched from his nose to his mouth, though the mouth itself was attractive, with full lips and even teeth. His eyes were hidden behind spectacles – an owlish pair with tortoiseshell frames, and his clothes were conventionally correct rather than snappy or exciting. Okay, he wasn't exactly plain, but after Elizabeth's build-up, she'd been expecting some sort of cross between Clint Eastwood and Lord Byron. She watched him stroll up to the bar, scattering greetings like confetti.

'Well?' She nudged Elizabeth. 'Aren't you going to hurl yourself into his arms?'

'Ssh! He'll hear you.'

'Don't be silly. We're miles away. And anyway he's far too busy talking himself. He's obviously very sociable.'

'Oh yes, he always was.'

'Well, he'll be thrilled to see you, in that case. Go on – say hello. I can't think why you're holding back.'

'I . . . I'm not sure either,' Elizabeth faltered. 'I know it sounds pathetic, but I feel almost as shy as when I first met him.'

'Okay. *I'll* go. We can't both sit here like a couple of boobies.'

'No, don't. I . . .'

Beattie pretended not to hear, jumping up from her chair and elbowing her way to the bar. 'Hugo Clayton-Brown?' she asked, putting out her hand.

'Yes, that's right.' He shook the hand enthusiastically and flashed her a winning smile. The hair might have receded, Beattie thought, but certainly not the charm.

'You must be Jackie Holdsworth,' he said, in that well-bred tone of voice she had come to expect from anyone connected with Elizabeth. 'I understand we're playing in the mixed foursomes next weekend.'

'No, alas. I'm Beattie Bancroft and I've never played golf in my life. But I have got someone over here who's dying to say hello to you – someone you haven't seen for thirty years.'

'Oh, you mean Fiona Walters. They *said* she might be coming back to . . .'

'No. Wrong again, I'm afraid! The name's Elizabeth Hargreaves.'

'*Who?*'

'Sorry – Elizabeth Stanford. She wasn't married then.'

Hugo still looked blank. His eyes were an unremarkable blue – she could see them now behind the glasses, creased up in bewilderment.

'She worked at your father's gallery in the sixties, when you were both about eighteen.'

'Oh, *Elizabeth* – of course I remember. Good God, how extraordinary! Where *is* she?'

'Hiding in the corner.' Beattie led him over and watched the two appraise each other. Hugo did his tactful best to conceal his immediate reaction, but she could tell that he was shocked. He probably remembered Elizabeth as a slip of a girl with long fair curls and a mini-skirt, and here was a middle-aged woman with salt-and-pepper hair scooped up messily on top and an unflattering tweed suit. As for Elizabeth herself, she was blushing – yes, really blushing; her cheeks flaming with embarrassment, or nerves. Beattie found it hard to believe: the professional psychotherapist, fazed by some almost-stranger from her past.

'Look, this calls for a drink,' she said, hoping Hugo would return to the bar and give Elizabeth a chance to cool off. But he didn't appear to have heard. The two of them were already deep in reminiscences – did Elizabeth remember old so-and-so, and had she heard about yak-yak-yak? Well, she'd better go and get the drinks herself – Elizabeth looked as if she could do with one. She turned on her heel, almost colliding with a tall and leggy redhead, dressed in a dazzling white sweater and well-cut navy slacks.

162

'Oh, do excuse me,' the woman said. 'I'm Hugo's wife, Anna. You must be Jackie Holdsworth.'

'I'm beginning to wish I was!' grinned Beattie. 'But I'm afraid I'm strictly a non-golfer. I'm Beattie, Beattie Bancroft.'

'I'm sorry, do forgive me. We're meant to be meeting Jackie here and we were told to look out for a stunning girl with dark eyes and a spiky haircut.'

Now it was Beattie's turn to blush. Could Anna really think she was stunning? She warmed to her at once, especially as she was so attractive herself – a woman with a near-perfect figure (who knew how to show it off), blessed also with dramatically high cheekbones and striking grey-green eyes. Elizabeth wouldn't stand a chance against such competition. She introduced her to Anna, and Hugo sprang to his feet, explaining to his wife where and when he'd known Elizabeth and what a surprise it was to see her again. Then he and Elizabeth gave each other a brief résumé of the intervening years: marriage, children and career; Anna chipping in occasionally to correct her husband's story. Finally, he clapped his hand to his head and said, 'I'm sorry, we should be doing this over drinks. I blame *you*, Elizabeth! I was so taken aback at seeing you again, I've quite forgotten my manners.'

He took their order and strode off to the bar, nodding and waving at people he knew – which meant almost everyone. By the time he returned with four glasses on a tray, Anna and Elizabeth were deep in conversation on the subject of psychoanalysis: was it a con, or an indulgence, or the best route to nirvana? Beattie felt excluded. Anna sounded too clever by half, making facetiously witty remarks as if she were appearing on some intellectual chat-show. It was a relief when Hugo came to the rescue, passing her a gin and tonic with another of his engaging smiles and pulling his chair up close to hers.

'Now then, Beattie, I want to hear the story of your life.'

'How long have you got?' she grinned. 'Two weeks?'

'Good heavens! Is it *that* bad?'

'Oh, worse than you could imagine! I wouldn't dare reveal the half of it.'

'I say, that *does* sound intriguing! Don't leave out a thing. Start at chapter one and work right on through to the grand finale.'

'Well,' she said. 'I was born in an enchanted castle and my mother was a Persian princess.'

'I can see we're made for one another! *I* was born in Kwangchow and my father was the Celestial Emperor.'

She realized they were both shamelessly flirting. This man was damned seductive, receding hair or no. It was his voice, his smile, his manner which attracted, and she could well understand how a naïve seventeen-year-old could fall for him hook, line and sinker. She ought to leave him to Elizabeth, but *she* was still being monopolized by Anna, who was now talking in a low confiding whisper; her former sparkling witticisms replaced by a more serious mood.

'So, what are you doing in Cheltenham?' Hugo asked, once they'd concluded their brief but fantastical life-histories by agreeing to move to Madagascar together and set up home in a Moorish palace.

'Oh, we came for the racing – the Mackeson Gold Cup. I'm introducing Elizabeth to a lot of different vices, and gambling's one of them.'

'Well, I hope you have better luck than I did! I tried to lead her off the straight and narrow thirty years ago and had no success whatever.'

'What's that you're saying about me?' Elizabeth laughed.

'That you were impervious to my manifold charms,' Hugo bantered, touching his glass to hers.

'*That*'s unusual,' Anna put in tartly.

'Well, you did start her smoking,' Beattie remarked. 'Or so she told me.'

'Filthy habit,' Hugo tutted.

'You hypocrite!' said Anna. 'You've only just given up yourself.'

'Oh dear,' said Elizabeth. 'I hope I'm not going to weaken your resolve, Hugo, but I've simply got to have one. Whenever people mention smoking I seem to respond like Pavlov's dogs.'

'No, please do go ahead. I'm proof against temptation now. Anna says I've only just given up, but it was at least two years ago.'

'Congratulations.' Elizabeth offered a cigarette to Anna, who refused with a grimace, then lit one for herself.

'Well, it was more a matter of *having* to,' Hugo said, passing her the ashtray. 'I was laid low with a few health problems, which made life a bit of a pain. And I must admit I do feel better. In fact, I'm a reformed character altogether. I used to be a workaholic, but now I've taken up jogging, and go sailing once in a while. And we even went skiing last Christmas – something we haven't done for years.'

'Hm,' said Anna, raising a sarcastic eyebrow. 'I seem to remember you spent most of your time drinking *Glühwein* in the bar.'

'Slander!' Hugo protested. 'The ski instructor told me I was almost ready for the red runs.'

'Whatever's that?' asked Beattie. 'The result of drinking too much *Glühwein*? It sounds absolutely revolting.'

Hugo laughed, then lolled back in his chair. 'No, red's the colour-code for a moderately difficult run. All the ski-runs are graded, you see, and marked on the piste-maps in different colours. Green's the easiest, black's the hardest, and red comes in between. Actually, I have to confess you've got me on one of my favourite subjects. I may not be the world's best skier, but I'm definitely a fanatic. I only gave it up because I thought I was getting too long in the tooth. And then I met this wonderful old boy of seventy-three who said he still went every year and had no intention of stopping until he was a *hundred* and three, at least! Do you *share* my passion, Beattie, by any chance?'

She wished she could say yes – she spent her winters in St Moritz, or Val d'Isère, and had recently graduated to the black runs. 'I'm afraid I've never actually been. Though I've always wished I could. I sometimes watch it on the box and it looks wonderfully exciting.'

'Well, you'd better join us on our next trip. And how about you, Elizabeth? Shall I book for four?'

'No thanks! I've only tried it once, but that was quite enough to put me off for life. It's so . . . so uncomfortable! And I hated all those clothes. I felt like Michelin man.'

'You want to choose your resort. *I've* been skiing in a tee-shirt with a hot sun blazing down.'

'Before my time,' Anna said dismissively. 'As far as I recall, it was freezing cold last year and we had a really horrendous snowstorm.'

Elizabeth filled the awkward pause by switching from skiing to golf – was Hugo equally impassioned about *that*?

'Oh lord, yes! Though I'm afraid my handicap's disgracefully high. But I'm working on it. If only there were more hours in the day . . .'

Beattie saw him glance surreptitiously at his watch. Were they keeping him from his golf at this very moment, or was he bored with them already?

Elizabeth hadn't noticed and was now asking about his current exhibition. 'I had a peep through the gallery window, and it looks a fascinating show.'

'Well, it certainly should be. We've been putting it together for the last couple of years.'

Elizabeth leaned forward, leaving her cigarette smouldering in the ashtray. 'Was that a Gertler I could see hanging in the back?'

'You mean the still life? Yes, I picked that up a month ago. You used to like Gertler, didn't you?'

Who the hell is *he*, Beattie wondered? However many artists' or writers' names she got to know, there were always hundreds more waiting to confuse her. To tell the truth, she preferred Hugo the flirtatious charmer to Hugo the knowledgeable gallery-owner. He and Elizabeth in tandem made her feel not only ignorant, but spare.

'I *still* like him,' Elizabeth was saying. 'And I loved the Keith Vaughan in the window. Is that the only one in the show?'

'We've got a couple of watercolours – another nude male figure and a very early work: a rather romantic landscape, dark and bleak and brooding – you know the sort of thing. You can see the influence of Sutherland and Palmer.'

Look, will you kindly stop spouting all these names, Beattie muttered *sotto voce*, almost relieved to see Hugo glancing at his watch again.

He drained his scotch and soda, then rose to his feet. 'I'm terribly sorry to break up the happy party, but Anna and I are lunching with friends the other side of Cheltenham and we really ought to make a move. But perhaps we can meet you later on? We'll be tied up till seven at least, but how about coming round for a bite to eat this evening?'

'Sounds great,' said Beattie, at precisely the moment Elizabeth was murmuring, 'I'm sorry, but . . .' Both of them broke off, embarrassed.

'I'm afraid we have to get back,' Elizabeth continued. 'It's a good three hours' drive, and I have a patient booked at half past six in the morning.'

'Good Lord!' exclaimed Hugo. 'Do you always work such ungodly hours?'

Elizabeth smiled. 'Well, I try not to encourage it, but this chap starts work at eight, and he can't come in the evenings.'

Beattie kicked Elizabeth under the table. 'We'd be back by midnight,' she whispered in a pleading tone. She had really warmed to Hugo and it would make a perfect climax to the weekend to see his house, get to know him better.

'Well, actually,' said Anna, trying without success to catch her husband's eye, 'it's a bit tricky for me as well. I promised I'd meet Val this evening.'

'You could always put her off.'

'No I couldn't,' she retorted. 'But perhaps Beattie and Elizabeth will be coming up another day . . .'

'Oh, I'm *sure* we will,' said Elizabeth diplomatically.

'You absolutely must,' said Hugo, hovering by her chair. 'We've so much to catch up on – your family, to start with, and your work as a psychologist, and . . .'

'A psycho*therapist*,' Anna corrected. 'And she even knows *my* shrink, would you believe!'

'Everyone knows your shrink, darling. He puts himself about.'

'What's that supposed to mean, Hugo?'

'Look, we mustn't hold you up,' said Elizabeth, ever tactful. 'It's already nearly half past one.'

Hugo seemed unwilling to drag himself away. 'It's such a shame we didn't know you were coming. You should have phoned us first and we'd have kept the weekend free.'

'But I didn't know that you still *lived* here, Hugo.'

'Well, you could have rung the gallery. Anyway, never mind. Make sure you phone *next* time. Here's my card. And do give us your address. Scribble it in here.' He produced a diary from his pocket and passed it to Elizabeth, then turned to Beattie, gazing deep into her eyes. 'See you in Madagascar!'

'Oh, definitely,' she grinned. 'I'll make sure the slaves springclean the palace and that I've got my tiara on!'

Anna said a more conventional farewell, and once she and Hugo were safely through the door, Beattie grabbed Elizabeth's arm. 'He's great!' she said triumphantly. 'Congratulations.'

'What on?'

'Your taste in men, of course.'

'But he's changed – enormously.'

'Well, what do you expect? He's not likely to be a gangly fresh-faced student after all these years.'

'No, I don't mean so much physically – though I must admit his glasses rather threw me, when he always had such lovely eyes. But more the way he behaved. He seemed very sort of . . . defensive.'

'Defensive? What do you mean?'

'It's difficult to explain. He seemed to be play-acting half the time.'

'Oh, *that* didn't bother me – I liked it. I liked him altogether.' Beattie took an olive from the small bowl on the table and nibbled it reflectively. 'I'm not sure about the wife, though. She's terribly glamorous and all that, but rather a bitch, I imagine.'

'Yes, she kept on putting him down.'

'Most wives do – that's nothing new. But I wonder why she sees a shrink. Did she talk to you about it?'

'She mentioned it briefly, yes.'

'Shit!' said Beattie. 'Now you've got your "don't-ask-me-about-my-patients" look on. And Anna's *not* your patient.'

'No, but she's actually very interesting. She knows much more about analysis than the average patient does. She's even read that new book on . . .'

'Well, then, why didn't you want to have supper with them? It would have been quite fun.'

'I'd rather have supper with you, Beattie – a nice quiet meal at home.'

'Oh, Elizabeth . . .'

'What?'

'You do say lovely things.'

'In fact, if you wouldn't mind, Beattie dear, I'd like to set off fairly soon. It's been a wonderful weekend, but I'd rather not be back too late.'

'But we haven't even had *lunch* yet, and there's that marvellous restaurant just down the road.'

'I'm afraid I couldn't eat a thing, not after such an enormous breakfast. Why don't we wait till supper-time and have something really simple like scrambled eggs, or soup?'

'Okay.' Beattie crammed three more olives in her mouth. *She* was hungry – now.

'And why don't you let me drive? You must be feeling tired after getting up at the crack of dawn this morning.'

'No, *I'll* drive.' It was important that she did. Elizabeth had told her once that Jeremy never used to let her share the driving, and that she actually *preferred* him to do it, old-fashioned as it might sound. Yes, it did sound old-fashioned – positively antediluvian – but if she wanted to be married to Elizabeth, she had to take the man's role, play husband to her wife. And a nice quiet supper at home did make them seem like a married couple – almost pipe and slippers by the fire. Unfortunately they hadn't consummated the marriage, but that would happen, given time. It *must* happen, she thought desperately, and I must provide the opportunity.

'Listen, Sophie, we'll just have to come to Cheltenham again. Otherwise it'll seem awfully rude when they've invited us and everything.'

'Well, you and Hugo certainly hit it off. I could tell he was attracted to you.'

'To *me*?'

'Oh yes . . . Funnily enough, you're not unlike his first wife. *She* was dark and pretty and had a marvellous sense of fun.'

'Bloody hell! All these compliments! They'll go to my head.'

'Well, don't let that *gin* go to your head, if you're driving. Perhaps you ought to leave the rest.'

'Okay.' Beattie moved her glass to the far side of the table. 'And as soon as we get home I'll be a model of abstemiousness. No booze or swearing or gambling, and no lazing in the bath all evening.'

'Promise?' Elizabeth laughed.

'Promise.' Beattie pushed the bowl of olives out of reach. She didn't need such paltry pleasures when she could feast on the approval of Anna, Tony, Elizabeth, and now even Hugo too. The weekend had turned out better than she had ever dared expect.

17

Beattie lay back on the bed, trying to work out the logistics of what was going on. She had counted at least a dozen bodies, but they were all in such extraordinary positions it was difficult to know who owned the various arms and legs, genitals and breasts. And the more excited they became, the more turned off she felt herself. They were obviously close to orgasm; breathing very heavily with exaggerated gasps, which crescendoed into moans and cries of ecstasy. She watched the six men climax within seconds of each other; come spurting into faces, dribbling over buttocks; the camera moving in salaciously to savour textures, details.

Max seemed no more aroused than she was. He was standing by the television with his limp penis in one hand and the video control in the other, looking the picture of misery. She felt sorry for him really – he'd had a nightmare of a week, with crises both at home and at work, and on top of everything else he'd pulled a muscle in his back. Yet she resented the fact that he had resorted to a porn movie without bothering to ask her if she minded. It seemed he did need help, though. Last time they'd met he hadn't managed to perform at all and so it had become a vicious circle: he was now creating failure by expecting it. He would be better off at home – not in *her* bed but in his own – with a hot water bottle to ease his aching back.

'Listen, darling,' she said in her most persuasive tone, 'it's probably just because you're in pain. I mean, you can't expect to . . .'

'Wait! There's a better one – I'm sure there is. Kevin said if you ran it on for long enough . . .'

He punched the fast-forward button and the action speeded up like the silent films of the past; limbs jerking as if electrified, and the various combinations of couples, threesomes, foursomes, bonking at breakneck pace. It made the whole thing even more ludicrous; a rapid-fire succession of flailings and contortions. She covered her breasts with the duvet, wondering what the time was. She didn't have her watch on, but her stomach kept reminding her that it was long past dinner-time. 'Max, why don't we go out and eat? Then come back here afterwards. You'll be better once we've . . .'

He didn't answer, too preoccupied with the video controls. 'Christ, look at that!' he said, holding down the pause-button and giving a long appreciative whistle. A young girl loomed into close-up, with full lips, voluptuous breasts and dramatically dark hair cascading round her shoulders. All at once she hitched up her skirt, revealing an eight-inch prick, erect.

Beattie stared in disbelief. Above the waist she looked convincingly (and even glamorously) female, and as the camera moved in closer, it lingered on her genitals: a normal clitoris and vagina in addition to the penis, and tucked just underneath.

'A hermaphrodite!' Max exclaimed, backing towards the bed. He sat down heavily on the end of it, riveted by the screen. The girl was joined by another: a crop-haired blonde called Bella, who appeared to be her room-mate at some improbable American high school. The dark girl, Stacey, was saying in a Texan drawl that she felt like a freak and never dared go out with a man for fear of his rejection and disgust. Bella told her that *she* knew just the guy to help: her own boyfriend, Ted, a gym instructor.

Beattie glanced from the screen to Max. He appeared to have forgotten her existence; his full attention on Ted and Stacey as they were introduced to each other. It was clear that Ted regarded Stacey as a perfectly normal female, dressed as she was in a clingy angora sweater, a mini-skirt and thigh-length shiny boots. Bella was also wearing long black boots, and a backless dress with side slits. Beattie brushed a hand across her own bare and boring skin. She should have made more effort herself, but she felt increasingly unwilling to cavort around in tacky Ann Summers gear, or dress up like a school-girl or a tart. The last time she'd tried it, it hadn't even worked, and besides she was now seeing everything through Elizabeth's eyes – which was confusing, to say the least. She knew from ploughing through all those therapy books that her view of sex and Elizabeth's were worlds apart, and it left her stranded in a limbo, no longer sure of *what* she believed. She was beginning to feel uncomfortable about

171

the things she did in bed, yet had very little patience for the analytical theories which made sex so *serious*, a minefield of problems, compulsions, complexes. After reading stuff like that, *any*one would need a shrink.

Back on screen, Ted was slavering over Stacey, who had stripped off to her boots. He stared at her naked body with the same incredulity as Max had shown, but having recovered from the initial shock, he went down on her with alacrity, tonguing both her sets of genitals. Beattie looked at the wall instead. The close-ups were grotesque, and anyway she felt a mixture of pity and revulsion for the girl. If she was a genuine freak of nature, it seemed insensitive to gawp at her. Of course she could be a transsexual who'd had surgery, but that was pretty sad in itself. Or maybe just some ordinary girl (or man) who'd been fitted out with false anatomy in order to make money. Whatever the truth, it riled her that Max should find it such a thrill. If he needed a woman with male equipment to get him going, she might as well give up. And he *was* excited now, leaning forward and all but touching the screen.

'Boy!' he said. 'This is really way-out. If it's a put-up job, it's bloody clever. But I don't see how it *can* be, when the camera's so close.'

Stacey had an audience of four now: Max, Ted, Bella and the girl in the next-door room who had come to join the party, flinging off her clothes with wild abandon.

'Look, I'm feeling a bit spare here,' Beattie muttered. 'I'll go and make some toast.'

'Oh, don't be a spoilsport, darling. I only borrowed the thing from Kevin because I thought it would turn you on.'

Rubbish, she thought. You brought it to turn yourself on, to salvage your drooping pride. Porn movies did nothing for her – they were utterly unreal. She knew from her stint as a so-called glamour model how easy it was to fake; to screw up your face into a lascivious smirk, when actually you were worrying about your tax return. But the girls she'd worked with had been pretty second-rate, whereas the characters on this video were all depressingly gorgeous, as if they spent every spare moment at the gym or beauty parlour. How could she compete? She pinched the skin of her thighs. She had put on weight since leaving Kent. Without Elizabeth's magical presence, she could no longer eat what she wanted and get away with it. In fact, her body looked repulsive altogether: pale and sort of doughy, as if she'd been fished out of a stagnant pond. And she could feel a spot erupting on her chin, whereas the girls on screen had perfect complexions (or perfect make-up, anyway, despite all their exertions). She wondered if Max felt similarly inadequate. Both Ted and his mate (who had dropped in for a drink and stayed) were tall, young, slim and incredibly athletic, with rippling muscles and deep bronze tans. And, needless to say, both extremely well-endowed. But Max probably felt he was just as good as them. Men were so blind about their shortcomings.

She became more and more annoyed just watching him: his great stomach sticking out, his flushed face and hairy back, and the way he seemed oblivious to everything but the gymnastics on the screen. He was creditably stiff now – though no thanks to *her*, of course. She drew her knees up to her chest and hugged her arms around them. Why was she so angry? Max was her *lover*, for God's sake. He had even invited her to a big do at the Savoy, and the tickets were like gold dust. She should be all over him (in every sense), not begrudging him a bit of pleasure.

'Beattie . . .'

'Mm?'

'Can you lie the other way, sugar? I want to have a bash at what they're doing.'

'Which ones?' she asked sarcastically. At least four couples were now disporting themselves on the screen.

'The fair one and the black guy – Leroy, I think he's called.'

She glanced back at the video, surprised to see a black guy there at all. She hadn't noticed him come in, but then porn movies were like that – people materialized from nowhere, just to increase the number of sexual permutations. Leroy was lying on a fur rug in the corner, entangled with an eager Bella, and all but hidden by the other heaving bodies. The position he was in looked lethal for Max's back, but she kept her mouth shut and lay down as he wanted. They'd already had an argument when he'd turned up unexpectedly at well past nine o'clock, and she couldn't face another row. It was all very well for Elizabeth to say he shouldn't treat her badly, but what did 'badly' mean? He'd always been extremely generous as far as cash and presents were concerned. And anyway she was just as much at fault this evening for not responding; refusing even to cuddle up to him and watch the film companionably. That Savoy do was important. It wasn't just the occasion itself, but the fact that it made her special too, and might give her the chance to meet some famous journalists.

'Beattie, are you okay?' Max was trying to lock his legs around her waist, imitating Bella and Leroy.

'Mm. Just a bit worried about your back, that's all.'

'Bugger my back! It's all right now.'

'But I thought you said you'd sprained it.'

'You just don't seem yourself tonight. I mean, if you're not in the mood, there's no point us . . .'

'No, honestly – I'm fine.' She did her best to copy Bella's actions, right down to the provocative smile. Max was also watching Bella, his eyes continually flicking back to the screen. She found it insulting that he was more excited by a phoney celluloid stranger than by the flesh-and-blood woman he was actually making love to. (Though 'love' seemed hardly the right word.) She could feel her resentment swelling like the music on the soundtrack; drums and brass thundering to a climax, to accompany the actors' throaty moans. All the assorted couples had reached the height of pseudo-passion, yet *she* felt utterly despondent. The position was a strain, for one thing. If it didn't hurt Max's back, it certainly hurt hers, and his legs were sweaty and uncomfortable, too tight round her waist. She was severely tempted to get up and turn the sound down. The people in the flats below would start complaining next.

It was impossible to relax whilst fretting about the neighbours, but she did her best to fake, letting out a gasp or two – which didn't sound convincing. She just wasn't in the mood. Never before had she felt such a total lack of interest. She kept imagining Elizabeth watching her with a concerned expression on her face. She was concerned about her*self*, for heaven's sake. Perhaps there was something really wrong with her and she *did* need to see a shrink. She shut her eyes in desperation, determined to block out all those writhing squalling bodies – and Elizabeth as well – concentrate only on Max and his enjoyment. He had managed to slide in now and was trying to thrust against her – not easy with so little leverage. She shifted position slightly, using her hands to stroke his stomach, feathering them gently down to his greying pubic hair. 'He's too old for you,' a voice whispered in her head. Elizabeth's voice, or . . . ?

Oh God! He was going soft again; must have picked up on her mood. She tried a twisting, rolling motion to prevent him slipping out, squeezing her legs together and gripping with her muscles. Too late.

Neither of them spoke, just remained lying in that fatuous position. She glanced down at his small and squashy penis, now coiled in on itself. They'd stopped using the name Maximus. *Last* time it had seemed inapt, and this time almost a mockery. Poor Max. His face was tense, defensive; his eyes closed, avoiding hers. It *was* her fault. She knew perfectly well how much he hated failing, yet she'd done almost nothing to help.

'I'm sorry,' she murmured, hoping he would say sorry in return. But all she heard was the video playing to itself. She bit her lip to stop herself from crying. Sex was meant to make you *happy*, for God's sake. If only Elizabeth was here – someone who would comfort her, someone she could cling to. But Elizabeth had never seemed more distant, as if she were living on a different planet.

Max unhooked his legs and stood up very gingerly, rubbing the base of his spine. He switched off the video, then retrieved his boxer shorts, turning away from her to put them on. Even from the back, he looked totally defeated – shoulders hunched, body sagging. She picked up her own clothes from the floor and dressed in wary silence.

'Any chance of a drink?' he asked listlessly. 'Just orange juice or something? It's so hot in here, I'm parched.'

'Yeah, I'll get some.'

Glad to escape, she dived into the kitchen and poured juice into two tumblers. She stood staring at the speckled lino, the stained and tatty cupboards. Everything was so grotty compared with Mile End House. And so small and mean and cramped. Her spell in Kent had made her feel a stranger in her own home or, worse, a prisoner, cooped up in a rabbit hutch with barely room to breathe. And it wasn't just the flat – even her friends seemed shallow, judged by the standards of the cultivated Hargreaves. She had already quarrelled with Sal, who said she was turning into a snob and speaking in a stupid stuck-up accent.

She kicked sullenly at the table: an ancient rickety thing covered in mustard-coloured Formica. Elizabeth's kitchen table was solid pine, and old in the right sense. If only she could stay in Kent for ever, with Elizabeth as her mate, and James and Margaret as the grandparents she'd never had. James had been teaching her Greek and she missed the time he spent with her. She loved the fact that he had taught Elizabeth the same way as a child, even using the same book. She had learned the word '*metanoia*', which meant a change of mind or heart, a turning in a new direction. That's what she longed to do – to turn in *Elizabeth*'s direction; to change so fundamentally she actually became one of the Hargreaves. But the opposite was happening: she was back in London with her witless crowd and living in a tip.

It was Elizabeth who had persuaded her to go – kicked her out, to put it bluntly. Driving back from Cheltenham they'd had a long talk about her future: Elizabeth felt she should spend more time with people her own age and devote more effort to her writing, instead of putting everything on hold. On *hold*, for heaven's sake, when the two of them had spent the most miraculous weekend together. But however much she'd argued, Elizabeth still maintained that she was frittering away her energy and talents, and that now she was no longer ill she should get back to work of some sort. In the end, they had reached a compromise: she would leave Kent the following week, but return for Christmas and New Year; then later on in January they would go away for another weekend together. It all sounded fine in theory, but the reality had been vile. Temp work was very scarce at present and despite touring round the agencies, she had landed only a dreary job in a reinsurance office, working for a sixty-year-old martinet. And as for her writing, although she'd turned out four long articles, Max hadn't so much as glanced at them.

She trailed back to the bedroom. He was fully dressed now and sitting slumped on the bed, staring at the blank television screen. Okay, she knew it was humiliating for him if he couldn't get it up, but what about *her*? If she didn't make it as a journalist, she was no one and nothing; just a second-rater who had wasted her life on a succession of dead-end jobs. Elizabeth had said as much – well, not in so many words, maybe, but that was the implication. She *had* to succeed, to gain Elizabeth's respect, to be worthy of her, accepted in her circle. A writer and a journalist sounded infinitely more impressive than a glorified typist. Max was probably conning her, *pretending* he'd help so she'd continue sleeping with him. Three months had passed since he'd first raised her hopes sky-high by hinting that she might even get her own column, worth fifty grand a year. Yet here she was, trying to exist on a measly seven pounds an hour for banging out tedious lists of figures.

She handed him his glass of orange, noticing he'd bought new shoes – again. If he was so incredibly pressured, how did he find time to get out to a shoe-shop, or to all those other menswear shops, for that matter? Every time she saw him, he seemed to be sporting a new shirt or tie.

'Right,' he said, draining the juice in one mammoth gulp and wiping his mouth with his hand. 'Let's go and eat.'

'I'm not hungry.'

'You said you were.'

'Well, I'm not now.'

'You're not sulking are you, Beattie?'

'*No.* I'm just not hungry, that's all. Anyway it's too late to eat.'

'Late, at half past ten? We've had dinner at midnight before now.'

'Yes, but not when I've been up since six. I have to be in the office at the crack of dawn, and it's the other side of London. If only you'd do more to help, I wouldn't have to take these rotten jobs.'

'I'm *busy*, Beattie. I've told you – up to my sodding eyes!'

'Not too busy to watch porn, though.'

'So *that*'s what's bugging you. Why didn't you say so, before I put the thing on?'

She banged her tumbler down. He hadn't given her a chance, that's why. And, besides, it would only have led to an argument, which he'd have won, of course. It was like the central locking on his car: one snap of his fingers and doors and women opened to him – or so he arrogantly assumed. 'You don't consult me about *any*thing, Max. You didn't even phone tonight to say you were coming.'

'I tried – three times – but it was constantly engaged. You're always yakking to your friends.'

'Well, I have to talk to someone. I never seem to *see* you these days except dead-beat after work.'

'You don't understand the pressures. It's not just work. Michèle's unwell again.'

'I know. You said. I'm sorry.'

'You don't sound the least bit sorry.'

'Well, you've never seemed exactly fond of her. I can't think why you mind so much about her getting a few headaches.'

'Because it means more bloody stress, that's why. She's scared it's something serious, so she's changed all our Christmas plans. I'd invited a whole bunch of people for a drinks party on Boxing Day, and now she's saying she can't cope.'

So the worm has turned, thought Beattie, touching a finger to the spot on her chin. It was getting bigger, definitely.

'In fact, she wants us to spend Christmas with Rory and Janine. She says it's the only place she can get some peace and quiet. Peace and quiet for *her*, maybe, but a bloody bore for me. My son's a wimp, at the best of times, and we've never seen eye to eye since he left his nursery school. And as for his prissy wife, she makes even Mary Whitehouse seem broad-minded.'

'Well, at least you'll get some sea air,' Beattie muttered tetchily. She could never imagine Max with a son, let alone an artistic one living in the wilds of Cornwall and trying to earn his living as a craftsman.

'Yeah, it'll be Christmas with the seagulls, and maybe the odd born-again. Apparently Janine's into religion now – the "clap-your-hands-for-Jesus" kind. That's *all* I need.' He picked up her glass of orange juice, drained that too, then took her hand in his. 'Look, I'm sorry, Beattie, you don't want all this family stuff. Christ almighty! It's boring enough for *me*, without my inflicting it on you as well. And forgive me if I snapped. I'm knackered, I admit it. And I'm probably taking it out on you.'

She was so surprised by the apology – *two* apologies, to be exact – she sat down on the bed beside him and made an effort to speak calmly. 'I'm sorry too – about your wife. And Christmas. But if you really want to know why I'm upset, it's because my life's a mess. I'm just not *getting* anywhere. Can't you understand that, Max? And it feels worse because you encouraged me. I mean, you told me I could make it, and then refused to help. I spent bloody hours writing those four articles, and you haven't even . . .'

'Yeah, they're on my desk at home and I must admit I haven't had a minute to look at them yet. But I *will* read them, I promise. I'll do more than that – I'll sort out the best one and give it to the features editor first thing Monday morning, tell him I expect some action – fast.'

'Oh, Max!' She threw herself into his arms and kissed him with something close to fervour. 'You *swear*? You're not just stringing me along?'

'I swear. And if I think it needs a bit of subbing before he gets to see it, I'll do it myself, tomorrow.'

'You're an angel, Max, honestly.'

'Yeah, I know I am. But listen – I've just had a great idea. We both need a break, that's obvious. You're working bloody hard and I'm close to cracking up. Well, if Michèle *does* go to Cornwall, why don't I persuade her to make the trip on her own? I can tell her it'll be more restful there without me, or give her some spiel about being needed in the office over Christmas. Then we can spend the week together – just you and me and Santa Claus. It'll do us both a power of good. In fact, I'll book us into the Ritz, if you like, then we need never crawl out of bed at all. We'll have our meals sent up – caviar, champagne, anything you fancy. Well, what d'you say, sweetheart?'

Beattie disentangled herself and went to stand by the mirror. She began studiously combing her hair, flicking it one way, then the other. 'But suppose Michèle *doesn't* go?' she asked.

Max got up and stood behind her. She could see him pondering in the mirror, his face still flushed and dampish. 'I'll think of something, darling, even if it means lying through my teeth. I'm determined to have some time with you. I mean, that's the whole damned trouble. We see so little of each other at the moment that when we *do* meet, everything goes wrong.' He eased the comb from her hands, as if jealous of the attention she was giving to her hair. 'If Michèle stays home for Christmas, then I'm afraid I'll have to be there too – at least for Christmas Day and Boxing Day. I can't get out of that, or I'll never hear the end of it. But maybe we could sneak off on the Monday.'

He clasped her waist with both hot hands and drew her round to face him. 'Yeah, I've got it! I'll say there's a problem with the house in France – the builders have fucked up or something. Or a pipe has burst and I've got to inspect the damage. She'll never know – she's so worried about her health, she's shown hardly any interest in the place. But I've been dying for you to see it, darling, ever since I signed the contract. Okay, it's not quite the Ritz, and I can't promise you hot sun, but at least we'll be on our own, with no work, no meetings, no bloody phone. In fact, let's go there anyway, whatever Her Indoors decides. It'll be safer out of London. I mean, the last thing I need is someone spotting us and blowing the gaff. Besides, I know you'll love Fayence. The village is incredibly old – medieval, I think they say – and it's on top of a hill, so you get these marvellous views of the countryside. Not that I intend to waste precious time gazing out of the window. I can think of better things to do!' He cupped her breast, to demonstrate, feeling for the nipple with his thumb. 'And if by any remote chance we do happen to want a change, we can always shoot down to the coast and hit the bright lights. It's only about half an hour to Cannes. Or we can even try a spot of gambling in Monte Carlo.'

Beattie pulled free of his hands, pretending she needed to reapply her lipstick. 'It sounds absolutely great,' she said, rummaging through her cosmetics bag. 'But I've ... er ... promised to spend Christmas with Sal. I mean the whole holiday, right up till January the fourth.'

'Whatever for? Didn't you go there *last* year? Yeah, I remember you telling me it was the worst Christmas of your life.'

'I know. But I can't\ let her down at this stage. I mean, she hasn't ...'

'Oh, bring the bloody girl along. There's a decent-sized spare bedroom and even a second bathroom, so she might as well join the party. The only thing is, I don't want her in our hair. Perhaps I'll invite another bloke to make the numbers up.'

'But ... but she's already got a boyfriend.'

'Perfect. Ask him too. And let's hope he keeps her busy!'

'I'm sorry, Max, it just won't work. They're both completely skint – they'll never afford the air fare.'

'Don't worry, *I*'ll look after that. I'll put in on expenses. And you can ease my conscience by zapping out a little piece about the dolce vita in France. Come on, let's discuss it over dinner.'

'Er ... wait a sec. I need a pee.' She barged out to the bathroom and locked the door. Max would go spare if he knew she'd arranged to spend Christmas down in Kent. She had assumed he'd be so busy at home with his wife and friends and family that he wouldn't even have to know. He already resented all the time she'd been away; couldn't understand the attraction of a dowdy middle-aged woman living in a backwater. He even blamed Elizabeth for his sexual difficulties. The first time he'd gone limp was when he'd found her in the flat, so now he connected her with failure. And however preposterous it sounded, she didn't completely disagree with him, but felt in some illogical way that if Elizabeth disapproved of Max, maybe she was castrating him long-distance. So, if she put the 'dowdy middle-aged woman' first, after he'd invited her to France, it would lead to a major bust-up. She would lose any hope of a writing career – any hope of impressing Elizabeth.

She jumped as he shouted through the door. 'Get a move on, darling! Everywhere'll be closed if we don't get cracking.'

'Coming!' she called, running the taps to make it sound as if she was washing her hands. Couldn't she somehow keep Elizabeth *and* Max – please them both, spend time with both? If she phoned Elizabeth tomorrow and suggested she came down straight away, instead of over Christmas, she'd have almost two weeks in Kent before she was due to leave with Max for Provence. In fact it would be better, in a way: she'd have Elizabeth more to herself than during the hectic Christmas period when she'd be forced to share her with the family en masse. And she could still keep Max sweet by . . .

'What on earth are you doing?' he asked, banging on the door. 'Having a bloody bath?'

She opened the door and almost fell into his arms. He kissed her on the lips, then groped a hand up her skirt. 'D'you know, I feel a damn sight better already just thinking about our French trip. It's exactly what the doctor ordered – six hundred miles between me and the bloody office, with nothing to do all day but screw, and no fucking editor putting me off my stroke. And you'll *die* when you see the bed! It's one of those old brass ones, with three huge great feather mattresses, so high you need a ladder to climb up to it. I can just see us lying there – you in your black suspenders and me . . . Christ, Beattie, I can hardly wait!'

III

18

Beattie parked by the church and got out of the car, gazing up at the moon. It was surrounded by a halo: a huge dramatic circle of shimmering white light which formed a perfect sphere. It looked magical, mysterious – a rare and striking light-effect laid on in her honour. The whole sky seemed so much vaster than in London: the stars brighter and more lustrous, and a silence so profound even the faint jingle of her car keys was obtrusive. Although it was only early evening, it felt more like the middle of the night: all normal life suspended and a sense that creation was still only in its infancy; nothing in existence yet except moon and stars and sky.

She had just driven from the West End – another world entirely: streets jammed solid with traffic and pedestrians; stores rackety and garish, pumping out taped carols to appease the frazzled shoppers. Christmas here was more modest altogether – more a genuine celebration than a vulgar commercial hype. And 'peace on earth' was no longer a sick joke: no 'Jingle Bells', no policemen using loudhailers to control unruly crowds, no hot red buses lumbering past or sirens screaming 'Danger!' The only sound was the creaking of the wooden door as a woman emerged from the church, and then her slow and rhythmic footsteps tap-tapping down the path.

'Is the church still open?' Beattie asked her.

'Oh yes. Daphne's doing the flowers. Do go in if you want.'

It seemed a weird time to do flowers, but she approached the heavy door and pushed it open nervously – she was still not at home in churches. This was *Elizabeth's* church, though, where all her children had been christened and the whole family had prayed almost every Sunday for over fifteen years. She nodded at the frumpy matron arranging white chrysanthemums in a large vase by the font, then sidled into a pew at the back and knelt down. Praying was a new and strange experience.

'Let this Christmas be special,' she whispered. 'Please God – Whoever – make it work.'

She remained kneeling for a few minutes, overawed by the atmosphere; the dim light casting shadows on the stone, the graceful pillars soaring up to the carved wooden roof with its cherubs and heraldic shields. She would be here again on Christmas Day, as part of Elizabeth's family: the first and only Christmas she had ever gone to church. And she was really looking forward to it – even to the day itself, after years of loathing the entire month of December because of that dreaded twenty-fifth. It was partly connected with failure. If you hadn't married, hadn't made it, then you spent Christmas on your own (or with *other* failures) slumped in front of the television, watching the rest of the successful world enjoy themselves uproariously.

She crept back to the door and stepped out into the cold again, shivering at the sudden change in temperature. The moon was still veiled in its mysterious misty halo. It seemed extraordinary, incredible, that man had ever set foot up there, and to tell the truth, she resented the intrusion. The moon belonged to poets, not to clumsy-suited astronauts blundering about and capsizing all its mystery.

Her neck ached from looking up and she was beginning to feel unsettled – there was almost too much sky to cope with. In London you were less conscious of it, safely cocooned by all the lights and noise and buildings. She got back into the car and drove, too fast, towards Mile End House, suddenly desperate to see Elizabeth. It was over five weeks since they'd met – thirty-eight days to be exact – she'd ticked each one off on the calendar. Yet she was also apprehensive. What if she wasn't wanted there, or had been invited only out of pity? After all, Elizabeth hadn't sounded exactly keen when she'd suggested coming earlier – just said that she was very busy until Christmas week itself, so it was best to leave the arrangements as they stood.

She slowed the car to a snail's pace, almost tempted to turn back. For some unknown reason she was remembering the first Christmas she had returned to Croydon after leaving home at sixteen and a half. She had arrived to find the whole house dark and cold, with no one to greet her at the door. Her mother had suffered a relapse

and was lying upstairs in the dark; her father was away, of course –
in Blackpool doing panto. She'd had to phone him at his digs, after
calling out the doctor. All that week she had played the roles of nurse
and mother: scuttling up and down the stairs with medicines and
trays; struggling with the ancient Hoover; throwing meals together.
When she'd had a moment to spare, she'd phoned her friends (to
make her feel less isolated), but they were mostly too busy with their
own families to want to talk for long.

She turned into the shadowy lane which led to Mile End
House. Suppose *that* was also dark and cold; Elizabeth not even
there?

No – she could see the reassuring glow of its lights as she bumped
along the drive; felt a huge surge of relief that the house looked so
hospitable and solid. Elizabeth had heard the car and was just opening the front door; another swathe of friendly light falling across
the path. Beattie jumped out of the car and ran towards her, tears
streaming down her face.

'Beattie, whatever's the matter?'

'N . . . nothing,' she sobbed, furious with herself. She had planned
the perfect reunion; imagined Elizabeth's rapturous greeting, the
pleasure in her face and voice – and instead her friend was frowning
in concern.

'What's wrong?' she asked again.

Beattie shook her head. How could she explain how miraculous
it was that the house was warm and welcoming, and that someone
was there to open the door to her. Elizabeth had been cooking, and
delicious smells were wafting from the kitchen – another sort of
welcome – freshly brewing coffee, hot mince pies, mulled wine. She
brushed her eyes with her sleeve. 'It's . . . it's just such a relief to see
you – I mean, I'm so glad you haven't d . . . disappeared.'

Elizabeth reached out to her and suddenly the two of them were
embracing, and closer than they had ever been before; her breasts
pressed against Elizabeth's, her cheek against her cheek. She could
smell the faint scent of her talcum powder; feel the loose untidy hair
tickling on her face. She hugged her even tighter, aware of her
smallness, her fragility, her amazing warmth and softness. If only she
could stay like that for ever, fuse with her until all her own sharp
edges and stupidities and ignorance simply disappeared and
she became a different person: sensitive and cultured, loving and
well-bred.

But already Elizabeth was pulling away. 'Well, er ... happy Christmas, Beattie,' she said, sounding slightly disconcerted.

Beattie was too overcome to speak, and anyway she didn't *want* it to be Christmas yet. Only for this one evening would she have Elizabeth to herself, before the rest of the family started trickling in. Emma and family were driving down from York tomorrow, Sarah arriving the day after (flying from Madrid), and Harriet expected early on Christmas Eve. And on Christmas Day itself the house would be straining at the seams to accommodate all the other relatives, including two stray aunts and a cousin who'd been recently bereaved.

Boz had trotted out from the kitchen and was winding himself ecstatically in and out of her legs. She bent down to make a fuss of him, glad of the chance to hide her face. She knew it was still flushed, her whole body reacting to the intensity of the hug. Had Elizabeth reached out to her simply because she was crying, the same way she might have comforted a child? Or was the gesture more significant? If only she *were* a child, she could demand a second hug, or sob and scream until she was comforted again.

'Boz has really missed you,' Elizabeth was saying, as the cat's throaty purr reverberated through the hall. 'After you left, he kept roaming round the house, wondering where you'd gone.'

But did *you* miss me, she longed to know? Did *you* roam round the house, wishing I was here? She was floating in a heady sphere where the two of them were lovers, whereas Elizabeth had reverted to the role of gracious hostess, waiting to take her coat, remarking on the dreadful traffic and the hold-ups on the London road.

Slowly Beattie unbuttoned her coat, unwilling to come down to earth or make trivial conversation. Besides, she needed to satisfy herself that the house was just the same as she remembered it – nothing changed or out of place. She gazed around the hall, noting each familiar detail: the two gold-framed landscapes and the portrait of a man and wife; the dried flower arrangement and brass umbrella stand; the inkwell on the antique desk, the Queen Anne chair with its hand-worked tapestry seat. Those were *her* possessions now – her paintings, acquisitions. She and Elizabeth owned the house between them. Satisfied, she walked into the drawing-room, exclaiming at the quantities of Christmas cards crowding every available surface. Elizabeth had far too many friends – lucky people she'd known and loved for years. Somehow she had to prise her away from that circle, become more precious than them all. Her eye fell on the tall Christmas tree standing in the corner, as yet undecorated.

'I thought we'd do the tree together,' Elizabeth said, following her glance.

'Oh, I'd love that,' Beattie said, darting over to the tree and drawing herself up to her full height. 'Look, it's even taller than me!' A tree so large must have cost a fortune. Christmas in her childhood had always centred round the cost of things: the wicked price of turkeys, the need to buy the cheapest cards (and preferably buy them eleven months early, half-price in the January sales). There had been no question of extravagances like crackers, or real Christmas trees, or expensive decorations, and even their few presents had to be unwrapped with great care, so the paper could be re-used the following year.

'Look, I'll go and fetch my stuff in from the car. I want you to open your presents.'

'What, now?'

'Yes, now! I know you, Sophie. You'll be so busy on Christmas Day, you won't have a chance to turn round.'

'Gosh! I'd forgotten about the Sophie. It *does* sound odd.'

Beattie stared at her in horror. How *could* she have forgotten? George and Sophie were their intimate 'married' names. Had she forgotten George, as well?

She strode out to the car and returned with two large cases, one containing her clothes and the other all the presents. She got down on her hands and knees and unlocked the second case, extracting a heavy oblong parcel wrapped in red and gold. She pushed it into Elizabeth's hands. 'That'll remind you of Sophie,' she said. 'Go on – open it.'

'But we never open our presents till Christmas Day,' Elizabeth objected.

'Oh please. I've bought you loads of other things. You can save *those* for Christmas Day.'

'Beattie, my love, I've told you over and over – you mustn't keep buying me presents.'

'Christmas is different. Anyway, they're to thank you for having me to stay, so it's only what I'll save on the housekeeping.'

Elizabeth laughed. 'You're incorrigible! Okay, but let's go into the kitchen. I ought to keep an eye on the oven.'

Beattie stopped at the kitchen door and took a deep breath in. 'What are you cooking? It all smells wonderful.'

'Lots of things. Mince pies for us and a Dundee cake for Daddy. And I'm brewing coffee for a coffee mousse – it's a new recipe I want to try. And the mulled wine is an old family favourite, so I thought I'd do some tonight, to welcome you. And there's a moussaka in the oven, too. I wasn't sure how hungry you'd be.'

'Starving!' She sank down on the settle, gazing around at the cheerful cosy room. 'Oh, Elizabeth . . .'

'What?'

'It's great to be back. I've missed you terribly. *And* the house. *And* Boz. And even Tolkien. Where is he, by the way?'

'Upstairs. I trod on his foot by mistake and he's sulking, I'm afraid. He's such a prima donna! Now what would you like to drink, Beattie? A glass of mulled wine, or a cup of tea, or . . . ?'

'Oh, wine please. Wine and presents. There are three for you to open now, and I'll put the rest under the tree.'

'Well, I hope they're only little things. You're far too generous, you know.' She dipped a ladle into the saucepan on the hob and poured wine into two sugar-frosted glasses. 'Cheers!'

'Cheers!'

'I thought we'd have supper about eight, so perhaps you'd like a mince pie now to fill the gap?'

'Mm, yes please!' She took one, hot, from the baking tray, then pushed Elizabeth's still unopened present across the table towards her. 'It's my first mince pie this year,' she said, 'so I'm allowed a wish.' Wishing was like praying – the same words, the same intensity. She bit into the pastry, almost burning her tongue. 'Let Christmas be special,' she murmured under her breath. At least it had *started* well. She relived the hug once more: the fantastic feeling of Elizabeth's body pressed so close to hers; the clean smell of her hair; the sense of having crossed some crucial barrier.

'Now, what can this be?' Elizabeth smiled, stripping off the paper to reveal a large and heavy book. She turned it right side up and read out the title: '*Wildfowl in Britain.*'

'I know it might seem rather boring,' said Beattie anxiously, 'but I went all over the place to find a book with illustrations which would show both George and Sophie. You know – our special ducks.'

Elizabeth looked nonplussed. Surely she remembered the *ducks*?

They were desperately important: living proof that two utterly dissimilar breeds could pair for life.

She leaned across and opened the book, determined to make Elizabeth understand. 'See – there's Sophie. I put a marker in for her, and one for George. *She*'s a rare species, apparently, but poor George is quite common or garden.'

'He doesn't look common or garden to me,' Elizabeth remarked, gazing at the photograph. 'He looks jolly smart – and special.'

Beattie gulped her wine in confusion. Could Elizabeth be *flirting* with her, paying her a sort of lover's compliment? But before she could respond in the same vein, Elizabeth began thanking her, politely but uneffusively, the same way she'd done at Cheltenham when she'd unwrapped the gold bracelet – no real excitement or enthusiasm. And she wasn't even *wearing* the bracelet, Beattie noticed despondently. For all she knew it was still in its box, or shoved at the back of some drawer.

She rushed out to the hall to fetch two other presents. Elizabeth probably had so many books she couldn't get worked up about another. But the racing presents would please her – they were different altogether. She put them on the table, next to Elizabeth's plate, keeping a careful watch on her face as she opened the first one: a pair of small but powerful binoculars in a snazzy leather case.

'Beattie, *no*! I can't accept these.'

'Of course you can. You *need* them. They're for when we next go racing, and everyone takes binoculars to the races.'

Elizabeth continued to protest about the extravagance, and looked more dismayed than delighted. Beattie slid her hand across the table and moved the final present out of reach. Best leave that unopened. It was a racing diary listing every single race-meeting up and down the country. Perhaps Elizabeth thought she was trying to control her, holding her to her promise about going racing again. Those dreary psychoanalytical books were always banging on about 'control': presents could be 'controlling', and relationships, and even love. But why make things so damned complicated? As far as *she* was concerned, presents were a way of bringing people closer, of saying things you daren't put into words, of proving that you cared enough to spend endless time and trouble choosing exactly the right thing. She had scoured the shops each lunch-hour, dithering and worrying, asking advice from snooty sales assistants, trying to pick out toys for Tim and Alexander, or find something original for people she hadn't even met, like Emma and her husband, and Sarah and the two aunts. And to pay off her credit-card bill she'd had to take an evening job (serving cocktails in a sleazy bar) on top of her nine-to-five one. Many nights she'd arrived home so late she had fallen into bed too tired to eat. All she wanted in return was Elizabeth's honest-to-goodness pleasure, not another of her cool impassive thank-yous.

She waved the lukewarm thanks away, trying to hide her disappointment by helping herself to another mince pie.

'Well, tell me all your news, Beattie,' Elizabeth said, passing her a paper napkin – one of Tim's, no doubt, since it was printed with pink dinosaurs.

'There isn't any. Life's been pretty foul. I'm still doing that ghastly job.' She didn't mention the evening work, or Elizabeth would only make more fuss about the presents.

'I thought you said you were going to get one of your articles accepted?'

'Yeah, I was.'

'So what happened?'

'Not a lot.' Beattie licked her finger and scooped up the last crumbs of pastry. 'Look, d'you mind if we don't talk about it?'

'No, of course not.'

There was a sudden awkward silence, but the last thing she wanted was to discuss the whole Max débâcle. The very day he'd promised to read her pieces, his wife had gone down with a particularly nasty virus infection, which confined her to bed for two weeks (and apparently explained her earlier headaches). Since Max relied on Michèle to cook his meals, iron his shirts, and even get him up in the morning, he could hardly be expected to keep his promise when plunged waist-deep in a major domestic crisis. Then Rory had phoned from Cornwall and offered to come up to London to look after the invalid. At first Max had hated the thought, but then saw it as a perfect chance to get away himself – with *her*.

The only problem was, she hadn't wanted to go. If she had to choose between Elizabeth and Max, Elizabeth would always win. And anyway it was beginning to dawn on her that Max would *never* keep his promises, never launch her into journalism.

'So, how's Sal?' Elizabeth was asking now, obviously keen to fill the silence.

'She's okay – more or less.' She had no wish to discuss Sal either. They'd quarrelled again last week, and Sal had accused her of turning into a completely different person. Elizabeth *had* changed her – it was true – but only for the better. In fact, that was partly the problem with Max: the more she took on Elizabeth's values, the more guilty she felt about deceiving his wife, especially now Michèle was ill. The occasional assignation in London didn't seem so bad, but a whole two weeks away in France was betrayal on the grand scale. She was becoming increasingly uneasy about the parallels between *her* involvement with Max and Jeremy's with Loretta, and was haunted by the thought of Michèle suffering the same jealousy as Elizabeth had done. In her previous entanglements with married men, she had never really bothered much about how the *wife* might feel. Wives were simply the lucky ones – or the *stupid* ones, for causing their husbands to look for sex elsewhere. But Elizabeth had made her much more sensitive; more conscious of her actions and their effects on other people.

Decisively, she drained her wine, suddenly tired of all the soul-searching. She would damn well enjoy the 'now', as she had vowed at Cheltenham – not keep harking back to Max, or Michèle, or her mother, or her rotten job. She had left all those behind; was doing exactly what she wanted: spending Christmas with Elizabeth in quite the nicest house in Kent, with all sorts of marvellous food to eat, a real Christmas tree to decorate, two cats to keep them company, and the bliss of knowing no one would disturb them till tomorrow afternoon.

'Let's drink a toast,' she urged, as Elizabeth refilled her glass.

'To George and Sophie?' Elizabeth asked, glancing at her book with a smile.

'Well, yes, to them, of course. But first to the *now* – to this actual perfect moment.'

'The tree looks great!' said Beattie, settling back on the sofa to admire it.

'Thanks to you. You're far more artistic than I am. Tim helped me do it last year and I'm afraid it turned out – well – not quite in *your* class, George.'

Beattie gave a modest shrug, secretly delighted. Glancing round the drawing-room, she felt like one of those smug people she had watched so often on television, enjoying a genuinely happy Christmas with everything near-perfect: a real coal fire crackling in the grate, tasteful decorations (unlike the lopsided paper chains which had featured now and then in Croydon, when her mother was well enough to put them up), Christmas goodies on every side – liqueur chocolates and marzipan, bowls of nuts and tangerines. The evening had gone wonderfully well. They had eaten supper by candlelight (which seemed deliciously romantic), and Elizabeth had even reverted to calling her George, prompted by the bird book.

She reached out for another chocolate, disturbing Boz, who was curled up on her lap. 'I'm sorry, Boz, but I've got to get up anyway. I'm dying for a pee.'

As she closed the cloakroom door behind her, she was jolted by the dark square of sky glaring through the uncurtained window. The moon wasn't visible from here and the sky looked almost menacingly black. She turned away, uneasy. She was safe with Elizabeth, happy with Elizabeth, but that precious safety and happiness suddenly felt threatened. Beyond the warm cocoon of Mile End House loomed hideous things she hardly dared to think about: big bangs and final crunches, chaos and black holes. Elizabeth might *die* – as randomly as stars died – leaving her widowed, orphaned, horribly alone. Those psychoanalysts might talk about control, but the brutal truth was that you couldn't control *any*thing, least of all relationships, or love.

Returning to the drawing-room, she was almost surprised to find Elizabeth still there, sitting quietly in her chunky navy cardigan and nibbling a marzipan fruit.

'Oh, Elizabeth . . .'

'What?'

'Do you ever feel . . . well . . . terrified?'

'Frequently! Especially on the M20 in the rush-hour.'

'No, seriously. I mean, just frightened that . . . that we're here at all. It's all so sort of . . . precarious. We don't know where we came from or where we're going when we die. Yet people just seem to *accept* it, without seeing how scary it is.'

'Oh, I don't think they *do*, my love. Several of my patients feel exactly that kind of fear.'

'Well, they're jolly lucky to have you there to help. I've felt a bit adrift since I was about fourteen or fifteen, but it's not something I've ever discussed. No one seems to want to talk about it.'

'That's because it *is* frightening, but they'd probably rather not admit it. I suppose religion is a way of dealing with it – a brave attempt to reassure us and make us feel safer in the world.'

'When we're *not* safe at all,' Beattie interrupted.

Elizabeth nodded. 'Yes, you're right. We're not safe.' She got up to put more coal on the fire and stood by the fireplace, gazing into the flames. 'I remember feeling that acutely just after Jeremy left. Often I couldn't sleep, you see, so I'd go down to make a cup of tea, and Boz would want to go out. I'd open the back door for him and I'd look up at the sky and think, "How can I *mind* so much about my husband leaving, when I'm only an infinitesimal speck?" But instead of that consoling me, I'd feel even worse. Okay, we *are* specks in the great scheme of things, yet we're also the centre of our own all-important universes, and both those facts together can be a bit too much to take.'

She returned to her chair, kicking off her shoes and stretching her legs towards the fire. 'I suppose it's all frightfully adolescent in a way – the sort of thing you're meant to agonize about when you're young and insecure. But perhaps we're *always* young and insecure, in one sense, anyway. I remember talking to my analyst about it – you know, the famous Dr Grübinger – and he called it "existential angst".'

'He would,' said Beattie tartly.

Elizabeth laughed. 'I don't know why you've got it in for poor old Grübinger. You bristle whenever I mention him.'

'Because he didn't help you, that's why – just talked a load of crap.'

'I doubt if *any*one can be much help in certain situations. You need courage and acceptance, and you can only find those in yourself. Though I must admit I used to get a bit annoyed with him myself sometimes. He was always giving things *labels*, as if that would cure them or explain them. I'm afraid it's one of the faults of my profession – too much jargon and dissection – and sometimes not enough humility to admit we actually know depressingly little about the psyche.'

'I do wish you'd finish your book,' said Beattie, picking up the nutcrackers and tackling a large walnut. 'There's been so much stuff in the papers recently about therapists and Freud and what-have-you, you really ought to cash in on it.'

'Yes, I suppose I should. Though actually I find it rather alarming. I mean, some of the things I've been reading are out-and-out attacks on the profession as a whole. Such as Freud being a charlatan who distorted the evidence and didn't care a fig about his patients, and therapy just a money-making con. It makes my own criticisms seem positively tame.'

'Yes, but your book would be topical and that would make it sell.' Beattie passed Elizabeth a few fragments of mangled walnut. 'Sorry! I'm not exactly a dab hand with the nutcrackers. I'll try a brazil this time.'

Elizabeth ate her walnut shreds, followed by a shattered brazil nut. 'Actually, I *have* written another chunk of the book. I watched this thing on television a couple of weeks ago, and it was so violently anti-therapy, it produced a sort of gut reaction and set my creative juices flowing!'

'Great! I'll type it tomorrow. How much have you done?'

'Oh, there's enough for another long chapter – maybe two or three. It depends on how I divide it up.'

'So the book's practically finished, then?'

'Well, no. This new bit isn't right for the end. It's more a sort of addition which needs slotting in earlier.'

'No problem. I'll sort it out in the morning on the computer.'

'I thought you said you'd booked a haircut?'

'Yeah, I have. That girl in Sevenoaks is a genius! The place I go to in London is nothing like as good.'

'And you were going to give me a hand with my Christmas shopping.'

'Most definitely. I'm the world's expert on shopping.'

'And you wanted to fly Tim's kite, remember? Up on Tandridge Hill.'

'Oh I *do*! I've never flown a kite.'

'And you promised you'd help me peel the chestnuts for the stuffing.'

Beattie nodded, laughing. '*And* try my hand at brandy butter.'

'Well, it looks as if we're going to have a pretty busy day.'

Not *too* busy, Beattie begged her silently. They needed time to simply *be* – to laze together, talk together, as they were doing so blissfully now. Sal might sneer at her pretensions, but then Sal was probably jealous at being stuck in a rut while *she* was learning and growing. Three months ago she wouldn't have dreamed of reading articles on Freud or psychotherapy. And she'd no more have ventured into an art gallery than into a Hindu temple, or read books on physics, or listened to Stravinsky. Over supper this evening they'd been talking about philosophy, for God's sake! But that's what Elizabeth had done for her – upgraded and refined her.

196

She had even learned to crack a nut – she passed a perfect un-broken almond to Elizabeth.

'No more, George my dear. In fact, I think it's time we went to bed. It's already after midnight and we've so much planned for tomorrow we'll need our beauty sleep.'

'Oh no! I can't bear this evening to end. It's by far the best evening I've had since the *last* time I was here.'

'Don't worry, we'll have plenty more evenings together.' Elizabeth got up from her chair and retrieved her scuffed blue shoes. 'Right, can you let Boz and Tolkien out and I'll damp down the fire.'

Plenty more evenings together, Beattie echoed, as she gently prodded the cats from their torpor. That was a promise, a commit-ment, the best Christmas present she could possibly imagine. She floated into the kitchen, surveying her handiwork: dishes washed and put away, neat uncluttered surfaces, oven sparkling clean. She had worked a miracle in here, turned chaos into order and been rewarded by Elizabeth's praises. The rewards were mounting up. By Christmas Day itself she would have received the CBE – the Closest Bond Ever with Elizabeth.

She let the cats out and stood by the back door, picturing Elizabeth standing in the very same spot and looking up at the sky, utterly wretched because Jeremy had left. She longed to make up for all her friend had suffered, to fill the void in both their lives by becoming a Jeremy-substitute.

She shivered in her silky blouse. She wasn't dressed for the middle of winter, but she'd bought the blouse in Elizabeth's honour, and it was far too pretty to hide beneath a jacket. Her breath turned to vapour in the freezing air and her hands were numb already. It was also oppressively dark, the former lustrous moon now wreathed in heavy clouds. The ring around it must have long since disappeared, she realized with a surge of disappointment. Such a rare and special moon had seemed to mean that Christmas would be rare and special too, and she had wanted it to last all night as her portent, her good omen. She stepped onto the lawn, willing it to return, but the clouds were obscuring everything except a faint wash of pearly silver.

She called the cats and walked back to the door, about to close and bolt it, when all at once the moon sailed out, complete with its majestic halo – now a translucent bluish white and more spectacular than ever.

'Elizabeth!' she shouted in excitement. 'Come and look at this.'

They stood side by side, gazing upwards at the sky. 'It's quite magical!' Elizabeth exclaimed. 'The only other time I saw a moon like that was on my twenty-first birthday – and it felt like an extra birthday present, the perfect end to a perfect day.'

Another good omen, Beattie reflected as she continued to look up. No longer did she feel such terror about the vastness of the universe or the catastrophes in space. Elizabeth would keep her safe. Just discussing her fears had helped to dispel them. She had never had a friend she could talk to about 'existential angst' (or whatever the fatuous Grübinger called it); one who sympathized as well as understood. With all her other friends she usually nattered about trivial things like clothes or make-up, or their boring jobs, or the latest scandal in *EastEnders*. But Elizabeth's world was infinitely wider – like the sky itself, full of stars and wonders.

'We'd better go in,' Elizabeth said, 'before we freeze to death.'

They bolted the doors and settled the cats in the kitchen, then walked upstairs to bed together. Like man and wife, thought Beattie – with the depressing difference that they'd have to separate once they reached the landing.

'Well, goodnight,' said Elizabeth. 'Sleep well.' She turned to go to her room but on a sudden impulse, Beattie stepped towards her and kissed her on the lips, hardly knowing what she was doing or where she'd found the courage. To her amazement, Elizabeth kissed her back – only very briefly, with the lightest brush of the lips, but still a kiss returned.

'Goodnight,' Elizabeth said again, but the word sounded far less casual now.

Beattie stood transfixed, holding her hand to her mouth, as if to preserve the last vestiges of the kiss. Elizabeth could have rebuffed her; recoiled in anger or disgust. Instead she had accepted the kiss, even responded to it – maybe feeling the same longing and affection she was experiencing herself. So why was she walking away, closing her bedroom door? Perhaps she was simply overwhelmed by what had happened; excited by the kiss, but also startled, needing time to sort out her emotions.

They *had* time – almost another whole day on their own. She needn't have her hair cut or go shopping or fly kites. If there was a chance of getting closer to Elizabeth, everything else must go by the board. They were already triumphantly close; had moved on light-years since September.

She drifted into her own room and knelt down by the bed – something she hadn't done since she was a small (reluctant) child, forced to say her prayers. 'Thank you, God,' she had been instructed to recite, for a whole string of things she didn't want and certainly wasn't grateful for. This time it was different.

'Thank you, God,' she whispered fervently. 'For Elizabeth. And for answering my prayer.'

19

'Happy Christmas, Elizabeth dear.'

'Happy Christmas, Charlotte! Oh, and happy Christmas, Jill and David – I didn't see you there.'

Beattie clenched her teeth. If anyone else says happy Christmas, she thought, I'll crown them.

In any case, it *wasn't* Christmas, but four days afterwards, and it *hadn't* been happy (at least, nothing like as happy as she'd hoped). She tried to hide her irritation and treat these new arrivals with a modicum of good grace. It was something in their favour that they were friends, not family. From Christmas Eve until today, every single person in the house had been related to Elizabeth in some way or another – except for *her*, of course. She was the odd one out in so many respects: wrong parentage, wrong accent, wrong education, wrong job.

'And this is Beattie,' Elizabeth said, ushering over a forbidding-looking woman – a mannish type with powerful shoulders and iron-grey hair pulled severely off her face. 'Beattie, this is Agnes Jennings, a colleague of mine. We trained at the same institute and then discovered we lived within three miles of each other.'

'Pleased to meet you,' Beattie lied.

'How do you do.'

They exchanged politely formal smiles as Elizabeth disappeared to welcome yet more guests. Beattie glanced about for support, but everyone else seemed to be otherwise engaged. She felt deeply uncomfortable in the presence of a shrink, who could probably see into her mind and detect her desire for every daughter, grandchild, aunt and guest to vanish into thin air, leaving her blissfully alone with Elizabeth.

'Did you enjoy your Christmas?' Agnes asked.

'Yes, thanks,' said Beattie. 'How about yours?'

'Oh, very quiet.'

They continued with the pleasantries, Beattie answering questions about her work and where she lived, sorely tempted to lie: 'I used to be the editor of *Playboy*, but now I've retired to a harem and my sole occupation is sucking the Sultan's toes.' 'I'm a famous racehorse-owner with a mansion in the Cotswolds and a penthouse in Manhattan, and I've had dozens of winners in the last few months alone.'

'Have you known Elizabeth long?' Agnes was enquiring.

Oh, a good ten years, she longed to say – or better still, since infancy. If only she could claim Elizabeth as her godmother, her childhood mentor and confidante, who had grown into her closest adult friend. She was jealous of the thought of Agnes knowing Elizabeth longer and better than *she* did; training with her at some prestigious institute; belonging to the same superior world – a world closed to outsiders.

'Hello, Beattie!' boomed a voice behind her. She swung round in relief, only to find it was bossy-boots Eleanor – a WI stalwart from the village. Eleanor had tried to recruit her when they'd first met in October, saying they needed young blood in the group. (She could just see herself making chutney, or learning to do patchwork-quilting with a gaggle of bored housewives, or listening enthralled to talks on Poultry Keeping or Identifying Woodland Fungi.) Hurriedly she introduced Eleanor to Agnes and took the chance to steal away – only to be collared by Jane, a churchy friend of the Hargreaves she had met at the Christmas service.

'Did you have a lovely Christmas, dear?'

'Yes, great.'

'And Elizabeth says you're staying for New Year?'

Beattie nodded. New Year's Eve was only forty-eight hours away: more guests, more celebrations, more damned jollity. That sounded really peevish and ungrateful, but her period was due and she invariably felt vile the week before. This time it seemed worse than usual and she was ready to snap at everyone. Actually, it wasn't just her period – she'd had a ghastly dream last night, which she couldn't get out of her mind. It had been Christmas Day in Croydon and she was nine years old and alone with her sick mother. Nothing unusual about *that*, but when they cut into the turkey, it was only charred brown paper which flaked into thin air. 'It's wicked to waste food,' her mother muttered, so they just sat there eating forkfuls of nothing, listening to the silence. And then her mother slowly crumbled away as well, until she was nothing but a pile of scurfy ash.

The dream had brought back other memories – of returning to school each January and boasting about the gifts she hadn't had; pretending she'd had *fun*, for heaven's sake, and that her father had given up a starring role in order to be home with her.

Her attention drifted back to Jane, who had now embarked on a discussion of the weather.

'I do hope it doesn't snow. The forecast's awfully bad, you know. My husband suffers terribly with arthritis and the cold and damp always make it worse.'

Beattie made a sympathetic clucking noise, and had a sudden vision of herself as a hen – cluck-cluck-*cluck*, cluck-cluck-*cluck* – or better still, a cockerel: cock-a-doodle-*doo*! She pictured the whole roomful of people turning into birds or animals, their tedious small talk transformed into a cacophony of cheeps, moos, baas, grunts, snorts. She suppressed a grin. 'Is your husband *here?*' she asked, picking up the thread of the conversation.

'Oh yes. Over in the corner there, talking to Emma. And doesn't she look marvellous – positively glowing!' Her voice fell to a confiding whisper. 'We're all so thrilled that she's . . . er . . . expecting.'

Beattie gave a noncommittal grunt. All the animal noises were converging into a deafening chorus, a furious roar of pain and indignation. Another wretched grandchild to tie Elizabeth down, claim her love, her time. Apparently Emma had had a miscarriage last year, so she was supposed to take things easy, but it was galling to see Elizabeth fussing round her daughter as if she were made of tissue paper.

'Why not come and *meet* Richard?' Jane suggested brightly, steering Beattie in the direction of a timid-looking little man deep in conversation with the radiantly pregnant Emma.

Beattie felt embarrassed at butting in, especially when confronted by Emma's cool appraising gaze. Emma had never been openly hostile, she just made you feel constantly guilty: for drinking gin, or wearing black net tights – most of all, for *being* here, intruding on a sacred family Christmas. Even her five-year-old daughter, Amanda (a depressingly gorgeous moppet with long golden ringlets and forget-me-not blue eyes), tended to be standoffish, as if she had inherited her mother's distaste for ill-bred interlopers. Of course Elizabeth *adored* Amanda, showered her with the hugs and kisses *she* craved for herself.

'I understand you're a famous journalist,' Richard said, with wide-eyed admiration.

'Well, I wouldn't quite say that,' Beattie mumbled, blushing. That was the trouble with a village: gossip spread like poison ivy. Her odd remarks to Margaret the day she'd first arrived at Mile End House had evidently been inflated, so that she was now the toast of Fleet Street. 'I . . . er . . . just turn out the odd article,' she said falteringly, conscious of Emma's raised eyebrows. She changed the subject quickly by asking Amanda the name of her doll – one she hadn't seen before.

Amanda gave her a baleful stare, hugging the doll closer to her chest. Beattie backed away, muttering something about needing a glass of water, and escaped into the kitchen. Hardly an escape – it was full of people, family for the most part: Caroline feeding baby Alexander with a jar of brownish goo; Harriet cuddling Tim on her lap; Emma's husband John decanting mulled wine into glasses, and a besotted Auntie Dora going into ecstasies over the guzzling Alexander. Why should babies be entitled to such non-stop adulation just for being small and helpless? She wished *she* were small and helpless, then Elizabeth would feed her with a spoon, rock her on her lap, settle her in her cot each night with kisses and caresses. She reached up to the cupboard for a glass, nervously aware that the conversation had stopped. Had they been discussing her; wondering when she'd push off?

'I've just come to get a glass of water,' she explained, to fill the silence, running the hot tap by mistake and beating a hasty retreat with her undrinkable drink.

She stood at the drawing-room door, glancing miserably at the Christmas tree, which had been subjected to various assaults by clumsy kids or careless guests. Several of its decorations had now been knocked askew, and the shining Christmas fairy dangled upside down at the top. Indeed the whole room looked tired and wilting: a wine stain on the carpet, the evergreens drooping in their vase, and at least half the Christmas cards knocked over on their backs. Christmas had gone on far too long and should have been chucked out with the turkey bones. And how about a complete spring-clean: the daughters consigned to the dustbin with the empties; the other guests all hoovered away, and the house restored to its former peace and quiet?

'Elizabeth,' she mouthed, watching the perfect hostess talking to a group of friends. 'Why not just sneak out with me? Let's leave these stupid people and drive down to the coast together, so that we can be alone again?'

The only response was a braying laugh from one of Elizabeth's circle – some balding buffoon who then had the nerve to put his arm around that slender girlish waist and give it a suggestive squeeze.

She crept into Jeremy's study, closing the door behind her and sitting down at the desk. At least this was a room where she felt some tie with Elizabeth. She'd been typing the book in here, and that made her part of Elizabeth's world, gave her a professional status. She knew more about the book than any of the daughters did, and anyway the daughters couldn't type – or only Harriet, who'd done a basic office-training course, but hadn't any speed or real experience. Also, the study was usually empty and during the past hectic week had proved a welcome refuge from the hordes. She only wished she had more chapters to work on, but Elizabeth had no *time* to write when she was rushed off her feet with all the cooking and entertaining.

All at once the door burst open and Sarah strode in, glaring at her accusingly. 'What are you doing?'

'Nothing.' Was she about to be charged with defacing the books or stealing the family silver?

'This is my father's study.'

'Yeah, I know.'

'Well you shouldn't be in here.'

'Who said?'

'*I* did.'

Beattie tried to hide her annoyance. Sarah was much younger than she was and had no right to throw her weight about, yet she'd been aggressive from the minute she arrived – not silently disapproving like Emma, but continually on the attack. 'Your mother lets me work here,' she said, with an attempt at a smile. If she got on the wrong side of two of the four girls it would only make things difficult for Elizabeth.

'Yes – like she let you sleep in my room.'

So *that* was it! Beattie was shocked at such childishness, and needled by the waspish tone of voice. Elizabeth's happy, loving family was not quite what it seemed. All the same, she did feel rather awkward sitting at Jeremy's desk. It was probably sacrosanct, like his special chair in the kitchen. And she was well aware that Sarah missed her father, and had been particularly upset that he hadn't come to her degree ceremony. There had been quite a row about it, Elizabeth had said. But that was no reason to take it out on *her*. In fact, she'd seen far less of her own father than Sarah had of Jeremy. Up till just two years ago, Jeremy had come home each night, eaten supper with the family, spent part of each weekend with them. Besides, Sarah had a loving mother – a mother who was *well*. Still, best not to argue the point – she didn't want a slanging match, or Sarah telling tales to Elizabeth.

Uneasily she got up from the chair and edged towards the door. Sarah stood her ground, monitoring her every movement as if she was a dangerous prisoner who might resort to violence. Unlike the ash-blond Emma, she was mousy rather than fair, and the only one of the family to wear glasses – an unattractive rimless pair which made her look schoolmarmish and prim.

'Caroline says you've been here since the summer,' she remarked coldly.

'I have *not*!' retorted Beattie. 'I didn't even meet your mother till September and for the last six weeks I've been slaving my guts out in London.'

'That's not what Caroline told me.'

'Well I'm sorry if I'm in your way – *and* Caroline's.' She slammed out, close to tears. Caroline had always been charming to her face, but what on earth had she been saying behind her back? Did they *all* resent her – Elizabeth included – regard her as a sponger and a gatecrasher?

She blundered up the stairs, taking them two at a time in her haste to get away. She would retreat to her bedroom in the attic; stay up there all day, if she wasn't wanted downstairs. The room was small and poky, and got very little light, but it was the only space available with the whole family in residence. Emma and John were sleeping in the consulting room; Sarah had doubled up with Harriet to make room for one of the aunts. The second aunt and the elderly cousin were in Caroline's old room, while Caroline and her husband had been allocated the spare room (which had its own en suite bathroom and was therefore handy for the baby). She hated all the upheaval.

The house seemed alien, and she was separated from Elizabeth by this long flight of narrow stairs.

She trudged on up despondently, tears smarting on her cheeks. There were only two bedrooms on the top floor of the house. Hers was a glorified boxroom, while Tim and Amanda shared the bigger one next door. Elizabeth had asked her if she would be kind enough to look after them, and she had felt honoured at the time; pleased to be so trusted. Now, however, it seemed more of an imposition. She had turned into the au pair, the 'foreign' girl who didn't belong, but was a convenient form of labour who could be stuck up here alone with the kids, given the worst room in the house. She sat down on the edge of the bed, staring at the wall. It would have been better to have spent another Christmas with Sal than to be made to feel a nonentity. She was actually missing London, even missing television, ironically enough. In Mile End House, no one seemed to watch it. They preferred talking, or listening to music. Even the children were encouraged to look at picture-books rather than waste their time on game-shows or cartoons. She wished she had a TV up here, then she could switch on something mindless and forget her petty problems for a while.

She trailed to the window and peered down at the collection of cars parked outside the house. One car – James and Margaret's – was just manoeuvring out of the gates. They hadn't said goodbye to her. Well, no doubt they'd been so dazzled by the charms of their great-granddaughter they'd forgotten everything else. Amanda charmed *everyone*, with her long dark lashes and lisping voice.

She watched Elizabeth waving goodbye to her parents. They were leaving early for a lunch appointment in Westerham – a grand affair, apparently, with some local bigwig and his wife. *She* didn't want lunch. She had already put on almost half a stone, which made her feel flabby and depressed. The fridge was full of left-overs, yet Elizabeth kept on cooking. For the drinks party today, she'd made vol-au-vents and quiches, three different pâtés and a whole variety of dips. Strangely though, the food didn't taste as good when it was prepared for other people. What she missed was the dishes cooked for her alone, and served with love, in private.

She rubbed the tiny windowpane, misted by her breath. The light was dull and grey outside, echoing her spirits. There had been no glint of sun all day, only oppressive clouds and a rawness in the air. She caught sight of Boz on the path below, skulking round the side of the house. She was surprised that he was out in such cold weather, but then Tim had been tormenting him, hauling him about, and the cat had made his disapproval clear by vanishing into the garden. She considered going to fetch him back, smuggling him up here so they could comfort one another. No – that would mean venturing downstairs again, and she had no desire to run into Sarah and risk a second row. She picked up her jade elephant instead. It accompanied her on every journey to Kent, and had become her magic talisman. Secretly she'd been hoping for a similar gift from Elizabeth this Christmas, something equally precious and original. What she'd actually received was a small and rather drab-looking book. It *was* a first edition and bound in tooled brown leather, but there was nothing remotely personal about it. The elephant had been chosen in direct response to her fears about being jumbo-sized, but a book on the history of Kent was surely more suited to James. And she was still hurt by the fact that not one of the daughters had given her a thing. It wasn't that she was a gold-digger expecting loads of expensive gifts – just a couple of tiny, silly things would have made her feel accepted. Apart from Elizabeth's book, her only present from the family was a box of chocolates, courtesy of Auntie Jean, with a picture of a black cat on the lid. Well, in the absence of Boz, it would be some consolation.

She tore off the cellophane and dipped into the first layer, picking a chocolate with a squiggle on the top which vaguely resembled an E. There was the sound of footsteps on the stairs, children's voices, laughter. Several people had brought their kids along and a contingent of them must be coming up here. Yes, she could hear Tim's piping voice, inviting them into his room. The door slammed shut and she listened through the wall to the excited screams and giggles which made her feel even more alone. She crunched another chocolate – a brazil nut – knowing she'd regret it later: chocolates made her fat. They also reminded her of Max, who usually brought her a box when he came round to the flat – often, she suspected, as a sort of compensation, either because he was hopelessly late or because he had barged in uninvited. She tried to picture him at home, playing nursemaid to his wife, or quarrelling with his son. He'd been angry with her, too, the day she'd finally confessed to him about spending Christmas in Kent. She had told him a whole pack of lies to justify herself – lies involving Sal as well. She wished she didn't have to lie, but sometimes it seemed the only way to stop people being cross, or to make them think more highly of her, or simply to avoid some dreaded duty.

Both Sal and Max felt very far away. It was not that she was missing them – far from it – just that she was all alone with that sense of disappointment she knew so well from childhood: the letdown after the huge pre-Christmas build-up; the feeling that Christmas hadn't really come at all, or not for her, at least.

She rammed the lid back on the box of chocolates and sprang up from the bed. What a selfish pig she was! Max and Sal had probably spent *truly* lousy Christmases, whereas she'd been totally indulged – waited on hand and foot, provided with all manner of diversion – yet she still had the cheek to complain. She ought to be keeping an eye on the kids next door, not gorging herself on chocolates and self-pity.

She went to see what they were doing; found Jill and David's twelve-year-old twins already playing nanny and making a good job of it. Eight faces turned to stare at her, evidently resenting the intrusion. None the less, she lingered at the door, attracted by the cheerful room with its polka-dotted curtains and fluffy sheepskin rug, the toys and games jumbled on the floor. Amanda was queening it in the one and only chair, still cradling her expensive doll, and exerting her charms on two little boys sitting cross-legged at her feet. Beattie observed the flirtation; frightened by the anger she felt. How could you hate a five-year-old whose only fault was to be cute? No, it wasn't the cuteness she minded, but Elizabeth's enslavement to the child – to *all* her precious grandchildren. She had watched her this morning cuddling Alexander, and had actually thought enviously of Herod, with his power to slay every baby in the land and get away with it.

She returned to her own room, guilty and ashamed. She must be thoroughly wicked to harbour such murderous thoughts. And grasping and ungrateful to carp about her Christmas presents. No wonder the daughters disliked her. And Elizabeth must have realized by now that she didn't know how to love – not unreservedly. If you genuinely loved someone, you loved their family as well. Except it was so depressingly difficult. If only the daughters weren't so *superior*, so well-bred and coldly smug. And if only Elizabeth would kiss her again, or call her George, or make time to talk to her alone, then she wouldn't feel so excluded. She glanced in the mirror, surprised at her normal appearance. She had somehow expected her vileness to show on her face, like a hideous sort of skin-rash. She was probably overreacting, as usual. She'd feel far less tense and scratchy as soon as her period had come, and once she and Elizabeth were on their own again. She just had to be patient, and more reasonable. Elizabeth could hardly lavish affection on her in front of all the family, or call her George in public and risk their scorn and derision.

She took up her position at the window, watching some of the visitors depart. Soon she'd be watching the family depart, and then her *real* and happy Christmas would begin. She heard the mother of the two small boys calling up the stairs to them, and then Jill's shrill voice, summoning the twins. The party must be over, thank God. At least the shrinks would be gone, and the village worthies, and a good half-dozen kids. And, with any luck, Harriet and Sarah would go out for their usual walk. Her spirits rose as each car pulled away. 'Good riddance!' she muttered as the final one drove off. She was about to move from the window when she spotted another car nosing in through the gates towards the house. Who on earth could *that* be – a guest who'd got the time wrong, or some new and tedious relative? Well, hardly tedious, judging by the car, which was low and sporty-looking and a zingy shade of yellow. She watched the driver climb out: a tall bespectacled man whose face seemed vaguely familiar. At first she couldn't place him, then suddenly the penny dropped. It was Hugo – the chap who ran the gallery in Cheltenham, and Elizabeth's first love. But whatever was he doing *here*, in Kent?

She raced downstairs to find out. She had warmed to Hugo instantly when they'd met at the golf club. He was the kind of man she liked: charming and flirtatious, and much more fun than Emma's stolid husband John, or Caroline's shy Anthony. She ran along the landing, skidding to a halt when she saw Hugo standing in the hall talking to Elizabeth. Something about the pair of them made her feel uneasy. They were standing too close, for one thing, and as she watched, unseen, Hugo slipped his hand into Elizabeth's, edging closer still. Beattie froze in horror. This wasn't the near-stranger Elizabeth had met at the golf club, after a gap of thirty years. It was obvious they'd been seeing each other since then and had renewed their earlier friendship. Except this was more than friendship. They looked like secret lovers, talking in whispers, and still holding hands, for Christ's sake. It was all she could do not to scream out an objection from the landing, or hurtle down and separate them by force.

Yet she had to admit they didn't seem desperately happy. Hugo was shaking his head and frowning, and Elizabeth's face was creased up in concern. She released her hand from his, glanced quickly around, then ushered him into her consulting room. Beattie could hardly contain herself. *No one* went in there – the consulting room was sacrosanct. Why should Hugo have privileges denied to everyone else? She was just frantically debating whether to burst in and surprise them, when Emma emerged from the bathroom and fixed her with her customary critical gaze.

'Have you seen my mother anywhere?' she asked.

'Er, no,' said Beattie. 'Sorry.' She turned her back on Emma and stumbled down the stairs, let herself out of the side door and dashed across the garden. She had no idea where she was going, but knew she had to get away before she did something reckless. Her mind was churning with speculations. And fear. How many times had Hugo driven down here since they'd met him in mid-November? Had he been *invited* today, or just turned up out of the blue? Most important, why had Elizabeth said nothing to her, not so much as mentioned his name? They'd talked for *hours* the day she'd arrived for Christmas, yet all that time Elizabeth had been concealing something central in her life.

She squeezed through the fence and ran towards the beech wood which stretched beyond the garden. She was freezing cold without her coat, and tripping on the uneven ground in her stupid high-heeled shoes. A few people out walking their dogs stared at her in astonishment. She ignored both the cold and the stares. There was too much else to worry about: why had Hugo and Elizabeth been holding hands like that, and what the hell had happened to his wife?

She ran blindly through the trees, which seemed to move in closer, as if to hem her in. She had lost all sense of direction and could see nothing but their tall grey naked trunks. Finally she lurched to a halt, feet hurting, fingers numb. Not only was she out of breath, but it was slowly beginning to dawn on her that there was no point in running away. She would have to return at some stage and face up to what was happening. Elizabeth couldn't deceive her and expect to get away with it. She'd go back now, this instant, and demand an explanation.

By the time she reached the gates of Mile End House, she was almost too cold to think. It was madness to have ventured out on a raw December day in only a thin dress. The sky was overcast still, and although it wasn't much past three o'clock, the light was grey and murky, as if the day had lost all hope and decided to put an end to itself before official twilight. She trudged in through the gates, stopping with a sense of shock. The yellow car had gone. A sudden image flashed into her mind: Elizabeth sitting in the passenger seat beside a triumphant Hugo as the two of them sped along the motorway towards the Channel ports or Heathrow. It made her feel so panicky she almost turned and ran away again. Without Elizabeth, Mile End House was nothing – simply a pile of bricks. She tried to imagine not just the house, but her *life* without Elizabeth.

No, she thought desperately, I *won't* give her up to Hugo. And of course she hasn't left with him. She's safe at home, sitting in the drawing-room with Tolkien on her lap. And I'm going straight in to confront her, to find out what in God's name's going on.

20

Beattie banged the front door, savouring the warmth of the house after the freezing air outside. She rubbed her arms to restore the feeling to them, stamped her feet, blew on her numb fingers. She needed a few moments not only to warm up, but also to prepare herself. It was no good barging in with all guns firing, yelling abuse at Elizabeth, embarrassing her in public. Best to take a quieter approach, but without playing down her sense of betrayal.

She strode into the drawing-room, to find only the two aunts fussing over baby Alexander. She apologized, backed out again. Next she tried the consulting room, knocking loudly on the door. No answer. But there was a sound of voices in Jeremy's study, so she swung round and knocked on *that* door.

'Come in.'

'Sorry,' she mumbled again as she saw Harriet and Sarah sitting on their own, one each side of Jeremy's desk. 'I was looking for Elizabeth. D'you know where she is?'

'No idea,' shrugged Sarah. 'I haven't seen her for ages.'

Beattie edged away, all her fears returning. She walked down to the kitchen, hardly daring to go in. If she drew a blank there too, then went upstairs and found no trace of Elizabeth, how would she bear the terror of not knowing where she'd gone?

She pushed open the door, trying to appear unconcerned. Amidst the blur of faces, Elizabeth's alone sang out, clear in every detail. She suppressed a whoop of joy, smiling dutifully instead at Emma and Amanda, Caroline and Tim, who were sitting round the table sipping tea. Her overwhelming instinct was to seize Elizabeth in her arms, hug her, kiss her, shake her. But she stood silent in the doorway, simply drinking Elizabeth in. She looked reassuringly normal in her frumpy khaki dress, standing at the worktop, whipping up something in a mixing-bowl.

'Heavens, you *are* flushed!' Elizabeth said, raising her voice above the whir of the beater. 'Have you been out for a run?'

Beattie shook her head, then nodded, feeling suddenly disoriented. Everything seemed so *ordinary* – life going on as usual: a saucepan steaming on the hob, the children munching slabs of cake, even Boz back on his cushion by the Aga. Perhaps she'd *imagined* Hugo, experienced some weird hallucination. No – whatever else, she wasn't mad, and anyway she could hardly have invented all the details: the double three on his number-plates, his arty purple tie, Elizabeth's small hand in his large masculine one, their eyes meeting for a moment before both of them looked down, embarrassed.

'E . . . Elizabeth?' she faltered.

'Mm?'

'I wondered if I could possibly have a word with you – on your own, I mean? If you're not too busy, that is.'

She was aware of the unspoken disapproval. Elizabeth *was* busy – anyone could see that – and it was a bloody cheek to impose on her. However, Elizabeth herself seemed unperturbed; immediately put the egg-whisk down and ushered her into the hall.

'Well?' she asked, smiling. 'What's the problem?'

Beattie glanced nervously around. The aunts might be eavesdropping or Harriet and Sarah emerge at any moment from the study. 'Do you mind if we go up to my room?' she asked. 'It's sort of . . . private.'

Elizabeth led the way upstairs, stopping every now and then to move various toys or obstructions from her path. 'Gosh! I really must start clearing up. The house looks as if a bomb's hit it.'

Beattie smiled half-heartedly. Her attention was turned inwards, worrying about what to say. She was determined to sound calm, but once they'd reached the privacy of her room, the words came out in a hysterical rush – angry and accusing words.

Elizabeth stayed silent for a moment, just stood by the window looking down. Then she turned to face Beattie, her expression strained, defensive. '*Nothing*'s going on between us, as you put it, Beattie. I'm merely trying to give Hugo some support. I'm afraid his wife's walked out on him and he's extremely shocked and upset.'

'God! I'm sorry,' Beattie muttered, torn between pity and relief.

It was awful for poor Hugo to be abandoned by his wife, yet she couldn't deny the euphoria she felt. Elizabeth was *hers* still. The fact that she had let him hold her hand was obviously only a comfort thing, just as she held her patients' hands if they were particularly distressed.

'I'm not breaking any confidences in telling you,' Elizabeth assured her, ever the professional. 'Apparently half of Cheltenham knows – which makes it much more painful for him. I know in my *own* case, the constant village gossip was almost as bad as the divorce itself.'

'Has Anna gone for good then?' Beattie asked.

'Well, Hugo seems to think so.'

'And is there another man involved?'

Elizabeth nodded warily, that familiar closed expression coming over her face. Beattie sat down on the bed, trying to swallow her resentment. She knew well enough by now that good therapists never gave away their patients' secrets (even if the patient was a friend), but she felt excluded none the less. How long had this been going on: these furtive visits, these dramatic heart-to-hearts? 'So what's Hugo going to do?' she asked, still wondering why he was in Kent at all.

'He's too depressed to know at present. *I* was just the same. You can't take it in at first, let alone make rational plans.'

Beattie eased off her muddy shoes and kicked them across the room. She had to take her annoyance out on something, though it was *Hugo* she would have liked to kick for dredging up all Elizabeth's grim memories. She herself had been trying to do the opposite: divert her with new pleasures, encourage her to *bury* the past. She also resented Hugo for changing from a charmer to a loser. But that was really callous and unfair and only proved – again – what a heart-less bitch she was. Elizabeth's first instinct had been to offer help and support; *hers* to think solely of herself.

'I'm sorry,' she repeated, trying to mean it this time. 'Is there any way I can help?'

'No, it's sweet of you to offer, Beattie, but there's not much anyone can do. I'm afraid it's just a matter of his accepting the inevitable and trying to adjust to it. Unfortunately, he's started smoking again. It seems such a shame when he managed to give up for so long.'

Beattie refrained from mentioning pots and kettles. Elizabeth smoked thirty a day.

'And he's taken to smoking cigars now, which I'm sure are worse than cigarettes – stronger, anyway. I mean, he gave up in the first place on medical advice, so he really shouldn't . . .'

Beattie pulled irritably at the bedspread. Elizabeth sounded like a fussing mother-hen. 'Where's he gone now?' she asked, hoping the answer would be the Arctic Circle. 'Back to Cheltenham?'

'No, he's staying with a bachelor friend only a few miles away. He can't leave the gallery too long, but he'll certainly be down here over New Year. So I've told him to phone whenever he likes, or to come and join us if he's up to it. The trouble is, other people's celebrations are the last thing you want when you're feeling so utterly wretched.'

Beattie noted the strain in Elizabeth's voice. It was clear that she was identifying with Hugo. They must have exchanged experiences, compared their sense of loss, their jealousy and anger. And she could see the saga continuing for months – or *years*, more likely, once the lawyers got their noses in the trough. 'Did he and Anna have kids?' she asked, dreading the thought of Elizabeth getting increasingly embroiled in battles over custody and access.

'No. He's lucky in that respect – or *un*lucky, I should say. In fact, *very* unlucky as far as having children is concerned. Apparently, his first wife had a lot of trouble conceiving, but refused point-blank to go through all the tests and things when Hugo tried to persuade her. I suspect by then she'd already embarked on her modelling career, and children would have only spoilt her figure. Then, when he married Anna, he was faced with rather the same problem – a glamour girl who didn't seem to understand how much he wanted a family.'

Beattie stared at Elizabeth in surprise. Not only was she giving away confidences, she was also making bitchy remarks – slagging off *both* wives. It was totally out of character, and made her sound jealous and even petty. But of course if she *was* in love with Hugo, then she'd naturally be hostile to all the other women in his life. Could she be concealing the truth, using her role as therapist as a smokescreen for an affair?

She sprang up from the bed. 'Elizabeth, listen – *please*! Can you absolutely swear to me you're not . . . you know . . .'

'What?'

'Involved with Hugo.'

'Beattie, I've never lied to you, and I don't intend to now. Yes, I

215

am involved with Hugo, but only in the sense of providing a friendly ear. You see, when a . . .'

She was interrupted by a tapping on the door. 'Who is it?' she called.

'Only me,' Caroline's head appeared round the door. 'Sorry to disturb you, Mummy, but there's a Hugo Clayton-Brown on the phone, and I wasn't sure if . . .'

'Yes, I'll take it.' Elizabeth was already on her feet.

Beattie tailed her halfway down the stairs, watched her disappear into the consulting room and close the door. No chance of listening in. She hung about on the landing for what seemed like half an hour, making a huge effort to see the situation from Hugo's point of view. Of *course* he needed to talk, and he was lucky to have found someone who was not only trained to listen, but could also understand his pain first-hand. All the same, it hurt. *She* had problems too, yet wasn't allowed to monopolize Elizabeth, or not when all the family were there. One of her chief problems, ironically enough, was Elizabeth herself – this terrifying need for her (which she tried to hide, for fear it would be 'analysed'). It was shameful being so dependent when she had always posed as a self-sufficient woman who lived alone from choice. She had never been the clingy type, nor even very jealous, yet she felt she could literally murder any rival, in order to keep Elizabeth for herself. It would be like an amputation if she lost her – some part of her own body hacked callously away. She dared not tell a soul about such feelings. It would make her sound pathetic, or totally screwed up.

And it *was* pathetic, wasn't it, to stand dithering on the landing like this, imagining the worst. But why was the phone call going on so *long*? Perhaps Hugo was begging Elizabeth to visit, to comfort him in person. And if she did, who knew what might happen; how that 'comfort' might develop?

Too restless to stay still, she mooched downstairs and went into the drawing-room. Aunties Jean and Dora were engrossed with Alexander, one jigging him on her lap while the other billed and cooed at him with a stream of adoring baby-talk.

'Isn't he a *darling*!' Jean exclaimed to Beattie.

'Yes,' she muttered tersely, listening for Elizabeth's footsteps in the hall. If Hugo was in such a state, he was bound to keep phoning all the time. She would never have a moment with Elizabeth, even after the family had gone.

'What's happened to your feet, dear?' Auntie Dora enquired.

Beattie glanced down at her laddered stockings and the red weals on her toes. 'I . . . er . . . went out in the wrong shoes.'

'You shouldn't wear those dreadful high heels, you know – not even indoors. They put a strain on the whole back and can permanently damage the spine. My chiropodist told me always to buy laceups. They support the foot, you see, and . . .'

'Yeah, thanks. I'll remember.' Beattie dashed out of the room. She could hear Elizabeth talking to Amanda just outside the door.

'Is everything all right?' she mouthed, grabbing Elizabeth's arm.

Elizabeth nodded, then returned to the kitchen, Amanda trotting after her. Beattie followed too, and joined the others at the table. Okay, she wasn't wanted, but she didn't intend to let Elizabeth out of her sight. Caroline poured her a cup of tea and offered her some cake. She chewed it mechanically, trying to work out how Hugo's separation would affect her own relationship with Elizabeth. It was horribly selfish to think that way, but she couldn't seem to help it. Her claim on Elizabeth was weak enough already (compared with adorable babies and enchanting five-year-olds), without this added threat. Sometimes she pictured Elizabeth as a beautiful, solid house with several storeys, and *she* was standing on the step, begging to be let in. But Elizabeth couldn't hear – too busy with the other people who occupied her various rooms to admit a tiresome stranger.

She jumped as the phone rang. 'I'll get it,' Elizabeth said, hurrying out of the room.

Beattie watched the door click shut, feeling increasingly despondent. Hugo had only just rung off, yet here he was bothering his 'therapist' again. New Year would be ruined. She'd been dreading it in any case, but with Hugo phoning every other minute, Elizabeth would be out of commission for hours on end. And each private phone call would draw them closer still.

'It's for you, Beattie,' Elizabeth said, returning to the kitchen.

'*Me?*'

'Yes.'

'Who is it?'

'A man. I asked his name, but he wouldn't say.'

Max, she thought, with alarm. She had given him her number under protest, making him promise to ring only in an emergency. Could his wife have died? Perhaps her illness was much worse than anyone had realized. She had no idea how Max would take the news, whether he'd be shocked, distraught, or secretly relieved? And what about the son? She knew he was close to his mother, and also a nervous, insecure type who might react extremely badly to her loss.

She picked up the receiver in the hall, praying Max wouldn't swear or shout. Harriet and Sarah were just coming out of the study and might hear his effing and blinding.

'Hello?' she said apprehensively.

'Hi, sweetie-pie!' boomed Max. 'How're you doing?'

'Er . . . fine. How about you?'

'I'm fucking awful, but never mind. Why I'm ringing is I've got some fantastic news for you: that break you've always wanted. How do you fancy being commissioned to do a piece for the woman's page – and I mean officially commissioned, this time – all expenses paid and a dirty great fee on top?'

Beattie could barely find her voice. Was he *serious*? 'Wh . . . what d'you mean? What sort of piece? And why have they asked *me*?'

'Because I've told them you write a damn sight better than most of the crappy columnists they use, including the prima donnas on a hundred grand a year.'

'Oh, Max, you *didn't*!'

'I did.'

'But how can I live up to it?'

'Look, stop making problems and go and pack your case. You'll need to get your arse to Devon by the day after tomorrow, and I insist on seeing you first – you owe me ten per cent!'

She tried to stall, desperate for more time to think. Why Devon, for God's sake, and what would she say to Elizabeth? 'Max, I'm really sorry, but . . .' she lowered her voice to a whisper, wishing he'd do the same '. . . I'm afraid I'll have my period by then.'

'Sod it!'

'And, anyway, the day after tomorrow's New Year's Eve.'

'Yeah, that's the whole fucking point, my sweet.'

'Oh, I see – it's supposed to be a piece about New Year?'

'Well, it's more complicated than that. But I can't explain it now. There's a crisis on at the moment and I'm up to my bloody eyes.'

'What, you're ringing from the office, you mean?'

Max's only rejoinder was a barrage of instructions, bellowed not at her, but at some dogsbody.

She waited till he'd finished. 'But you told me you had Christmas week off?'

'Well, that's newspapers for you! Thank Christ we didn't go to France. It was just as well you called it off, otherwise they'd have hauled me back to the office in the middle of our first French fuck. It's all right for *some* to fart around in Kent, but I'm working my arse off here.'

'I'm sorry, Max, honestly, but listen, I'm a bit concerned about getting away. You see, there's this big party planned down here and I've said I'd . . .'

'Look, do you want the job or don't you?'

She closed her eyes, saw her name and photograph emblazoned all over the *Herald*; heard the pride in Elizabeth's voice as she showered her with congratulations.

'Yes!' she shouted, no longer caring who was listening. 'Yes, yes, yes, yes, *yes*!'

21

Beattie parked outside the community centre and walked up to the entrance, her stomach churning with fear and elation at embarking on her first assignment as a professional journalist; the piece scheduled for next Thursday's woman's page. She could still hardly believe that a national newspaper with a circulation of over a million had actually commissioned her to write for them – a million plus people sitting over their breakfast next week, engrossed in Beattie Bancroft's deathless prose.

She stopped abruptly on the bottom step. But suppose it *isn't* deathless, she thought – or, worse, never sees the light of day at all. Max had told her that pieces were frequently spiked, even those by well-known columnists. She stared bleakly at the placard on the door: 'WELCOME TO FIRCROFT', and was tempted for an instant to jump into the car and hurtle back to London – to safety and stagnation.

'Hi there!' called a friendly voice behind her. 'Have you come for the rebirthing?'

She turned to see a large and rather shapeless-looking woman walking towards the building, her face only a blur in the darkness.

'Yes,' she called back. 'I know I'm a bit early, but . . .'

'Best to get here early, especially in this weather. Freezing, isn't it?'

'Mm,' said Beattie, sweating from sheer nerves.

The woman extended a welcoming hand. 'I'm Monica, one of the assistant trainers. It's really great to meet you. I don't know your face. You must be new.'

Beattie nodded, holding the door politely. Dead right – she *was* new: new to the whole weird set-up here, new to this benighted part of Devon, and a complete novice in the newspaper world.

'Have you done any rebirthing before?' Monica asked as they stepped into the entrance hall.

'Not really.' She daren't admit that she hadn't even *heard* of it until Max had phoned a second time to explain the details of the job. He had given her some bumph on the subject in general and a leaflet on this specific weekend course, and she'd also tried to do some homework of her own. But there hadn't been much time, and anyway, the few books she did manage to find were wildly at variance with each other. One, written in breathless California-speak, had described rebirthing as a biological experience of God, more pleasurable than food or even sex. Another, more sober, English tome had called it merely a method of conscious controlled breathing, designed to release the birth trauma.

Elizabeth took a different view again. 'It could be very dangerous, Beattie. Reliving one's birth is often quite traumatic in itself, and I honestly don't advise you to get mixed up in it.'

'But I'm only going as an observer,' she'd protested, 'you know, to send the whole thing up. I shan't get personally involved – no fear!'

As luck would have it, Hugo had phoned while they were arguing the toss, and for once she had welcomed his call. She didn't want Elizabeth ruining her first big chance before she'd so much as uncapped her pen. Well, it wouldn't be a pen. Max had lent her his laptop, so she could bang the thing out on Sunday night, should she feel the urge.

'Come and meet the others,' Monica smiled, taking off her duffel coat. Underneath she appeared to be wearing pyjamas – a faded blue pair worn incongruously with several strings of beads.

Beattie followed her into a large institutional hall, where at least a dozen people, mostly women, were greeting each other with what could only be described as rapture; kissing and embracing with near-orgasmic squeals of delight.

She stopped in her tracks, daunted by the passionate hugs, and also embarrassingly aware that her clothes were totally wrong. The leaflet had advised casual, comfortable gear, so she'd rushed off and bought a tracksuit in pink and purple velour. It had looked casual enough in the shop, but here it stood out as glaringly smart and new. Most other people were just in jeans or leggings, with tatty sweatshirts on top, and not a trace of make-up, whereas *she*'d put on the full works: lipstick, blusher, eye-gloss and mascara.

'Excuse me a moment,' she muttered, as Monica seized her arm and was about to march her into the mêlée. 'I need the . . . er . . . loo.'

'It's the first door on the left,' said Monica, pointing back the way they'd come.

'Thanks,' said Beattie, bolting straight out to the car. She had to change her clothes, scrub off all the make-up. The last thing she needed was to look conspicuous. Max had told her on no account to reveal she was a journalist – the slightest whiff of the press and they'd probably throw her out.

She wrenched the car into gear and careered off back to the hotel. The night was eerily dark, the landscape bleak and lonely. This tiny village was the last outpost of civilization before the wilds took over: a huge expanse of moorland stretching almost to the sea. She suddenly felt homesick: homesick for the now familiar countryside of Kent; homesick for Elizabeth. If only they hadn't parted on bad terms. Elizabeth was still worried about the effects of the rebirthing, and also disapproved of her intention to satirize a group of people who were committed and sincere, and even more of her underhand methods (posing as an ordinary course-member, instead of coming clean and admitting why she was there). The ground-rules for any kind of therapy, she had pointed out with unusual tartness, were openness and honesty.

She swung left into the narrow lane which zigzagged to the Huntley Arms. Elizabeth was so naïve in some ways, especially about the newspaper world. All the same, she wished they hadn't quarrelled. She had enough on her mind as it was, particularly the nagging fear that she might not prove up to the job. Originally, the *Herald* had commissioned a top-drawer Cambridge graduate with fifteen years' experience as a freelance, who also happened to be an expert on alternative therapies and had written witty pieces on everything from radionics to rolfing. But two days after Christmas she'd gone down with Asian 'flu, so Max had intervened, saying he knew *exactly* the right person to take over: a terrific writer with a fresh and unconventional approach, and the raunchy voice of youth.

She turned into the hotel car-park and left the car slap outside the door. *Youth*, for heaven's sake, when she was pushing thirty-one! But Max had gone completely over the top, telling the editor she was talented and brilliant, even though she was barely out of college. She was terrified she'd disappoint them both, especially as her period was late, so she still felt pretty lousy. But Max had come up trumps again and promised to knock the piece into shape himself before she sent it off. So she couldn't really lose.

Yet as she walked into the smart hotel with its thick-pile carpet and bowls of hothouse flowers, all her fears resurfaced. A single room here cost ninety pounds a night, paid for by the *Herald*, of course. Was she really worth it – *and* worth all the rest: her meals en route, her petrol allowance, and the exorbitant cost of the course itself (to say nothing of her fee)?

As she waited for the lift, two young couples in evening dress passed her in the corridor, presumably on their way to some New Year's celebration. Her mind swooped back to Kent once more. The family would be preparing for *their* party – a big do at Caroline's. To tell the truth, she wasn't sorry to miss it. She might be quaking with nerves about her own freakish New Year's Eve, but better that than a lot of Auld Lang Syne-ing with people who disliked her.

She unlocked her bedroom door and scrabbled through her suitcase, which was still sitting on the bed, waiting to be unpacked. *None* of her clothes seemed suitable, and she couldn't even follow Monica's example and put on her pyjamas. They were see-through, for one thing, and the neck was far too low. In the end, she kept her tracksuit bottoms on, but changed the appliqué top for a plain white tee-shirt. Next she dived into the bathroom and set about removing her make-up, cursing the indelible puce lipstick she had bought to match the tracksuit.

Five minutes later she was downstairs again. She stepped out of the lift, pausing by the door of the bar. A drink would give her courage, and anyway, she could have a last quick glance through the rebirthing information before returning to the fray. Armed with a double brandy, she sat at a table in the corner and took the leaflet from her bag. The course was being run by an American – Chuck Masters, who apparently believed in something called physical immortality, which meant he didn't intend to die. Well, that would make a perfect start for her piece – Live-Forever Chuck, who, according to the blurb, had healed his own birth trauma in a three-day rebirthing marathon way back in the seventies, and since then had grown younger every year. He must be a mere child by now, although the photo showed a bearded man with thinning hair and bags under his eyes.

She gulped her drink, scanning the names of the 'assistant trainers' and the details of the timetable. At the foot of the last page was printed in bold capitals:

NOW IS THE TIME TO TRANSFORM YOUR FONDEST DESIRES FROM FANTASY TO REALITY. YOU CAN TRULY HAVE IT ALL!

Great! she thought, downing the last of her brandy and striding to the door. That's absolutely fine by me.

Back at the centre, she sidled into the hall once more. The brandy had given her courage, and, by God, she needed it. The original dozen participants had swelled to a sizeable crowd and the room had taken on a churchy air, which was unsettling, to say the least. She found herself choking on a cloud of incense; her ears assaulted by solemn music booming from a cassette player. A cluster of joss-sticks were burning on a long low table, set up like an altar, with two lighted candles and a picture of an Indian guru, wreathed in plastic flowers. The 'congregation', however, were in more of a party mood, either standing around chatting in animated groups, or sprawled on the floor munching chocolate bars or apples. A good deal of hugging was also still in progress. In fact, judging by the time and effort devoted to it, hugging should have featured on the timetable as an officially scheduled activity.

She scanned the hall for Monica, her only point of contact in this intimidating herd of strangers, but there was no sign of her blue pyjamas. Though a few more *men* were now in evidence – rather peculiar types for the most part, including a punk-haired lad stretched out on a blanket in the corner, either fast asleep or in some sort of trance.

She took a hesitant step forward, whereupon two of the huggers hurried across to say hello, introducing themselves as Karen and Patricia. Whatever else, rebirthers were certainly friendly. Both women embraced her eagerly and promised to look after her when they discovered she was new.

'You'll never forget this weekend,' enthused Karen, a motherly type with a buxom figure and kindly blue eyes. 'My first rebirth utterly transformed me. I used to be an agoraphobic and I'd just sit at home crying all the time. Now there aren't enough hours in the day!' She clasped her friend's hand, smiling. 'And tell Beattie what happened to *you*, Patricia.'

Patricia was much younger and had stunning chestnut hair, reaching almost to her waist. 'Well, my first husband walked out after just three months of marriage, and my second used to beat me up. Before I discovered rebirthing, I just accepted all the misery because I saw myself as a victim – until I met Karen, that is. She took me to her own rebirther and that was a turning-point in my life.'

'She's overtaken *me* now,' Karen added. 'She's training to be a rebirther herself.'

Beattie did her best to memorize the details. It would all make marvellous copy, though she only wished she could record it here and now. She would have to stay up late each night jotting down everything she could. 'Whoa!' she almost shouted as Patricia launched into an account of her various rebirths: ten with a woman, ten with a man, three under water and seven in a group.

Then Karen took over, giving the date, venue and outcome of each of her *own* rebirths.

Beattie listened in surprise. She had assumed that a *single* rebirth was all you·needed, but evidently you could go on repeating the process more or less indefinitely.

'And in July we're going to the States together,' Patricia said excitedly. 'To San Francisco, the place where it all started.'

'Oh, that reminds me – where's Chuck?' asked Beattie, looking around for the bearded American guru.

'But surely you've heard? He's not coming after all. They announced it a few minutes ago. I'm afraid he's had a heart attack and was rushed to hospital. Everyone's desperately disappointed.'

The immortal struck down, Beattie mused wryly. Max would never *believe* this, not in a thousand years. 'What's going to happen, then?' she asked. 'Is someone else running the course?'

'Willow,' whispered Karen, gesturing to a skinny woman standing on their left. 'We're terribly lucky to get her. She rebirthed with Leonard Orr himself.'

Beattie had never heard of him, but judging by the reverence in Karen's voice, he was obviously some high priest of the movement.

'And considering she's stepped in at only two hours' notice, *and* on New Year's Eve, we've really got to support her all the way.'

Beattie murmured in agreement, her attention now distracted by a strikingly handsome man who was arranging chairs in a large circle, helped by two young girls. 'When do we start?' she asked.

'Oh, any minute now. Willow's not a great stickler for time – she prefers to go with the flow. I'll introduce you, shall I? She likes to meet the new people and have a little talk with them about why they're here and what they're hoping to get out of the course. This is a very personal training, you see, and how you interact with her could make all the difference to what you gain from the weekend.'

'Okay,' said Beattie nervously, making her face a guileless mask. But Willow barely glanced at her face; instead drew her into a protracted hug, which she found highly disconcerting. If *Elizabeth* had embraced her in such an intimate way, she would have responded passionately, but this woman was a total stranger. Besides, she didn't like the feeling of her emaciated body. Whereas Elizabeth was exquisitely frail, Willow was merely bony, with no breasts, no hips, no ounce of surplus flesh. She finally disengaged herself, but the contact wasn't over. Willow stood gazing at her with embarrassing intensity, as if she could penetrate the mask and see the lies and the deception. Beattie squirmed in irritation. These people carried on as if they were *lovers*, for God's sake. And for all she knew, they *were* – although the shortage of men might make things rather difficult. She had counted only seven so far, compared with thirty or forty females.

One of the males came rushing up to Willow at that moment, reporting that someone called Melissa had just phoned to say her car had broken down. 'Shall we wait for her?' he asked.

'No, I don't think it's fair to the others,' Willow replied. 'Some of them are already getting restive. I suggest we start straight away. Can you ask everyone to sit down.'

Beattie was riveted by Willow's voice, which she had expected to be small and feeble, in keeping with her tiny frame; on the contrary, it was melodiously deep and surprisingly assured. She might resemble a starveling sparrow, but there was also something of the eagle in her.

'Come on,' said Karen, 'let's bag some seats. I don't fancy sitting on the floor.'

She and Patricia ushered Beattie over to the circle of chairs and sat one on either side of her. She was glad of their company, and also extremely thankful that Willow hadn't asked her any questions – in fact, she hadn't said a word. Was that simply because she'd been interrupted, or because she'd realized at first glance that here was a traitor in their midst, unworthy of the usual 'little talk'? There wasn't time to speculate since Karen and Patricia were plying her with questions, some of them highly personal. Was she in a relationship, Patricia wanted to know. Beattie debated whether to tell them about Max. She could pretend he was her age and single – invent a new persona for him, as well as for herself. Except she felt distinctly uneasy even mentioning his name to two devotees of rebirthing when he'd been so scathing about it. He had dismissed the whole thing as a con and its practitioners as neurotic navel-gazers with more money than sense. In fact, Max was best left firmly back in London, especially after last night, when she had given him his 'reward' for getting her the commission. He personally was very pleased her period was late, so that she could gratify his every kinky whim.

'Well, there *is* a guy,' she began, 'but . . .'

'Right, we're starting!' yelled the good-looking man, rounding up the stragglers who were forced to sit on the scratchy brown cord carpet, since all the chairs were taken.

Willow followed more slowly, taking up her position in the centre of the circle, her limp fair hair falling over her eyes. Beattie found it hard to guess her age. Her pre-pubescent figure made her look joltingly young, but her face was gaunt and strained, and there were lines beneath her expressive grey-green eyes.

'Welcome!' she said in her ringing voice. 'It's wonderful to see you all. We weren't sure how many people would turn up on New Year's Eve. We feared you might all be rushing off to parties.'

A few people laughed, as if the very idea was absurd, and a man in pink leggings gave a nervous throaty cough.

'Actually, we chose the date deliberately because New Year is the perfect time for rebirthing. All those resolutions we keep making, but somehow never get round to keeping, can really *work* this year, once we succeed in giving birth to the person we were truly meant to be. In fact, we're hoping this weekend will prove to be a very special celebration in itself.'

Hear, hear, said Beattie silently, thinking of her new career.

'Many of you here,' continued Willow, 'already know the great benefits of rebirthing. It can heal a host of physical conditions, from haemorrhoids and acne to cancer and arthritis. That may sound an extravagant claim, but you see, a lot of diseases stem directly from the birth trauma. And sometimes we *cling* to our illnesses so that we

227

can play the role of helpless infant and use doctors as mother-substitutes. But rebirthing offers us the chance to break out of that cycle. I've seen people cured in just ten minutes of conditions they've been suffering from for ten or twenty years. The disease is literally pumped out of the body with the breath.'

So we're into the miracle business, Beattie reflected cynically. If the cures were as dramatic as Willow said, why hadn't the medical profession latched on to them – or the general public, for that matter? A pity her mother hadn't been on a course like this, then she needn't have died of multiple sclerosis.

'And it's just as effective with psychological problems. You don't need to spend a fortune on therapy. If you go to a shrink, it may take years and years – poking around your psyche, analysing everything, trying to "understand" it – but rebirthing allows you to throw out all that garbage in one fell swoop.'

Beattie suppressed a smile. Elizabeth, in her therapist's role, had attacked the rebirthers' methods, and they in turn attacked hers. Presumably shrinks and rebirthers were fighting for the same clients, the same small pool of cash, so no wonder they had to do each other down.

'Now, before I tell you any more about what I call Divine Orgasm and Pure Bliss, I'd like us all to introduce ourselves. Each person simply says their name, and tells us very briefly something they know about their birth, then shares with us their goal for the weekend.'

Beattie tensed in alarm. So much for her hopes of remaining anonymous.

'I'll start,' said Willow, 'to give you the idea. My name is Willow – your first name's enough, by the way – and I was born by Caesarian section, which left me feeling that I couldn't do things for myself, but always needed outside help, someone to "rescue" me, or take over. I'm glad to say I've conquered that, and my goal for the weekend is to help you come to terms with your *own* births and the wrong conclusions you might have drawn from them.'

Everyone applauded, Beattie joining in a little late, once she grasped the form.

'Isn't she amazing?' Karen whispered.

Beattie nodded, still working out what to say herself. Luckily it was nowhere near her turn. They were going round the circle clockwise, starting with a woman sitting opposite.

'I'm Donna, and my birth was perfectly normal. The only problem

228

was the Irish midwife was humming "It's a long way to Tipperary" through a good part of the process, which drove my mother nuts!'

Donna waited for the laughter to subside, then continued in the same jokey way. 'My goal is to attract loads of money into my life, so I can afford more rebirthing weekends.'

Beattie warmed to Donna. She, too, wanted loads of cash, though for rather different reasons. Again, she joined in the applause too late, only realizing now that *everyone* was clapped, not simply the trainer.

'I'm Jon – without an h. I was born with the cord looped round my neck, which has left me with a sense of struggle. Oh, and I've always hated wearing ties! My goal is to let go and trust the Universe.'

More applause.

'I'm Geraldine. My birth was a total disaster from beginning to end, and everything that could go wrong *did* go wrong. As a result, my mother felt no love for me. My goal is to learn to love *myself* and to try to . . .'

A blood-curdling scream cut through her soft voice, followed by a succession of shorter screams, no less terrifying. Beattie almost jumped out of her skin. Every eye was directed at the screamer: a small dark man sitting cross-legged on the floor, still emitting violent yells.

Willow's expression remained completely unperturbed, as she walked over and knelt in front of him. She held his face in both her hands and smiled at him serenely. Gradually his wild shrieks subsided into sobs. Beattie watched in astonishment. She had never seen a man cry, let alone in public – there must be fifty people in the room. But maybe this was a normal part of rebirthing. In any case, it would make fantastic copy. She could even open her piece with the scream, get it off to a rousing start.

However, nothing more transpired for several minutes, except a whispered dialogue between Willow and the man. And then suddenly he started laughing – his laughter almost as hysterical as his screams. He must be really disturbed, thought Beattie nervously, although everybody else seemed delighted by his change of mood and broke into spontaneous applause. Willow kissed him on the forehead, then returned to her position in the centre of the circle, whereupon the introductions continued as if nothing had happened to disrupt them.

'I'm Jo . . .'

'I'm Monica . . .'

'I'm Anne-Marie . . .'

'I'm Patricia . . .'

Oh God! thought Beattie, it's *my* turn.

'I'm . . . er . . . Beattie,' she stuttered, as everyone turned to smile at her. 'And my birth was . . .' She broke off in confusion. Her mother had made a mess of the birth, the same way she had cocked up her whole life, but she didn't intend pursuing *that* depressing saga. 'Well, actually, I . . . I don't know what it was like. My mother never told me and she's dead now, I'm afraid.'

'Don't worry, Beattie,' Willow soothed. 'You'll find powerful memories coming up as you relive the birth experience. Often we suppress the memories deliberately because they're simply too traumatic. But once we've succeeded in releasing them, we're free to live in peace, without all our former hang-ups and defences.'

'Oh, good,' said Beattie, uncomfortably aware of Karen's hand coiling into her own and giving it a sympathetic squeeze.

'And what about your goal, Beattie?' Willow prompted.

'Ah yes, my goal . . .' Beattie cleared her throat to play for time. She wished she could release not her birth trauma, but Karen's clammy hand. 'To . . . er . . . get to know more about rebirthing,' she finally murmured lamely.

The applause was thunderous. Lame or no, it appeared to be the right response, and now Patricia clasped her other hand. Beattie felt a total idiot sitting there with her hands trapped, while the entire circle beamed at her. She realized she was blushing like a school-girl, and even when it was Karen's turn to speak, she missed most of what was said, except the final bit about breast-feeding and inner hunger.

'That phrase "inner hunger" is crucial, you know,' Willow interjected. 'Some of us feel empty all our lives, as a direct result of what happened at our birth. You see, in the womb we're safe and snug and have all the nourishment we need, but we're born into a harsh, cold world, with glaring lights and booming voices and clumsy obstetricians slapping us on the back. If the cord is cut too quickly and we take in our first breath with a sense of pain or panic, we may conclude "life's a struggle", or "I can't get enough air". We then go on to feel a *constant* lack. There's not enough of anything, whether it's love, or food, or sex, or time, or attention.'

'I know exactly what you mean,' Jo said feelingly. 'I'm sure that's why I used to be so fat. However much I stuffed myself, I still felt basically empty, and I'd bolt my food like a starving dog, in case someone snatched it away.'

Beattie glanced at Jo's slim figure – she must be another of the success stories. But if all these people like Patricia, Karen, and now Jo, were cured or transformed or whatever, why did they keep coming back?

'What we need to realize,' Willow emphasized, 'is that our birth experience can make an enormous difference to how we see the world. If it's a *negative* experience, we may go on to lead an unfulfilling life, or even be downright miserable. For example, if we're put into an incubator, we might feel a sense of abandonment, or believe we have to crash through a glass wall to get any love or contact. Or a forceps delivery could leave us with a strong fear of manipulation, combined with a continual feeling of inadequacy. Or it may give us chronic headaches, and make us feel that life's a headache itself.'

'But what if we had a normal birth?' Donna interrupted.

'Well, we could grow up to feel we're very ordinary, and find ourselves deliberately creating drama in our life.'

'That's me!' said Donna, laughing.

You can't win, thought Beattie, if even a normal birth fucks you up. Actually, she was damned lucky to have a commission like this – it was a piece of cake, a laugh a minute. She could have been asked to write about something really dreary, like waste-disposal units, or the shortage of nursery schools. The only problem was, the *Herald* had specified fifteen hundred words, and she already had enough material to write a *book*, for heaven's sake.

The introductions continued with three foreigners in turn: a Malayan girl, a man from Yugoslavia and a Polish woman with so little English she couldn't progress much beyond her name. Rebirthing was clearly international. In fact, Patricia had said earlier that she'd done a few of her sessions in Germany, and one or two in Greece, and then there was her trip to San Francisco. Why had no one mentioned Chuck, Beattie wondered suddenly? Surely Willow should have apologized for his absence in her introductory talk, or explained that she was standing in for him, for the benefit of those (like her) who had missed the first announcement. Maybe his heart attack was too much of an embarrassment, undermining the whole spirit of the weekend, which emphasized renewal, not decay.

'Now,' said Willow, moving to the back of the hall and standing by the picture of the guru. 'I want everyone to come up here and pick a card. Don't agonize about it – just take the one you feel is right. And it *will* be right, I assure you. Your choice is divinely inspired.'

Beattie trooped up with the others, inspecting the array of cards laid face-down on the carpet. They weren't playing-cards, nor Tarot cards, nor any cards she'd ever seen before, but had dramatic pictures on the back of goddesses and wizards, mythic beasts and birds. She picked a scarlet dragon and returned with it to her seat.

'Each card has a number on it,' Willow was explaining. 'And that number determines who will be your buddy for the course. You'll be doing a rebirthing with your buddy, and looking after each other throughout the whole weekend, so that person's very special. How it works is this: one and two pair up, and three and four, and five and six, and so on up to forty-eight. We've got forty-eight people on the course, including the assistants. So just spend a few moments now finding your buddy, and whoever they turn out to be, rejoice, because it's *meant*. That person has been chosen for you at a karmic level because you *need* them in some special way – maybe to help you with your spiritual growth, or to release certain blocks, or perhaps to mirror something in yourself which you couldn't see on your own.'

Beattie turned her card over: number twenty-two. She was reminded irreverently of Bingo: twenty-two, two little ducks. Well, where was her fellow duck? She could hardly wait to find him – or to start her article. With material as good as this, even a novice couldn't fail. And 'buddy' – what a word! So American and *twee*, probably imported by Chuck. Poor Chuck, she thought – languishing in hospital and missing all the fun. Everyone was milling around calling their numbers out loud, as if involved in some party game. Well, all except the Polish woman, who was clearly at a loss. One of the assistants was trying vainly to explain the process to her, and also to the bewildered-looking Malayan girl. They needed a simultaneous translation system, like they had at business conferences (and someone to translate for *her* terms like 'karmic level' and 'spiritual growth').

'Has anyone got twenty-two?' the small dark man was clamouring – the one who'd screamed so wildly, and had later introduced himself as Jazz.

Oh God! thought Beattie, not *him*. She'd been hoping to get Monica, or Karen or Patricia – someone safe and supportive. To tell the truth, she felt quite scared of Jazz. He had a frightening look about him, as if he wasn't right in the head. She approached him reluctantly, proffering her card.

'Brilliant!' he said. 'I hoped it would be you.'

'Why?' she asked uneasily.

'Because you're a bloody attractive woman – that's why.'

'Gosh, thanks,' she muttered, though she couldn't return the compliment. Jazz was little more than five-foot-four, with lank greasy hair and pimply skin. She certainly didn't fancy him as her midwife, but if it had been decreed by the Powers Above, who was she to complain?

'What star sign are you, Beattie?' he asked, pawing her with a small sweaty hand.

'Virgo.'

'Great! I'm Pisces with Virgo rising, so we should really hit it off.'

She mumbled some inanity, suddenly realizing that it *was* great. Why go for someone *safe* as her buddy, when fate had offered her this screwball, who would provide her with marvellous copy all weekend? Elsewhere in the room, other buddies were falling on each other's necks, fondling, stroking, groping. If the course hadn't called itself Rebirthing, she might have been forgiven for thinking she'd stumbled into an orgy.

Willow and the assistants helped the last few people who hadn't yet found their buddies (either through language difficulties, or because – as one man claimed – there were two number thirties but no twenty-nine). Eventually everyone was sorted out, then instructed to sit in pairs – on the floor or in two facing chairs – and keep eye-contact with their buddy.

'We're going to give you some paper and a box of coloured crayons, and I want you each to draw yourself as a new-born baby, just seconds after your birth.'

'I can't draw,' objected Denise, one of the oldest women there, a tall imposing type with iron-grey hair scooped up in a chignon.

'Everyone can draw,' Willow countered serenely. '*And* sing and write and paint. We just grow up to believe we can't. Anyway, the point of this exercise is not how well we draw. It's to convey what sort of baby we felt we were at birth – insecure, or frightened, or full of rage, or starving. Then you swap your picture with your buddy's and try to interpret what you see in each other's drawing – what you feel the mood is, what impression's coming over to you.'

'Help!' Jazz hissed at her. '*I* was born with only one kidney and half my lower bowel missing. How the hell do I draw *that*?'

And how do I interpret it? Beattie wondered, gloating inwardly. This was getting better and better.

'We're also going to give you notebooks, so you can jot down anything you're told which provides an insight for you. In fact, we encourage you to take notes the whole weekend – after each rebirthing, for example, then you can record whatever comes up for you.'

Brilliant! Beattie crowed, borrowing Jazz's word. Fate truly was benign. Now she could scribble down everything that happened without arousing any suspicions.

She opened her box of crayons, chose the brightest one she could see, and drew a perfect new-born baby, with *nothing* missing, and an extra-large brain. Only *she* could interpret it – this was the baby she was meant to be: the journalist, the genius, who would be born to huge acclaim this very weekend.

22

Beattie stared in horror at the screen. If this was natural childbirth, she'd opt for drugs and epidurals, even a general anaesthetic. It was obvious that the mother was in agony; the camera switching gloatingly from close-ups of her contorted face to shots of the baby's head emerging. Judging by the screams, it would be born any second now, in full gory Technicolor. Beattie hid her eyes, and when she looked again, the slimy infant had been placed in its mother's arms. The mother looked ecstatic, but *she* felt nauseated. How could anyone want to cuddle such a repulsive blood-stained mess? As far as she was concerned, the human race should have long ago progressed beyond this primitive stage and learnt to have their babies by some more hygienic and less painful method – or, better still, not have them at all. She was clearly in the minority, though: a cold unnatural woman, devoid of the maternal urge. Everybody else seemed to be sobbing with emotion.

'Wasn't that beautiful?' whispered Monica, as the curtains were drawn back and daylight filtered into the hall once more.

'Mm,' said Beattie, who was sitting next to Monica, with Jazz the other side. The purpose of the video was to demonstrate an ideal birth: soft lights, no anaesthesia and a loving obstetrician who greeted the baby the moment it arrived: 'Welcome to our wonderful world!' Apparently it *worked*. Babies born without the usual trauma developed into happy balanced adults.

She wished she could believe it – wished even more that they could do some actual rebirthing. How could she write a piece about it when she hadn't yet witnessed a single rebirth? They had been cooped up in this over-heated hall until ten o'clock last night and a good six hours today, but most of that time had been spent doing exercises in pairs or groups, and then 'sharing' any insights. (Sharing here meant endless talk about embarrassingly personal problems.) They'd also spent ages on breathing – first the theory, which made it sound more complicated than space travel; then the practice, working through a whole set of variations on something called conscious connected breaths. For thirty years she had managed to breathe quite automatically, without sparing the process a thought, but by the time she'd mastered such contortions as breathing through the nose with the tongue between the teeth and the lips closed, she had come to realize it was a rarefied skill.

It had been followed by an hour of 'affirmations', which seemed alarmingly close to brain-washing. You had to tell yourself you were beautiful, or incredibly rich, or talented, or immortal, regardless of whether it was true. Apparently the mind would accept more or less anything you fed into it, so long as you repeated it often enough. They'd each had to choose a dozen affirmations and write them out twenty or thirty times, like being given lines at school. Hers had been completely over the top, since she'd copied them from Monica, who in turn had acquired them from Chuck.

'I love myself and the whole universe, and the whole universe loves me.'

'I feel blissful all the time.'

'I rejoice in everlasting life – my body renews itself totally and eternally.'

Well, if they all came true, she wouldn't need commissions from the *Herald*. Alas, the reality was rather different. There was still no sign of her period, so she was feeling as tense as ever, and also starving hungry. Meal-breaks on this course were few and far between, and the food was mainly cold and wholly vegetarian. Now she understood why Willow was so thin. She wasn't anorexic, merely on a 'health diet' which forbade almost every kind of normal food, even many fruits and vegetables. She drank nothing but hot water, and had toasted the New Year in a cup of steaming H_2O, while the rest of them sipped non-alcoholic punch. Beattie grinned, despite herself. This was the first New Year's Day in fifteen years she wasn't suffering from a hangover, so perhaps she should be grateful for small mercies.

'If only *I* could have been born like that,' Jazz was saying wistfully, 'instead of being pumped full of drugs and then carted off to intensive care.'

'Well, now's your chance to overcome the trauma,' Willow told him gently, 'because we're going to do a group rebirth.'

Beattie was thankful for some action, at last. She was aware of a subtle change in mood; an air of barely suppressed excitement as the assistants started moving the chairs and spreading sleeping-bags and blankets on the floor. Soothing music floated from the cassette player and more joss-sticks were lit, emitting a heady smell of sandalwood and musk. Several people had already stretched out on the rugs and were making themselves comfortable with pillows and duvets.

'Just lie anywhere you want,' instructed Willow, 'No, Denise, you don't have to pair up with your buddy. We'll be doing the buddy rebirth tomorrow. This is a group rebirth, which means we all do it on our own, and yet together. The assistants and I are here to help and support you, and we'll be going round the room making sure you're all okay and reminding you of the breathing. You look a bit cramped there, Patricia. Why not move into this larger space – that's it. Right, is everybody settled?'

Beattie chose a place in the corner, hoping it would be relatively inconspicuous. She lay back on her rug and pulled the two patchwork covers right up to her chin. Thank God Max wasn't here to see her. She imagined him making some crack about her enjoying a siesta in the middle of the afternoon and passing it off as work. But it *was* work – serious work – and she was already worried about missing crucial details. She couldn't take notes while she was lying on the floor cocooned in blankets, and anyway it was difficult to see much because the curtains had been drawn once more, plunging the hall into the same twilight gloom as when they'd watched the video. She only hoped she'd stay awake. She had hardly slept at all last night – the Huntley Arms had laid on a New Year's Eve dinner-dance which had lasted till the early hours. She had felt distinctly out of things: a Cinderella not invited to the ball. Her double bed was too big just for her, the room too stiff and formal, and she had lain awake thinking enviously of the others, whose sleeping arrangements involved a lot less luxury but a good deal more companionship. No one else was booked into a hotel. One large contingent had clubbed together and hired a house in the village; quite a few were local (including Monica and Willow), and those who came from farther afield had somehow managed to cadge a bed from Willow's friends and neighbours. Still, at least she had escaped Jazz. After half an hour's acquaintance, he had asked her to sleep with him, though she wasn't sure whether it was sex he wanted, or merely someone to comfort him when he woke from his nightmares (which he had described in graphic detail during one of the 'sharing' sessions).

'Now let me just remind you,' Willow was saying in a softer voice than before – a hypnotic tone in keeping with the darkened room – 'the purpose of rebirthing is to re-experience the moment of that first breath you took as an infant, and to release the trauma of it. You may feel some pain or fear, but simply breathe it out and let it go. All discomfort in rebirthing comes from holding on to misery. If you allow new energy to flow in, any panic or distress will be swept away by the breath.'

All around, Beattie heard the exaggerated mouth-breathing they had been practising earlier on. The noise was like a gentle bellows, which gradually grew stronger. Not wanting to arouse suspicion, she made a show of doing it herself, although she hated breathing in that forced unnatural way. It made her feel dizzy and light-headed, when really she needed to concentrate on what was going on. It would make a fantastic scene for her article: the huddled shapes lying in the gloom, the soft background music competing with the wheezing noises, and the assistants creeping round from prone body to prone body, whispering instructions and encouragement. One of these assistants tiptoed up to her: a dumpy woman called Sylvia, with unflattering thick glasses and hair cut in a bob.

'All right, Beattie?' she murmured.

'Yes, fine,' she whispered, quickly breathing with new vigour.

'Don't breathe quite so fiercely,' Sylvia cautioned. 'Otherwise you'll hurt your throat. And try not to pause between the inhale and the exhale. It's *continuous* breath, remember, pet.'

Pet, thought Beattie, suppressing a grin – a new endearment to add to 'darling', 'love' and 'sweetheart'. (Rebirthers used such terms continually, to help create an atmosphere of what they called unconditional love.)

'That's good, pet,' Sylvia whispered. 'But try to relax more as you breathe.'

It was almost impossible to relax when the man beside her was threshing about in his blanket-cocoon, shrieking abuse at some invisible midwife. And he wasn't the only one. The noise was getting louder all the time – sudden screams and cries, people retching as if they were about to choke or vomit, and one girl howling like an animal. Willow had assured them that all pain and panic would be swept away by the breath, but the hall seemed *full* of pain, and she was beginning to find it frightening. She was relieved when Sylvia moved on and she could snatch a rest from the breathing. No one else seemed to need a break, though the breathing noises had become extremely fraught and laboured, like the mother on the video, just seconds before giving birth.

'What's wrong, darling?' whispered Colin – another of the assistants, now hovering beside her.

'Er, nothing.'

'Are you finding the breathing difficult?'

'Y . . . yes, I am, a bit.'

'Maybe you're afraid to face your birth trauma. That often happens the first time. It all seems too overwhelming, so you resist unconsciously.'

Beattie nodded. Colin was probably right. She had no desire to dredge up painful memories from the past. There was enough trauma in ordinary adult life without returning to the maternity ward. And anyway, she mustn't lose her professional detachment when she was being paid so highly to maintain it. 'Look, I'm perfectly all right.'

'I don't feel you *are*, love. I'm aware of you holding back. Can you open your mouth a bit wider? That'll help to relax your jaw.'

'I'd rather do it on my *own*, if that's okay.'

'But, don't you see, Beattie, that's your whole problem? If you were induced or born by Caesarean, you *couldn't* do it on your own, so ever since then, you've probably insisted on your independence, even if it meant missing out on love or intimacy.'

She grunted in response. Conversation wasn't easy when it had to be conducted in a stagey whisper and against a background of disturbing noises from elsewhere in the hall. The man beside her was still fighting with his midwife, judging by his continued violent flailing movements and the fury in his voice.

Colin leaned closer to make himself heard. '*Did* you have a difficult birth, Beattie?'

She shook her head and tried to relax her jaw. It was simpler to obey than argue. And then unaccountably she started to yawn – a series of unstoppable yawns, one after the other.

'That's great!' said Colin. 'It's really getting to you, Beattie.'

'I think I'm just tired. I couldn't sleep last night.'

'Do you often feel tired?' he persisted.

'Yes,' she whispered, recalling the last week in Kent – the

exhaustion of Christmas and the strain of feeling Elizabeth's whole family despised her.

'It may be because you were drugged at birth. Do you find you have a drink problem?'

'*No!*'

'Why I'm asking, darling, is because babies who were drugged often turn to drink in adult life, to deaden pain or fear. What they're really doing is re-creating the numbness and disorientation which got them through the ordeal of their birth.'

'Look, I don't know anything *about* my birth – I keep telling everyone.'

'Yes, I'm aware of that, and it's all the more reason why you should try to retrieve the memories. They could be wonderfully healing. Listen, I'm going to fetch Joyce, okay?'

Oh God! she thought, now I *won't* escape. Joyce was Willow's second-in-command: a rebirther in her own right, who'd had years of experience in both Europe and the States. She seemed decent enough – a kindly sensitive woman who'd been marvellous with Jazz in the more manic of his phases, but who would probably show less patience with those she regarded as slackers. Beattie could see her small neat figure already hurrying over.

'Colin says you're having a bit of trouble with the breathing.'

'I've . . . er . . . just lost the rhythm, that's all.'

'Well, why don't we breathe together, then you can follow me.' Joyce seated herself cross-legged on the floor and began breathing in and out to a slow deliberate rhythm. Beattie had no choice but to copy her, although secretly she was scared of losing control, or being 'taken over'. The others had long since succumbed, but far from experiencing Willow's promised release, appeared to be trapped in some place of torment – sobbing, gasping, and in one case actually throwing up.

'I'm picking up a lot of fear,' Joyce whispered. 'Just relax and trust the process, Beattie. The more you resist, the harder it becomes – like birth itself. If the baby holds back, the whole thing becomes a struggle.'

'I'm *not* resisting.'

'Okay, let's continue with the breathing. Try to keep in time with me. You're exhaling a little too fast. That's better – yes, that's great! Now slow the inhale down as well. Fantastic! You're really getting the hang of it.'

240

Joyce's calm caressing voice was surprisingly relaxing. It reminded her of Elizabeth: the same aristocratic accent and gentle intonation. And she had to admit she did like being praised.

'You're doing brilliantly, my love. You're so much more relaxed now. I can really feel the difference.'

She lay lapping up the praise, like a little kid at nursery school being awarded her gold stars. But then praise was rare enough in life, so she might as well lie back and enjoy it.

'Well done, Beattie! Your jaw's a wee bit tight still, but I think we can solve that. I suggest you close your eyes, then you can shut out everything except the sensation of the breath itself.'

Beattie did as she suggested, but what she *couldn't* shut out was the sensation of the woman's gentle hand. It was gliding over her face, stroking back and forth along the eyelids, then down the cheeks, and to and fro across the jaw, loosening and relaxing it. No one had ever touched her with such tenderness, as if she were a precious fabric which might be damaged by more careless handling. She had hated being pawed by the others on the course, but this was somehow different. She could turn Joyce into Elizabeth – and the two *were* alike, in fact, not just in the way they spoke, but in their age, their build, their manner.

She squinted through her eyelids, almost surprised to see Joyce's Californian tan rather than Elizabeth's pale skin, and completely taken aback by the look on her face. Joyce was gazing down at her with what she could only describe as love, however unlikely that might sound. It was as if she were gazing at a beloved child, fixing it with the same entranced and doting scrutiny as Elizabeth gave Amanda.

'What's happened to the breathing?' she smiled.

'Oh, sorry,' Beattie whispered in confusion. 'It keeps sort of . . . petering out.'

'It's because you don't trust it – or yourself. But it'll come in time, don't worry. Look, instead of closing your eyes, try looking into mine. That's what we call an eye-gaze rebirth, and it can be very powerful.'

Beattie tensed in embarrassment. Gazing into another person's eyes was incredibly intimate – hard enough with a lover, let alone a virtual stranger. Yet how could she regard Joyce as a stranger when there was such affection in her eyes – no, more than affection – 'love' really was the only word for that outpouring of concern, devotion and tenderness. If only she *deserved* it, instead of being a fraud. She fidgeted and glanced away, fearing Joyce could see right through her, but then she felt still *more* guilt because she wasn't keeping contact with those magnetic hazel eyes.

Joyce began to stroke her hair. Her touch was so exquisite Beattie found her worries subsiding and began to savour the experience. The fingers feathered slowly down her head, pausing at the nape of her neck to ruffle the soft hair there, then traced the coil of her ear. Far from being an intrusion, Joyce's touch was like the expression in her eyes: gentle and adoring. It turned her into a child – a small and precious Amanda who must be cosseted and fussed, told she was an angel. The hand continued stroking: smoothing the hair from her brow, lingering on the forehead to soothe away any frown-lines, then sweeping slowly down the scalp before returning to the brow again. It was so rhythmic, so relaxing, she felt an extraordinary sense of peace. And Joyce's steady breathing must be affecting her as well, because almost without thinking she, too, was taking deep connected mouth-breaths, just as she'd been taught.

'Good girl,' said Joyce, delighted.

Beattie frowned in bewilderment. If anyone else had called her a 'good girl', she'd have found it acutely condescending. Yet on Joyce's lips it seemed the most perfect phrase in the world. She was being praised for simply existing, like an animal, or a baby. No one had ever called her good, and deep inside she believed herself to be *bad*.

'Never forget,' Joyce whispered, as if reading her mind, 'that you're a good, loving, innocent, beautiful woman.'

Beattie shook her head, protesting and yet thrilled. She wanted the words repeated, to ensure she'd heard them right, then shouted from the rooftops by everyone she knew: by Elizabeth and her daughters, by Sal and Max (and even Max's wife), above all, by her parents. She had been waiting all her life to hear herself described in such terms – it was the missing key, though to *what* she hardly knew. She began to feel a strange tingling in her arms, and her mouth was opening wider and wider, as if demanding more, more, more – more words, more food, more air, more love, more stroking. The hunger felt insatiable, disgusting. How could anyone so greedy be innocent and good?

'Yes, *greedy*,' her mother repeated, 'selfish and self-centred.'

'Innocent,' Joyce insisted. 'Good and full of love.'

The rival voices were shouting each other down; her own voice joining in as well, whispering silently to Joyce: 'Of course I can't be innocent. I'm here under false pretences. I've only come to sneer at you all. My mother's right – I'm rotten to the core.'

But the words couldn't seem to make themselves heard. Instead she wailed aloud: 'I'm hungry. I'm so *hungry*.' She was astonished by the tremor in her voice: a child's petulant cry, verging on despair.

'Of course you are,' Joyce murmured, 'but I'm feeding you with love, Beattie. Can't you feel my love? That love will always be there for you, so you'll never be hungry again.'

All at once, something snapped inside her. Joyce's gentle loving voice was now grating on her nerves. It was ludicrous to promise everlasting love, when love *never* lasted long – she knew that from experience.

'For Christ's sake!' she shouted, suddenly beside herself with fury. 'Why promise what you can't give?' She *would* send these people up, and Joyce in particular – devote a whole sarcastic paragraph to her sentimental platitudes.

'If you'll only open your eyes, Beattie, you can *see* my love and know it's there for you. Just inhale it with the breath.'

'There *isn't* any love,' she yelled. 'The whole thing's a con. But don't think you'll get away with it. I'm going to expose the lot of you, tell the world rebirthing *stinks*!'

She flung aside the patchwork covers and struggled to her feet, stumbling over bodies in her haste to get away. She pushed past Joyce – and Willow, who had come rushing up to help – and stormed out through the door, sobbing uncontrollably.

23

'Would you like some grapes now, Beattie? They're those lovely little seedless ones.'

Beattie opened her mouth. Warm fingers slipped a grape in, then another and another, their flesh soft and deliciously sweet.

'And how about a drink?'

She nodded. A cup was held to her lips and a kindly arm supported her while she sipped cool refreshing fruit juice. This *couldn't* be happening – she must be dreaming it: people huddled protectively around her, feeding her with titbits, massaging her hands and feet. Far from being driven out as a traitor and impostor, she had been lapped in love and sympathy the whole afternoon and evening, then invited to spend the night in the large house in the village hired by Dawn and Sylvia for a number of the group. It was now almost midnight and they were all in their pyjamas, enjoying a late-night snack in the kitchen.

Karen peeled the lid off a raspberry yoghurt and stood over Beattie, smiling, with the pot in one hand and a teaspoon in the other. 'Do you like yogurt, darling?' she asked.

What should she reply? If she said no, it would sound churlish, but if she said yes, she'd be fed like a baby. This extraordinary crowd actually believed that grown-ups should be spoon-fed – literally – when they were feeling insecure. It was all part of their philosophy of nurturing and love. A few minutes ago, she had watched Patricia 'nurture' Jazz: cutting a peanut butter sandwich into tiny fingers, which she fed him one by one. Then she'd peeled an orange for him, easing each segment between his lips.

Impulsively she opened her mouth. If Karen wanted to mother her, she might as well go along with it. It would be another gem for her article – though she was becoming increasingly uneasy about writing the piece at all. These people had showered her with devotion, yet she was continuing to deceive them. They hadn't seemed to understand her reference to exposure; realize she was threatening to denounce them in the press. Her outburst had been treated as simply a reaction to the breathing. Apparently the process was so powerful, it *could* engender wild emotions, including fury and hostility. They were used to it, expected it (especially from a newcomer) and had been trying to reassure her ever since.

Even now, Colin was recounting his own traumatic first experience. 'I felt it was actually *me* in labour, as if I'd somehow become my own mother. I had these tremendously strong contractions which went on for hours and hours, but all I produced in the end was a tiny blood-stained cricket ball.'

Everybody laughed, Donna squeezing his hand in sympathy.

Beattie paused a moment to swallow another spoonful of yogurt. It was difficult to contribute to a conversation when one was being fed. 'But ... but why do you *do* it,' she asked, 'if you find it so upsetting?'

'Because in time you release the pain,' said Donna. 'And then it's really wonderful. I mean, in the group-rebirthing today, I had an experience of total bliss, like the most amazing orgasm. I could hear myself laughing out loud for minutes on end.' She laughed again, recalling it. 'And last year was even better. I went home from the rebirthing course on the Sunday afternoon, and on the Monday morning I met a really caring man, who proposed to me a fortnight later.'

'And did you accept?' asked Beattie.

'Of course. It was *meant*, you see. I'd always had a problem with relationships until I was rebirthed that time and made to see that my hostility to men was the result of being hurt at birth by an arrogant young doctor.'

Beattie sucked the spoon clean. She had to admit she was rather enjoying the experience of being a good and gorgeous baby surrounded by doting mothers. Yet if her friends could see her, she'd die of shame. She felt torn all ways: one part of her longing to submit and be nurtured to bursting-point; another part too tired to think at all, and her professional self determined to glean more details for her piece. The professional self would have to win – she wasn't here to guzzle, but to do a job of work.

Once her mouth had been wiped by Karen, she decided to take the plunge and ask some questions. There hadn't been much chance so far. Although they were encouraged to talk in the sessions, that meant long-winded discussions of 'blocks' or 'negativity' or 'break-throughs', not learning basic facts. 'I still don't quite understand,' she said, 'what triggers off the rebirth. I mean, is it just the breathing?'

Several people chipped in at once, eager to explain that yes, it *was* the breathing, but the process was also greatly helped by the presence of a skilled rebirther who could make the person feel secure enough to re-experience their birth.

'You see,' said Colin, in his usual earnest tone, 'the rebirther has worked through his own birth-trauma, so in effect he's saying to the rebirthee: "You'll be okay. *I* came through it safely and successfully and so will you."'

'But suppose you *don't*?'

'You're still frightened, aren't you, Beattie?' Karen murmured. 'But whatever happens, you mustn't give up. A lot of us felt exactly the same when *we* were new to it. But you see, the more pain you release, the more you're able to undo your past conditioning and write a different life-script. Look, give it another try tomorrow, and you'll probably find it's easier already.'

'And talking of tomorrow,' Sylvia interjected, 'we really ought to go to bed. We've got an early start.'

There was a murmur of agreement and a general move to tidy up the kitchen; cheese and yogurts returned to the fridge, biscuits to the tin. Sylvia took Beattie's arm and led her into the sitting-room, where a dozen bed-rolls were laid out on the carpet.

'Lie down here, pet. There's plenty of spare blankets.'

Beattie did as she was told, watching as the others trickled in and lay down on the makeshift beds. Many of them began cuddling up to each other, not in a particularly sexual way, but more like animals or children, following their natural instinct for safety, warmth and closeness. She found it touching, despite herself. Most of her life *she* had slept alone. The room was spartan and practically bare of furni-ture – in contrast to her luxurious hotel – but she felt much safer here, and certainly less isolated. Sylvia tucked the blankets round her, then spread a coverlet on top.

She lay on her back, taking in the scene: the motley of strange nightclothes: tracksuits, tee-shirts, kaftans and, in Colin's case, long-johns and a vest. He had set up a miniature shrine on the windowsill, with a picture of a Buddha-figure and a tiny vase of plastic flowers, while, on her left, Eve was giving a back-massage to a dark-haired girl called Lee. Fortunately the room was warm, as Lee had taken off her pyjama-top and was wearing only a pair of leggings. It was freezing outside, with a strong wind and sleety rain, though 'outside' seemed another world entirely, as if the group had been transported to a different planet. The usual New Year's Day diversions had completely passed them by: race meetings and pantomimes, bargain sales or ice-shows, were of little consequence here.

'Comfy?' Sylvia asked.

Beattie nodded. She *was* comfy – surprisingly – though maybe she'd been brainwashed. How could the cynical Beattie Bancroft, potential unmasker of all this mumbo-jumbo, feel so much at ease? Should she give her piece a different slant, she wondered; not so much a hatchet job, more a beginner's guide. But the *Herald* would probably regard that as too tame. She *could* play up the contrast between rebirthing and psychoanalysis; make the thing more serious, even bring in one or two points from Elizabeth's book. After all, Elizabeth herself had admitted that *her* type of therapy could sometimes be too cerebral, so that patients were left craving physical contact or tender loving care. *Here* they'd have it in excess.

'Goodnight then, pet,' Sylvia whispered. 'Sleep well.'

'Goodnight,' said Beattie, doubting whether she'd sleep at all with a dozen other people in the room. Anne-Marie had a ticklish cough and Colin had admitted that he often talked in his sleep. Jazz, mercifully, was absent – staying the night in Willow's house. Willow herself was sharing a bed with Joyce, an idea she found bizarre.

She turned over on her side, imagining herself and Elizabeth *also* sharing a bed, lying in each other's arms. Elizabeth seemed dreadfully far away, but at least she would have her to herself when she returned to Kent in two days' time. She shut her eyes, smiling at the prospect of the family's departure – daughters, babies, cousins, aunts, all leaving Mile End House. The smile turned into a yawn: a yawn of sheer exhaustion. Some of the others had already dropped off to sleep. The sound of their muted breathing contrasted singularly with the vehement rebirthing breath she still found such a strain. Yet she was determined to go through with it tomorrow. That was her last chance and she had no intention of messing things up a second time. In fact, she would try to take it seriously; do whatever she was told and simply see what happened. After all, the *others* had survived, in spite of their initial pain and panic. Even Jazz regarded his rebirthing as an unqualified success, and said he'd found his '*real*' mother, who was quite different from the one who had actually given birth to him.

She peered across at Dawn, who gave her a reassuring smile. Indeed, she was aware of a growing confidence, as if the presence of so many loving rebirthers was exerting some strange influence on her.

'Goodnight,' she whispered to Dawn, stretching out luxuriously. She was amazed to realize she did truly feel – dare she say it? – happy.

'Ready, Beattie?' asked Kim, settling himself beside her on a folded tartan rug.

She nodded. His voice was almost lost in the sad, slow music issuing from the cassette player. They were about to start the buddy-rebirth, though she was paired not with her buddy Jazz but with Kim, the male assistant. Willow had decided that she needed more support than Jazz could give, and had selected Kim as the best person to provide it; he was the most experienced rebirther there, after herself and Joyce.

And by far the best-looking, Beattie thought, with his sensuous face and thick dark hair. She'd noticed him the first evening as being the only really attractive man around. Since then, she'd found his personality equally attractive – kind, considerate, sensitive. It would be no hardship to be close to him, in any sense. They were upstairs in a smallish room, away from the main hall – a relief after the cramped conditions yesterday. Two other difficult cases had been brought up here as well: Jazz himself, who was going to be rebirthed by Joyce, and Anne-Marie, who'd suffered an extremely traumatic experience in the group-rebirth and hadn't yet recovered. The three of them had their own small altar, with a flickering night-light casting eerie shadows on the walls, and their own joss-sticks and cassette player.

'Let's start the breathing together,' said Kim. 'Remember, you're absolutely safe, Beattie. We've created a little womb up here and all you have to do is breathe.'

'Okay.' She opened her mouth and followed his rhythm, trying to ignore the discomfort in her throat. The breathing didn't seem to hurt the others, so she was probably doing it wrong.

'That's great!' said Kim. 'Absolutely brilliant.'

Encouraged, she continued, though the breathing was still a struggle. Her throat felt constricted and she couldn't seem to take in enough air. Then a peculiar sort of tingling began vibrating through her hand. 'My hand's tingling,' she complained. 'A bit like pins and needles, but much stronger.'

'Don't worry. Just surrender to it. Tingling is only energy. Try to relax into it, and it will help you push out the blocks in your body.'

She wished she had his confidence. The tingling was intensifying, becoming close to pain. And it was in her *right* hand, which seemed distinctly threatening – perhaps a form of retribution. How could she type her article if her fingers refused to function?

'It feels awful,' she winced. 'I've lost all feeling in it. My hand doesn't seem to be *there* any more.'

Kim took it in his own hands and massaged it for several minutes, using a gentle circular motion.

'Thanks,' she whispered. 'But now it's moved to my left hand.'

He smiled. 'That's because you need more massage. Your body's trying to tell you these things. You must *ask* for what you need, Beattie. I'm here to provide it.'

How incredible, she thought. It was rare enough in life to be encouraged to state your needs; even more unusual to have them instantly gratified. 'Well, could you possibly massage my feet?' she asked. 'The tingling's gone down there now. *And* to my legs. In fact, I'm beginning to lose whole sections of my body. There's almost nothing left of me except my middle bit.'

Kim moved to the end of the rug, pushed aside the duvet, and ran his hands slowly down her legs. Then he picked up each leg in turn and gently bent and stretched it, opening her thighs and moving them in slow and rhythmic circles. For a man to touch her in that way seemed extraordinarily intimate, yet she had no sense of his taking advantage of her. The word which came to mind was service – gentle loving service to a fellow human being. The men she knew in ordinary life would be incapable of such a thing. Any touch from *them* was invariably sexual.

However, it wasn't easy to relax, or enjoy what Kim was doing. The tingling was too intense and she was beginning to feel faint as well. Rebirthing seemed more like *death* – a gradual slipping-down into a terrifying realm where you might finally lose consciousness. The others sounded no happier: Anne-Marie was making high-pitched whimpering sounds, which were horribly distracting, and out of the corner of her eye she could see Jazz threshing violently, as if he were in the throes of an epileptic fit.

'Beattie, stay with the breathing,' Kim urged. 'Let go on the exhale, and try to take it easy on yourself. *Love* your body, *love* your breath.'

Her teeth began to chatter. Not only had the tingling spread, even to her stomach now, but she was shivering with cold. The strength of her reactions was almost unbelievable. How could a simple breathing process trigger such extreme effects? A freezing wind seemed to be blowing on her naked skin, yet she was dressed in several layers of clothes and lying in a well-heated room with all the windows shut. 'I'm c . . . c . . . *cold*,' she managed to stutter. 'Colder than I've ever been in my life.'

'Cold is really fear,' Kim explained, replacing the duvet over her and spreading two thick blankets on top. 'These physical reactions are all part of the process. But no matter what you're feeling, Beattie, remember you're completely safe.'

She continued to shiver, despite the weight of blankets. Her hands were frozen into rigid claws and her jaw was so tight she could barely speak or swallow. She also hated lying on her back. It made her feel vulnerable and stranded, like some helpless creature washed up by the tide. And her body was still tingling, as if she had lost the last vestige of control and was about to fall apart, or plunge into a panic-attack. Kim kept assuring her she was safe, but it was Elizabeth's word 'dangerous' which echoed in her head. She struggled to sit up, determined to stop before it was too late.

'Kim, I . . . I'm sorry, but I've had enough.'

He smiled at her, unruffled. 'Don't worry, Beattie. That's just another reaction. Accept it and breathe through it. Accept *whatever* comes up, whether it's pain or anger or an urge to run away. I'm here to help you, darling, so trust my love and support.' Tenderly, he settled her back down, stroking her face and neck. 'Let's continue with the breathing, okay? And really open the throat this time. Don't push the cold and fear back into your body, but release them, let them out. Concentrate on your *breath*, and not your feelings.'

Feeling powerless to resist, she did as he instructed, opening her mouth wider and wider, and taking in great gulps of air. Suddenly and startlingly, waves of pain began to shudder through her body, all but overwhelming her. She could hear frenzied cries – a baby's cries – yowling from her own mouth. She was fighting to be born, and the pain and horror of it had literally taken her breath away.

Her lungs were bursting with the strain, and the iron band clamped around her throat was gripping tighter, tighter.

'Breathe into the fear,' a faint voice urged, but the words were drowned by her cries. She was beyond all help, trapped in a restricting passage, with something blocking her way: something leaden, solid and bloody. She raged at the obstruction – kicking it and butting it, and still half-suffocating from the lack of air. Her back arched up in a spasm of pain, but with a final desperate effort, she managed to thrust the obstacle aside and force her own way out.

She recoiled in shock from the sense of limitless space; the new glaring, brutal world where everything was too loud, too bright. Cruel pincer-claws clutched at her head, and she was suddenly swung upside down and slapped so hard she choked. Unfamiliar noises reverberated around her, but through their clamour she heard a muffled whisper; a softer, more despondent voice: 'The other one's dead, I'm afraid.'

Only then did she understand, and was so horrified at what she'd done she tried to struggle back into the safe enfolding darkness she had left. 'I *killed* you, George,' she cried. 'I was so greedy I took everything for myself.'

Oblivious to her distress, they tore her from her twin and flung her, alone, into a cell: a cramped prison with glass walls. She tried to scream in protest, but tubes were forced into her throat, and her arms and legs were strapped down. She lay in isolation, watching the blurred giant-shapes looming on the other side of the glass. Now life was only blinding lights, deafening whines and bleeps, violent shocks jolting through her body. Her mouth made frantic sucking motions, searching for some comfort it somehow expected to be there. But no comfort came, no food came, and no one spoke her language. This must be the punishment for murdering her boy-twin. Her parents didn't want a girl, so they had kicked her out, abandoned her. Her mother didn't want a child at all. She had tried to abort her babies when they were scarcely bigger than shelled walnuts; had begun to bleed so heavily that she and George had clung to each other, to avoid being swept away on the scarlet tide. It was so vivid in her mind, she could actually feel her mother's blood flowing out between her legs; its warm wet stickiness soaking into the rug.

A new voice whispered in her ear: 'I think your period must have started, darling. Do you want to go and clean up?'

'What?' she stammered, totally confused. She groped a hand

between her legs and brought it up scarlet to her face: *her* blood, *her* abortions. She had no right to blame her mother when *she* had been every bit as callous, not just once but twice. She could see the shabby room in the clinic where she'd sat propped against the pillows, once it was all over, wolfing cottage pie and trifle, and still feeling desperate hunger.

Not hunger, *greed*. Greedy, even then. A disgusting greedy pig.

'Forgive yourself,' a voice was saying, a kindly gentle male voice. 'Release the grief and guilt, then tell yourself you're innocent.'

Suddenly, Jazz began to cry out: a terrifying jagged noise, rising to howls of despair.

Beattie sat up with a start. 'That's *him*!' she shouted. 'That's George. I'm *not* innocent, don't you see? I killed him. I'm a murderer.'

'Hello? Hello? Elizabeth, please answer.' Shit! The damned thing's out of order. No, she must be there. She's got to be. 'Elizabeth, come and fetch me, *please.* I can't drive back to London. I'm too upset. And scared. And the weather's terrible. Christ! Why does no one *answer?*'

24

Beattie was practically forced onto the hard shoulder as a huge lorry blundered past, flinging a shower of slush over the windscreen. Visibility was bad enough as it was. She was half-blinded by the whirling snow, and her windscreen wipers, sluggish at the best of times, were now juddering and complaining. A second juggernaut overtook her: a macho roar, a whoosh of spray and again her tiny car shuddered in its wake.

'Services 1 mile.'

Thank Christ, she thought, turning off at the slip-road and following the 'Welcome Break' signs. She parked as close as she could to the main building and ran, head down, towards the entrance. A harsh wind slapped her face, snow stung her lips and lashes, and she had trouble keeping her footing on the ice-rink of a path. It was a relief to get inside and let the fuggy warmth thaw her numb hands and feet.

She made straight for the row of public phones and dialled Elizabeth's number. Still nothing but that frustrating high-pitched whine. She had reported it on Sunday night. It should be repaired by now, for God's sake. Cursing, she rang the engineers again.

'This is British Telecom Fault Repair Service. Your call is being held in a queue and will be answered as soon as possible. Please hold the line.'

The voice was followed by tinkling music: the 'Dance of the Sugar Plum Fairy'. She recognized the tune – Elizabeth had played it for Amanda over Christmas, while the child pranced around in her ballet dress.

'Come on!' she muttered. '*Answer*, will you?'

'This is British Telecom Fault Repair Service. Your call is being held . . .'

She banged the receiver down. She had listened to the same maddening message a dozen times on Sunday, with the same maddening music sandwiched in between. She'd better have some lunch, then try again.

She walked into the restaurant, breathing in its healing sanity: normal cheerful people eating hamburgers and pizzas; the tantalizing smells of fried onions, greasy chips. Since Sunday night she'd been snowed up in the hotel, too shaken by the rebirthing to leave her room (or even ring down for meals); surviving on the mini-packs of biscuits they had provided on the welcome tray. She had sat alone, staring at the walls, then suddenly, in the early hours, she had got out her laptop and poured all her grief and horror onto the page. Ordinary life vanished altogether as she relived her violent rebirth. She found herself writing the piece not as she'd intended – dispassionately and even cynically – but recording her own personal trauma in equally feverish prose. Only now, nearly two days later, was she calming down, re-entering the real world.

She went up to the counter and inspected the array of food, feeling she could wolf the lot. There seemed to be a huge hole inside her, impossible to fill. She chose a cheese and chutney sandwich, a slice of chocolate gâteau and a giant-sized bag of crisps, and went to sit in the most crowded area. She needed to be close to people after her painful isolation.

She bit into her sandwich; tore the bag of crisps open. Even yesterday, she had been too worried about her article to bother with proper meals. She had faxed it straight to Max, who, although impressed, had said it sounded as if she'd written it while she was on an acid-trip. Fortunately, he'd managed to do a salvage job: cutting it to the bone and injecting some black humour, and he was now awaiting a verdict from the editor of the Woman's Page.

She finished her sandwich and started on the gâteau – must fill the hole, fill the hole. Then she drained her coffee, crunched the few remaining crisps, and went to find the toilets. Her period was still terribly heavy, almost like an abortion in itself. She *had* to speak to Elizabeth, ask her advice about losing so much blood. She hated being out of touch like this. It seemed ages since they'd last seen each other and there was such a tremendous lot to tell her. Besides, she owed her an apology – rebirthing *was* dangerous, as she'd discovered for herself. It had affected her more radically than she could ever have thought possible; left her almost shell-shocked. Even now, when she was beginning to recover, the smallest thing could set her off again. The flush of the cistern and the whirr of the hand-dryer jarred her ears grotesquely, and when someone dropped a hairbrush, she jumped as if she'd been shot. How much longer might she be like this, she wondered in alarm. She would never cope with editors – or with Max himself, for that matter – in such a fragile state.

She emerged from the ladies room and tried British Telecom once more.

'Your call is being held in a . . .'

Useless! There was nothing for it but to drive to Kent. Elizabeth must *know* she'd been delayed: the appalling weather was the first and longest item in every news report. And surely she wouldn't mind her just turning up? True, she had left things rather vague when she'd dashed off after Christmas, but Elizabeth had nothing planned – no more visitors or relatives – not even any patients till next week.

She buttoned up her coat, pulled on her thick gloves, and went outside to brave the elements. The car started easily, thank God, and she set off on the motorway, battling through the snow. After twenty slow and hazardous miles, she saw the first sign for the M25.

'Elizabeth, I'm on my way,' she murmured into the snowy wastes. 'Kill the fatted calf!'

Dusk was falling as she pulled into the drive of Mile End House. The snow was much less heavy in Kent, and Elizabeth's garden looked really picturesque. Every dead brown flower-head on the hydrangea bush was coated with a frill of snow, like a delicate new flower. The beech tree was a masterpiece of light and dark effects, and the stone owl by the birdbath was resplendent in his new white plumage. She got out of the car, stretching her cramped limbs, then walked up to the door and rang the bell. No answer. She rang again before fumbling for her key and letting herself in. Boz trotted up to greet her, purring like a lawn-mower.

'Where's your mistress?' she asked, bending down to stroke him. He was obviously trying to tell her, responding in his cat-language, which she couldn't translate, alas.

'Elizabeth!' she shouted, moving to the foot of the stairs. She called again, her voice echoing through the house, but only Tolkien appeared, sauntering along the landing with his usual haughty air. Elizabeth must be out, though she couldn't have gone far – she hadn't set the burglar alarm, and most of the lights were on.

She removed her coat and hung it in the cloakroom, not wanting to untidy the place. The hall looked miraculously neat in contrast to last week – no longer cluttered with all the family paraphernalia: toys, pushchairs, presents, gumboots, coats. She put her head round the drawing-room door, cheered by the sight of the empty chairs, then went to look in the kitchen. The remains of Elizabeth's lunch-for-one were still lying on the table: a single plate, knife, fork and mug. This evening it would be supper for two, simple and serene.

She ran upstairs to Sarah's room – *her* room. The only trace of its last occupant was a forgotten navy sock, which she tossed into the laundry basket. She removed her shoes and stretched out on the bed. She was exhausted from two sleepless nights, but just couldn't seem to relax. Within minutes she was up again and prowling about the house, relishing the fact that John's shaving gear was no longer in the bathroom, nor Amanda's dolls simpering on the landing. She walked on to Elizabeth's bedroom and stood outside the open door, gazing at the double bed. Would she and Elizabeth ever share a bed, as Joyce and Willow had? Joyce, a stranger, had shown her such great tenderness: stroking her face and smoothing her hair, looking adoringly into her eyes. And Kim had been unbelievably kind, treating her like a beloved child who needed unstinting devotion to make up for her ordeal. If only Elizabeth would do the same – cherish her and cosset her, hold her close all night.

Suddenly her eye was caught by something draped across the foot of the bed: a purple tie with a distinctive swirly pattern. She recognized it instantly as Hugo's – the one he'd been wearing when he called in after Christmas. She glanced nervously over her shoulder, then sidled into the room and snatched it up. What the hell was it doing *here*? She remembered Elizabeth inviting Hugo for New Year, but only casually; to pop in for a drink if he found himself at a loose end. So why should she bring him to her bedroom, for God's sake? And why should he remove his tie? What *else* had he removed – his jacket, shirt, his . . . ?

Don't be ridiculous, she told herself. You're jumping to conclusions without a shred of evidence. Except the tie itself was evidence. Elizabeth never took people to her bedroom. And if Hugo *had* stayed the night on New Year's Eve, where else could he have slept? The only other room free was her own glory hole in the attic, but Elizabeth would never stick him up there. A man six foot tall couldn't be expected to sleep in such a narrow bed, and next door to rowdy kids. There was only one other explanation: they must have spent the night together – several nights, for all she knew. The minute she was out of the way, Elizabeth had deceived her.

No. That was too far-fetched. Elizabeth had told her categorically that she had never had an affair in the whole of her life, so she was hardly likely to embark on one now, with all her family in residence. What about last night, though, when the family had gone? She would have been alone last night – alone except for Hugo, conveniently abandoned by his wife. Wouldn't he need comfort, somebody to turn to?

She stood wretchedly by the bed, the two conflicting voices raging in her head, neither quite convincing her. She swung round in alarm at a sudden noise from downstairs. Elizabeth! She mustn't be found in here – only *Hugo* had that privilege. She dashed down to the hall, struggling to control herself. It was no use confronting Elizabeth the minute she walked in. Better to say nothing, and see how *she* reacted.

But Elizabeth wasn't there. The *Kent Advertiser* was lying on the doormat, along with a few brochures. The noise she'd heard must have been the rattle of the letter-box. Mechanically, she picked up the paper and put it on the desk. What could Elizabeth be *doing*? She never went out for more than a few minutes without setting the alarm. Or had Hugo so bewitched her that she was mooning around in an adolescent daze?

She sank down at the desk. There was no way she could compete with him – a sophisticated gallery-owner, who was clever, wealthy, *male*. The pictures grew more painful in her mind: Hugo shagging Elizabeth in the tangled bed upstairs, or grinding into her on the couch in the consulting room.

She jumped to her feet. The consulting room! The only place she hadn't checked. They might even be there now – so caught up in each other they hadn't heard her prowling around.

She stumbled along the passage and burst in. The room was empty but smelt faintly of cigars. *Hugo* smoked cigars, or had done since his wife left. Three half-smoked panatellas lay in the ashtray, snuggled up to Elizabeth's cigarette-ends. As she stood staring at them, they began to blur and tremble, distorted by her tears. It was pathetic to cry, but she felt so desolate. Even their smoking excluded her – an intimate and private ritual, conducted in this sanctuary where she was forbidden to set foot. She picked up Elizabeth's empty cigarette-packet, clutching it for comfort, inhaling its familiar smell. Her longing for Elizabeth was almost a physical pain. *Someone* must know where she was – Caroline, maybe, or James and Margaret. Instinctively she reached for the phone, but the line was dead. Of course. It all made sense now. Elizabeth had disconnected it on purpose, so she and Hugo wouldn't be disturbed.

No, the idea was quite insane. She was overreacting to a ludicrous degree. Whatever else, Elizabeth was responsible. She wouldn't take the risk of being out of touch with all her family and patients just to gratify a man she hardly knew.

But she *did* know him, didn't she? – and rather well, in fact. He was the first man she'd ever fallen for; the romantic figure she had worshipped from afar. And now they were much closer. For all she knew, they could have been seeing each other for *weeks*: wandering round galleries together, going to the theatre, listening to highbrow modern music – two cultured connoisseurs talking a language she couldn't hope to understand. She remembered the artists they'd discussed at the golf club whose names meant absolutely nothing to her. What a fool she was ever to imagine *she* could be Elizabeth's mate: an ignoramus who had left school at sixteen without an A-level to her name. Hugo and Elizabeth belonged naturally together. It was to do with birth again: the genes they'd inherited, the values and good breeding they'd absorbed with their mothers' milk.

She gripped the edge of the table. The memories were surging back – unbearable, grotesque – her own mother's desperate efforts to get rid of her; the spate of blood: her *twin*'s blood. She snatched up the receiver again, tears streaming down her face. 'Elizabeth, you *must* be there! Please speak to me. It's George.'

George. Her brother's name. She had murdered him and stolen his name. Because she had to be a boy to please her parents – to please her father, especially.

'Elizabeth, Elizabeth . . .' She heard her own voice, shrill and pleading, wailing down the phone, as if by some miracle Elizabeth would hear her and come back. She realized she was shivering just as she had at her rebirth; the same raw panic threatening to engulf her.

'*Elizabeth!*' She was hoarse now, frantic; trying to make the words carry; reach as far as Cheltenham.

No answer. Elizabeth had gone; probably disappeared for ever.

She flung the phone down, wincing as it hit the floor. Now it was beyond repair – it had cracked right across the base. She swept the ashtray off the table, watching ash and cigarette-ends scatter everywhere. She hardly knew what she was doing, only that she must destroy all trace of Hugo. She darted over to the couch, wrenching off the coverlet, pummelling the cushions. Hugo had lain there, leching with Elizabeth – untidying it, defiling it, when it was sacred to her patients. Christ! The patients were as bad, though: selfish, grasping morons who monopolized Elizabeth. They, too, must be destroyed. She heaved the top drawer right out of the bureau, searching for their case-notes; found only piles of stationery, old diaries, paperclips. She up-ended every drawer in turn – letters, notebooks, diaries, folders, cascading to the floor. She left the room in chaos and blundered on to Jeremy's study. She had spent ages closeted in there, typing Elizabeth's book; lavished such devotion on it. Yet what did Elizabeth care? She had run off with Hugo and not even bothered to say goodbye.

She marched over to the desk and turned the computer on – she would damned well get *rid* of the book. Fingers shaking, she typed in a command.

'Are you sure – Yes or No?' flashed up on the screen.

'Yes,' she typed, without a moment's hesitation, and in a matter of three seconds every single text-file was totally erased. The speed of it was terrifying, but there was still the back-up copy – that must go as well. She opened the desk drawer and snatched up the disk: such an insignificant-looking square of dull grey plastic, yet containing all that survived of her weeks of laborious work. She rammed it into the machine and repeated the delete command.

'Are you sure?' the computer asked again.

This time she hesitated, hands poised over the keyboard as she recalled the sheer effort of the task: deciphering Elizabeth's scrawl, continually consulting the dictionary, noting all the cross-references for the index, taking endless pains with the layout. A labour of love, Elizabeth had called it.

She pushed her chair back and walked slowly to the window. She *did* love Elizabeth, more than she had loved anyone before. Elizabeth understood her, accepted her with all her faults, was always ready to listen – had taught her what love *was*, for heaven's sake.

She returned wearily to the desk. The cursor was still blinking at her. 'Yes or no? Y or N?'

It had to be no – she couldn't kill that love. Her finger moved towards the N key, when, suddenly, horrifically, Hugo burst into the study, naked and dishevelled. She shrank back from him in horror, but whichever way she looked, she could see him with Elizabeth: screwing on the sofa, making gloating love on the floor.

Savagely, she jabbed the Y key, watching in grim silence as her command was carried out. Again it took just seconds. Three seconds to delete three hundred pages.

She stared at the screen, still not fully comprehending what she'd done. Then, in desperation, she pressed the N key, hitting it over and over again: No No No No No No No No *No*.

Too late. The book was dead.

IV

VI

25

'Well,' said Max, crunching into a caviar tartlet, 'how does it feel to be a famous journalist?'

'Great!' said Beattie. 'Absolutely great.' She closed her eyes against the brilliance of the sun, seeing in her mind again her photo in the *Herald* and the six long columns of newsprint with *her* name underneath. Not only had it been published, but the Women's editor (a dynamic-sounding female called Fenella Ferguson) had actually invited her to lunch to discuss writing other pieces. The minute she was back in London they were going to arrange a date – in fact, she'd already worked out what to wear for the occasion.

'More champagne, madam?' drawled a sultry voice.

A willowy blonde with an ice-bucket was smiling down at her, already topping up her glass. She looked more like a film star than a wine waitress, but then this whole glitzy world was straight out of a movie. How else could the hysterical wreck who'd left London in a snowstorm now be calmly soaking up the sun on a luxury yacht in Cannes? She had never set foot on *any* yacht before, let alone such a grand one, with acres of gleaming brass and chrome, a suede-lined stateroom complete with four-poster bed, at least four other cabins, and even a sauna, a jacuzzi, and a helicopter pad.

She relaxed back in her chair, surveying the full splendour of the scene: the forest of masts in the marina (literally hundreds of boats, doubled by their shimmering reflections); the improbable blue of sea and sky, stolen from a holiday brochure; the palatial hotels on the famous La Croisette, where one small cup of coffee could set you back fifty francs.

'Oh Max,' she said, squeezing his arm. 'This is *heaven*, honestly. I wish *I* had friends with yachts in Cannes.'

'Well, they're not exactly thick on the ground! Most people I know think themselves lucky to have paid off their mortgage. And between you and me' – he lowered his voice – 'I suspect Dave only bought the thing with the proceeds of insider trading. That's one of the perks of being a big shot in the City. Mind you, even when he was still slaving away in the exchange, he was notorious for siphoning his money into tax havens.' He helped himself to an asparagus roll and demolished it in a single bite. 'What I envy him most, though, is being able to retire at fifty-three. He's got bugger all to do now, so he can spend his time swanning around the Med like Onassis, while *I*'m stuck in London working my balls off.'

'Ssh, he's coming back!' she whispered, as Dave sauntered across the deck towards them – a stocky figure in a white designer sweater and white slacks, his grey hair contrasting dramatically with his near-mahogany tan.

'Sorry to be such an age. There was an urgent fax from London.'

Heavens, thought Beattie, a *fax* on board as well! Maybe Dave was not as idle as Max had just suggested. Or perhaps it was his broker with news of a Van Gogh for sale.

Dave sank into the chair beside her and pulled on his navy yachting cap. 'In case you're wondering about lunch,' he said, 'we should be eating in about an hour, so long as everyone turns up on time. There'll be twelve of us in all – no one desperately exciting, I'm afraid. The sparky people tend to vanish from the scene after Christmas and New Year, back to their sparky jobs. And of course the *seriously* rich decamp to Florida or Barbados for the winter. This is very much the dead season on the Riviera.'

Dead! Beattie's eyes swept from the turquoise sea, bright with sails and wind-surfers, to the exotic feathered palms along the promenade. Dave ought to see Southend.

'I hope you both like seafood, by the way. We're having *langoustines* for lunch.'

'Mm, sounds great!' said Beattie, wishing she could remember what it was. 'Though I must admit I'm rather full already.' She laughed, gesturing to the empty tray beside her. She and Max had been stuffing canapés since noon: exotic things glistening with black beads of caviar, or decorated with tiny ripe red strawberries. Dave had invited them early, so he could show them over the boat before the others arrived. The *Princess Prudence* – named after his mistress – was a recent acquisition and obviously his pride and joy. Pru herself had gone to the Hilton health club for a facial and a massage, and was expected back at any moment. She must be frighteningly glamorous, Beattie thought – or hopelessly neurotic – if she needed a long session in the beauty parlour before she could face a lunch party on board.

'How's that old fraud Fred the Red?' Dave enquired of Max. 'Still up to his tricks?'

'God, no! You should see him – he's a reformed character. D'you remember his first wife, that frightful old bag who . . .'

Beattie left them to reminisce while she sipped her champagne and drank in lungfuls of the intoxicating air. Everything seemed so amazingly bright after the grey sludge of London's streets, and there was a sense of movement all around as the boats bobbed on the water and a skittish breeze tugged at sails and pennants. Some of the larger yachts looked like overweight tycoons themselves, lying indolently at anchor and baring their plump girths to the gold fingers of the sun.

She inspected the back of her hand for signs of a tan. The mornings and evenings were cool – real winter-coat weather, in fact – but by midday it was almost warm enough to sunbathe. Yesterday they had gone walking in the hills, a few miles from Max's house, and she'd felt poetry welling up inside her as she gazed at the distant mountain peaks, barred with gold and purple, and beyond them the French Alps, sun glittering on snow. The moment she'd set eyes on it, she had fallen in love with Fayence – its higgledy-piggledy red roofs, perched up on the hill; its narrow cobbled streets with their artists' workshops and flower-stalls; the Saturday morning market selling local goat's cheese and huge untidy bunches of mimosa. Max's house was set high, with a view which took your breath away, and there were wild flowers in bloom (in *January*!) in his tiny jungled garden, and smug brown lizards sunning themselves on stones, and she had even seen a dragonfly one morning.

'You're very quiet,' said Max, breaking into her thoughts.

'Come off it, Max,' laughed Dave. 'The poor girl can't get a word in edgeways with us rabbiting non-stop.'

'I *like* my women silent and subservient.'

'So what are you doing with *me* then?' Beattie gave him a playful punch on the arm.

Dave put his glass down and waved to a couple just stepping onto the gangplank. 'Aha!' he said. 'The first arrivals.' He strode off to greet the pair, who were dressed in elegant white trouser-suits. Both also had white hair: hers blue-rinsed and bouffant, his natural but thinning.

He ushered them over. 'May I introduce Annabel and Harry Charlton. They moved here from Blackheath and wouldn't live in London now if you paid them a million pounds. Isn't that right, Annabel?'

'Absolutely,' Annabel smiled, displaying a set of perfect teeth.

'And this is Max Gillespie, executive editor on the *Daily Herald*, and a very old friend of mine. We've known each other for – how long is it now, Max? – fifteen years? Good God! I'm giving away my age. And Beattie Bancroft is also from the *Herald*, one of their leading columnists.'

Beattie didn't bother to correct him. You *had* to be rich and famous (both, ideally) to gain acceptance here. She shook hands with Harry, instantly attracted to him – the distinguished older man, oozing wealth and charm – though he was evidently more interested in Max. The two men were soon deep in a discussion about the dangers of the Murdoch empire, while she was left with Annabel. She racked her brains for something suitable to say. Asking about work would hardly be appropriate when both the Charltons must have long ago retired. Anyway, Max had told her that for many of these people 'work' was a dirty word, implying that they weren't quite rich enough to support a life of total leisure. Fortunately Annabel got in first.

'I do envy you being a journalist. It must be an exciting life!'

Beattie shrugged. If she was meant to be the toast of Fleet Street, she'd better affect an air of nonchalant sophistication – and certainly not reveal the fact that she'd rushed out and bought thirty copies of the *Herald* the day her piece appeared.

'Do you write books as well as articles?' Annabel enquired.

'Yes, I'm . . . er . . . working on one now.' It wasn't quite a lie. An idea for a raunchy novel had sprung to mind last night while she and Max were making love in the famous feather bed.

'Oh, do tell me what it's about! I *adore* reading books by authors I've met. It makes them much more interesting, don't you think?'

'Well, it's only at a very early stage. You see, I . . .'

She was rescued by Dave, who arrived at that moment with someone else in tow – a nondescript-looking girl, wearing dingy jeans and a faded navy sweatshirt.

'May I introduce my girlfriend, Pru,' he said.

Beattie hoped her astonishment was not too glaringly obvious. She had expected Princess Prudence to be an out and out glamour-girl, dressed by Versace and loaded with expensive jewellery. She simply couldn't understand how someone who'd spent the morning in a beauty parlour could look quite so unprepossessing: her face bare of make-up; her short straight hair falling in her eyes.

'Hi,' she said, noticing that Max was also giving Pru the once-over; probably comparing the two of them. Well, at least she'd made an effort – taking ages over her face and hair, and changing her clothes half a dozen times before she was satisfied. Perhaps Dave preferred youth to glamour. Pru couldn't be more than twenty-five, with an almost childish face and big innocent grey eyes. Actually, she and Pru were the youngest there, by a long chalk.

Another ancient-looking couple had turned up (again dressed in the statutory white), plus a woman in her forties with a miniature poodle on a garish diamanté leash, and two florid-faced men of Dave's age, talking rapid-fire French – who might be anything from stockbrokers to film producers to local mafiosi. Her confidence began to flag in this cosmopolitan company. They all seemed to be bilingual, whereas even her *bonjours* sounded wincingly English. And everyone except Pru looked sort of . . . lacquered, as if they were on display in some millionaire's museum, far removed from the real and messy world.

The woman with the poodle had come over; the dog as impeccably groomed as its owner. She introduced herself as Gabriella, half-Italian and half-French.

'Isn't this weather amazing?' she said, with barely the trace of an accent. 'It's the warmest I've ever known it here in winter.'

'Yes, I must say I can't remember a sunnier January,' Beattie said truthfully, thinking back over her thirty dreary winters in Croydon, Penge and Westbourne Grove. By choosing her words carefully, she could probably give the impression that she spent her life jetting from one playground to another. The scene across the bay provided a wealth of inspiration: a flotilla of small dinghies with brilliant scarlet spinnakers; a lone jet-skier slicing expertly through the water; the billowing sails of a schooner out at sea, and, nearer the shore, three bronzed and hardy surfers pitting their skills against the waves.

'Were you here last Christmas?' Gabriella asked.

'Er, no.' Beattie swiftly suppressed the memory of her drunken 'celebrations' in Sal's shabby basement flat.

'We were frightfully disappointed. It was overcast most days and

269

even when the sun did shine, there was a bitterly cold wind. And the year before that, we had . . .'

'Excuse me, ladies,' Dave interjected, 'I don't think you've met Elizabeth.'

Beattie froze at the name. She had been doing her utmost to leave Elizabeth in England, to forget that hideous week before Max whisked her off to the airport. The night she'd run riot in Mile End House (then fled before Elizabeth's return), she hadn't dared go back to her flat, in case Elizabeth phoned her there, or – worse – turned up in person. She had stayed holed-up at Sal's, numb with guilt and misery, until Max finally lost patience and said if she intended hiding indefinitely, she had better hide with *him* – in France. He had been a tower of strength, not only taking her side against Elizabeth, but handling every last arrangement, so that all she'd had to do was pack her case and get herself to the airport. Once she was safely ensconced in his house in Fayence, the whole drama seemed utterly remote, as if it had happened in another life and to a completely different person – some demented stranger.

Yet now, faced with Elizabeth's namesake, she found her guilt resurfacing; the full horror of what she'd done at Mile End House. *This* Elizabeth even looked like hers: petite, blue-eyed and rather dowdily dressed.

'What a gorgeous dog!' Elizabeth said, smiling at Gabriella. '*I* used to have a poodle once, but he was one of those big shaggy ones. Yours is really sweet.'

Beattie left them talking dogs and fled into the deck saloon. She could feel herself unravelling; the happy confident person she had become this last week in France reverting to the half-crazed London wreck. She ran downstairs to the lower deck and locked herself in a bathroom. Its midnight-blue walls seemed oppressive rather than opulent; closing her in, matching her dark thoughts. In only six days she would have to return to England – and Elizabeth. The idea filled her with dread. She longed to stay in France for ever, secure in her own glass case.

She sat despondently on the edge of the bath, trying to avoid the array of mirrors – four of her, five of her – looking anything but sophisticated: hair tousled by the wind, a grease-spot on her jacket. The Queen of Fleet Street was a complete and utter fraud. Even the one article she *had* produced would never have been accepted without Max's wholesale editing. He had sharpened it up, transformed her adolescent outpourings into a meaty piece of prose, satirical and succinct.

She ran some water in the basin to sponge the stain off her jacket. She might as well try to make herself presentable – if only on the outside. The basin was real marble, the taps flamboyant golden swans' heads. Elizabeth wouldn't approve of all this ostentation, and even *she* was beginning to find it pretentious. If only she could work out who she was, or what she really wanted – to be part of this exclusive world, or to share a quiet existence with Elizabeth. Except that Elizabeth wouldn't want her any more; might have already invited Hugo to install himself instead. She would be banished to her flat, cooped up on her own with only her jealousy as companion. Hugo's mere name was enough to spark it off again, and when she thought back to New Year there were still more frightening memories to contend with. Here in France, in Max's cheerful company, the gruesome images of her dead twin George had more or less receded, but . . .

'Beattie? Are you in there?'

She tensed. Max's voice, followed by a loud rap on the door. Reluctantly she let him in.

'What's wrong? Too much champagne? You got me worried, rushing off like that. I thought you were going to throw up.'

She shook her head. 'Not *enough* champagne.'

'What do you mean?'

'Oh, I don't know. I'm probably being stupid, but I seem to be getting all worked up again.'

'Kiss me.'

She obeyed half-heartedly. His mouth tasted of fish – caviar, smoked salmon.

'Look, sweet, we're on *holiday*. We're supposed to have left all the shit behind in England.'

'Yeah, I know, but if Elizabeth starts . . .'

'Beattie, I don't want to hear that woman's name again. She's really fucked you up, if only you could see it. It's not your fault – it's *hers*. She's got you in her power. Shrinks do have that effect on people. Remember what they did to my son? He got worse, not better, and in the end he was literally enslaved.'

'Elizabeth's not my *shrink*, Max. She's my . . . my . . . friend.'

'Some friend!'

'Oh, Max, that really is unfair.'

271

'Look, she's standing in your way, darling, stopping you from fulfilling yourself. I mean, here you are, with your name in print at last and everything going for you, and what do you do? Lock yourself in the bathroom and tear yourself apart over some middle-aged frump who can't hold a candle to you in terms of looks, talent, style, or . . .'

'You don't understand, Max. She's . . .'

'I *do* understand. Just take it easy, darling.' He bent down and kissed the deep V of flesh between the lapels of her jacket. 'Christ! You look so fucking beautiful today. Dave said the same. He took me aside earlier on and said if I wasn't one of his oldest friends, he'd drag you off to his stateroom and make wild impassioned love to you.'

'You're kidding!'

'No, really. He's definitely got the hots for you. I can always tell with Dave.'

'But . . . but what about Pru?'

'Oh, *Pru*. She's not in your class, my sweet. You never seem to realize how stunning you can look. Even Leon said what a knock-out you were, and he must be eighty if he's a day. Oh, and by the way, Yves read your piece in the *Herald* and thought it was terrific.'

'Eve? Who's she?'

'*He*, not she – the guy in the white polo-neck. He's the editor of *Quotidien Azur*, so he should know what he's talking about.'

'Did he *really* like it, Max?' She ran her hand distractedly through her hair. 'I mean, that's another thing that's bothering me. I keep feeling it's a sham.'

'What on earth d'you mean?'

'Well, *you* wrote it, not me.'

'Come off it, Beattie. You're getting paranoid. All I did was knock the thing into shape and flam it up a bit. It's a matter of technique, that's all – writing to a formula, giving the buggers what they want. You'll soon get the hang of it, once you've had more practice. And as for style, you're a natural. Yves saw that straight away.'

'Honestly? You're not just trying to cheer me up?'

'Look, I'll give you chapter and verse, if you want. He said it was *vif* and *dynamique* and a few other words I can't pronounce. Which roughly translated means bloody fucking marvellous.'

'Oh, Max!' She hugged him. 'You're a wonder. You *have* cheered me up – no end.'

272

'Thank God for that! Now come on, let's get back on deck, or Dave will think *I'm* making wild impassioned love to you in his stateroom.' He slipped a hand inside her bra and ran his thumb across the nipple. 'Which is not a bad idea, come to think of it.'

She grinned and pulled away. 'Max . . .'

'What now?'

'I've been thinking. Couldn't we stay in France a bit longer? I mean, a fortnight's hardly anything, and half of it's already gone.'

He took a bottle of cologne from the shelf and dabbed some on his wrists. 'I'd love to, sweetie, but I'll never wangle a third week. Not with Clive in such a state about that wretched meeting. And anyway, what about Michèle?'

'I thought you said she was enjoying it in St Ives?'

'Yeah, she is – poor sod.'

'Well, she'll be glad of another week there then. And as for Clive, can't you say you've sprained your ankle or gone down with some bug or something, and need more time to recover? I mean, it's doing you the world of good out here. You're much more relaxed than in London.' Less irritable as well, she thought – in fact, almost a new-model Max: attentive, complimentary, and more generous even than usual. He had wined and dined her each evening at the best restaurants in the area, and had promised to drive her to Monte Carlo for a night of serious gambling.

'Well, I suppose I could invent a reason for staying on.' Max sniffed his wrists appreciatively, then returned the cologne to the shelf. 'Find some story that needs following up, maybe. Actually, I've got to phone Clive anyway.'

'What, again?'

'Yeah, there's a problem with our next serialization.'

'Bloody cheek! If they can't even leave you in peace when you're meant to be on holiday, you jolly well deserve a longer break.'

He laughed. 'Try telling that to Clive!'

'Actually, that's not a bad idea. I've a good mind to ring him now and say you're too busy to take his calls. Where's the phone?'

'Knowing Dave, there's probably one in here. He seems to have them all over the show.'

'No, wait, I'll send a fax. And maybe one to my broker, while I'm about it. I wouldn't mind another million shares. Where d'you think he keeps the thing?'

'Don't be silly, sweetheart. As far as Clive's concerned – *and* Her

Indoors, for that matter – I'm here strictly on my tod. And sorting out a duff drainpipe, not living the life of Riley.'

'Well, *you* get on the phone, then. Oh *please*, Max! I'll make it worth your while.' She pressed herself against him, hands groping for his zip. 'Wow! Look at Maximus. He obviously agrees with me. He's performed brilliantly all week, darling.'

'Yeah, amazing how it helps to be away from all the pressures.'

'Well, there you are. You admit it yourself.'

'God, what are you *doing*, sweetheart? No, don't stop. It's fantastic.'

'I will unless you promise to ring Clive.'

'I promise!'

She knelt on the floor in front of him and took Maximus in her mouth, grazing very lightly with her teeth, squeezing with her lips, then making her tongue as frenzied as a lizard's and swirling it round and round the tip. The marble floor was hurting her knees, but she tried to ignore the discomfort and focus only on Max. She owed him such a lot. Not only had he rescued her when she was at her lowest ebb, but he had launched her on a fantastic new career. She was determined to make it better for him than it had ever been before; more intense and more arousing. All her own senses seemed sharpened: the salt taste of his prick somehow fusing with the lemony cologne; his muffled gasps of pleasure echoed by the throbbing of a powerboat somewhere far across the bay. She could even hear the faint hum of the generator, and the cry of a gull as it swooped down past the porthole.

Then suddenly Max's urgent voice cut across the other sounds. 'Christ, I've *got* to have you, woman!' He prised her mouth away, drew her to her feet. 'Quick – let's go and find Dave's stateroom.'

'Max, we *can't*.'

'We can.'

'But what if he comes in?'

'Too bad. *He* was the one who gave me the idea.' He yanked his zip up and practically pushed her out of the bathroom.

The master cabin was only two doors down. Max swept in as if he owned it, hardly pausing to shut the door. He made straight for the four-poster and threw himself diagonally across it.

'God, what a turn-on! Just imagine when you're out at sea – all that extra pitching and rolling!'

Beattie glanced nervously over her shoulder, knowing they ought to be on deck, especially as Dave had arranged the party in their honour. But Max had already unzipped his flies and was now taking off his jacket.

'Max, *no* – you mustn't undress. Supposing someone finds us.'

'They won't. Dave's busy playing host and no one else would come in here.'

'But what about Pru?'

'Oh, *she* can join in.'

'Over my dead body!' Beattie edged towards the bed. She had to admit she was tempted. It would be great to tell Sal that she had made love in a four-poster with carved mahogany posts and a ruched canopy in a sea-green velvet and *yards* of matching coverlet. The whole cabin was outrageously flash: gilt-framed pictures on every wall, a huge L-shaped leather sofa, and a dressing-table and wardrobe which would have looked at home in Buckingham Palace. She had assumed naïvely that yachts had small and spartan cabins, not ones this boastful size, with cocktail bars and satellite TVs.

'When you've quite finished admiring the joint, sweet, perhaps we could get back to business.'

She pulled her pants off and climbed onto the bed. She might never get another chance to play at millionaires. 'Listen, Max,' she said, giving him a teasing kiss on the lips. 'This has got to be a quickie, okay? I'm not undressing any further than this.'

He rolled her over onto her back and started unbuttoning her jacket, kissing away her protests and reaching round to unhook her bra. 'Hey, let's pretend I'm Dave and you're Pru – no, *Prudence*. Prudence sounds like a real tight-arsed virgin. Yeah, it's your first time, Prudence, and you're very very nervous.'

'Too right,' said Beattie, clamping her legs together and giving another anxious glance at the door.

'So I'll have to coax you, won't I, sweetheart?'

'Yes. *Please* don't be too rough, Dave,' Beattie lisped. She might as well enter into the spirit of the thing. After all, she was pretty good at fantasies (though she did get tired of virgins – all men seemed to crave them, especially schoolgirl virgins).

'Dave, I'm only just fifteen. Perhaps you didn't realize. And I'm feeling awfully scared. We shouldn't really be doing this.'

'I know, sweet. Don't breathe a word to your parents, for God's sake. In fact, you mustn't tell a soul. It's our little secret, Prudence. And there's no need to be scared – I promise I won't hurt you. We'll take things nice and gently. Now that feels good, doesn't it?'

'I'm, er, not sure, Dave. You're so *big*, you see, and . . .'

'Close your eyes and relax. The first time's always difficult. But you just wait, sweetums. Once we get our act together, we're going to be absolutely great!' He traced her lips with his finger, then moved his hand slowly, slowly down. 'Have you ever had your breasts kissed?'

'N . . . no.' She made her voice tremulous, with just a hint of excitement.

'Well, you're really going to love this, kid. And you've got such darling breasts – just tiny little buds.'

'Yeah, I wish they'd grow.'

'Don't worry – the more I kiss them, the bigger they'll become.' He demonstrated, pulling gently on the nipples, then sucking them into his mouth. Prudence responded dramatically, gripping with her muscles and rocking her pelvis wildly back and forth.

'Wow! What the hell are you up to, Prudence? Good God, you're learning fast, you little hussy! If you're not careful, you'll make me come before I've even . . .'

There was a sudden noise outside the cabin: the sound of footsteps approaching, then Dave's voice – the real Dave's voice – echoing past the door. 'Beattie! Max! Where *are* you? Lunch is served.'

26

Beattie turned the corner into Rainham Road, glancing with distaste at the row of bulging dustbin bags spewing litter onto the pavement. Although she had been home four days, the place still seemed depressingly grotty after the charms of Max's house in France. She could hardly wait for Easter, when he had promised to take her back there, if only for the long weekend. And if things went well, she might even be able to find herself a more salubrious London flat. She already had another commission from the *Herald*, and Max was trying to interest the travel editor in her satirical piece on Cannes.

She let herself in and unloaded her shopping onto the kitchen table. The huge sheaf of flowers she'd bought this morning hadn't seemed quite enough, so she'd gone out to get more presents: a whole French cheese, a box of nougat and a bottle of Provençal wine. She hoped Elizabeth would assume that she'd bought them in France and accept them as a peace offering. She had been too apprehensive to phone to say she was coming, although the two letters postmarked Sevenoaks waiting on the doormat had been models of restraint: merely enquiring as to her whereabouts, not expressing any anger. All the same, she planned to keep the meeting short – she would apologize profusely, blame the trauma of the rebirthing, then return to London and get on with her own life. Max had advised her to see much less of Elizabeth: it was a total waste of her talent, he'd said, to loaf around in the sticks with a woman old enough to be her mother, when she could be making a name for herself.

She went into the bedroom and sorted through her wardrobe. She wanted to impress Elizabeth as the up and coming journalist, smartly dressed and heading for success. She chose the suit Max had bought her in Toulon: red with a slit skirt. He had showered her with gifts in France – driven her the whole length of the coast for shopping trips and sightseeing, and when they'd landed at Heathrow and were about to go their separate ways, he'd become almost sentimental, loath to say goodbye.

Impulsively she picked up the phone and dialled his number at the *Herald*. 'Max – it's me! I just rang to thank you again.'

'That's okay, sweet. Any time.'

'By the way, Max, you don't think Fenella's forgotten about that lunch she promised?'

''Course not. She's just busy, that's all. Up to her eyes – like me.'

'Sorry. I'll leave you in peace.'

'No, hang on, I've got a minute. Actually I'm seeing Fenella this afternoon, so I'll give her a nudge.'

'Thanks.'

'So what are you doing, sunshine? Reclining on the old chaise-longue, spoon-feeding your chihuahua?'

'Yeah, something like that.' She squinted in the mirror, smoothing her unruly hair. She had no intention of telling him she was going down to Kent, when he had warned against Elizabeth so strongly.

'Christ, I miss our daily workouts! Maximus keeps popping up and asking where you are.'

'Give him my love.'

'And mine to Miss Blackberry Bush. 'Bye, sweet. Must rush.'

She replaced the receiver and checked her watch. If she set off now, she'd be in Kent by three. She had chosen both the day and the time with care: avoiding the weekend, when half the family might be there, and mealtimes, so that Elizabeth wouldn't feel obliged to lay on any food. Tuesday was the obvious choice – the only day free of patients – so they'd be able to talk in peace.

She grabbed some biscuits from the tin and ate them while she collected up her things, including two copies of the *Herald*: one for Elizabeth and one for James and Margaret. She scanned her article again, feeling a mixture of pride in her achievement and horror at the memories. The next commission should be less traumatic – a piece on a pet cemetery in Cobham. Max had already discussed it with her; dug her out some other pieces, so she could copy the general format.

She packed everything in a carrier bag, picked up the flowers and made her way downstairs, careful not to damage the extravagant bouquet. She'd chosen irises, narcissi and some exotic speckled lilies, then added several bunches of Elizabeth's favourite freesias, in shades of cream and yellow. She laid them gently on the back seat of the car, then walked round to the driver's door, glancing up at the sky. The dismally grey morning had changed to a bright afternoon – the fierce light making all the colours deeper, as if Cannes had come to London. It was already the first of February. Next month would be spring, and who knew where she'd be by Easter? Not just back in Fayence, but maybe several rungs up her career.

As she turned into the Marylebone Road, she was feeling almost light-hearted. She needn't actually *grovel* to Elizabeth. After all, a broken phone and a few upended drawers weren't exactly criminal. And as for the aborted book, well, Elizabeth wouldn't even know it had disappeared from the disk. She would simply have to retype it – a big job, admittedly, but a way of making amends, and after that she could forget the whole palaver.

She stopped at some pedestrian lights, admiring the tall West Indian guy crossing the road in front of her. It seemed extraordinary to think that she'd been in such a state about fancying a woman. It had been just an aberration, a crazy teenage crush, and the gratifying sex in France had drummed it out of her system, thank God. Funnily enough, she happened to be passing a church at that moment, and grinned to herself at the words on the poster outside: REJOICE IN YOUR SALVATION.

'Yeah, I *will*!' she said. 'Don't worry.'

She rang the doorbell twice before Elizabeth appeared.

'Hello! It's me. I'm back,' she said, stepping into the hall. Boz had rushed to greet her, but she hardly noticed him. She was too concerned with Elizabeth, who was looking almost hostile, her mouth set in a grim line. She thrust the flowers across, but there was still no smile, no thaw.

'Beattie, I don't want flowers, I want an explanation.'

'Yeah – 'course. I . . . I know. That's why I'm here.'

'And couldn't you have phoned before you came? More to the point, couldn't you have phoned four weeks ago?'

She was shaken by the cold, brusque voice. Elizabeth sounded as if she were talking to an *enemy*. 'Look, I tried to ring. Loads of times. Your phone was out of order.'

'Only for a couple of days. And I haven't heard a word from you for a month. I wrote to you – twice – but you failed to reply. For all

I knew, you might have had an accident, or have landed up in hospital, or . . . or worse. Didn't it even occur to you that I'd be worried?'

'Well . . . no. I thought you'd be more angry, to tell the truth.'

'I *was* angry. I still am – if it was you that did that damage in my consulting room.'

'I'm sorry, terribly sorry. I know it was an awful cheek, but . . .'

'No, it's not a cheek. It's much more serious than that. In fact, I'm extremely distressed about it. I'd have thought by now you might have grasped that my work as a therapist is based on confidentiality. My patients expect me to keep their records totally private. That's the whole basis of my relationship with them. Otherwise there'd be no trust between us. So if a third party tampers with their notes . . .'

'I *didn't* tamper with them. I didn't even look at them, for Christ's sake!' Beattie heard the indignation in her voice, but it hurt to be referred to as a third party and to be kept standing in the hall like some unwelcome stranger and addressed in such an acid tone. 'Look, couldn't we sit down and talk?'

'I'm not sure I want to talk.'

'Elizabeth, please don't be so . . . so hard on me. I've said I'm sorry. What else can I do?' Beattie put her bags down. The dark green walls seemed to be closing her in; the familiar surroundings now menacing, oppressive. And Elizabeth herself had all but changed her character; become unreasonable and stern. 'I didn't realize you'd worry or . . .'

'No, you don't appear to have thought at all. Perhaps you didn't realize, as you put it, that you left the house unlocked when you came back here after New Year.'

Beattie stared at her incredulously. She remembered almost nothing about her wild dash from the house, but surely she couldn't have been so careless?

'You can imagine how upset I was when I returned to find the front door open and then saw my wrecked consulting room. Naturally I assumed there'd been a burglary, so I got straight on to the police.'

'Oh God, no!'

'*Yes*, Beattie. And it's worse than that. The police asked if any of my patients would be capable of doing such a thing.' Elizabeth broke off for a moment, as if the memory appalled her. 'I do in fact have one rather violent patient, so the suspicion fell on him, of course. I phoned his psychiatrist to find out where he was, and meanwhile the police began a thorough search to see if anyone was still on the premises. It was then they found your suitcase – up in Sarah's room – and I realized . . .'

'Hell! I'm *sorry*,' she muttered again, but it sounded more hollow with every repetition. Trite apologies were useless; she had to make it up to Elizabeth for all that worry and upheaval. But *how?* In desperation she held out the bag of presents. 'These are for you. I brought them back from France.'

'So you've been in France?'

She nodded.

'With Max?'

'Er, yes.'

'And I imagined you in the mortuary.'

Elizabeth hadn't taken the bag. Beattie banged it down on the floor, hearing an ominous clunk from the bottle. 'I only went because I was scared – I didn't dare to face you. Can't you understand that?'

Elizabeth let out a long sighing breath. 'Yes, I *do* understand. And of course it crossed my mind that you might be avoiding me on purpose. But I didn't think you'd be so irresponsible – I mean, to vanish for a month without a word.'

Beattie couldn't meet her eyes. All her feelings were suddenly flooding back – desire, excitement, love and longing, overlaid with guilt and shame. She was utterly bewildered. How could she be affected like this when she'd got *over* her obsession; accepted Max's view of it as sick and even dangerous? Yet face to face with Elizabeth, his words seemed sick themselves. This was the woman she *loved*; the person who meant most to her in the world. In fact, it was all she could do not to rush over and hug her.

She took one hesitant step forward, still fearing rejection. 'Elizabeth, *please* let's talk,' she begged. 'I mean, sit down and discuss things properly. I can't even think straight, standing here in my coat.'

Elizabeth led the way into the drawing-room and sank into a chair. She looked even paler than usual, Beattie noted wretchedly, aware of her own healthy South-of-France glow. She could hardly scrub off her tan, but she should have thought twice before breezing in here dressed up to the nines. Elizabeth's sober skirt and quiet blue top seemed a mute reproach to her own brazen scarlet swank.

'Beattie, perhaps it would be wiser if we discussed things a bit later, when we've both had a chance to calm down. I have to admit I did feel quite outraged. I mean, it was an unforgivable thing for anyone to do.'

Outraged. Unforgivable. The words cut her like steel knives. 'Oh, *please* don't say unforgivable. It makes me feel like . . . like shit. Look, I promise faithfully I'll never set foot in your consulting room again, if you'll let me off the hook this time.'

'It's not a question of letting you off the hook. You still don't seem to understand the principles involved. If we're going to remain friends, Beattie, you've simply got to accept that my patients have their rights as well, and have to be considered.'

'I *do* accept it – truly. Just say you forgive me.'

Elizabeth picked up her cigarettes and sat in silence for a moment with the packet in her hands. 'Look, I'm sorry if I was sharp,' she said, no longer sounding angry, only infinitely tired. 'I probably overreacted. It was quite a shock, seeing you there on the step, when I feared you might be . . . be . . .' She clicked her lighter open, then shut it again without lighting her cigarette. 'Shall we call it quits? You've apologized for your part, so let's leave it at that – all right?' She gave a rueful smile. 'Actually I'm extremely relieved you're not dead.'

'Oh, *Elizabeth*!' Beattie hurled herself into her arms. 'I love you, honestly. I know you won't believe it after the awful way I've behaved. But there's so much I haven't told you. You say *I* don't understand, but *you* don't either. If you only knew what I'd been through before I drove back here. Let's talk *now* – I need to. I mean, the rebirthing was horrendous, and I think it drove me . . . sort of . . . mad.'

'I did try to warn you, Beattie, dear.'

'I know, and you were right. You can say "I told you so" as often as you like.'

Elizabeth smiled and said nothing. Beattie sat down on the carpet at her feet, trying to work out where to start. She had never told anyone that she'd had a twin who died. And no one had told *her* until she was nearly fifteen. Even then, her father had approached the subject with such obvious pain and despondency, she hadn't liked to pursue it. And when she finally plucked up courage to question him more deeply, he'd seemed equally resistant, saying he had promised her mother never to discuss the matter. Only now did she realize that *he* was the one who probably found the loss unbearable: his longed-for son stillborn.

She looked up at Elizabeth. Now she was so close, she could see how utterly drained she was: dark rings under her eyes and a tautness about her face, as if she hadn't been sleeping properly. Perhaps she'd been unwell or overworking, or maybe Hugo had exhausted her with all his wretched problems. Before she launched into her own trauma, she ought at least to find out how things were *here*. 'How's ... Hugo?' she asked dutifully, though his name was still anathema.

'He's okay.'

'Recovering from the shock?'

'What shock?' Elizabeth herself looked startled. She had sat up straighter in her seat, one pale hand gripping the chair-arm.

'Well, his wife walking out, of course.'

'Oh, I see. Yes. Yes ...'

'Elizabeth, are you all *right*? You sound sort of ... weird.'

Elizabeth lit her cigarette at last, then got up slowly and walked over to the window. 'Beattie, dear, there's something I need to tell you. Perhaps now is not the ideal time, but I've been ... worrying about it for some days.'

Don't tell me, she implored, overwhelmed by a sudden irrational burst of fear. She too stood up, but kept absolutely still, her eyes fixed on the carpet, as if by avoiding Elizabeth's eyes she could somehow stop her talking. Let the phone ring, she prayed, or someone come to the door.

Elizabeth opened her mouth to speak, cleared her throat, began again. 'Hugo and I ... are ... are going to be ... er ... married.'

Beattie could hear herself screaming in the silence. She put her hand over her mouth to stop any sound from actually emerging. Whatever happened, she mustn't lose control this time. All she had to do was wipe out that last sentence, simply tell herself she'd imagined it. In any case, it *couldn't* be true. Elizabeth would never be so impulsive as to agree to marry a virtual stranger. Besides, she had stated categorically that she intended never to remarry, so why should she change her mind now?

She steadied herself on the back of the chair. Perhaps she had imagined the whole last month, including the rebirthing, and she and Elizabeth were together again, enjoying the happy time they'd promised themselves once the Christmas upheaval was over. She shut her eyes to make it seem more real. Yes, the family were gone and Hugo had driven back to Cheltenham, leaving the two of them alone. And they'd spent a blissful afternoon, revelling in the peace ...

'Beattie, are you all right, my love?'

My love. She sucked the words like a sweet, rolling them round and round her mouth, extracting all their flavour. 'Yes . . . fine. Just . . . er . . . thinking. Sh . . . shall I make some tea?'

'Good idea. *I'll* make it.'

'No, you look tired. Let me.'

Beattie went out to the kitchen and began to fill the kettle, but her hands were shaking too much so she left it in the sink. Everything would be all right in a moment. She was cold, that's all – seemed to have lost the feeling in her body. She sat down on the settle. Boz was dozing there on a cushion and stretched his limbs languidly, purring with his eyes still closed. She picked him up and held him tight against her. 'I love you, Boz,' she whispered. 'You do understand that, don't you? I mean, even though I went to France and let Max persuade me you were horrible and dangerous, I didn't really believe it. I loved you all along.'

Boz struggled to get down. She must be hurting him, clutching him too tightly. She did that all the time – hurt the people she loved. Then they went away.

She let him go, staring dully at the table. Two cups and saucers had already been set out, one in Jeremy's place. She scrutinized the pattern of tiny blue-grey flowers; the gold rim round the cup. No one sat in Jeremy's place. Only Elizabeth's husband. Only Hugo.

Just at that moment Elizabeth appeared at the door. 'I've come to give you a hand.'

Beattie's eyes didn't move from Hugo's cup. 'Y . . . you said you'd never marry again.'

Elizabeth smiled. 'Oh, did I?'

Beattie pummelled her fist on the table. 'You *must* remember! You must, you must. It was our first day out together. That day we went to Sandown. You told me you'd made up your mind straight after the divorce and you'd no intention of changing it.'

Elizabeth gave an embarrassed shrug. 'Yes, I do recall it now.'

'Well, what happened?' Beattie demanded. 'I mean, you gave me all these reasons why you *preferred* being single – not having to dress up for someone, or entertain their friends, or consider *them* all the time, instead of being independent and doing what you want.' There were a million other reasons churning in her mind: more serious and pressing ones. She had to save Elizabeth, stop her making a terrible mistake. 'And what about your work?' she persisted. 'Your patients will be totally bereft if you move to Cheltenham and leave them in the lurch. Or perhaps you've persuaded Hugo to come *here?*

Christ! Your family would loathe that. You told me yourself Harriet and Sarah haven't got over the divorce. Well, they'll hardly welcome some stranger muscling in and taking their father's place. And the grandchildren won't understand. They're bound to be jealous and . . .'

'Beattie, I don't think . . .'

'Please don't interrupt. This is terribly important. I mean, have you even thought how little *experience* Hugo has of children? He's never had any himself, and he's an only child, isn't he? So he'll probably find *your* lot a bloody imposition.'

'But Beattie dear, he always *wanted* children.'

'Okay. All the more reason why he should marry a younger woman and start his *own* family. I remember you saying how upset he was that Anna didn't want kids and his first wife couldn't have any. Well, *you*'re hardly likely to produce any, are you? I'm sorry if that sounds blunt, but I can't bear to think of you making yourself unhappy.'

'But Beattie, I . . .'

'Listen – Hugo's had two failed marriages already. You'll be failure number three, unless you change your mind. I mean, you didn't even *like* him when you met him at the golf club – or have you forgotten that as well? You said he was defensive, and . . . and . . . oh, lots of other things.'

'Yes, well, perhaps I didn't know him then.'

'You *still* don't know him, do you? You've only been seeing him a few weeks.' She suddenly recalled him turning up out of the blue, four days after Christmas – the shock she'd felt spying from the landing, and then her heart-to-heart with Elizabeth. 'Shit! You *lied* to me!' she shouted, springing to her feet. 'That time we talked in my room in the attic. You said the only reason you were seeing him was because he needed someone to listen.'

'Beattie, I *didn't* lie – that *was* the only reason.'

'You don't expect me to believe that, do you? I saw you holding hands, for God's sake.'

'Yes, that's true, but . . .'

'I . . . I can't bear to think of you lying.' Tears were sliding down her face; her voice choked and indistinct. 'You were the only person I've ever known who always told the truth. That meant more than anything. So many people lie. But you were different. You . . .'

'But I *haven't* lied, Beattie. I know it must seem odd, Hugo visiting me here, but he only came originally because he just didn't know

285

who to turn to. After that, things . . . changed. It does sometimes happen – and happen very quickly. And it can take you by surprise. To tell the truth, I was . . .'

'I don't want to hear.' Beattie turned to face the wall. The obscene *speed* of it was almost the worst thing. 'He's marrying on the rebound,' she sobbed. 'That should be obvious to anyone – except you. Once he's got over his divorce, he'll feel completely different. I mean, you're a *therapist*, for fuck's sake, and you can't see what's under your nose!'

Elizabeth had come up to her and put a hand on her shoulder. 'Let's talk about this later, Beattie, when you're feeling less distraught.'

'No. I want to talk *now*. You keep trying to put me off.' Furiously she brushed her tears away. It was mortifying to cry, and anyway she must look quite revolting with all her make-up streaked. She took a deep breath in, to try to calm herself. There was so much she burned to say, but it was all jumbled in her mind, and she wasn't sure if she was even making any sense. 'Elizabeth, you've *got* to listen. Don't you see – I'm the only one who cares enough to tell you what a mistake you're making. I mean, you and Hugo have almost nothing in common. Okay, art and music, maybe, but look at the huge differences. He's a sports fanatic, to start with – golf, skiing, jogging – you name it. You've never played golf in your life; you detest the thought of skiing, and you'd jump in the car and *drive* to the village rather than walk a mile.'

'People don't have to share *all* their interests, Beattie. They need some time away from each other.'

'Not when they're married, though.'

'Oh, yes – perhaps especially then. If Hugo wants to play golf, that's fine by me. I don't think he's expecting me to caddie for him!'

'Elizabeth, you're not being serious.'

'I'm completely serious. It often helps to have different hobbies, then you're not in each other's pocket all the time.'

Beattie kicked out at the chair-leg. She wasn't getting anywhere. 'Anyway, that's not the only problem,' she said, trying a different tack. 'Take something much more personal. I mean, hasn't it occurred to you that Hugo likes glamorous women? You've only got to look at Anna. D'you honestly imagine he won't compare you both? I'm sorry to be brutal, but you're always wearing tatty clothes and you're *years* older than her and . . .'

286

'Beattie, I'm going to make the tea, all right? And I suggest we sit down quietly and . . .'

'Okay. I'm sitting.' She slumped down at the table, deliberately choosing Jeremy's chair. It was no good ranting on – Elizabeth was blind. Either way she'd suffer. If Hugo forced her to go to Cheltenham, she'd lose her home and patients. And if she dragged him here, her entire family would be up in arms. And all for a marriage that was doomed. Hugo was *using* her, that's all, clinging to her for support, lapping up her sympathy. But as soon as he recovered from the divorce, he'd realize what a fool he'd been and drop her like a hot potato. 'Elizabeth, I'm only trying to *save* you,' she said desperately.

'I understand.' Elizabeth joined her at the table, took her hand. 'But I'm not in any danger,' she said gently, 'and nor are you, my love. If you're worried about losing me, let me reassure you – as far as you and I are concerned, nothing's going to change. We'll still be very good friends.'

'*Friends!*' Beattie spat the word out, pushing Hugo's cup to the far end of the table. *He* wasn't a mere friend, but Elizabeth's partner and beloved. There was a terrifying sense of Elizabeth receding from her, literally – no longer sitting next to her, but moving further and further away; the blue of her jersey fading into grey. 'Elizabeth,' she panicked, 'please come back.'

'I'm here, Beattie, beside you.'

'No, you're not. You're *not*. I'll probably never *see* you again. You'll be with Hugo all the time and . . .'

'Beattie, dear, if you're so upset, maybe you should talk to someone.'

'What do you mean, "someone"?'

'Well, perhaps it might help if you went to see a therapist.'

Beattie stared at her, appalled. Elizabeth *was* a therapist, one who'd counselled Hugo, not sent him packing to some prying stranger who would make money out of his grief. And besides, hadn't Elizabeth written a book questioning the whole business of psychotherapy, pointing out its drawbacks? Hugo, it appeared, must be protected at all costs, whereas *she* could be dispatched to any bloody charlatan.

'Thanks,' she said coldly, 'but I don't need a shrink.' She blundered over to the kettle, switched it on and started banging cups around, simply to keep busy. She was terrified she'd lose control. Already she could feel herself disintegrating: her hands clumsy and unco-ordinated and a strange numbness in her limbs. She opened the fridge to get the milk, but there was only a dribble left. She stood holding the empty bottle, the fridge's cold breath chilling her legs.

'Did Hugo finish the milk?' she asked. Her voice sounded unfamiliar – strident and embittered. 'I suppose he had it on his cornflakes. Or don't you bother with breakfast? No, I expect you prefer to lie in bed. It must be so exciting, getting to know each . . .'

She swung round at a noise from the hall. Someone was coming in. Hugo! He was certain to have a key. She'd be forced to watch him with Elizabeth – kissing her, embracing her. No. She'd blow his brains out first. The thought appalled her, because it *wasn't* just a thought: she knew she was capable of murder, could feel red violence flowing through her veins. She stood her ground, waiting for him, waiting . . .

'Mummy?' called a female voice. 'We're back.'

Caroline bustled into the kitchen with Alexander in her arms. Tim rushed on ahead to greet his grandmother, stopping in his tracks when he saw Beattie.

'We thought you was *dead*!' he accused.

'You look wonderful,' said Caroline diplomatically, trying to fill the awkward silence. 'Anything but dead! Where did you get the tan?'

'Fr . . . France.'

'Beattie, d'you like my new dinosaur?' Tim clamoured, holding out a handsome velvet creature: green with orange paws. '*Hugo* bought it for me. We went to the shop together. He took me in his car. Isn't it great?'

'Y . . . yes,' she whispered, pushing it away. 'It . . . it's absolutely great.'

27

Each day comes
Each day goes
We miss you more
Than anyone knows
Beloved Bruno
We miss your wet nose

Beattie copied the lines into her notebook. That should make her readers laugh – the non-pet-owners, anyway. The dog-lovers would probably cry. She was crying herself, tears falling on the page and smudging the black ink. So many of the inscriptions reflected her own feelings for Elizabeth: 'I love and miss you more than words can say'; 'You will always have a place in my heart'; 'My life, my love, my happiness'. Indeed, Elizabeth seemed as hopelessly lost as the pets buried in this cemetery; their marble headstones stretching all around her.

She closed her notebook and slumped onto a bench, wishing she could go back home to bed rather than continue with this job. It was a difficult commission and she wasn't sure what line to take – satirical or sympathetic. 'Make it punchy,' the *Herald* had said, but her thoughts kept creeping back to Elizabeth and Hugo, wondering what they were doing; imagining them together, absorbed in one another to the exclusion of all else. They even had the power to influence the weather, to celebrate their engagement. February should be bleak and grey, with lowering skies and the threat of snow, yet today was bright and spring-like – romantic wedding weather.

'Excuse me, dear. D'you mind if I join you?'

A shapeless middle-aged woman was standing over her; her hair scragged into a bun; six inches of drab blue skirt showing beneath her khaki coat.

'No, please do.'

The woman lowered her bulk onto the bench, placed her string bag in her lap, and folded her hands across it: gnarled arthritic hands, bare of any rings. 'Forgive me for intruding,' she said, 'but I couldn't help noticing how upset you were. Have you lost a loved one?'

'Yes,' said Beattie listlessly. 'Last Tuesday.'

'I'm *sorry*, dear. I know what it's like, believe me. I've got four babies buried here. I come every day to see them.'

Beattie bit her lip to stop herself from crying again. She ought to *use* this woman, pump her for facts to help flesh out her article. Well, there was no real need to pump her – she was already in full flow.

'Yes, I'm quite a regular fixture here. I only live down the road, you see, so it's nice and handy for visiting. Some people come *miles*, you know. I met a couple from Glasgow once, and this sweet old lady from Holland. She'd brought her cat here – well, just his ashes in a jar. She'd had him on the mantelpiece at home, but she said she wanted a proper resting-place – you know, somewhere she could visit, and a bit of dignity and ceremony. Well, you can understand that, can't you?'

Beattie nodded, shading her eyes against the sun.

'Was *yours* a cat?'

'No.'

'Don't worry, dear' – the woman patted her hand – 'I can see you'd rather not talk about it. I was just the same when Sheba passed away. I didn't speak to a soul for almost a week. I didn't even go out.' She fumbled in her red string bag and extracted a large Thermos flask. 'Would you like a cup of tea, dear? I always bring some with me, especially in the winter. Mind you, it's lovely today, isn't it – cold, but nice and bright.' She poured tea into a plastic cup and handed it to Beattie. 'I'm Thelma, by the way. Thelma Smith. I'm not that keen on Smith – they're ten a penny, aren't they? – so do call me Thelma. Everybody does.' She poured tea for herself, put the cup down on the bench, then began unwrapping something in grease-proof paper. 'I've got cake here too, if you fancy something to eat. Go on, have a piece. It's a shame to see you so upset – a lovely girl like you.'

Beattie was touched by the concern in her voice. One of the awful

things about losing Elizabeth was that she had received no shred of
sympathy, because she couldn't confide in anyone. It would hardly
do to admit to her friends that she was in love with another woman,
whereas if she'd split up with a *man*, they would have rallied round
in comfort and support. The only person who knew was Max, whose
reaction had been 'Bloody good job too!'

'Thanks,' she said, accepting a slice of ginger cake. 'My name's
Beattie – Beattie Bancroft.' It was the least she could offer in return.

'Nice to meet you, Beattie. I don't think I've seen you before, have
I? Do you live round here?'

'No . . . er . . . Kent,' she said, sipping the over-sugared tea. She
refused to give up Mile End House, if only in fantasy.

'That's a fair old trek! Still, it's worth it, don't you think? It's so
peaceful when you get here, and such a lovely atmosphere. Have you
bought your plot yet?'

Beattie shook her head.

'Of course it *is* expensive, isn't it, especially if you have a proper
coffin, on top of all the rest. I didn't stint on anything for my four.
Well, you've got to do it properly, if they mean that much to you.
They've each got a solid oak coffin with brass handles, a marble
headstone and surround, and those nice blue marble chippings, to
add a bit of colour. And I've left provision in my will to pay the
upkeep for ten years after I've . . . I've gone. It's worth it for the
peace of mind. It stops me worrying that their graves will go to rack
and ruin, or someone might . . . might dig them up.' She returned
the remainder of the cake to its crumpled greaseproof paper. 'I'll
take you to see them, if you want. They're all together, over there by
the hedge. I made sure they were close to one another, so they
wouldn't get too lonely.'

'Yes, I'd like that,' Beattie said, draining her tea and handing back
the cup. 'It'll give me some ideas.'

Thelma stood up gingerly, rubbing her left hip, then led the way
along a grassy path, edged with clumps of heather.

Beattie opened her notebook. 'I'm just jotting down some of these
inscriptions,' she explained. 'You know, to inspire me when I come
to compose my own.'

'Good idea,' said Thelma. 'I did the same with Sheba. I found
these lovely words on an Irish setter's grave: "Thank you for choosing
us, your devoted Mum and Dad". I copied them for Sheba, without
the Dad, of course. I met the owners later on and they didn't mind

at all. In fact, we became quite pally in the end. Oh yes, I've made some lovely friends. You see the same faces Sunday after Sunday. It's a bit early in the day yet, but give it another hour or two and there'll be quite a little crowd here. Some people stay the whole afternoon, especially in the summer – you know, bring a picnic, make it a day out.'

Beattie glanced towards the cemetery entrance. A large family party was just filing in through the gates: mother, father, grandparents, several small children and an overweight black labrador. She made a few surreptitious notes before returning to the inscriptions and recording the range of pets. 'Topsy the terrapin', she scribbled. 'Our beautiful bunny Blossom', 'Pretty Polly, never lost for words'. There was even a family of rats (commemorated with a large brown marble cross), though most of the burials appeared to be dogs and cats – 'Sampson, gone for long walkies', 'Puss-Puss, we loved you to bits'.

She suddenly thought of Boz and Tolkien; how upset they'd be if Elizabeth moved to Cheltenham. Cats hated change – Elizabeth had told her that herself. They were bound to fret, especially Tolkien, and might even try to run away. Perhaps she should buy them plots here – and one for herself while she was about it. Then Elizabeth might pay for her memorial, inscribe some passionate message on it: 'No stronger love', perhaps, which she'd just seen on a wolf-hound's grave. Or '*ALWAYS*', which she'd noticed earlier on, engraved in black italic on a large white marble heart. 'Always' was a sham, though. Nothing ever lasted.

'Right, here we are,' said Thelma, stopping by a cluster of head-stones. 'That's my precious Charlie. He lived until he was almost sixteen, but I still call him my baby.'

Beattie bent down to read the inscription: 'The most beautiful dog in the world.' And there was his picture to prove it, hand-painted on a porcelain plate.

'And this is Bess, my Sealyham. I took her with me everywhere – church, shopping, even to the toilet. She wouldn't let me out of her sight.'

Beattie hoped she'd remember the details. It seemed insensitive to make notes in front of Thelma. She certainly *wouldn't* forget the dog-bowl placed tastefully on the marble chippings, and the big red rubber bone.

'And Timmy's just two down. He was only an ordinary moggie,

but very special to me. He died of cancer, bless his heart. The last few weeks were terrible.'

Beattie scrutinized the grave: the two grinning gnomes holding fishing lines – presumably to catch his dinner; the inscription: 'Gone with the angels'.

'And Sheba, last but not least. She was a real bundle of love. Today's the anniversary of her death – that's why I brought the flowers.'

Expensive flowers, Beattie noted, not unlike the bouquet she'd bought Elizabeth. What had happened to those flowers? Had they been left to die, stifling in their cellophane shroud?

'I never forget their birthdays either. *Or* Christmas. I bought them each a little tree last year, decorated with fairy lights. Several people came up to me and said how pretty they were.' Thelma stooped to remove a sweet-wrapping from the path, then laid her hand on Beattie's arm. 'Now, if you'll excuse me, dear, I'll just stay here on my own for a while. I always like to talk to them in private – tell them what they mean to me, make sure they know I'll be coming back tomorrow.'

'Yes . . . yes, of course.' Beattie edged away. She had no desire to ridicule this woman. In fact, as things were going, she would probably land up the same way: on the shelf, with no one to love but some furred or feathered 'baby'. In the last few days, her sense of isolation had veered frighteningly close to panic. Elizabeth had phoned to ask how she was, and had invited her down for a meal and to stay overnight if she wanted. But she couldn't face the thought of Hugo. Even if he wasn't there, his presence would pervade the house like a dangerous gas-leak, invisible but lethal. And as for Max, they seemed to do nothing but quarrel. He had told her – sharply – that if she was still determined to be miserable when everything was going for her, then she must bloody well *enjoy* depression. Their three weeks in France seemed as vacuous now as a holiday brochure; even their enthusiastic romps in bed like scenes from some crude video. Secretly she blamed him for persuading her to go at all. If she had only stayed in England – stayed in Kent – she might have prevented the engagement.

She sat down on a tree-stump, turning up her coat-collar and pulling on her gloves. It was cold out of the sun; her hands too numb to hold the pen. The weather was a sham as well: all glitter and no warmth. On the plot beside her a bedraggled teddy bear lay propped against the headstone. It looked more like a baby's grave and immediately reminded her of George. She had dreamed about her twin last night and he'd been alive and actually *part* of her, joined in mind and body, as if they were one being and one flesh. She closed her eyes, desperate to relive the dream. If George had survived, she would have had a soul-mate, someone who understood her, and who could take away the frightening feeling of being an uninvited guest in the world.

She looked up at the sound of footsteps. A man was strolling along the path, holding a little girl by the hand – his daughter presumably, since both were blue-eyed and fair-haired.

'Good morning,' he smiled as the pair of them walked past.

'Good morning,' she mumbled mechanically, suddenly longing to see her own father – the only person left who had a genuine blood tie with her, a tie which couldn't be broken. She had sent him a copy of her article and he had written back by return, full of pride in her achievement (and obviously assuming she was already in the money, since he'd suggested she fly over for a visit). She had been tempted to drop everything and go. Apart from anything else, she wanted to ask him more about George – and her own birth. She couldn't broach the subject in a letter, and even phone calls were slightly constrained. It would be much easier face to face. But she just didn't have the money for the air fare, and would never earn it unless she kept plugging away at her writing. Besides, it would be better to go to Australia at the time of Elizabeth's wedding, then she could escape the whole hideous affair. She could hardly bear to think of it: Hugo and Elizabeth joined officially and legally; one being and one flesh.

She forced herself to get up. She would never afford to go *anywhere* if she didn't get on with her article. More people had begun to trickle in and she ought to be observing them, eavesdropping on their conversations. Scarcely anyone was on their own: most were families or couples, and even Thelma had been joined by another woman, the two of them chatting companionably on a bench. She watched the ritual with the Thermos, feeling even more excluded; craving another cup of tea, another slice of cake. Her sense of panic was threatening to return, as if Elizabeth was her life-blood and her oxygen, and without her she had been sentenced to death.

Don't be so *pathetic*, she told herself. You're behaving like a tragedy queen, and anyway, if you really loved Elizabeth, you'd be *pleased* at her engagement.

'No!' she said aloud, slamming her notebook shut. The r
ship just wasn't right and was bound to end in disaster. It w
she loved Elizabeth that she was determined to rescue her – n.
repeat of her first marriage: all those cramping duties and restrictions
which had turned her into a chattel. She still found it quite extraordinary that a therapist could be so blind about herself, and also so
impetuous. To rush into a marriage with a man she barely knew
seemed completely out of character – more the act of some madcap
teenager than a sane and sensible grandmother. It was up to her to
intervene, to *save* Elizabeth, before it was too late.

She began pacing along the path, her mind teeming with wild
schemes: how to dispose of Hugo without actually doing violence.
There seemed no possible solution, unless she simply *willed* him to
die, used some sort of voodoo curse.

She stopped by a white marble urn, her eye caught by the inscription: 'In loving memory of my beloved pony Rex'. A pony! She had
no idea they buried such large animals. A pony would be twice the
size of Hugo. She crouched in front of the grave, a plan forming in
her mind. If she bought a plot here for Hugo, that might *work* like
voodoo and somehow bring about his death. It sounded quite insane,
but such things did happen sometimes. She had read about a case
where a woman 'murdered' her perfectly healthy husband merely
by inserting his death notice in *The Times*. Three weeks later, he was
dead – from unknown causes, according to his mystified GP.

She took the cemetery brochure out of her bag and made a few
rough calculations. If she dispensed with all Thelma's extras, it
wouldn't be too expensive. But perhaps she *shouldn't* cut corners.
The process might work better if it really cost her dear, demanded
every penny she had. She ought to make it realistic like a proper
human burial, with a full-sized coffin and an elaborate headstone
engraved with the date of his death. Instantly a date flashed into her
head: March the twelfth, the day her mother had died. Grotesque
perhaps, but did that really matter? At least it would give her time
to work on Hugo, to exert her influence on him and succeed by
sheer force of will. And then there were all the preparations to
make: deciding on such details as the type of coffin, the form of the
inscription. Something dignified but final would be best – maybe
simply 'Rest in Peace', which was written on the pony's headstone,
underneath its name.

She reached out to touch the letters; the solidity of the marble abruptly shocking her back to her senses. What in God's name was she thinking of – plotting someone's death in cold blood? She must be stark raving mad. No wonder she'd lost Elizabeth – in fact, had never had any permanent relationship, either with a woman or a man. People could probably see into her mind, see how unutterably evil she was. She knelt hunched over the grave, wishing she could vanish into the earth and rest in peace like the beloved pony Rex. But peace was a lie, like the other fancy words here. The only times she had experienced it were – ironically – with Elizabeth: her convalescence at Mile End House, way back in the autumn, and their one weekend away together. She remembered kneeling beside her in the little church near Cheltenham and experiencing an *incredible* peace. Secretly, she had regarded that service as their wedding, so she *hadn't* lost Elizabeth – they were already married, symbolically, at least.

The thought was so tremendously consoling, she felt the peace of that church service beginning to steal back. She could even recall the words: 'The peace of God which passes all understanding ... and the blessing of God Almighty be among you and remain with you always.' Could she really be unutterably evil if she'd been blessed by God, or Whoever? And wasn't it strange that the exact words should return to her out of the blue, when it was three months since she'd heard them? Perhaps it was a sign that she must concentrate on good, not evil – give up all idea of revenge and focus instead on love.

'Beattie!'

Startled, she sprang to her feet. Elizabeth – calling her, telling her she was right: that love would indeed win her back. She turned to see not Elizabeth but Thelma, accompanied by a couple more old dears.

'Come along,' clucked Thelma. 'You mustn't sit here moping on your own. I've brought some friends to meet you who'll understand exactly how you feel. They've been through it too, you see – poor Vera just six weeks ago. She lost her darling Toby in December and of course it ruined the whole of Christmas for her. And this is Winifred – her lovely little Barnaby passed away in January last year.'

Beattie said hello, touched when both the women immediately offered their condolences. Then Thelma launched into a long account of Barnaby's last illness, though Beattie was barely listening; too elated by the notion that she and Elizabeth were *meant* to be together. It was as if someone – something – was telling her that if she only worked on the relationship (and worked on *herself:* established her career), she would prove a worthy partner for her, and had no need to despair.

'But you see, after his last operation, the vet said there was nothing else anyone could do. The only comfort was that Winifred had already bought her little plot here. That's right, isn't it, Winnie?'

Winifred nodded sadly.

Thelma turned back to Beattie. 'Come and see his grave, dear. It's really beautiful – an open book with a lily for a bookmark.' She steered Beattie towards the beech tree in the middle of the cemetery, then down a grassy path, Winifred and Vera following arm in arm. 'Oh, look!' she cried. 'The first crocuses are coming out. That means spring is on its way. You'll feel better in the spring, dear – just you wait and see. Time does heal, you know, though you probably won't think so at the moment.'

'No, I *do,*' said Beattie. 'I'm feeling better already.' Instead of fixing on a date for Hugo's death, she would choose the time for her reunion with Elizabeth – and spring would be ideal. In fact, it was almost here already: forsythia in flower, a green glaze on the willows, the slender spears of daffodils swelling into bud. When she'd slunk into the cemetery half an hour ago, she'd been blind to everything, loath to write the article at all. But this commission – and all the others after it – were her way back to Elizabeth.

'There!' Thelma stopped triumphantly beyond a clump of rhododendrons. 'That's Barnaby.'

Beattie gazed down at the open marble book, reading the inscription on the left-hand page: 'WAIT FOR ME'.

'Wait for me,' she mouthed, and could almost hear Elizabeth responding, echoing the words engraved beside the lily.

'TOGETHER AGAIN FOR EVER'.

28

'And then I met this television producer. Well, he already knew my work, of course, and he'd read the novel and liked it. So, to cut a long story short, I did an adaptation and it'll be on the box next year.'

'Congratulations,' said Beattie, spooning in the last mouthful of *soufflé glacé* Grand Marnier. Almost all the courses had been awash in alcohol: sea bass with a champagne sauce, *suprême* of guinea fowl marinaded in port, and three different wines already. 'Which channel will it be on?' she asked. 'I'll make sure I watch it.'

'BBC2.'

Naturally, thought Beattie. She couldn't imagine any of these glitterati churning out down-market stuff. When Max had first shown her the guest list she'd felt a mixture of excitement and sheer terror. It was like something out of Debrett's: judges and QCs by the score (hardly surprising, since this was Middle Temple Hall), a good scattering of Honourables and Sirs, a Professor of Comparative Philology (whatever *that* might be) and another of Jurisprudence, and any number of writers, actors and other VIPs. And now here she was sitting in their midst. She had been placed between a novelist called Quentin, whose parents had been close friends of Evelyn Waugh, and the principal of an Oxford college (which she'd never actually heard of, but then she didn't know *many* Oxford colleges). Further down the table were a Lord and Lady Someone, and the man opposite was a literary agent, who'd been engaged since the fish course in earnest conversation with his neighbour.

He looked up at last and smiled at her. 'Do forgive me, Beattie. You must think me very rude. But Hamish and I have just discovered we were at Balliol together, and we've been reminiscing about student life in the fifties.'

'It must have been fun,' said Beattie, wondering if fun was quite the word. She knew little about the fifties, but they conjured up an image of struggle and austerity. 'How come you never met before this evening? Is Balliol very *big*, or . . . ?' She broke off to stop the waitress overfilling her brandy glass, worried that her accent might slip if she drank any more. Even now, with all her months of practice in modelling herself on Elizabeth, she couldn't afford to drop her guard, especially in such company.

'No. Giles read English and I was a biologist, so our paths never crossed, you see.'

'What he really means, Beattie, is that *he* was a worker and *I* was a drone. All the Balliol scientists were such *drudges*, for God's sake! They'd cycle off to the labs at the crack of dawn, when any halfway civilized chap would be in bed nursing a hangover.'

'Slander – absolute slander!' Hamish laughed, swirling the brandy round in his glass. 'Were *you* at Oxford, Beattie?'

'Er, no,' she said, cautiously sipping from her own glass. She had fielded off that question twice already. The evening had been organized by one of the poorer (poorer!) Oxford colleges as part of a mammoth fund-raising drive, so Oxford graduates were thick on the ground.

'Beattie's a journalist,' Giles explained to Hamish. 'She writes for the *Daily Herald*.'

'And the *Express*,' Beattie added. It would be true in a couple of weeks if her meeting with the features editor went well. He had phoned her after reading her various pieces in the *Herald* and asked how she felt about doing something for *him*. She was highly flattered that two national dailies were actually making overtures to someone without an A-level to her name. Yet her new career was so fragile – well, not a career at all yet, just three short pieces published and the prospect of a fourth. Still, it was a step in the right direction. Elizabeth was delighted and had sent her a congratulations card with a genuinely loving message. And the fact that she was here this evening meant she was slowly advancing towards Hugo's cultured world. Of course she owed it all to Max (who'd been persuaded into coming by the *Herald*'s literary editor, herself an Oxford graduate), but with any luck these were some of the people she would soon be mixing with in her own right. They seemed quite at home in such magnificent surroundings, whereas *she* felt overawed and had to stop herself from gawping at the amazing hammer-beam roof and the pan-elled walls with their row upon row of carved heraldic shields. Queen Elizabeth I had sat in this very hall, and scores of other history-book people, like Walter Raleigh and Francis Drake – even Shakespeare, Max had said. She must read it all up afterwards, to impress Elizabeth. Middle Temple Hall was every bit as grand as Hugo's Cambridge col-lege. Some of the paintings were worth *millions*, just hanging there as casually as the dog-eared posters tacked to her kitchen wall. And an all-female string quartet was playing on the dais, wearing full-length dresses in damson-coloured velvet, with matching velvet ribbons in their hair. She only wished she knew what they were playing and could make some scintillating remark about the piece or the composer, as *Hugo* would have done. But at least she was working on herself: borrowing cassettes of classical music from the library and reading books on modern art. Alas, she hadn't been to Oxford, but she *had* enrolled in her own private university whose patron was Elizabeth.

'I think the auction's about to begin,' said Hamish. 'Look, Jeffrey's getting up.'

Beattie glanced over to the top table, where Jeffrey Archer (*Lord* Jeffrey Archer) was sitting among fellow millionaires and the most eminent of the academics. He had been persuaded to play auctioneer for the first dozen items in the catalogue before handing over to Bonham's.

Giles consulted his gold fob watch. 'No, there's still ten minutes to go. He's probably busting for a pee, that's all.'

'And I have to admit that *I* am too!' Beattie pushed back her chair. 'So if you'll please excuse me . . .'

She stopped behind Max, who was sitting between the literary editor, Ruth, and a distinguished-looking poet whose name she'd stupidly forgotten.

'Going home for an early night?' he joked.

'No fear! Not when the bidding's about to start. Don't forget lot twenty-four.'

'Darling, how *could* I? You've reminded me enough times. And frankly I'm in something of a sweat about it. I mean, what if we're outbid? Will it all be over between us?'

'But of course!'

'What *is* lot twenty-four?' Ruth asked, scooping a dab of cream off her low-cut black silk dress.

300

'It's called the Book of Fate,' said Beattie, 'and it was once owned by Napoleon.'

'Good God, Max!' Ruth exclaimed. 'You *are* aiming high. You'll have to mortgage the house, by the sounds of it.'

'Yeah, that's what worries me. But luckily it's in pretty poor condition.' He opened his catalogue and jabbed a finger at the entry. 'See? "Light soiling throughout, half the cover missing, and the title and margins torn". Thank God you didn't choose the Alexander Pope, darling. They reckon that'll go for at least ten grand.'

'You could always change your mind,' Ruth stage-whispered to Beattie. 'That would really land Max in trouble.'

'No, I've set my heart on the Book of Fate. I don't know why, but . . .' She *did* know why: she wanted the book for Elizabeth, who had told her once that she'd hero-worshipped Napoleon when she was still a dumpy schoolgirl, and had a picture of him above her bed, in preference to the pop-star photos her classmates idolized. It would make a perfect present – something even Hugo couldn't match – the translation of an ancient Egyptian manuscript found in a royal tomb near Mount Libyas, according to the blurb in the catalogue. Even the title was significant. Fate was favouring her just now, and not only in relation to her work. Ever since that occasion in the pet cemetery, when an extraordinary peace had descended on her, she'd had the feeling – weird as it might sound – that some power or presence was guiding her. She actually felt much calmer (amazing in itself) and had even started praying, in a fashion, that Elizabeth's God would prevent the disastrous marriage. There had been several little hints of late that the prayers were starting to work: that things between Elizabeth and Hugo were no longer all sweetness and light. Not that she'd seen them together, but Elizabeth had referred to him – and only half in jest – as a typical male chauvinist. Besides, she still looked dreadfully pale and tired; nothing like a radiant bride-to-be. And, most encouraging of all, she had made no move to join Hugo, but was continuing as usual with her busy life in Kent, while he spent most of his time in Cheltenham. Maybe they were coming to realize that it simply wouldn't work – that the fundamental conflict between her patients and his gallery would put paid to any permanent relationship.

'Back in a second,' she said, ruffling Max's hair and envying him the ability to sit through a long dinner without needing to take a leak, as he called it. Much to her embarrassment, this was the second time she'd slipped out – though slipping out was hardly the right phrase. It involved a long trek down the hall, past endless rows of tables, and up two flights of ancient wooden stairs.

She washed her hands and leaned against the basin, suddenly realizing just how tired she was. Despite her achievements and her new-found peace, this last month had been a strain. She worked nine to five at her temp job, then poured her heart and soul into her writing most evenings and weekends. Lunchtimes, she tried to read, ploughing through the books on art and music, while munching a Mars bar or a sausage roll. The weather had been foul – snow and sleet and gales – and even her new resolve to be positive and loving required a constant effort of will: not to give up hope, nor shift from love to revenge; not to dwell on painful subjects such as Hugo, or her twin.

'Are you all right, madam?' The attendant had appeared at the door – an anaemic-looking woman whose dyed black hair only emphasized the pallor of her skin.

'Yes, thanks,' said Beattie. 'Just feeling a bit tired.'

'I know what you mean. These late do's take it out of you. I must admit I'll be glad to get home myself. I didn't finish yesterday till well past midnight, and tonight will be worse, by the looks of it.'

'Have you far to go?'

'I live in Streatham, so yes, it *is* a bit of a trek, but luckily I've got a lift. One of the stewards is driving back that way and he's promised to drop me home.'

'Well, I hope it won't be *too* late,' Beattie smiled, leaving a large tip. She'd done enough low-grade jobs herself to know how thankless they were. She peered at her reflection in the mirror. The crêpe de Chine dress was flattering – one Max had bought for her in Cannes – with a swingy pleated skirt and daringly low back. She looked the part, thank God – no cracks showing (yet). But how long could she keep it up? Life was so frighteningly arbitrary, and if fate stopped smiling on her, she might go crashing back to her former world, when she had earned her keep by posing nude for tawdry magazines or washing dishes in a late-night caff. She wondered if the people in the hall downstairs ever lay awake at night worrying that their cushy lives might suddenly collapse. But no, it probably never crossed their minds that they might find themselves wiping toilet-seats or disposing of soiled sanitary towels.

On impulse, she put a five-pound note in the saucer, on top of the three pound-coins she'd left already. The attendant was nowhere to be seen, so she opened her handbag and took out Elizabeth's card. She carried it with her everywhere – another lucky talisman, like the tiny jade elephant. She removed the card from its envelope and read, for the thousandth time: 'I'm so thrilled for you, Beattie dear, and wish you every success. Fondest love, Elizabeth.'

Fondest love – the best present she'd had in her life, infinitely more valuable than jade or crêpe de Chine. She mouthed a quick prayer of thanks, begging God to let it all come right; feeling stupid as she did so, almost an impostor. She still found it odd to pray. God seemed very much a stranger, not for the likes of *her*. He preferred genuine believers – well-bred virtuous people who wouldn't let Him down.

She stowed the card away and hurried back to the hall, which was buzzing with excitement: waitresses scurrying about, refilling glasses before the auction started, and Lord Archer already positioned at the podium.

'I'd better change places with you, Beattie,' said Ruth. 'Come and sit by Max and make sure he does his stuff.'

'Thanks.' Beattie slid into the empty chair and opened her catalogue. Max started playing footsie with her, and she nudged his knee in response. He was looking rather good tonight in his dinner jacket and rakish red bow-tie, and his recent shorter hair-cut was a definite improvement.

'You've met Stephen, haven't you, Beattie? He's just published a novel in verse form, which is tipped to win the Booker.'

'Fantastic!' she said, hoping her enthusiasm would mask her ignorance. She had no idea people wrote novels in verse, but that would have to change. However busy she was, she must find more time for study; borrow literary novels from the library – the sort Hugo would read himself.

Max was smiling dutifully at the woman sitting opposite, who looked at least a hundred, and whose bony wrists and fingers displayed the family jewels: a formidable array of gold bracelets, diamond rings. 'Lady Chandor, I don't think you've met Beattie Bancroft. Beattie's . . .'

He was cut short by Lord Archer, who banged his gavel dramatically on the podium and produced an instant hush.

'My lords, ladies and gentlemen. First of all, may I welcome you this evening and say just a few words about the aim of tonight's dinner. The historians among us may know that in the elegant world of eighteenth-century Oxford, book sales were often preceded by lavish banquets. Those occasions weren't just commercial events, but became very important socially. I'm afraid our twentieth-century society is much less elegant and more stressful altogether. Which is why I'm so delighted that one of Oxford's most go-ahead young colleges is reviving the tradition . . .'

Beattie waited impatiently for the speech to finish and the bidding to begin. Fortunately Lord Archer kept it fairly short, concluding with a brief accolade on the college and its many famous graduates. Whereupon a more recent graduate (female, blonde, and stunning) brandished the first item in the auction – a book by Joseph Addison.

'Now, ladies and gentlemen, I hope you've got your chequebooks at the ready, because here's something really meaty to kick off with. Okay, it's not in mint condition, but what can you expect when it's dated 1761?'

Polite laughter from his audience, and a rustle of catalogues as people set aside their liqueur glasses for the more important business of the evening.

'Now who's going to open the bidding for me at three hundred pounds? You, sir? Thank you. Any advance on three hundred? Yes, the lady in the blue. Three hundred and twenty. Fifty. Eighty. Yes, three hundred and eighty, the gentleman with the beard. Four hundred – thank you, madam. Four hundred and twenty. Fifty. Eighty . . .'

Beattie squeezed Max's hand. It was so terribly exciting – and so *fast*. The book was knocked down to a man at the top table for a cool six hundred pounds. The next item was only an ordinary modern novel, yet it went for over a hundred. (Most of the books *she* bought cost 10 or 20p, from the bargain bin in the Oxfam shop.) She longed to join in the bidding – to buy a thank-you present for Max and a whole *crate* of books for Mile End House – but she had to save her money. Once she'd won Elizabeth back, she would need to compete with Hugo; pay for treats and outings, become a good provider. Anyway, according to Max, the antiquarian book-dealers were out in force, so she would be bidding against the professionals – not to mention the Oxford contingent, here to support the college with their wallets. She glanced around the tables, struck by the stern attentive faces. It was almost like being in church: an air of seriousness and solemnity as people hung on Reverend Archer's every word, following every nuance of the bidding. By now, they had reached Lot 7: the complete works of Byron, bound in grey-green calfskin. Elizabeth had been reading a biography of Byron when they'd met at Ashley Grange, and it was one of the first things they had ever talked about.

'. . . Two hundred and fifty. Two hundred and eighty. Come along now, ladies and gentlemen, surely you can do better than *that?* Byron must be turning in his grave! Do I hear three hundred? Three hundred, anyone? All right – bid me two hundred and ninety. What, no more takers, not even for two hundred and ninety? Disgraceful! All right – going, going, *gone* to . . .'

Beattie pretended that *she*, not Lady Chandor, was the successful bidder, smugly taking possession of her book. She had watched her ladyship nodding her white head and holding up a thousand-carat finger every twenty seconds or so, and had felt quite a pang of envy. She continued to pretend that she was bidding for each lot – and invariably successful. Her stack of books for Mile End House was growing by the minute: an impressive addition to her and Elizabeth's library.

Archer's twelfth and final item was the Alexander Pope, undoubted star of the show. It had an entire page to itself in the catalogue and a reserve price of £7000. Beattie peered at the insignificant-looking volume being held aloft. She simply couldn't imagine having seven thousand pounds to splurge on a single book. It was wicked, in a way, when you thought of the starving millions – or even of one lavatory attendant.

'Damn!' she muttered, feeling a sudden urge to pee again. Fatal to think of lavatories, with such an unsociable bladder and all that drink swilling around inside her. It would be terribly embarrassing to leave at this key moment in the auction. Worse though if she didn't. She edged her chair back and stood up.

'What's wrong?' Max frowned.

'Er, nothing. Won't be long.' Fortunately every eye was focused on the podium and she managed to slink out without attracting undue attention.

The attendant recognized her as she opened the cloakroom door. 'Are you sure you're feeling all right, madam?' she enquired solicitously.

'Yes, fine,' Beattie mumbled, secretly wishing she could stay up here and rest. She really did feel whacked. But it wouldn't do to be

away too long. People might start talking about her: 'You know –
that girl who keeps disappearing.'

By the time she got back, Nicholas Bonham had taken over as
auctioneer and the bids were rising fast and furious from the floor.

'Everything okay?' Max whispered.

She nodded. 'What did the Alexander Pope fetch?'

'Twelve and a half grand.'

'Wow!'

'I'm surprised you didn't hear the applause – the whole hall went
mad.' Max drained his brandy and helped himself to a chocolate
mint. 'Not long till *yours* now, sweetie. I'll have to keep my wits about
me. This guy's more on the ball than Jeffrey. Here, have a mint.'

'Thanks.' She unwrapped the crinkly gold foil and sat pleating it
between her fingers. Max had told her that two hundred pounds was
his limit – which was tremendously generous, in fact, and far more
than she deserved. She felt guilty about him paying for a book
intended for Elizabeth. But he'd said Ruth would expect him to bid,
and since there was nothing he fancied particularly, she could choose
a present. She knew that if he got the book, *she* would get Elizabeth.
It was all part of the fate thing – the book wasn't just a present, but
a 'wedding' present.

Once the bidding started, she was almost too nervous to listen. It
reached eighty pounds in seconds, then climbed more slowly to a
hundred and twenty. Max was frowning in concentration, one finger
tapping the table.

'Any advance on a hundred and twenty? Come on, ladies and
gentlemen, this is a most original item. Thank you, sir – a hundred
and fifty. And you, madam, yes, the lady in pink over there – a
hundred and eighty. Any advance on a hundred and eighty? Two
hundred. Thank you, sir.'

Oh *God*, thought Beattie, that bloody woman in pink – she's bound
to outbid Max again. It's over before it's begun. And Lady Chandor
will probably bid as well – she's obviously made of money. Max
doesn't stand a chance. 'Please God,' she begged, 'keep them quiet.
Sew up their mouths. Strike them dumb.'

'Ladies and gentlemen, *please*! This is worth a lot more. Come on
– have another go. It was owned by Napoleon, remember.'

Don't remind them, she implored. It's a *revolting* book – you can
see that for yourselves – torn and dirty and battered. No one in their
right mind would want to own such an eyesore.

'Any advance on two hundred? Do I hear two hundred and twenty? You, sir? Madam? Well, how about the young gentleman with the beard? Dear, dear! It seems that poor old Napoleon isn't held in very high esteem here. All right – nothing for it. Going, going, *gone*, at two hundred pounds, to the gentleman in the red bow-tie.'

Beattie fell on Max and hugged him. 'Oh, Max . . .'

'Do I get my reward tonight?' he whispered.

'Anything you want, darling!'

He squeezed her thigh, only relinquishing his hand when a Bonham's minion materialized beside him to collect his money and present him with the book. He sat up hastily, wrote the man a cheque, filled in some form or other, then handed her the volume with a flourish. She sniffed the ancient leather, inhaling ecstatically. She was a collector, like Hugo, the proud new owner of a book hallowed by its link with Elizabeth's beloved Napoleon, a Book of Fate which had just decided her own fate. Someone *must* be looking after her. Why else should the bids have stopped? Elizabeth's God clearly wanted what *she* did: to spare Elizabeth years of misery with a man totally unsuited to her.

'*Now* where are you off to?' Max hissed, as she suddenly jumped up.

Blushing, she lowered her voice. 'I think I'm getting that ghastly cystitis again.'

'God! How awful for you. Look, we can push off soon, if you like. I warned Ruth I wouldn't stay to the end. Shall we leave in half an hour, say?'

'I'll see how I am, okay? Sorry – got to rush.' She was desperate for a pee, even though it was only twenty minutes since the last time. She dashed up the second flight of stairs and barged straight into a cubicle, ignoring the attendant. The urine burned and stung, and she sat biting her lip in pain. It *was* cystitis – the symptoms were all too familiar: that excruciating sensation of passing razor blades or liquid fire. At length, she stood up gingerly, horrified at the sight of blood in the toilet-bowl, and instantly recalling the doctor's warnings about the risk of permanent kidney damage. Instead of following his advice, she'd been living on junk food and drinking pretty heavily, and hadn't even bothered to keep the appointment for her last check-up. She *couldn't* be ill again – not now. It would ruin everything, including her meeting with the *Express* man. He probably wouldn't bother asking her again, and anyway, how could she write articles if she landed up in hospital?

Wretchedly she unbolted the door. It seemed a bitter irony that just as she'd acquired her Book of Fate, fate had turned so cruelly against her.

The attendant bustled over and passed her a clean towel. 'Why don't you sit down, madam? You do look ever so pale. Can I get you a glass of water?'

'No thanks,' said Beattie listlessly, slumping onto the chair.

'Was it something you ate, d'you think, madam? Or perhaps you're going down with 'flu? There's a lot of it about.'

Beattie shook her head, wishing the woman would stop talking. An amazing idea had suddenly flashed into her mind. Suppose fate *wasn't* being cruel, but this illness was simply part of the plan? After all, when she was ill before, she had spent five glorious weeks convalescing at Mile End House. In fact, only then had her relationship with Elizabeth really taken off. So perhaps this was her *second* chance, dictated by that mysterious force which seemed to be watching over her. Now she had a perfectly good reason to seek Elizabeth's help and return once more to Kent. She knew Hugo wasn't there at the moment, but back in Cheltenham, supervising the hanging of his latest exhibition. So Mile End House was free for her, and Elizabeth would have no conflict of loyalties.

She rummaged in her purse for some 10ps for the phone. She could be in Kent by midnight, safe and warm in bed, with Elizabeth sitting beside her, maybe staying with her all night.

The attendant was still hovering, offering aspirin and Alka-Seltzer. Beattie declined politely – all she wanted was a phone-box.

'I'm afraid it's two floors down, madam. Do you need to call a taxi? Look, let me do it for you. I really don't think you're well enough to cope with all those stairs.'

Beattie stood up slowly, jingling her fistful of coins. 'No,' she said with a smile. 'I'm feeling remarkably better already.'

29

Beattie peered out of the window in the hope of spotting Elizabeth's green Volvo. But there was only the troop of navvies who had spent all morning digging up the road, driving her mad with the whine of their drills. She shivered and returned to bed. The central heating had broken down and the flat was freezing cold. She checked her watch again – almost noon already. Everything had gone wrong. Instead of lying in bed in Mile End House, she was stuck here on her own, waiting for Elizabeth to make a flying visit. At this rate, she'd only have an hour with her before she left again for Kent – *if* she turned up at all.

She took a gulp of water from the glass on the bedside table. Elizabeth's doctor-friend Lofty had advised her to drink plenty of fluids. If only she could see him again, have him visit her in Kent and give her all the time she needed, treating her like an equal, not a pain in the neck. The doctor last night had stayed a scant five minutes and made no secret of his annoyance at being called out in the early hours. He had diagnosed pyelitis, informing her tartly that it could have waited till the morning, and no, her kidneys weren't at risk – goodnight. Despite the drugs he'd prescribed, it still stung really viciously every time she peed, and all her limbs were aching, as if she were going down with 'flu. And on top of the physical symptoms, she couldn't stop worrying about Elizabeth. Why wouldn't she discuss things on the phone? And where had she been last night? Where was she *now*, for heaven's sake?

She winced at the bombardment from outside. The drills were accompanied by hammering and banging, and the men were shouting over the din. Mile End House would be so peaceful: no noise except the birds singing and Boz's rhythmic purr as he lay curled up on the bed beside her. And there would be meals on trays, beautifully prepared; not just a paltry glass of water and a Kit-Kat. Before he left last night, Max had offered to buy her food from the all-night shop round the corner, but she'd told him not to bother, assuming she'd be in Kent by lunchtime. She still didn't know why Elizabeth had refused to let her come.

She dragged herself out of bed once more and stood by the window, watching a pigeon peck avidly at a crust. It was pointless mooning around like this, feeling sorry for herself. And why the hell should she expect to be waited on, like some pampered little princess? Okay, she might feel lousy, but she wasn't at death's door. She snatched up a pen and a shorthand pad and took them back to bed. She'd do better using the time to draft her piece for the *Express*; work out a dramatic opening, to make her readers sit up. She frowned in concentration, but nothing seemed to come. She doodled a long row of Es, growing smaller, smaller, smaller, then crossed them out and began again. After fifteen minutes, she had produced a dozen words. She tossed the pad aside in disgust and trailed into the bathroom for a pee, holding her breath to make the pain more bearable. She washed her hands and stared at her face in the mirror. Last night's successful journalist had vanished, leaving only a washed-out wreck.

She had almost given up hope of Elizabeth when the bell rang. She rushed downstairs to let her in, then stood in the doorway, simply looking at her. Yes, everything was right: the drab blue sweater and unfashionable beige jacket, the long untidy hair and – thank God – no engagement ring. Elizabeth stepped into the hall and kissed her lightly on the cheek. Beattie breathed in the smell of her hair and skin, wishing the kiss could be more intimate, more special.

'How *are* you, Beattie dear?'

'Not too bright.'

'Well, you'd better get back to bed. This hall's like an ice-house.'

Beattie led the way upstairs. 'I'm afraid it's like an ice-house everywhere. The heating's on the blink.'

'Haven't you got a fire?'

'Only an ancient one-bar thing.' She ushered Elizabeth into the flat. 'I've got it on in the bedroom. Look, would you like a cup of tea or . . . ?'

'No, you shouldn't be waiting on *me*. I've brought some hot soup for us both. And a few other bits and pieces. Shall I put them in the kitchen?'

'Yes, do. Sorry it's such a mess.' She watched Elizabeth unpack two plastic carriers. She'd thought of everything: lemon barley water; a large Thermos flask of soup; apples, grapes and tangerines, and a few frozen meals-for-one, which she began stowing away in the top part of the fridge. Beattie heard her voice making the right noises, saying 'thank you' and 'how thoughtful', while another silent voice was howling: 'Elizabeth, I don't *want* meals-for-one. I want to be at Mile End House, sharing food with *you*.' She leaned against the worktop, pulling her dressing-gown around her. 'I suppose, er, Hugo's there, is he?'

Elizabeth looked up from the fridge. 'Where?'

'At home with you, in Kent.'

'No, Beattie, he's not.'

'But you're expecting him later? I mean, that's why you can't stay?'

'No, I have to get back for a patient.'

'Patients? On a Saturday?'

'Oh, this is a one-off. Someone who missed a lot of her appointments because she's doing jury service, so I said she could come today. Now, off you go to bed and I'll bring the soup in. Where would I find bowls?'

Beattie got two out from the cupboard and stood hovering beside her. 'Elizabeth . . . ?'

'What?'

'Can't I come back *with* you? I mean, if Hugo isn't there? I won't be a nuisance, I promise. You don't have to look after me or anything. I'll just lie in bed and keep out of the way.'

'No, I'm afraid I . . .'

'Oh *please*, Elizabeth! Just for the weekend?'

'But Beattie dear, I shan't be there.'

'Wh . . . what do you mean, not there?'

'Look, if we're going to talk, let's do it in the bedroom. You'll catch your death, with those bare feet on the lino. You go and tuck yourself up and I'll bring the soup on a tray.'

'I'm sorry, I couldn't eat a thing. It's sweet of you to have gone to all this trouble, but . . .' She had been feeling ravenous, until Elizabeth's 'not there'. 'You have yours, okay?'

'Actually, I'm not hungry either. Never mind – it'll keep.'

Beattie returned to the bedroom, realizing with dismay what an utter pigsty it looked: clothes strewn on the floor and a cluster of dirty coffee mugs huddled on the bedside table. She kicked Max's latest unsavoury video under the bed, then pulled up the stool for Elizabeth. 'Perhaps you'd like a more comfy chair? I could bring one in from the sitting-room.'

'No, I'm fine. You get into bed. That's it, pull the duvet round you.' Elizabeth did it for her, then glanced out of the window. 'Gosh! What a racket those men are making. I'm surprised they're working on a Saturday.'

Beattie was hardly aware of them any more. All else had faded beside the alarm-bells triggered off by Elizabeth's words. She clutched her hand impulsively. 'Why . . . why did you say you wouldn't be there?'

'Well, I'm . . . er . . . going to Inverness – leaving first thing in the morning.'

'*Inverness?*' Beattie closed her eyes and saw Inverness right at the top of the map, hundreds and hundreds of miles away.

Elizabeth nodded. 'Now, what are we going to do about getting someone to look after you? How about that friend you sometimes mention? What's her name . . . Sal?'

'Sal's away.'

'Well, surely there's someone in the house here? I spoke to a lady just now and she seemed a fairly friendly type. She was coming out of the gate as I walked in and I stopped to say hello to her two boys. Couldn't you ask *her* to help?'

'Mrs Tobin? You must be joking! The only reason she'd come up here would be to borrow a tenner or dump the boys on *me*.' Beattie took a sip of water, her hands gripping the glass. 'Please tell me why you're going to Scotland. I hate you having secrets.'

'It's not a secret, Beattie.' Elizabeth glanced at her watch. 'It's just that there isn't much time, and I don't want to leave before I've made sure you're all right.'

'Well, I'm *not* all right. I feel terrible. That's the only reason I phoned. In fact, the doctor said that if I didn't have anyone to look after me, he'd have to admit me to hospital.'

'Surely not with pyelitis? It isn't that serious, is it?'

'Well, he . . . he wasn't sure if it *was* pyelitis. He said I . . . I needed more tests. I was hoping Lofty could do them. After all, he *knows* me and . . .'

'But they can do them just as well here. Look, I'll ring Lofty for you, if you like, and get him to suggest a good kidney chap in London.'

Beattie shook her head, hating herself for lying. She had made such an effort lately to be truthful, and now everything was falling apart. She ran a hand through her hair, feeling it still stiff from last night's lacquer. 'You're going with *Hugo*, aren't you? To Inverness.'

Elizabeth opened her bag and took out her cigarettes. She spent some moments lighting one. 'Yes, I am,' she said at last.

'For a holiday?'

'Not really. Well, not for him, in any case. He's going to see some paintings.'

'Big deal.'

'Yes, it *is* a big deal. One of the most important art-collectors in Scotland is selling up his house and most of the contents – you know, pictures, sculpture, furniture and so on. There's going to be a big auction on the estate and he's asked Hugo to advise him on reserve prices for the paintings.'

'But why do *you* have to go?'

'Hugo's my fiancé, Beattie. You really must accept that.'

She recoiled as if she'd been slapped. Elizabeth had never used the word before. 'Yes, I . . . I know. But if it's just a work thing?'

'Well, it's not entirely work. Andrew's an old friend of Hugo's, so he and his wife have asked us both to stay.'

Beattie stared down at her hands. No wonder Elizabeth wasn't keen to hang around playing nursemaid when she'd been invited to some millionaire's mansion. 'How . . . how long are you going for?' she asked.

'Ten days.'

'Ten *days?*'

'Yes. Hugo wants to stop en route in Nottingham and see a dealer there, and he's arranged to call in at a gallery in Edinburgh. Anyway, it's such a long drive, it's hardly worth going for less.'

'You're driving? All that way?'

'Well, Hugo needs the car, you see, in case he buys any pictures. It's much easier and cheaper for him to bring them home himself.'

Home. Another dangerous word. Which home did Elizabeth mean? 'He's keeping the gallery, then?' she said, making a huge effort to control her voice. 'Does that mean you're moving to Cheltenham?'

Elizabeth shook her head.

'I wish you wouldn't keep stalling. I feel so shut out.'

'But Beattie, dear, I know you find it upsetting and I don't want . . .'

'It's more upsetting *not* to be told.'

Elizabeth suddenly plucked the cigarette from her mouth and stubbed it out. 'I'm sorry, I wasn't thinking. I shouldn't smoke in a sick-room.'

'Go ahead. I don't mind. The only thing I care about is knowing what's going on. I thought we were meant to be friends.'

'We *are* friends, Beattie. And I haven't been hiding anything. These big decisions take a long time to work out and we've only just come to a solution.'

'But *what* solution?' She gripped the glass so tightly, it was in danger of breaking in her hands. Instead of Hugo and Elizabeth gradually drifting apart, it appeared they were closer than ever, with *decisions* and *solutions*.

'Well, Hugo's decided to give up the gallery and deal from home, instead.'

'Wh . . . whose home?' Beattie watched Elizabeth put her cigarettes away. She seemed uncharacteristically nervous; shifting on her seat and clearing her throat. Maybe she knew she'd made the wrong decisions and didn't want to talk about them. Which meant there was still hope. Wrong decisions could be changed, given time. '*Whose* home?' she repeated softly.

'Mile End House.'

'So Hugo's moving in with you?'

'Mm.'

'And bringing all his pictures with him?'

'Well, yes he is, but Beattie dear, it's *you* I'm most concerned about at the moment. Look, if you give me your GP's number, I might be able to arrange for someone to pop in, if only every couple of days.'

She shook her head wretchedly. 'No thank you.'

'Beattie, you're making it very hard for me. I hate leaving you like this, but it's extremely awkward to change the plans at this stage.'

'I . . . I'll be okay – don't worry.'

'And, anyway, I'm meeting someone in Aviemore. A friend I haven't seen in years. I can't let her down.'

'It . . . it's okay, I told you.'

'Oh, Beattie, don't *cry*, my love.'

'I'm not.'

'Here, have my hankie. Gosh, your hands are freezing! Look, we must get you a decent fire. This one's hopeless. I can barely feel any heat from it at all. Why don't I go out and buy one?'

'No, *please* don't go.' Beattie wiped her eyes, suddenly close to panic. If she let Elizabeth out of her sight now, she might never see her again. 'There's things I haven't told you – things you've got to know before you leave. About my . . . my twin.'

'Your twin? What *do* you mean?'

'He . . . died. At birth.' Once again she relived the nightmare journey, pushing past the corpse, then lying screaming in the sound-proof cell where she'd been confined as punishment. 'He was called . . . George, like me. I should have *been* him all along. And then things would . . .' Abruptly she broke off. Stirring up all that trauma would only intensify the fear, and if Elizabeth was going away for ten endless hopeless days, she had somehow to endure it.

'I'm sorry, Beattie. I don't quite follow.'

'It doesn't matter. I . . . I'm only talking nonsense. Just . . . just call me George, okay? I liked it when you did that. It made me sort of . . . special.' She gave a sudden jolting laugh. 'D'you remember those two ducks – the George and Sophie ducks? They were so . . . so devoted.'

Elizabeth smiled and nodded. 'Funnily enough, I was looking at your bird book only the other day – the one you gave me for Christmas.'

'Really, Elizabeth? *Were* you?'

'Yes. And I found those two markers you'd put in, one for George and one for Sophie. What a wonderful pair! Now, *George*' – she stressed the name – 'I'm going to get that soup and I want you to try to eat some. It'll warm you up, apart from anything else.'

'*No!*' She didn't want Elizabeth to go anywhere, not even into the kitchen. It was childish, crazy, totally unreasonable, but she couldn't seem to help herself. 'Sit here for a minute. *Please*.' She patted the duvet to coax Elizabeth over, then captured her hand, gripping it painfully hard. She could only exist when plugged in to that life-supply. The mere thought of Inverness froze her into a terrifying numbness, as if *she* were disappearing, not Elizabeth – slipping away, dispersing, reduced to a smear of cells, a blur. Yet how could she stop her going? It would be monstrously selfish to expect her to cancel the trip. Hugo would be livid, to say nothing of Andrew and his wife. Anyway, she'd despise her*self* if she wrecked Elizabeth's plans, chained her down like a prisoner. If only she didn't feel such overwhelming terror, or could think of something to make her *want* to stay.

With a flash of inspiration, she leapt out of bed and dashed into the sitting-room, calling over her shoulder, 'Wait there, Elizabeth. I'll only be a second.'

She tugged the bureau drawer open. There, in its tissue-paper cocoon, lay the Book of Fate. How could she have forgotten it? She unwrapped it carefully, shocked to see how worn it looked – more like a reject from the Oxfam shop than a rare historical treasure. Elizabeth might be insulted rather than impressed by such a tatty present.

Yet it was all she had and time was short. Elizabeth would be leaving any moment and either she must stop her or go with her.

Decisively she swung round, and was on her way to the bedroom with it when the phone rang. She was tempted to ignore it. Suppose it was Sal, when she'd just told Elizabeth she was away? Or Max. He'd be furious if he discovered that the 'bloody woman' was here again.

'Beattie, are you all right?' Elizabeth was calling. 'Or do you want me to answer that?'

'No thanks. I'll get it.' She snatched up the receiver. She could always tell Max she was too ill to talk and would ring him in a day or two.

'Hello, is that Beattie Bancroft?'

'Speaking.'

'Do forgive me bothering you on a Saturday, but this is Simon Christie from the *Sunday Times*.'

'Oh . . . *hello*!' She hoped her voice conveyed more enthusiasm than she felt.

'I'm the editor of the new Modern Living section and I've just read your piece on date-rape in the *Herald*. I really liked your approach.'

'Gosh, thanks.'

'I was wondering whether you'd be interested in writing something for us?'

No, she thought instantly, I *can't*. I feel terrible, and in any case, I . . .

'We're planning a feature on rather similar lines – how bad sexual experiences can affect a woman's subsequent view of men, and make her wary of marriage or relationships. How d'you feel? Would you like to give it a go?'

'Well, yes, I'm . . .' She ought to be overjoyed. The *Sunday Times*, for heaven's sake, and a subject practically *made* for her. But all she felt was fear: she would let them down; they'd discover she was a fraud without a grain of talent. Only this morning she had drawn a complete blank with her *Express* piece.

'About a thousand words, okay? And what I'd like is . . .'

She couldn't concentrate. The whole newspaper world seemed trivial and unreal. Had he rung a few days ago, or even yesterday, she would have been over the moon. But now nothing mattered except the threat of losing Elizabeth.

'Could you let me have it by Tuesday?' he was saying. 'I know that's a bit tight, but I'd like to get it in for next week.'

'Er, yes, okay.' Tuesday was impossible, and anyway she hadn't even taken in what he'd said. All through the conversation she'd been straining her ears to hear the click of the front door, terrified Elizabeth might leave.

The instant he'd rung off, she rushed back to the bedroom, clutching the Book of Fate. Elizabeth was still there and tidying up the room. She had remade the bed and picked up most of the clutter from the floor.

'Elizabeth, I don't know what to do. That was the *Sunday Times*. They want me to write for them.'

'Oh, Beattie, how exciting! Congratulations. The *Sunday Times* – I say! You *are* getting famous!'

'But you don't understand. I can't do it. I'm ill, and . . .'

'Calm down.' Elizabeth took her arm and led her back to bed. 'Look, I know you're feeling low at the moment, but those antibiotics do work surprisingly fast. Even by tomorrow you'll be more your normal self.'

Beattie said nothing. Elizabeth *wanted* her to be better, then she'd be able to leave for Scotland without the slightest twinge of guilt. Perhaps she was even beginning to hate her and couldn't wait to put five hundred miles between them. The thought was so appalling she felt another wave of panic. She wouldn't be able to write a word – or even survive at all – with Elizabeth that far away, and publicly acknowledged as Hugo's future wife. And yet she had accepted the commission. Why, for heaven's sake? She could have admitted she was ill, or pretended *she* was going away.

'Oh, Elizabeth, I'm in such a dreadful muddle. I've told the guy I'll do it, but I've completely lost my confidence – if I ever had any. Those earlier pieces were flukes. I'll have to phone him back and say I've changed my mind. But then that'll be the end of . . .'

Elizabeth sat down on the bed, with a quick glance at her watch. 'Why not leave it till the morning and see how you are then? I'm sure you'll feel much better after a good night's sleep. I mean, you were frightfully late to bed last night, and that always leaves one drained.'

Beattie turned her head away. Elizabeth was dying to get off – that was pretty obvious. She was mouthing platitudes, trying to convince her that she wasn't ill at all, simply overtired. Clearly she'd run out of patience and could no longer be bothered with these petty little problems. No wonder. It was infinitely more exciting to go zooming up to Scotland in Hugo's jaunty yellow car and hobnob with millionaires.

She reached out for the Book of Fate, which she had put on the bedside table, held it for a moment, then let it drop quietly to the floor. It couldn't help her now. Elizabeth was lost to her.

'What's this?' Elizabeth stooped to pick it up.

Beattie burst into tears. 'It . . . it was meant to be for *you*. I got it almost by . . . by . . . by a miracle. I thought it could change everything. But it's changed things the wrong way. And now I feel so miserable I wish I was' – her voice rose to a howl – '*dead.*'

30

Beattie rubbed her eyes. They were aching after hours of non-stop typing, and her fingers were beginning to stiffen up. Quite apart from feeling tired, she wasn't even sure that the task was worth doing in the first place. Elizabeth appeared to have lost all interest in her book, so that putting it back on disk for her was probably a complete waste of time. Yet it had once been their joint project, a bond which drew them closer, giving each of them a glimpse into the other's world; a chance to appreciate the other's expertise. How could things have changed so much?

She got up to stretch her legs and stood at the window, watching the relentless rain. It was only early afternoon, yet the day was so overcast she had been working with the desk-lamp on for the last half hour or so. The garden was a sodden jungle, and an overflowing gutter spouted an angry hiss of water on the path. Elizabeth had no time for gardening these days; no time for anything but her patients – and running Hugo's errands.

She went into the kitchen to make a cup of coffee. Coffee was still forbidden, with her urinary infection, but what the hell – Elizabeth wasn't there to see, and anyway she needed something to wake her up. There were over a hundred more pages to type and she could only do it when Elizabeth was out or closeted in her consulting room. Besides, better to keep busy than sit brooding over the difference between her time here all those months ago and this last desolate week. In a way history had repeated itself: once again she was convalescing at Mile End House and typing Elizabeth's book, but there were few other similarities. No kind supportive Margaret waiting on her hand and foot; no blissful sense of growing daily closer to

Elizabeth. James and Margaret were away in York, visiting Emma and John; Caroline hadn't so much as shown her face, and even Elizabeth seemed constantly preoccupied. Worst of all, Hugo's presence and possessions were beginning to take over the house. Although he was still away in Scotland, there were signs of him in every room: his Earl Grey tea here in the larder, his whisky on the sideboard, his art magazines on the desk in the hall.

She walked over to the table while she waited for the kettle to boil, and sat down in Jeremy's place. Presumably it was now *Hugo*'s place – head of the table, head of the house. Already Elizabeth was forfeiting her precious independence, something she had resented in her first marriage. Today, for instance, she was driving all the way to Bournemouth to collect a picture for him, despite the fact that it was Saturday and meant to be her day off.

She took her coffee back to the study with a couple of chocolate biscuits. The house seemed depressingly empty; no noise except the drumming of the rain. Even when the phone rang, it was always for Elizabeth. (The only call *she'd* had so far was from an acrimonious Max.) Last night she had hoped against hope that Elizabeth would suggest she went to Bournemouth too, but this morning she had left on her own, saying only, 'Goodbye. Take care.'

She licked the chocolate off her biscuit. She would allow herself a five-minute break – no more. Futile or not, the retyping was her recompense to Elizabeth and she was determined to complete it. In any case, she had no other work to do. She had told the *Sunday Times* man *and* the man from the *Express* that she'd developed a serious kidney problem and might have to go into hospital. That should let her off the hook for several weeks at least. Writing was impossible. Her confidence had completely gone and she was sure that anything she *did* produce would be instantly rejected. It was all connected with Elizabeth, of course. The first three pieces had succeeded only because she'd written them for *her* sake – hoping to impress her, to wean her away from Hugo. Having failed in that, there seemed little point in anything else.

Boz sprang onto her knee and she bent her face close to his, smiling as he nuzzled her chin. He alone was still loving and devoted, still happy to be near her. She stroked his silky fur, wishing she could confide in him, make him understand how upset she was by the changes in the house. Elizabeth had been rearranging everything, turning out rooms to make space for Hugo's pictures. This study was to be his office and the shelves were already bare, awaiting his books and files.

On impulse, she got up, depositing Boz gently on the sofa, then darting upstairs to Elizabeth's bedroom. With a guilty glance over her shoulder, she opened the door and slipped in. One quick look round the room put her mind at rest – there were no signs of Hugo *here*, thank God, only the familiar things: a scattering of hairpins on the dressing-table, a pot of Pond's cold cream, the toy giraffe still propped against the pillows, the shabby candlewick dressing-gown hanging on the door. All this week she had pictured the room turning into Elizabeth's and *Hugo*'s: the giraffe banished to make way for his pyjamas; the smell of cigars and after-shave drowning Elizabeth's flowery talc.

She opened the wardrobe, feeling an urgent need to touch Elizabeth's clothes, since she couldn't touch Elizabeth herself. She ran her hand along the rail of hangers, reliving the memories – the green suit evoking Cheltenham, and the red and white checked shirt Elizabeth's first visit to the flat. Tenderly she stroked the fabrics, inhaling their elusive smell: part lemon soap, part Silk Cut. At the end of the rail, she came upon a man's jacket – *Hugo*'s. She wrenched it out as if it were radioactive. How dare he leave his clothes with Elizabeth's, especially this great hairy thing. Without thinking, she slipped it on. It reached almost to her knees, the thick tweed weighing her down. There were several things in the pockets, making it heavier still: a silver cigarette-lighter, two blank cassettes, a bag of peppermints. She fastened the buttons and began striding about the room, snapping the silver lighter on and off. Now she *was* Hugo: six foot tall and powerful. It felt better being a man. She was growing stronger by the minute, more imposing and authoritative. Her voice was different, too – effortlessly cultured, a blue-blooded Cambridge graduate's. And best of all, Elizabeth adored her, slept with her at night, planned to spend her whole life with her.

She started as the phone rang. God! Not Hugo, she prayed. He had rung every single day this week. But no – he knew Elizabeth wouldn't be back from Bournemouth yet. It could be Margaret, who also phoned fairly regularly. She picked up the receiver and said a hesitant hello.

'Is that you, Beattie?'

'Er, yes.' It wasn't Margaret, but the voice did sound familiar.

'Good! It's you I wanted to speak to.'

'I'm sorry, who's that?'

'Sarah. Sarah Hargreaves. I'm ringing from Madrid. I'm so *furious* I just had to phone and tell you what I think of you. Caroline's been on to me, and I've never heard anything so . . . so despicable. I mean, didn't you *realize* how much Mummy was looking forward to that Scottish trip? She's desperately tired – she hasn't had a break for months. She didn't get away at all last year, except for that weekend at the health farm where she first got lumbered with *you* – God help her! You've been a perfect pest since then. Do you think you *own* her or something? Anyway, you don't *need* a bloody nursemaid. Caroline says there's nothing really wrong with you.'

'That's not true. I . . . I . . .'

'Don't interrupt! It's about time someone told you a few home truths. The others are too mealy-mouthed, and my mother's an utter *saint*. That's why I hate you taking advantage of her. She's got enough on her plate as it is. I don't suppose you're the remotest bit interested, but Harriet's feeling lousy again and has just chucked in her job, and my grandfather is booked into hospital for an operation next month. Mummy won't have a minute to *breathe* then, with all the visiting and stuff. And if Harriet decides to come home for a while, she'll have *two* invalids to cope with. So the least you could have done was let her have a few days' break beforehand.'

'B . . . but I didn't even . . .'

'Listen, Beattie, these phone calls cost a bomb and I don't intend to waste any more time arguing. All I want to say is that if you dare to show your face at the wedding, I . . . I'll *kill* you. Have I made myself clear? We don't *want* you there, d'you understand? – not one of us. Knowing you, you'd somehow manage to be ill again and expect Mummy to cancel her honeymoon.'

'Look, that really isn't . . .' Before she could finish the sentence, the receiver was slammed down. She stood paralysed with shock, Sarah's words still spitting through the room. Her first reaction was fury at such outrageous accusations. The bloody cheek of the girl! What right had she to talk like that? It was all lies anyway, vile malicious lies. But no, she thought, as she sank onto the bed, her rage subsiding into deepest shame – it's *true*. Hadn't she known in her heart how unforgivably selfish it would be to expect Elizabeth to forfeit her holiday? And she'd only made things worse by trying to justify herself; banging on and on about her terror at being left alone, as if she were a child of three, for Christ's sake. She had even resorted to *blackmail*, becoming near-hysterical and saying she wanted to die. And of course Elizabeth, the loyal friend and caring therapist, had had no choice but to stay with the potential suicide.

'But it wasn't *like* that,' she insisted, continuing to speak into the mouthpiece as if Sarah were still there. 'I was only trying to save her. I couldn't bear the thought of her marrying again and making herself miserable.'

'Bullshit!' Sarah's imagined voice snapped back. 'It's *you* who's making her miserable. You've kept her here, tied to the house, just to play nursemaid to a neurotic selfish bitch, when she could have been having the time of her life.'

'There'll be *other* holidays,' she pleaded. 'Hugo will see to that. He'll take her everywhere.'

'That's not the point, though, is it? She needs a break *now*, before James's operation. She didn't even *mention* that, or tell you about Harriet's job. Oh, no! Poor darling Beattie must be spared the slightest worry. Elizabeth's the one who has to cope with everything, however tired she is.'

She suddenly looked down at her sleeve, startled by the sight of Hugo's jacket. She had no right to be wearing it; no right to be in here at all. If Sarah could see her now, sprawling on Elizabeth's bed, snooping through her private things, she'd be beside herself with rage. She tore off the jacket and thrust it back into the wardrobe. Then hurriedly she smoothed the bedspread, which seemed polluted by her touch. She felt such a wave of self-disgust, she wanted to crawl away and hide, dig a deep hole in the garden and bury herself like . . . like shit.

She slunk back to her own room – except it *wasn't* hers, it was Sarah's. Nothing in the house was hers – not Elizabeth, or Boz; not the biscuits she'd just eaten or the coffee she'd just drunk. She ought to leave this instant, never set foot here again. Yet all her energy had drained away and she simply crumpled onto the floor; no longer daring to lie on Sarah's bed, or sit on Sarah's chair. Even here, the angry voice pursued her, repeating those vile words: '. . . perfect pest . . . despicable . . . If you dare to show your face at the wedding . . .'

She pressed her face into the carpet, trying to stop herself from thinking of the wedding. But the images were already swarming in: Elizabeth radiant in white; Amanda an angelic bridesmaid; Tim the perfect pageboy; the village church thronged with friends and family – everyone but her. She had always told herself it wouldn't happen

– the engagement, yes, but not the actual marriage. Yet now Sarah had made it a certainty, even mentioned the honeymoon, for Christ's sake. No doubt everything was arranged: the date fixed, the hotel booked. She eased up to a sitting position, her forehead smarting from the rough cord carpet. She had to have a drink – a shot of Hugo's whisky – to numb her misery.

Halfway down the stairs, she stopped. She was helping herself again, to something which didn't belong to her – stealing, in effect. She had tried to steal Elizabeth, commandeered her time and devotion when they weren't hers by right. Elizabeth belonged to her family. And to Hugo.

She gripped the banister rail, suddenly realizing that was *fact* – cold brute fact which she had no power to change. All this time, she had fought against it, talked herself into a state of almost madness, convinced that Fate was on her side and would help her win Elizabeth. Even this last week, she had managed to persuade herself that Elizabeth didn't *want* to go away, that it was too tiring and too far, and that Hugo would be so busy with his pictures she would hardly see him anyway. God! She was a monster – ignoring other people, bulldozing her selfish way through their lives and happiness. And she had even had the cheek to wail about the family ignoring her, expecting all and sundry to dance attendance on her, when they clearly loathed her guts. Well, if she was so crass and self-deluding, she deserved everything she'd got.

Slowly, she turned round and walked back upstairs to Sarah's room. She would leave quietly this time, with no scenes, no tears. She'd simply write a note of apology for Elizabeth, and then go away – anywhere – it didn't matter, so long as it was far enough.

She heaved her suitcase onto the bed and started collecting up her clothes, packing everything in a jumble: shoes on top of underwear. She had just closed the case when the phone rang. *Let* it ring, she thought. It was probably Sarah again. Or maybe Harriet or Emma, equally outraged. She couldn't bear a second round of accusations. She felt ashamed enough already, the lowest of the low. If she grabbed her coat and car-keys, she could be gone in a matter of minutes.

She lurched downstairs with her case, deliberately slowing as she reached the hall. She must behave responsibly this time, not just cut and run. There was the burglar-alarm to be set, lights and fires to switch off, doors to lock, Elizabeth's note to write. It was difficult to think, though, with that wretched phone shrilling on and on. Suppose it *was* Elizabeth? She had said she'd be leaving Bournemouth at three o'clock sharp, but perhaps the car had broken down and she was stranded on the road.

She reached for the receiver, changed her mind, stood dithering a moment, then finally picked it up. 'Hello?' she said nervously.

'Am I speaking to Mrs Elizabeth Hargreaves?' The voice was unfamiliar – a woman with a strong Scots accent.

'No, I'm afraid she's out.'

'Do you know when she'll be back?'

'Not till five at the earliest, she said.'

'Oh dear. Is there any way I can reach her? It's a matter of some urgency.'

'No. She's driving back from Bournemouth at the moment.'

There was a slight pause the other end. Beattie shifted from foot to foot. Perhaps it was a patient. As far as she knew, patients never phoned on Saturday, but this could be an emergency. 'Can I help at all?' she offered.

'Do forgive me sounding rude, my dear, but may I ask first who you are?'

She hesitated. Who *was* she? A selfish bitch. A thief. A nothing and a nobody, with no rights in this house. 'I'm ... er ... Mrs Hargreaves' daughter, Sarah.'

'Hello, Sarah. This is Staff Nurse Clifford at Kinloch Hospital in Inverness. I ... need to get hold of your mother just as soon as possible.'

'Why? What ... what's happened?'

'Well, I'm sorry to have to tell you that there's been an accident involving Mr Hugo Clayton-Brown.'

'*What?*'

'He *is* all right. But he's in Intensive Care. So if you could ask your mother to phone me the minute she gets in.'

No, thought Beattie, I can't, I *won't*. Elizabeth mustn't hear this – it's just too terrible. She struggled to find her voice. 'Wh ... what sort of accident?'

'Look, if you don't mind, Sarah, I think it would be better if I spoke to your mother direct.'

'But she won't be back for ages. Besides, I *need* to know, to ... to prepare her. I mean, was it a car crash – one of those awful pile-ups?'

'No, nothing like that.'

'Well, *what* then?'

'He was . . . skiing.'

'*Skiing*? But he . . . he wasn't going skiing. He . . .' She broke off in confusion. What did *she* know of Hugo's plans? It was the same as Harriet's job or James's operation. Why should they tell *her* when she only made things worse? 'How badly is he hurt?' she asked.

Another nerve-racking pause.

'Well, he's as comfortable as can be expected. But the doctor will know more, and can give your mother all the details. So will you be good enough to ask her to ring this number as soon as she gets back? Have you got a pen handy?'

She picked up the biro by the phone. Strangely, she was still able to function, her hand and brain responding correctly as she scribbled down the number. She heard her voice asking for directions to the hospital and where the nearest airport was. She sounded calm and capable; a supportive daughter taking charge in her mother's absence. But as soon as she'd rung off, she collapsed into a chair, struggling between shock and disbelief. This *couldn't* have happened – she must be dreaming it. And how would she ever find the courage to tell Elizabeth? She checked her watch, willing time to stop. Let her never arrive, she prayed; let her drive an endless road from Bournemouth, still happy, still not knowing.

She shut her eyes, instantly picturing the accident: a helpless figure spinning out of control, crashing into a boulder or hurtling down a ravine; blood spurting onto treacherous white snow. If Elizabeth had been with him, he wouldn't have gone skiing in the first place – Elizabeth hated skiing.

She went icy cold at the thought. That meant *she* was responsible. If she hadn't kept Elizabeth here in Kent, the pair of them would have stuck to safe pursuits: walking in the country, visiting museums. Hugo would never have left Elizabeth on her own while he went waltzing off to the ski slopes – not on their first trip together.

She sat rigid with horror, barely able to take it in; the enormity of what she'd done. Hugo might *die*, and she would be his murderer. He was obviously in a critical condition. There might not even be time for Elizabeth to see him before he . . . he . . .

She forced herself to stand up. She *had* to get hold of her, however much she dreaded it. There was just a tiny chance she hadn't yet left Bournemouth – some change of plan, some unexpected delay.

She darted into the consulting room in the hope of finding the number. If she could reach Elizabeth there, she could tell her to drive straight to Heathrow to catch the next flight to Scotland. Frantically she rummaged through the papers on the desk, but there was absolutely nothing connected with Bournemouth or the painting. She didn't even know the name of the collector, so she couldn't get his number from directory enquiries. Elizabeth's diary was lying on the bureau. After a moment's guilty hesitation, she opened it – scruples had to be sacrificed in an emergency like this. But, no, the number wasn't there. The page for Saturday was blank – only the printed date: March 12.

Oh lord! The anniversary of her mother's death and she'd totally forgotten it. Normally she made a point of phoning her father on that day, but today she'd obliterated everything except her own petty little concerns.

She sat staring at the page, all the colour draining from her face as she remembered something *else* about today: that plan she'd concocted in the Pet Cemetery. She had actually *willed* Hugo to die, even fixed the date of his death – for the twelfth of March. So the voodoo curse had worked, and precisely to time.

Her body began to shake. This new crime was far beyond even the wildest and most extreme of Sarah's accusations. Surely no one could even conceive of her being so . . . so *evil*. Never again could she face Elizabeth. She must leave at once, vanish to the ends of the earth.

Somehow she reached the hall. There, by the phone, was the hospital number she had written on the pad. Again, she heard the nurse's voice; saw the gruesome images. If Hugo was still conscious, he might be asking for Elizabeth at this moment. How could she walk out on her? She had to help her reach him, *then* she would escape.

Angrily she wiped her eyes. Tears were a luxury, a weakness, and it was essential to keep calm. She had a lot to do – first, phone the airport and enquire about flights. She picked up the receiver, trying to stop her voice from stuttering out of control. Yes, there *was* a flight this evening, and yes, she could book a seat over the phone. She went to fetch her credit card, forcing her mind away from thoughts of horror and onto practical details. Elizabeth needed a taxi to Heathrow. She rang the local minicab firm and booked a car for six o'clock. Somehow she was managing, talking sense, arranging things. It required a huge effort of will not to give way to panic and despair, but those too were luxuries.

She wiped her tears off the phone directory and replaced it in the drawer. She must pack Elizabeth's case next. She had no idea where the suitcases were kept, so the best solution was to unpack her own. She lugged it back to Sarah's room, clinging to the banister for support. Her legs felt strange and weak, as if they were coming loose from her body. Too bad. She emptied her things out on the bed, then took the case to Elizabeth's room, pausing at the door. This quiet and cosy room – soft magnolia walls and plush beige carpet; lovingly polished chest of drawers with its photo frames and posy of dried flowers – was about to be marked indelibly with grief; the whole house changed and scarred, and solely through her wickedness. How *could* she have willed a death, brought such anguish on anyone?

She slunk into the room and set about packing; handling Elizabeth's things like priceless treasures, as if that might afford some tiny recompense. Nothing must be creased or spoilt; nothing else broken beyond repair. She wrapped the toiletries in tissue paper; folded the clothes with infinite care. Then she ran through a mental check-list, ticking off each item in her head: underwear and night things, warm jerseys, tights and shoes. She laid the toy giraffe on top, tucked a sweater round him. He would provide some comfort, especially in the night. But where would Elizabeth stay? The plane didn't get in till ten. Or might she spend all night at the hospital? The awful pictures swarmed back into her mind: Hugo lying deathly pale beside the bleeps and whines of a life-support machine. Or maybe worse: the life-support machine turned *off* . . .

She banged the suitcase lid shut. *Stop* it, she told herself, and get on with your work – find Elizabeth a place to stay. She remembered seeing a hotel guide in the drawing-room. Slowly, she made her way downstairs again, frightened by the feelings in her body. It had become old and very heavy, and no longer seemed to belong to her; even her fingers clumsy as she fumbled through the book. She picked out two hotels in Inverness and rang them to confirm they both had rooms. Then meticulously she wrote down their names and addresses on the pad, under the details of the flight. Everything must be done as well as possible – done with love. Though how could she even *think* of the word, when she'd killed the person Elizabeth truly loved?

She thrust her guilt away once more and limped into the kitchen to make some sandwiches. Elizabeth probably wouldn't feel like eating, but better to have them ready, just in case. And a flask of hot coffee prepared. And the cats must be fed, and someone in the village alerted to look after them. And she ought to do the washing up, make sure the house was clean and tidy for Elizabeth's return. If her body protested at the task, she'd *force* it into action. Physical work would be a damned sight more use than sitting around weeping and wailing.

An hour later, everything was done: the sandwiches and suitcase ready in the hall; the house tidier than it had ever been; the central heating re-set; lamps and fires switched off. All she had to do now was to write a note to Elizabeth explaining what had happened. But the pen shook uncontrollably in her hand. It refused to write those terrible words – accident, intensive care – as if unable to inflict such pain. And yet time was short. Elizabeth would be back in half an hour and she herself must be gone by then. It would be impossible to speak to her in person; watch her face as she heard the news. Of course, *someone* should be there, so she had arranged for Jane from the village to come round at quarter to five, to provide some moral support. (She'd only met Jane twice, but she seemed reliable and kindly, and had known Elizabeth years.) She'd told her she couldn't stay herself – she had a plane to catch. Which happened to be true: she had decided to go to Melbourne, to her father. Only Australia was far enough. She would simply disappear, then she could never harm Elizabeth again.

She picked up the phone in the drawing-room and dialled her father's number. It was the early hours in Melbourne, but he wouldn't mind being disturbed. He had always told her to ring him any time, day or night, if she had a serious problem. He was a poor sleeper anyway, and often spent half the night awake.

She let the number ring for several minutes. No reply. Strange he wasn't home at half past two in the morning. Of course he might be out with some woman, or sleeping at her house. Even at the age of sixty, he was still partial to the girls. But it was the anniversary of her mother's death, so surely he . . . ?

She put the phone down. Not only her mother's death, but *Hugo*'s – the day she had chosen for him to die. She stumbled to the window, as if to summon help from outside. Dusk had fallen early, a pall of cloud settling on the garden and shrouding any natural light. It would be pitch dark in an hour or two. Dark like death.

She fought against the panic: her father would be back soon. All she had to do was ring again at a more reasonable hour; maybe wait till she got to the flat. But, no, she couldn't go to London – Elizabeth would find her there. And, anyway, suppose he *didn't* come back; suppose he never answered? He, too, might be ill or . . . or dead.

Frantically she snatched up the receiver. Perhaps she'd got a wrong number. She dialled again, checking every digit. He *had* to answer, *had* to be there. Where else could she hide herself? She had no other relatives, no mother, sister, brother . . .

No, whatever happened, she mustn't think about her twin. She was too distraught to handle that. Yet already a fierce tingling was spreading through her hands, just as it had at the rebirthing. And it was moving up her arms, intensifying into pain. Oh God, she thought, what's happening to me? Why should all these symptoms flood back now? The last thing she could cope with was a repeat of that experience – lying in that huddle of retching screaming bodies – and without support this time; no loving Joyce or Kim. She took in a great gasping breath, in the hope of regaining control, but the tingling had affected her whole body and she felt faint and dizzy, as if she were slipping into unconsciousness. Even the room itself was closing in; contracting into a narrow passage, dark and claustrophobic. Why was there no air? Her jaw went tight, her lungs constricted, and she was fighting for each breath, fighting for her life. Waves of pain shuddered through her body as she struggled vainly to push her blind way out. But she was obstructed by her twin, trapped behind his corpse – terrified, alone.

'Kim!' she cried. 'Please come. Please help.'

Suddenly he seemed to be there – rescuing her, releasing her; his arms a refuge as she wept; her midwife and her mother, utterly loving and devoted.

She groped towards the table. She had to find his number, had to talk to him. She scrabbled through the pages of her diary – it must be there, it must be. He had written it down for her himself.

Oh yes, thank God, she'd got it. And it was a London number, so he wasn't far away. She picked up the receiver, which was lying where she'd dropped it, and pressed it to her ear. She could hear its mournful cry, still wailing through the empty Australian night. There was no one there, no bolt-hole, nowhere she belonged. Shivering, she clicked it dead and slowly dialled Kim's number, panic-stricken in case he too was out. But after two brief rings, he answered.

She all but wept with relief. 'Kim, it . . . it's Beattie Bancroft. I . . . I need to see you . . . urgently. I wondered if . . .'

'What's wrong, Beattie? I can hear how upset you are.'

'I can't tell you – it's too terrible. I . . . I've . . .' She shut her eyes and saw the headstone in the cemetery – *Hugo's* headstone – the marble slab she had planned for him.

'Rest In Peace,' she mouthed, knowing at that instant that all hope of peace was lost to her for ever.

31

Beattie drew up in the narrow street and shone the torch on her map again. For the last half-hour she had been meandering round in circles in this godforsaken part of London, searching for Kim's street. The sheeting rain made it difficult to drive, let alone read road signs. But it looked as if she'd actually found her way at last: Beech Road should be the second on the left. She nosed cautiously along, watching for the turning. There were no beeches to be seen, nor trees of any sort; nor even any front gardens, just a row of tall cramped houses in sallow brick, one or two derelict with boarded doors and windows. She parked outside number 20 and made a dash for the front door, blinded by the rain. She stood shivering on the step, feeling weak and insubstantial. The drive had been exhausting and she supposed she must be hungry, though it would be impossible to eat. Since leaving Mile End House, her thoughts had been fixated on Elizabeth, imagining her horror as she arrived home and read the note; her mounting worry as she was driven to the airport; her taut distracted politeness when confronted with the painted smile of the stewardess.

She consulted her watch once more. The plane would be well on the way to Scotland now, and then Elizabeth would be driving to the hospital, walking into Intensive Care. Please God, she prayed, don't let her be too late.

Her finger hovered over the bell-push. Was she crazy to have come here? What could *Kim* do to help – either Elizabeth or her? Anyway, he might still be upset and angry about her article on rebirthing. He was bound to have seen it in the *Herald* (or at least been told about it by someone on the course), and would regard her as a traitor for taking such a satirical line.

The rain was soaking through her lightweight cotton jacket as she stood indecisive, wondering whether to jump back in the car and drive off – anywhere. Perhaps she should have phoned Max, not Kim, except he was annoyed with her as well. And Sal would never understand – ordinary friends were useless – yet she simply didn't have the courage to go back to her flat and spend the night alone.

Nervously she pressed the bell, still fighting a desire to run away. Within seconds, Kim appeared at the door, wearing a silky black kimono. His sensuous dark eyes held hers for a moment, then he reached out and clasped her in a hug. She pulled away, realizing with a twinge of fear that he was all but naked beneath the flimsy robe; no longer the kind devoted mother, but alarmingly male. She could see whorls of coarse dark hair curling up from the V-neck of his kimono, and could smell his musky cologne. Why was he undressed? Why that seductive scent?

'Darling, you're soaked to the skin! Come in and get dry.'

As he closed the door behind her, she felt still more uneasy. The house appeared to be empty – no reassuring noises, no signs of family or flatmates. The hall was bare and shadowy, not much better than the oppressive night outside.

'Let me take your jacket, darling. And look – your sweater's damp as well. Can I get you some dry clothes, or a dressing-gown?'

'Er, no. I'm fine.' She stood rigidly in front of him. Those 'darlings' seemed more intimate than they had on the rebirthing course. There, she had accepted them as simply part of the ambience, whereas here they were intrusive. She should never have phoned him, still less asked if he'd be alone. He had obviously jumped to the wrong conclusion.

She edged towards the door, feeling even more exposed without her jacket. 'Listen, Kim,' she said, 'that . . . that thing I wrote for the paper. I didn't really . . . I mean, what I'm trying to say is, it must have seemed an awful cheek, a betrayal of trust and everything, but . . .'

'That's not what you're here for, Beattie. You didn't come to apologize. You came for help.'

'Yes, I know, but . . .'

'Well, first things first. Let's get you warm and dry. Come and sit in here and I'll make you a hot drink.' He opened the door into a dimly lit room which, like the hall, was bare of any furniture, apart from an upturned wooden crate. A large double mattress was laid out on the floor, heaped with rugs and blankets.

'Look, Kim, I really can't stay. I've got to . . .'

'Relax! I suggest you stretch out on that mattress and just let your body go. You look utterly exhausted. I won't be long.'

She steered clear of the mattress and squatted on a cushion, glancing nervously around. A pack of Tarot cards was fanned out on the crate, along with various lumps of crystal and a small picture of some Indian guru. On the wall hung a much larger painting, unframed and daubed in crudely coloured oils, depicting a headless man floating in space, surrounded by black starbursts. The walls themselves were painted a dark red, like blood. She thought instantly of Hugo. Suppose he was already dead? How would Elizabeth react? How was she at this moment?

She got up and walked to the window, in an effort to distract herself. The rain was slamming against the glass, obscuring any view. She rubbed the pane with her sleeve and peered out at the street. She could still see very little; only distorted shadows from a lamp-post and the oily sheen of puddles. A car lumbered past, then another – faceless drivers in a foreign land. The whole area seemed alien, unreal; the splintered headlights destroying any sense of solidity or substance.

She heard the door-handle turn and darted back to her cushion as Kim came in with a towel over his arm, and carrying a tray.

'I've made you some hot milk and honey. I think you'll find it soothing. And here – use this for your hair.'

'Oh, thank you.' She took the towel and rubbed her wet hair, eyeing the large mug on the tray with apprehension. She hadn't drunk hot milk since childhood, but it would seem churlish to refuse.

'And this is my attempt at chocolate brownies. I'm afraid I'm not the world's best cook, but I thought they'd be nicer than shop-bought biscuits. I made them while I was waiting for you.' He passed her a plate of small misshapen brown things.

She took one dutifully, touched by the pathetic object. It was soggy one side, charred the other, and seemed to be crying out for help and comfort.

He sat down on a cushion next to her, so close their elbows were touching. 'Well, aren't you going to try it?'

She took a tiny mouthful, but it stuck obstinately in her throat. 'Kim, I *can't* eat. You don't understand. I . . . I've *murdered* someone.'

'Could you try to tell me about it?'

She held the biscuit tightly in her hand. He sounded so amazingly calm, just sitting there and smiling, for God's sake. Yet how *could* she tell him? He'd be absolutely horrified, and anyway it would mean explaining the whole business about Elizabeth, when she didn't really understand it herself. But then, suddenly, impulsively, she found herself blurting out the story, from her first meeting with Elizabeth to Hugo's skiing accident.

'So you see, I . . . *killed* him – twice over, you could say.'

'Like you killed your baby brother?'

'Yes, that's right. You see, I . . . I'm terribly destructive. I must be. I can't seem to do anything but harm people.'

'Drink your milk.'

The voice was soft, but she recognized it as a command. She took a reluctant sip, frightened she'd throw up. Fortunately she didn't gag, so she drank a little more. Far from making her sick, the milk seemed to calm her stomach.

'Better?' he asked.

She nodded gratefully, then almost at once shook her head. 'I'll *never* be better. Never. There's no forgiveness for what I've done.'

'But Beattie, darling, there's nothing to forgive. You haven't killed *anyone*. Tragically, your twin died, but he would have died anyway.'

'No, *I* took all the food.'

'Look, there wasn't enough for you both. In fact, you were only a tiny scrap yourself when you were born, and had to be put into an incubator for – what was it, twelve weeks?'

'Fourteen.'

'Well, there you are. And you didn't kill Hugo, either.'

'But I did, I *did*. I . . .'

'Hold on a second. One thing at a time.' He put his arm around her and began gently stroking her still damp hair. 'First of all, he's *not* dead. You said he was injured in a skiing accident and he's in Intensive Care.'

'Yes, I know, but . . .'

'*You* were in Intensive Care. For over three months, yet you're still alive. What you need to understand is that all these fears are simply the result of your birth-script. You had an extremely traumatic birth which left you feeling that you're never safe, but abandoned and alone, and that invariably you hurt people.' He feathered his hand across her temples, then slowly down her cheek; his touch as gentle

335

as his voice. 'In order for you to live, your twin brother had to die, so you continue to feel responsible for other people's deaths. And because your father wanted a boy and your mother didn't want *any* children, you've always concluded that you're a mistake, a burden, and a terrible disappointment.'

She pushed his hand away. 'Kim, this is a *crisis*. I can't go into all these way-out theories now.'

'They're not way-out and they're not just theories. I've proved them for myself, Beattie. You may not realize this, but my own life was a total mess. I was trapped in bad relationships and never really healthy. Christ! I even became addicted to dope and alcohol, and I often wanted to die . . .'

'*I* want to die.'

'I know, my love, but that's all part of it. You see, you're affected by your mother's feelings. You told me she wanted to abort you.'

'Yeah, but I've no real *proof* of that.'

'You don't need proof. The feelings that come up in a rebirth are true in the most fundamental sense. And even before your birth you may have had nine unhappy months. Your mother's womb would hardly be a welcoming place if she didn't *want* a baby.'

She banged her mug down impatiently. What fucking *use* was all this? 'Kim, this is getting ridiculous. You'll be saying next I was unhappy as an egg-cell.'

'No, Beattie, what I *am* saying is that a foetus is exceptionally sensitive to its environment, so . . .'

'Look, I'm sorry, but it's *Hugo* I'm concerned about. In any case, you don't know the half of it.' She turned her face away from him, locking her hands together. 'I hardly know how to tell you. It sounds so . . . so monstrous, but . . . well, when the hospital rang, I felt . . .' She gave a despairing shrug. 'It's no good. I just can't say it.'

'You felt *glad*, no doubt.' Kim's voice was utterly calm. 'You'd got what you wanted, after all.'

'But that's wicked, unforgivable.' Her voice rose in agitation. 'I mean, even now a bit of me is still . . . well, if not exactly glad, then . . .' She picked up her biscuit and began crumbling it between her fingers, hardly aware of what she was doing. 'I hate myself for feeling that. That's why I *deserve* to die.'

'But at least you're being honest, Beattie. You'd be surprised how many people take pleasure in others' misfortunes, but they seldom have the courage to admit it. I suppose it's only human nature. And especially understandable in your case, because you saw Hugo as a tremendous threat.'

He continued stroking her hair, and she found the rhythmic movement was beginning to relax her. How wonderful that he understood and hadn't damned her (as she damned herself) as evil. He had showered her with kindness, offered her a soothing drink, even made those biscuits for her, like a mother in a storybook. And yet she was still troublingly aware of his maleness – the dark bulk of his body pressed so close to hers; the hairs on his bare feet; that cloying scent lingering in the air; the deep seductive voice.

'What you need, sweetheart, is another rebirth, to . . .'

She jerked free from his arms, the hypnotic spell now shattered. 'No! I'd rather *die.*'

'Beattie, sweetheart, you want to die anyway, which is terrible and tragic for you. But another session could take away your despair.'

She hunched her arms round her knees. It suddenly dawned on her that he was probably touting for business. Individual rebirthing sessions cost up to a hundred pounds, depending how long they took and how experienced the rebirther. Kim was *very* experienced, and might keep her here all night on some pretence or other.

She stole a glance at him. Yes, it was quite obvious that he was trying to win her over, using his hands, his eyes, his mesmerizing voice.

'The most powerful form of rebirthing, Beattie, is what we call the hot-tub method. It's done under water – which is why I asked you to come here. There's a hot tub in the basement that was built specially for . . .'

'You mean this . . . this isn't your home?'

'Oh, no. It belongs to an American friend, a fellow-rebirther who commutes between here and California. He lets me borrow the house when he's away.'

She avoided his compelling gaze, uncertain now whether he wanted her as a client or was just hoping for a quick lay. He could well have lured her here not for the hot tub at all, but because he knew they would be undisturbed – no wife or flatmates barging in. Part of her was flattered. After all, he was tremendously attractive – unlike most of the men she'd been with. She realized to her horror that she was actually becoming aroused by the thought of sleeping with him. How *could* she, when Hugo was facing death? Whatever excuses Kim might offer, it was just another example of her wickedness.

'Kim, I . . . I'm worried about Elizabeth. It seems awful for us to be messing around in hot tubs when she's . . .'

'But it's *not* messing around. Far from it. You've got to understand, Beattie, this could be the most important step you've ever taken in your life. And you'll be doing it not only for yourself, but for other people too. You see, you can't help anyone else – and that includes Elizabeth – unless you release yourself from this negative spiral. Your birth-script has always told you that you're a destructive person who's bound to screw things up. So that's what happens – and always will, until you write *another* birth-script.'

She continued looking at the floor, now thoroughly confused. He sounded so committed and sincere. Perhaps she had imagined the whole sexual thing, jumped to the wrong conclusions, as she'd suspected *him* of doing. In any case, if she listened to what he was saying, it was startling in its relevance. She *had* screwed things up – the whole of her life, in fact. She had never had a decent job or a permanent relationship; had no confidence in her looks, her brains, or her future. And as for the present, everyone was angry with her: Caroline and Sarah and all of Elizabeth's family, Max and Sal, her recent boss . . . What had she to lose?

'Okay,' she said abruptly.

Kim rose to his feet and enfolded her in his arms. She stood awkwardly and stiffly, terrified of responding. If they were doing this rebirthing for Elizabeth's sake, the last thing she wanted was the distraction of his body – its dangerous warmth and solidity beneath the silky robe.

He squeezed her hand and smiled into her eyes, then ushered her out of the room and across the dingy hall. Warily she followed him down a flight of steep stone steps and through a heavy door. She reeled back at the heat. The room was panelled in pine-wood like a sauna, and every bit as stifling. In the centre a wooden tub had been set into the floor. It was much bigger than she'd imagined – about eight feet in diameter – though she couldn't tell its depth, since it was covered with a plastic sheet. Beside it lay another double mattress, again heaped with rugs and pillows.

'There's a changing-room through there, Beattie, so if you'd like to take your things off . . . It's more effective if you're completely naked.'

Yeah, I bet it is, she thought, all her suspicions surging back. These peculiar rebirthers probably managed to convince themselves that shagging their clients was simply part of the whole procedure. All that spiel about birth-scripts could be just the ploy they used to put people off their guard. Well, who cared? She was too tired to argue any longer, and besides, it hardly mattered. What was one more screw? In fact, it would be a relief to screw, in a way; to become a rutting animal, untroubled by conscience or self-loathing.

She crept into the changing-room and peeled off her skirt and sweater, unhooked her bra, pulled down her pants and tights. She emerged again, holding one arm across her breasts, the other shielding her pubic hair, and still feeling a certain resentment that he had to go to these ridiculous lengths for the sake of a quick grope. He was naked now himself and standing with his back to her, arranging something on a ledge. Slowly he turned round and she saw he had a hard on; blatant proof of his intentions. Her first hunch had been right, then. So much for the disinterested rebirther.

'I'm going to light this candle, darling. You see, what we're doing is really a sort of ritual, and the candle symbolizes the baby being born from the darkness of the womb into the light of life.' He lit the plain white candle and placed it in a jar, next to a smouldering incense-stick. He had made a sort of altar on the ledge. There was a vase of lanky daffodils and a bronze statuette of a Buddha figure. Shadows from the candle flickered on the walls, becoming more dramatic when he turned off the main light. She began to feel more and more unreal, as if she too were being extinguished. There were no windows in the room, no sense of any outside world. Even the rain was silenced, and she had long since lost track of time. She and Kim seemed marooned in some strange dreamscape, cut off from normal life.

He pulled the plastic cover off the tub and a fierce cloud of steam erupted from it, shrouding his body from sight.

'Kim!' she called in panic, suddenly fearing he might disappear for ever, leaving her a prisoner in this stifling basement cell.

'It's all right, darling, I'm here. This steam will clear in a moment. But it *is* quite hot, so do take care when you get into the water.'

She groped towards him and let him hold her close. Anything was better than that sense of total abandonment. His erection had subsided and she felt almost disappointed. At least with sex she knew what was expected. And she would still be *real* – a flesh-and-blood

339

person coupled to another – not cast adrift in some blurred and shifting world. She pressed against his warm perspiring body in the hope of arousing him again; lifted her mouth expectantly to his. But gently he released her, smiling and shaking his head.

'Beattie, we have work to do.'

Disconcerted by his rejection, she let him guide her towards the shallow wooden steps leading down into the tub.

'Have you any objection to using a snorkel?' he asked, pausing on the top step. 'We *can* do the rebirth with you floating on your back, but it's more powerful if you go right under. You see, that's closer to the experience of actually being in the womb.'

'Oh God, Kim! This sounds worse and worse. I've only used a snorkel once and I hated it. I just don't feel safe under water.'

'Don't worry, you can float then. And you *will* be safe because I'll be holding you up. You'll be literally in my arms.'

She dipped one apprehensive foot into the water, but hastily withdrew it. 'It's boiling! It'll burn me.'

'There's no danger of that, believe me. In fact, this is exactly the temperature of the womb.'

'No wonder I hated being in my mother's womb, then,' she murmured.

He smiled. 'I'll get in first, to show you it's okay.'

'But it's all right for you – you're used to it. Anyway, you haven't just been ill. I've barely recovered from this kidney thing, so I probably shouldn't . . .'

'But Beattie, don't you see, illness is simply part of your problem. When you were born, you were premature and sickly, so of course you picked up the feeling that there was something wrong with you. Then you carried that idea into your subsequent life and *continued* to be ill or depressed. I did just the same myself, so I know what I'm talking about. But I broke the pattern, and now I'm as fit as a fiddle. And I want that to happen for you.'

Still unconvinced, she stepped in after him, flinching in shock at the heat. The water was already up to her knees and inched higher as she descended another step. Despite his reassurances, she could feel the fear returning – fear of the rebirthing process, fear of fear itself. Her body seemed to be on fire, her breathing shallow and unsteady. 'I'm so *hot*, Kim. It's horrible. I'm scared I'm going to faint.'

'You won't faint, sweetheart. You'll be absolutely safe.' From somewhere behind him he produced a bottle of water and sprinkled some on a flannel, which he held against her burning face. 'There, that's better, isn't it? And would you like a sip of water?'

She nodded. Anything to delay the horror of going any deeper. How would she endure that overpowering heat against her breasts?

He held a paper cup to her lips and she gulped the water gratefully, touched by his kindness when all she had done was resist. She wiped her mouth and forced herself to brave the last few steps, until finally she was standing on the bottom of the tub. The water, lapping at her waist, looked dark and treacherous, and was so intensely hot, she registered it as pain. Kim's continual assertions that she was 'absolutely safe' were beginning to sound hollow. She remembered the rebirthers on the Devon course trotting out the same formula, regardless of whether the person involved was calm, or shrieking in terror. *She* was certainly terrified, and as she closed her eyes to distance herself from what was going on, she was suddenly plunged without warning into claustrophobic darkness, a trap-door snapping shut behind her. Desperately she struggled to escape. This cramped and fetid prison was becoming hideously familiar, a place of untold fear.

'Oh God!' she cried, 'I'm there again, inside her. It's *terrible*, I'm suffocating. I can't bear it.'

'Beattie, it's all right, darling. You're absolutely safe.'

She clung to him in panic, hiding her face against his shoulder. 'But I can't breathe or see or anything. Get me out, please get me out!'

'Breathe into the fear, darling. Breathe into your feelings. You can leave the pain behind.'

'I can't. I can't. I must get out.' She threshed wildly through the water and blundered up the steps.

Kim gripped her by the arm, but she shook him off and sank down by the side of the pool, hunching herself over her knees. How the hell could she know what it felt like to be in her mother's womb? It made no sense at all. Yet the feelings were so vivid, and coming from so deep a level, she knew she hadn't imagined them. And that made her more afraid than ever.

'I'm sorry, Kim,' she said wretchedly, 'I just can't cope with all that trauma again. The first rebirth was bad enough.'

'But that's the whole point, sweetheart. You released so much in the first session, this one could be a real turning point. You've been through the worst already. And remember you can actually *choose* to have a peaceful happy birth – to make it different this time, a joyful experience instead of a harrowing one. It's basically a matter of trust.' He came and sat beside her, took her hand in his and stroked it tenderly. 'Oh, I'm well aware that trust is a difficult thing for you, but I'm asking you just this once to trust *me* and trust the process.'

'But I *don't* trust,' she retorted. 'Not you or anyone.'

'You trust Elizabeth.'

'That's different. And anyway, she's not here.'

'Beattie, darling, it doesn't matter whether she's here or not. What matters is that you've found someone who's never let you down.'

Beattie pressed her face into her knees, trying not to see Elizabeth. But her small and solitary figure was just walking into the hospital, dwarfed by its brutal buildings, swallowed up in its heartless bustle. Kim was right – Elizabeth had always put her first, even forgoing her trip to Scotland to stay with her at Mile End House. Only to be repaid by Hugo's accident.

She suddenly knew she had to go through with the rebirthing, for Elizabeth's sake – and Hugo's. She had willed his death, so now it was up to her to will him back to life, and this ritual seemed the only way. Kim had told her she couldn't help Elizabeth unless she wrote another birth-script. She wasn't even sure what he meant, but she *had* to help Elizabeth. And the very word rebirth offered a shred of hope: resurrection for a dying man. Okay, it might sound crazy, utterly deluded, but far worse to sit idly by and do nothing for the one person she could trust. And it was no good being half-hearted about it, or recoiling from the dangers or the heat. Pain and fear were part of the process. Elizabeth and Hugo were both suffering, so why should *she* be spared?

She lifted her head and met Kim's eyes – he was looking at her anxiously. She reached out and pulled him to his feet, her new determination effectively reversing their roles. 'Kim, I . . . I'm ready now. And I . . . I want to use the snorkel. I want to do it the most powerful way.'

'Oh Beattie, that's wonderful!'

He guided her back to the tub, going over the breathing instructions once more. She hardly heard his words, bracing herself to re-enter the scalding water. Impatient of his restraining arms, she would have preferred to dive straight in, not take it step by frightening step.

'Now, don't forget, darling – whatever happens, you're *safe*. I want you to surrender completely, and trust me to be here for you.'

She returned his smile uncertainly, then picked up the snorkel and clamped it between her teeth. Kim helped her with the nose-clip, reminding her to breathe through her mouth and to relax as she went down. She shut her eyes and ducked under the surface, the heat blazing through her face in a spasm of scarlet pain. She could hear the sound of her breathing, amplified through the snorkel to a sort of gasping roar. She was spluttering and choking, but she tried to fight the sense of panic; accept the relentless heat. *Trust*, she thought, trust Elizabeth – you're doing this for her.

Gradually her breathing quietened and the roar of the snorkel grew steadier and softer, more like a rhythmic heartbeat. But it wasn't her mother's heart. That had always beat too fast, jolting and unsettling her. This heartbeat was calm, and strangely reassuring, despite the turmoil all around her. Everything was bursting open, and she appeared to have no choice but to surrender to the violent motion and let herself be pushed along. Her dark confining home was opening out to a vast and brilliant world beyond, a world she'd never dreamed of. Already she could catch glimpses of it; heard a voice she recognized murmuring gentle words of encouragement. She felt a mounting excitement as she was shunted convulsively along. She knew that someone was waiting for her, someone immeasurably important, who was part of her and would be central to her life. She longed to join that person, who had become precious and familiar during these last months – the sound of her, the taste and smell and rhythm of her – but always at some great remove. Soon they would be meeting face to face, and she would feel at last the soft curves of her body, the texture of her skin.

She was surprised how long the journey took and how much strength it seemed to demand. Yet there was no danger this time, nothing in the way – she was absolutely safe. The gentle voice was still urging her on, telling her not to panic as she was propelled through a narrow tunnel, which squeezed her tighter, tighter, constricting the soft bones of her head. Disoriented, she fought for breath, and was suddenly pitched through the white-hot barrier from darkness into light. Strong hands reached out to receive her and she gave a cry of joy as she was laid rapturously in Elizabeth's waiting arms.

She pressed against the warm and naked body. Their hearts were beating to the same rhythm, their breathing at one, drowsy after great exertion. New sensations washed over her: peace, happiness, fulfilment. She was the wanted child, the only child, the long-awaited girl-child; cocooned in love, born into a welcoming world. The body beside her was her anchor in that world, and would be there for her for ever – a resting place, a home.

She found the breast again, her lips closing round the nipple. Milk flowed into her mouth, unstinting, inexhaustible, and with it deep contentment. She knew that life was sweet, and very safe.

She was the perfect precious baby cradled in her perfect mother's arms.

32

Beattie opened her eyes. She was lying in Kim's arms, her head against his chest. He was holding a baby's bottle to her lips, tilting it to give her the last few drops. She pushed it away, incredulous, although Kim continued to gaze at her with an expression of near-reverence.

'You *were* hungry!' he smiled.

'Wh ... what's happening?' She struggled to sit up, wondering where she was and why it was so dark.

'It's all right, darling. Just lie back. It's only just past midnight.'

She sank down again beside him. They were lying on a mattress on the floor, both completely naked. Beyond him, she could see the wooden tub. The candle had burned down to a dribble of distorted wax, but a small lamp in the corner cast a shadowy pool of light.

'Has the tingling gone?' Kim asked.

She looked at him, perplexed. She could remember only bliss. 'Elizabeth,' she murmured.

'I'm here,' a soft voice answered, and again she felt those loving arms enfold her as she drifted back into warm and blissful sleep.

When she next woke, Kim had disappeared. She blinked and rubbed her eyes. She was still lying on the mattress, but now swaddled in a blanket and with a pillow under her head. She groped to her feet, surprised how weak she felt; her soft infant bones barely strong enough to support her. It was some time before she found her clothes – still longer before she had managed to dress. Everything was an effort and seemed to require skills she didn't have. She fastened the strap on her watch, peering at the dial in bewilderment. The hands were pointing to quarter to five, but was that morning or afternoon?

There was no daylight in this basement room so it was impossible to tell and, besides, she had lost all sense of time. For all she knew, *days* could have passed, or maybe no more than an hour. The only time-scale which meant anything was before her rebirth, and now.

She walked slowly to the door and climbed the stairs, pausing on each step. On reaching the hall, she saw that it was dark still – the glass panel in the front door reflecting only a square of inky black.

'Kim?' she called uncertainly. Perhaps he could help her regain her strength; restore her to the real world.

'Oh, Beattie, you're awake!' He appeared at the door of the kitchen, dressed in his kimono. 'How's my beautiful baby? I was just making you another bottle.'

She flushed, avoiding his eyes. The thought of him feeding her made her cringe with embarrassment.

He took both her hands in his. 'Beattie, never forget, you *are* beautiful. And what happened last night was very special for both of us. Don't ever be tempted to play it down, or deny it.'

'No, I won't,' she said truthfully. 'I couldn't. It was . . . over-whelming.'

He smiled and stroked her hair. 'You needn't have got dressed yet. It's only very early still. Why don't you go back downstairs and I'll bring your bottle as soon as it's ready?'

'No, honestly, I'm . . . fine.'

'Well, come and sit in here, darling, while I finish warming it up.'

Nervously she followed him into the small untidy kitchen and sat down on a rickety chair. 'Er, if you don't mind, Kim, I'd rather have some – you know – ordinary tea or coffee.'

'Of course. Whatever you want. But let me give you it in the bottle. It's important that you're fed, Beattie, because you were deprived as a new-born baby – wired up to all those dreadful drips and tubes, with no loving mother's arms to make you feel secure. I want to try to undo that, so you can feel what it's like to be given everything you need, and given it with love.'

'I *did* feel that – all night.'

'Darling, I hope you'll feel it for the rest of your *life*. And you *can*, you know, if you'll only change your thoughts and expectations. Now that you've been reborn to a loving mother, you can begin to see the world as a safe and loving place.'

She longed to believe him, but what proof was there, for heaven's sake? Her friends would die laughing if they knew she'd been bottle-

346

fed by a brawny 'mother' with chest hair and a stubbly chin. Yet, for all that, Kim had proved himself to be genuinely loving, and undoubtedly her experience last night had been the most intense of her life.

She watched him fill the kettle at a deep old-fashioned sink. The whole kitchen seemed to belong to another era, when fitted units and modern boilers were unknown luxuries. And there was still that sense of being cut off from the outside world. The one small window looked out on a back yard, and beyond that reared a high brick wall, enclosing them in their own private space. She was rarely awake at this early hour, and it seemed a sort of nothing-time; a no-man's-land between night and morning, with no certainty of light, no noise from traffic, or reassuring human sounds. Did anyone else *exist?*

Kim lit the gas on the ancient stove, and got a chipped white teapot out of the cupboard. His movements were calm and unhurried, but he rarely took his eyes off her, as if frightened she might slip away unless he held her with his gaze. 'The change won't happen by magic, Beattie. You have to work at it each day. It's like breaking an addiction – in your case, an addiction to unhappiness. What you need to understand is that if you focus on fear, you attract bad experiences and people who mistreat you. But if you focus on love, you attract happiness and good relationships.'

'Look, surely that's a bit pat?' she objected, torn between a longing to believe him and the cynical voices of her friends.

'Maybe. But it's true. You see, we don't *have* to think in our usual negative way. We can actually choose our thoughts, and decide to believe that life is safe, and that we're good, loving, innocent people.'

Innocent. The word struck her like a blow. 'Oh, God,' she said, clapping a hand over her mouth. '*Hugo!* How could I have forgotten him?'

'Don't worry, he's all right. He's going to pull through.'

She stared at him, astonished. Had he been in touch with the hospital, somehow persuaded them to talk to him? 'How . . . how do you know?'

'I *don't* know. But we've got to trust. It's part of the rebirth, part of your new thinking, Beattie – a shift of focus from death to life.'

She slumped back in her chair. He had allowed her a brief instant of hope, only to snatch it cruelly away. How could mere trust save a man in Intensive Care?

'And I think it would be a good idea if you went up there, to the

347

hospital, to help Elizabeth. The two of you are so important to each other. You were calling out her name last night in your sleep.'

Beattie hid her face in her hands. 'She wouldn't want me,' she said wretchedly. Elizabeth would surely blame her for the accident; might even refuse to speak to her at all.

Kim crouched by her chair and gently prised her hands away. 'But Beattie, you could be a great comfort to her. And not only that – you could help in purely practical terms. I mean, if you went by car, you could drive her to and from the hospital.'

She refused to meet his eyes. 'But . . . but it's a *hell* of a way to Inverness. I know, because I looked it up when Elizabeth said she was going there, and it's almost off the map. I just couldn't drive that distance. And, anyway, my car might let me down. It's a real old crock, and, knowing my luck, it's bound to conk out in the middle of nowhere. Besides, even if I *did* make it, suppose I arrive too late? I mean, I could slog my bloody guts out and then find that Hugo's already . . . you know . . .'

'What's happened to your *trust*, Beattie? Don't you see, you're focusing on the negative again – all the things which might go wrong? But if you look at it in a more positive way, this could be your chance to show Elizabeth the love you say she's always given you; to be *there* for her, in every sense. And the very fact the journey's such a long one makes it all the more valuable – a sort of present for her, if you like.'

'But I still feel rather faint and . . .'

'Don't worry about that, my sweet. It's quite normal after a rebirth, and it'll soon pass off. I'll get your tea – that should help.'

He returned to the stove and took the bottle out of the saucepan of hot water. 'I've made it nice and milky,' he said, swathing it in a tea-towel. 'Let's go into the other room, then you can lie down on the mattress.'

'*No*, Kim. I don't want to be fed. And anyway, I . . . I really ought to be going home. I know it's only the crack of dawn, but I never meant to stay all night. Oh, don't think I'm not grateful,' she added hastily. 'It's just that . . .' She stopped. How could she explain her sense of terror at the thought of seeing Elizabeth again? It was as if Kim had given her a commitment, a solemn duty she had no right to refuse. Yet he obviously didn't understand her feeling of inadequacy. It wasn't just the driving and the distance, or even the state of her car, which, despite its age, hadn't given her any more trouble since the trip to Ashley Grange. No, it was the risk of being rejected, or treated with a cool resentment. Besides, if she went up to the hospital she could only be a burden – a constant reminder of how different things might have been if Elizabeth and Hugo had gone away together.

She walked slowly to the window and stared out at the yard. Couldn't one of Elizabeth's *daughters* step in and help their mother? But no, none of them was free. Caroline and Emma were tied down with young children, Sarah was abroad, and Harriet unwell again. So Elizabeth was on her own. Her ordinary friends weren't likely to drop everything and travel six hundred miles. And even Margaret couldn't go – she'd hardly leave James alone when he was about to have an operation.

She trailed back to her chair and sat hunched over the table. Last night she had been lying in Elizabeth's arms, experiencing what she could only describe as perfect happiness, while Elizabeth herself was probably stuck in some godforsaken hotel, grappling with the deepest depression.

'What's wrong?' Kim asked, seating himself beside her at the table.

'Nothing.' It was *Kim* who had stayed up with her all night, forfeiting his sleep to tend her every need. And he hadn't so much as mentioned her cruel piece in the *Herald*, when he could easily have condemned her as a Judas and a shit. Yet, despite his devotion and his decency, she hadn't said a single word of thanks. 'Kim,' she burst out, 'you must think I'm really awful, taking all this for granted. I just don't know how to thank you. I mean, no one's ever . . .' She broke off in confusion as she realized with a jolt that she would have trouble even paying his bill, which must be astronomical by now. 'Look, there's . . . there's something I wanted to ask you. Would . . . would you mind awfully if I paid you half now and the rest a bit later – say in three weeks' time? I'm afraid my bank account's not exactly . . .'

'What d'you mean, *pay* me?'

'Well, the fee for the rebirthing.'

He shook his head, laughing. 'There isn't any fee.'

'But I couldn't possibly take it for nothing. I mean, all your time and trouble and . . .'

'That's the whole point, my love. I'm trying to make you see that you don't *have* to pay for everything, either with pain *or* with money. No, listen – I insist. I'm not Mr Wonderful. Far from it! Someone did the same for me – my own rebirther, Duncan. He was a fantastic man who transformed my life, but he refused to accept a penny. He told me that somewhere along the line I'd meet a person whose birth had been as difficult as mine, and that I could repay my debt to *him* by helping *them*. And you're that special person, Beattie. So thank you, darling, for phoning me last night.'

She hugged him fiercely, blinking back her tears. This whole approach was so different from the outside world, where everything had its price. Time is money, Max always said, yet here was a man she barely knew who had spent *hours* with her, for free. And despite her earlier misgivings, he hadn't tried anything on – she was quite certain of that now. So what had been in it for him? Only the chance to repay love with love.

'Kim,' she said suddenly, her voice muffled against his chest.

'Mm?'

'I *will* go up to Scotland.' She, too, had a debt to repay. And if Elizabeth didn't want her there, she wouldn't agonize or argue, but simply drive back home again. At least she would have made the effort, offered some form of recompense.

She remained in Kim's arms, hoping his love and generosity might have the power to change her. 'I'm sorry to be so clingy,' she said, still reluctant to let him go. 'It's just that I need some . . . some courage.'

He held her gently at arm's length and looked into her eyes. 'You *have* courage, Beattie, if only you could see it. You have everything you need – love and strength and beauty and . . .'

'Ssh! You'll embarrass me.' She pulled away, at last. 'And anyway, if I'm going to Scotland I'd better get down to practicalities and start working out the route and things. Actually, it would probably make more sense to go direct from here. We must be near the motorway – I seem to remember seeing it on the map. In fact, it could almost be *meant*, my being in north London, poised in the right direction. And I've even got my stuff in the car. I crammed it all in plastic bags when I left Elizabeth's.'

He stroked her hair affectionately. 'Well, by the sounds of it, you're all ready to go.'

'Yes. I'd better set off this instant. Then, with any luck, I should get there before dark.'

'Hold on, Beattie darling. If this is going to be your new start, you need to be kinder to yourself. You told me you were feeling faint, so you really should take more time to recover.'

'No, I'm fine now, honestly. You've given me new heart.'

'Well, I certainly didn't intend you to rush off before it's light.'

'All the better – there won't be any traffic.'

'Beattie, darling, you don't *have* to do the journey in one day. You could put up somewhere overnight and take it much more slowly, especially if you're worried about your car.'

'I'm not. That was just my negativity speaking.' She laughed. 'See, Kim, I'm a reformed character already. No, seriously, now you've put the idea in my head, I'm champing at the bit! And I don't like the thought of Elizabeth being alone up there another night.' Anyway, she didn't add, the longer I delay, the more chance there is of Hugo being . . . being . . . No, she mustn't even *think* it. If she was going to make this mammoth journey in a new spirit of trust, she had to change her outlook, focus on hope, not death.

Kim was tugging open the dresser-drawers and sorting through their contents. 'Well, at least let me find you a decent map. And you'd better take some food for the journey. I'm afraid Jake keeps his cupboards rather bare, but if you don't mind Ryvita sandwiches and maybe the odd muesli bar . . . Actually, you ought to have something *now*. You must be feeling hungry.'

'Don't worry, Kim, I can always stop on the way.'

'But it's only five to five and most places will be shut. Besides, it's very dark and chilly at this time of the morning, and you need something hot inside you before you set off.'

She grinned. 'Oh hell, Kim – I can see you're absolutely determined to give me that damned bottle!'

'Well, actually, I was going to suggest breakfast, but yes, the bottle, if you want it.'

'I *don't* want it. It's humiliating being fed. I'm sorry, that sounds very rude after all you've done, but . . .'

'Don't worry, I understand. In fact, we're so alike, I have to laugh! You probably won't believe this, Beattie, but I used to be every bit as sceptical as you. When I first met the rebirthing crowd, I thought they were completely round the twist. I fought poor Duncan tooth and nail before he finally made me see sense.'

'I bet he didn't feed you with a bottle, though.'

'Oh yes he did. He even put *whisky* in it once. He said it was the only way to shut me up!'

She sat down at the table again, trying to picture Kim, the rebel, being force-fed with a baby's bottle of scotch. He had certainly progressed since then – from alcoholic, junkie and potential suicide, to someone totally at peace with himself, who had transformed his life and relationships.

'Okay,' she said suddenly, picking up the bottle and pushing it into his hands. 'Let's compromise. I'll have the bottle, *and* some breakfast too, if you like, but I simply must be on the road by quarter to six.'

'All right, if you insist. But listen, Beattie, my sweet, don't saddle yourself with too many "musts". You need to give yourself time for things, instead of living in a constant rush and frazzle. It's all part of being kind to yourself and accepting that you're a decent person who deserves a decent life.' He helped her to her feet and steered her towards the door. 'Let's go back downstairs. It's warmer down there and you can stretch out on the mattress and take this chance to relax. I feel you need a little more cosseting before your long hard slog.'

The instant he closed the basement door, she felt enfolded in peace again. The room was warm, dark and secluded – the perfect womb. Almost in a dream, she lay down on the mattress, remembering those loving arms, that amazing sense of bliss. She closed her eyes and let him slip the teat between her lips. There was no need to be embarrassed – this was simply sustenance for her journey, comfort before she left. Warm sweet liquid began flowing into her mouth, and soon nothing else existed save the body cradling hers and an unending stream of milk. Once again she had entered that exquisite world which held no fear nor danger, and where nothing would be snatched away, nothing grudged or rationed.

She could lie here, safe, for ever, reunited with her perfect loving mother.

33

Beattie turned off the motorway and took the road to the nearest village. She'd made such good time, she'd decided to stop for lunch in a friendly country pub, instead of some huge impersonal motorway café. Well, she was only following Kim's advice and being kind to herself. Just before she'd set off, he had urged her to relax and think of wide, safe, empty roads, rather than traffic jams or breakdowns. And it had worked surprisingly well: she was already almost halfway to Inverness, and her ancient car seemed itself reborn as it rattled heroically along. The M1 had been more or less a doddle – none of the usual road repairs or lane closures – and although she had run into some traffic on the approach to Coventry, it had thinned out again once she'd joined the M6. She had even got used to the jugger-nauts, refusing to be browbeaten as they thundered past her gnat of a car; their slipstream slowing her down. And anyway, now that she'd passed Lancaster, the lorries were far fewer and the scenery fantastic.

She drove into the village along a winding tree-lined lane; the craggy hills beyond merging into grey-blue haze. The triumphant sound of church bells suddenly broke the silence, as if applauding her good progress. She parked in the main street and got out of the car, glad to stretch her legs. Although the journey had been easy, and she'd stopped twice already before this, she still felt very stiff. Her back was beginning to ache, and it was a relief to breathe fresh country air instead of diesel fumes. She wandered along to the church – a squat and stolid building in weathered stone, surrounded by moss-furred tombstones standing guard. Rooks, startled by the bells, were exploding from the tall trees in the graveyard. She watched them dwindle into sooty specks as they flapped raucously away, black against the watery blue sky. The rain had finally cleared, leaving a calm and windless day, with occasional glints of sun piercing through the clouds.

'Help Elizabeth,' she prayed, as she walked up to the porch. 'Let everything be all right.' She remembered the little church near Cheltenham; herself and Elizabeth kneeling side by side, bonded, almost carefree then. '*Trust*,' she whispered. 'Things can be like that again. Maybe.'

She retraced her steps along the path, then crossed the road to the pub. The Golden Pheasant was built in the same stern grey stone as the church, though softened by the virginia creeper which tendrilled across its brows. The interior was old-fashioned, even neglected. Evidently no one had seen fit to repaint the gravy-brown walls, or replace the faded carpet, let alone introduce games machines or juke-boxes. As she made her way to the bar, she was aware of curious glances turned in her direction. Her haircut was too extreme, her clothes too wildly coloured for this sleepy Lakeland village. Yet she didn't feel an intruder – Kim's influence again. 'Smile at everyone you meet,' he had said. 'And treat them as brothers and sisters, not as strangers.' Again, his advice paid off: her smiles were generally returned, and the barman chatted genially about the weather and the local horse-show. However, once she'd got her lager and steak pie, she went to sit at a table on her own. She didn't want to talk, but to concentrate her thoughts on Hugo – something she'd found difficult during the long drive. He's *alive*, she told herself. He's doing well. Elizabeth doesn't blame me; it was an accident, that's all. He's going to pull through. I *trust*.

She could almost hear Kim praising her; see him smiling in encouragement. He had been with her all the way, an invisible but comforting presence. And beside her on the passenger seat were his provisions for the journey: a supply of his home-made brownies, packed in greaseproof paper; the waterproofs he'd lent her to prevent her getting drenched again; a rug to keep her warm; a flask of camomile tea. He'd also found her a marvellous large-scale map, and had written out the route for her on a separate piece of paper, to make sure she didn't go wrong.

She had been thinking of him constantly – reflecting on last night's rebirthing, which seemed extraordinary, incredible. How could such intense experiences (whether of pain or bliss) have taken her over so completely? In some ways it was like sex: the violent things you said and did in the white heat of the moment because some man

354

was rooted into you. Then afterwards, returning to cold reality, you could hardly believe those heights of passion, that complete lack of inhibition. But rebirthing *wasn't* sex, and she was determined to keep faith with Kim. Sitting over their offbeat breakfast (buckwheat porridge and rice-cakes), he had told her that she could 'resurrect' her twin by incorporating the male and the female within her. There was no more need, he'd said, to feel that someone or something was missing. She was enough in herself, and could learn to be her own mother, in the sense of looking after herself and treating herself with respect.

God! Max would despise such New Age psychobabble – but then, according to Kim, Max was part of the problem. It was because she didn't love herself that she always ended up in relationships with unsuitable (unloving) men. She supposed she'd have to phone 'unsuitable' Max, to tell him where she was, but he'd only be furious with her again for running after Elizabeth like a bloody cat on heat. She tried to imagine having a different sort of lover – a tender devoted man like Kim – but then felt instant guilt about her disloyalty to Max. Besides, she wasn't exactly tender herself, let alone devoted.

She extracted the two lone pieces of meat from the gravy-slush of her pie, then tackled the leaden pastry. Not quite the delicious lunch she'd envisaged, but never mind – she'd stop somewhere nice for tea and order scones and cream.

The sound of a crying baby brought her abruptly back to the present. Its mother was sitting alone in the corner, trying to finish her drink, while the child squirmed on her lap. She was a scraggy pallid woman with dark rings under her eyes, who was becoming more irritable by the minute, snapping at the still howling brat and glaring at the people round her, as if defying them to complain. Then, all of a sudden, she pushed her drink away, hoisted the baby roughly over her shoulder and stalked out of the pub.

You need *Kim*, thought Beattie, to calm you and rebirth you; Kim to explain why you're unhappy, give you new hope. On impulse she jumped up and ran after the woman, who was standing outside on the pavement looking lost. She appeared to have no coat for herself and no pushchair for the child. It was still writhing in her arms, a bald and runny-nosed creature in a grubby Babygro.

Beattie edged a little closer, wondering how to break the ice. Kim would doubtless have offered help in a spirit of universal love, but she didn't have his knack.

355

'What you starin' at me for?' the woman said aggressively, thrusting out her chin.

'I was just . . . er . . . admiring your baby.'

'Piss off!' The woman spat the words at her, then marched off down the street, muttering to herself. Beattie leaned against the creeper-clad wall, watching the scrawny figure disappear round the corner. She was reminded of her own mother – the same thin body and pale unhealthy face, the same irrational anger and air of sullen misery. Her mother too had usually been alone; her father leading his double life miles away in digs. He had told her once that he'd missed great chunks of her babyhood. He would return home between shows, surprised to find she'd sprouted hair or teeth, or learned to walk or talk, while he'd been away playing Nanki-Poo in Liverpool or Buttons in Southend.

Hell, she thought suddenly, it must have been bloody awful for my mother – no support, no company, and unwell even then. The multiple sclerosis which killed her wasn't diagnosed for years. She was simply labelled a hypochondriac and told to pull herself together.

For the first time in her life, she felt pity for her mother; longed to sweep into the realm of the dead, track her down and tell her she was sorry. Since the age of eleven or twelve, she'd been so busy feeling sorry for her*self*, she hadn't spared a thought for how it might have been for a woman struggling on her own with lousy health, very little money, and a husband who fancied the young actresses he worked with. Her mother had never had the luxury of anyone like Kim, never been held or loved or cherished, and for all she knew, might have suffered a horrendous birth herself. It seemed inhuman now to have blamed her so relentlessly, shown so little compassion. And even if she *had* attempted to abort her twin babies, wasn't that understandable in the circumstances? She must have known in her heart that she wasn't well or strong enough to withstand the strain of giving birth and coping with young children.

Two men were just walking into the pub and held the door for her. She followed in a daze and sat down at her table. Her glass had been cleared away, although she had left it three-quarters full. She went up to the bar and ordered a port and lemon – her mother's favourite drink (on the rare occasions she *did* drink). She took it to a new seat in the window and raised her glass to Sonia. How odd that her mother had actually had a name, an independent existence of her own. She had only ever thought of her as pathetic boring Mum; never got to know the real person underneath.

She would drink a toast to Sonia, not health and happiness – those were now impossible, alas – but belated recognition of all she'd had to put up with, including her bolshie daughter.

She sipped the warming drink, experiencing a genuine sense of peace, as if she had indeed said sorry and settled all the old scores with her mother. She had a suspicion that Kim was behind it, influencing her again in some peculiar way. He'd talked a lot about forgiveness as an essential part of rebirthing, but it hadn't really registered till now. *He* would claim, presumably, that last night's breakthrough experience had enabled her to release a lifetime's bitterness.

Well, true or no, she certainly felt energized, as if she'd become lighter and less encumbered; the two-hundred-odd miles ahead of her no longer quite so daunting.

She drained her port and, with a smile at the people nearby, strode out to the car. If Kim was accompanying her on the journey, then why not her mother as well? It was high time they got to know each other.

She had almost reached the summit of the hill when her engine stuttered and then stalled. After a few false starts, she finally got it going again, praying it wouldn't conk out before she hit Inverness. She must be nearly there, and it would be horribly ironical if something went wrong at this late stage. She was still amazed by how easy things had been so far, as if Kim had stage-managed the whole trip; preventing any accidents or hold-ups, restraining the weather, making sure the visibility was good. Even on this last lap of the journey, with the A9 switching disconcertingly between dual carriageway and single, she hadn't encountered any real problems, and the traffic was surprisingly light. And whenever she'd stopped for petrol or a snack, people had seemed remarkably friendly, as if Kim had staffed the service stations with his own brand of Good Samaritans.

Suddenly, she braked, drawing in her breath. Ahead of her, the road fell steeply away to reveal an expanse of dazzling water, gilded by the sunset and spanned by an elegant suspension bridge which seemed to float in space. This must be the Moray Firth, and displayed at its dramatic best. The sky blazed red and orange, as if someone had set it alight; sparks showering on the water and igniting that in turn. And shimmering on her left lay a city built of flame – Inverness, at last. Beyond it, on the far side of the water, fields and mountains smouldered in the fierce glare of the sun; the whole scene glowing like a huge flamboyant painting.

She thought instantly of Hugo, feeling guilty at her callousness in feasting on the scenery while he lay injured in hospital. But perhaps this was her reward for the long drive – the longest drive she had ever attempted in her life. Admittedly it had left her pretty shattered. She was stiff all over, especially her back; her eyes were aching, and her clothes felt creased and grubby. Occasionally, on seemingly endless stretches of the motorway, she had found herself almost dropping off to sleep and had come to with a start. How wonderful it would be to stop at the next hotel, enjoy an indulgent soak in the bath, then crawl into bed and stay there for a week. But she hadn't come to Inverness to sleep. Elizabeth would be feeling worse than *she* was – not just exhausted, but overwrought, despairing. She hadn't spoken to her yet, although she'd stopped three separate times to phone the hospital. But each time, her nerve had failed her before she'd even dialled the number; not knowing what to say. Maybe it would be better simply to turn up and find out how Hugo was before she spoke to Elizabeth at all. Her confidence was beginning to crack now she was so near the end of her journey. Perhaps it was crazy to have driven such a hell of a way without knowing if Elizabeth wanted her there, or even if Hugo was . . .

Trust, she told herself. Why spoil all you've achieved? You've got here safely, *and* in record time, and (miraculously) the car's still in one piece.

She took the left-hand fork for Inverness, half-blinded by the brilliance of the sun. She realized she was driving at a snail's pace, less on account of the frail state of the car than because of her reluctance to arrive. So long as she was on the road, she could cope. She might be stiff and tired, but she had nothing more to do than steer the car and think positive thoughts. Once she walked into Kinloch, it would be a different matter entirely. She would have to face Elizabeth – and the risk of being rejected; would have to overcome her lifelong fear of hospitals. The very thought of blood had always made her feel sick, so how in God's name would she manage in Intensive Care, of all places?

You'll *forget* your fears, that's how – think of Elizabeth, not yourself.

Now get a move on and stop dawdling or they won't let you in at all.

She put her foot down again, surprised to see how ugly the road had become. The awe-inspiring scenery of sombre forest and snow-capped mountain peaks had given way to dismal urban sprawl. Even when she reached the town, it was nothing like the quaint place she'd imagined, but really rather nondescript, with the usual boring shopping malls and characterless modern buildings. And now that the majestic sunset had faded into dusk, it was no longer built of flame, only of functional grey stone. True, the river was impressive – broad and swiftly-moving, and flanked by attractive houses and hotels whose glittering lights sparkled on the water – but once she'd crossed the Ness Bridge, she was back to dreary streets again. She also had a feeling that she was going the wrong way. She spotted a middle-aged man ambling along the pavement, so she pulled in to the side of the road and asked him for directions.

'Sorry,' he replied. 'I'm a stranger here myself.'

There were few other people around. The whole place seemed stifled in Sunday inertia, shops closed, streets deserted; the only noise the mournful keening of gulls. There was nothing for it: she would have to get out and ask at a pub or restaurant – anywhere with some signs of life. She eventually found a pizza place and parked gratefully outside. The cold hit her like a blow as she opened the car door. It had been almost spring in London – here it was mid-winter. She turned up her coat collar and limped inside, her legs cramped and barely functioning after the relentless hours of driving. The waiter she spoke to was friendly enough, but his broad Glaswegian accent was practically impenetrable and made her feel she needed a translator.

Back on the road, she realized his directions paid scant regard to the actual layout of the town. It was a good fifteen minutes before she found the turn-off he'd described, and even then she couldn't locate the street he had assured her would lead directly to the hospital. When she finally pulled up in the car-park, she was beginning to wish she'd stayed in the pizzeria and ordered a stiff drink. Like the town itself, the hospital was quite different from how she'd pictured it – not a bleak impersonal tower-block dwarfing all who approached, but a straggle of low buildings plonked down together any old how, like a clumsy child playing with its bricks.

She switched off the engine and sat watching the main entrance. People were walking briskly in and out, going about their business, but *she* felt paralysed, unable even to open the car door. Suddenly, with a shrill blast of its siren, an ambulance drew up, blue lights flashing ominously. She averted her eyes, so as not to see another victim being carried in on a stretcher, as Hugo must have been. She unscrewed the Thermos and with unsteady hands poured the last of the camomile tea. 'Camomile to calm you,' Kim had said. She also unwrapped his brownies and, too nervous to eat, held one tightly in her hand to give her courage.

A car nosed into the parking space beside her, an old banger with a dented wing, almost as dilapidated as her 2CV. She glanced at the young couple inside, and saw the man lean over and give the girl a long protracted kiss. At once she felt envious, not so much on account of the kiss, but because the girl wasn't on her own – she had a partner to lean on; someone to support her and shepherd her safely into the hospital.

The minute they got out of the car, Beattie did the same, then followed them to the entrance, keeping a pace or two behind. They looked a sympathetic pair and it eased her sense of isolation to pretend that she belonged. They were walking very slowly, with their arms round each other's waists; the girl's eyes gazing into his. That's how Hugo and Elizabeth would have been, she thought, if they'd gone away together – strolling hand in hand, kissing in the car, eyes only for each other. She suddenly knew that if Hugo lived, she had to accept his marriage to Elizabeth. No, more than that – she must *rejoice* in it.

She stopped, confused, as if it wasn't just an intuition but someone actually speaking to her, making a pronouncement impossible to ignore. 'But I *can't*,' she muttered wretchedly. 'I haven't got that kind of courage.'

The couple in front had also stopped, and appeared to have forgotten something. The man took out his car keys and handed them to the girl, who ran back to the car. He stood waiting for her patiently, hands thrust in his pockets, shoulders hunched against the cold. Beattie watched in silence, making a pact with herself: I have to accept the marriage before that girl comes back and they go into the hospital – then Hugo will pull through. Otherwise, he'll *die*.

The girl was taking her time, as if giving her the chance to dismiss the idea as superstitious nonsense. But she knew it *wasn't* nonsense – it was the most important decision she would ever have to make.

She stood shivering and tense, half-hoping the girl would

disappear for ever. But all too soon she was on her way back, carrying a bunch of yellow freesias, Elizabeth's favourite flowers. Was that simply a coincidence, or some sort of extra sign?

Beattie kept her eyes fixed on the flowers. Yes, she murmured under her breath. I *do* love her enough to let her go.

The man kissed the girl again, drawing her so close he almost crushed the freesias. Even when he released her, he seemed scarcely aware of the hospital surroundings as he stepped inside, still caressing the girl's long hair; still lost in her, adoring.

Beattie followed, at a distance now. 'Yes,' she said aloud. '*Let* them love each other. I rejoice.'

34

Beattie trudged along the corridor, surprised how cheerful the place seemed. Of course, she was probably harking back to childhood memories of visiting her mother: the barrack-like ward with its depressing smells of pee and disinfectant; the gruesome cries she had heard on one occasion coming from behind a screen (and never forgotten in twenty years). *This* hospital was different. There were no repellent sounds or smells – only the soothing muzak playing in reception and the honeyed scent of freesias in the flower shop. Indeed, her first impression on walking in was that she had strayed into a shopping mall rather than a hospital. She had found a chocolate shop, a newsagent's, the florist's and a coffee bar, all open on a Sunday. Normal carefree people were drinking tea or buying sweets, children choosing comics, and a pair of old biddies gossiping contentedly on a seat, looking for all the world as though they were waiting for the evening's Bingo to start.

Even two floors up, there was little to suggest a place of suffering. She'd seen the odd nurse bustling past and glimpsed a woman in a wheelchair, but nothing worse than that. In fact, this long stretch of whitewashed corridor could just as well have belonged in a school. Yet she was beginning to feel more and more alone, especially when she arrived at the glass barricade marking the entrance to Intensive Care. She pressed the buzzer as the woman on reception had instructed. She had already told her who she was, and now spoke into the intercom, explaining all over again.

'So you see, if Mrs Hargreaves doesn't want me here, that's perfectly all right. I'll quite understand. In fact, perhaps I ought to . . .'

'Come through,' the disembodied voice invited, sounding encouraging and kindly. 'Just walk down the passage ahead of you and it's the first door on the left. I'll meet you there – okay?'

'Yes . . . yes, fine.'

The door opened automatically and she walked hesitantly through, terrified of what she might encounter. But still no smell or sound – just another corridor, with the same white walls and speckled vinyl floor.

A nurse was waiting for her: a plump, attractive woman, whose soft Scots accent seemed out of keeping with her dramatic Latin looks: burnt-almond eyes and jet-black hair.

'Hello, Beattie,' she said in her lilting voice. 'I'm Staff Nurse Jenny MacGrath. Shall we sit down and have a wee chat.'

She opened the door to a small neat room with lilac walls and a purple carpet.

The colour scheme suggested death, as did the vase of waxen flowers. Beattie perched on the edge of a chair, wondering why she'd been brought in here rather than taken to see Elizabeth. Despite the friendly tone and the use of her Christian name, the nurse was probably about to tell her that she had to leave at once, that Elizabeth didn't want her.

She cleared her throat, crossed her legs, uncrossed them. She ought to enquire about Hugo, but her voice refused to frame the question. The nurse was giving little away, merely asking a few questions about her relationship with Elizabeth.

Beattie was determined not to lie. From this day on, it would be the truth and only the truth. 'Well, I'm just a friend,' she said. 'But I'm very fond of her, so if there's anything I can do . . .'

'That's kind of you,' the nurse said. 'As soon as she's back, I'll let her know you're . . .'

'*Back?* Where from? They told me at reception she was here.'

'Yes, basically she is. She's . . . er . . . just popped out for a wee while.'

'Oh, I see,' said Beattie. She *didn't* see. The nurse was hiding something: her face had a guarded look, and she was already getting up. Evidently their 'wee chat' was at an end.

'Wait!' said Beattie, almost rudely. Perhaps Hugo had just died and Elizabeth had crept away to be alone with her grief. 'She *is* all right?' she probed, looking anxiously at the nurse. 'I mean, nothing's . . . nothing's . . .' She couldn't finish the sentence. She didn't have the words for death.

'Yes, she's fine, my dear. But she had to go to Casualty. Don't worry, it's nothing serious – just a minor injury.'

Casualty. Beattie felt the blood drain from her face. *Another* accident? The nurse was probably making light of it on purpose. They always played things down to stop you panicking. 'What happened?' she asked. 'What *sort* of injury?'

The nurse flashed her a bland smile. 'I'll leave her to give you the details, Beattie. But I assure you it's nothing to worry about. And she shouldn't be too long now. Just sit here and relax – you must be tired after all that driving.'

As soon as she'd gone, Beattie got up and prowled restlessly around. How could she relax when Elizabeth was in Casualty? Christ! Things were getting worse and worse. How awful for Elizabeth to have injured herself at the very time she needed her energies for Hugo. And if she was in pain on top of everything else . . .

She'd been freezing in the car-park, but now her hands were sweating. She wiped them on her skirt. She still had no idea how Hugo was, and felt angry with herself that she hadn't found the courage to ask. It was difficult to keep trusting, or to keep her mind off death, especially in this room, which seemed designed as a place of comfort for the bereaved: a Bible on the table, and a box of paper hankies; a picture of a gentle Jesus holding out his hands. Yet there was no real physical comfort, only an air of dour formality, as if no one had ever sat in these ramrod-stiff armchairs, nor dared to raise their voice above a funereal whisper. A clock was ticking ponderously, measuring a slower time than that in the outside world. On a table by the wall, a tray had been provided, with a kettle and some tea bags and a jar of instant coffee. Just the sight of it made her thirsty – she hadn't had a drink for hours, except for the dregs of the camomile tea. But if she helped herself to a cup of something here, it would imply she intended to stay, whereas, for all she knew, she might be unceremoniously shown the door at any minute.

She trailed to the window and lifted the mauve curtain. The night was dark and murky; clouds obscuring an emaciated moon. No, it was hardly night yet, only early evening, though it seemed much later, as if she'd been driving not just for a day but half a lifetime. It was incredible to think that she and Elizabeth had breakfasted together only yesterday morning. So much had happened in one weekend. And Elizabeth felt so far away, even now, when they were in the same town – in the same *building*, for heaven's sake.

She opened the door a crack and peered out. Two nurses were standing in the passage, talking earnestly together, but there was no sign of Elizabeth. She closed the door again, wishing she could wait somewhere else. This room seemed full of pain, as if a succession of grieving relatives had left their traces behind.

She glanced up at the clock. The hands had barely moved. Elizabeth might be kept for hours in Casualty, and when she eventually got out, would she really want the shock of coming face to face with an unexpected visitor – someone she *blamed* for Hugo's accident? She moved uncertainly towards the door again. Perhaps she ought to leave. Wasn't it the most awful cheek imagining she could help, when her presence might upset Elizabeth *more*? Kim probably hadn't really understood. In his blithe world *everyone* was innocent, and although she longed to believe him, the facts suggested otherwise, at least from Elizabeth's point of view. She stopped dead in her tracks as she saw the door-handle turning. The door was slowly opening and someone coming in: Elizabeth, hobbling on a stick.

Beattie stared in horror. She looked absolutely terrible – her face ashen pale, her clothes dishevelled, her lank hair scraped into an untidy bun. Her right ankle was bandaged, and the protruding bare toes were dirty, especially in contrast with the whiteness of the dressing. She wore a stocking on her other leg, but it sagged around the ankle, giving her the appearance of a bag-lady. These last two days seemed to have aged her several years.

For a moment they stood gazing at each other, Beattie tensing instinctively, expecting anger and recrimination. But Elizabeth limped towards her and clung to her like a frantic child.

'Oh, Beattie, I'm so *glad* to see you! When they said you were here, I . . . I simply couldn't believe it. I can't tell you what a relief it is. I've been feeling so . . . so . . .'

'Sit down,' said Beattie quietly. She led her to a chair and settled her in it carefully, placing a cushion beneath the injured foot. However moved she might be by Elizabeth's fervent welcome, or horrified at how ill she looked, she must keep her own emotions strictly under control. Elizabeth herself sounded near-hysterical, and was clearly on the verge of tears. Indeed, she seemed incapable of completing any sentences, or waiting for the answers to her questions as her voice ran on and on.

'Oh, Beattie, thank God you're here! You said in your note you'd gone away, so . . . Did you come by plane? My flight was late, and then I waited ages for a taxi, and . . . That's how I sprained my ankle. I was so desperate to get to Hugo, I tripped and fell right outside the hospital. They wanted me to go to Casualty there and then. But I just had to see Hugo first. And once I was sitting beside him, I couldn't seem to leave him, in case . . . in case . . .' Tears slid down her face. Impatiently she brushed them away. 'The nurses were so kind, Beattie. They said I ought to have an X-ray, and if I went to Casualty, they'd phone me there if they noticed any change in Hugo's . . . But I couldn't take the risk. Well, not till the pain got so . . . Then I knew I *had* to do something. So I've finally been down there just now. And it *isn't* broken, thank goodness. Only a bad sprain, they said, and . . .'

Beattie was shaken by Elizabeth's incoherent outpouring. She had never seen her so distraught. What had happened to the cool collected therapist, the level-headed mother of four? She was actually laughing and crying at once; obviously relieved at having someone to confide in, yet still in shock.

'Look, you really ought to rest,' she said, when Elizabeth finally paused for breath. 'Your leg looks very swollen, even above the bandage. And if you've been in pain since last night . . . Couldn't you try to have a nap – just for a little while?'

'Oh, *no*, Beattie, I wouldn't dare. Hugo's still unconscious, and I must be there the minute he . . . he . . .' She shifted on the chair, giving a sudden grimace of pain. 'You see, he skied off the edge of a track and hit his head on a boulder, as well as breaking his leg. And although he's had surgery and brain-scans, I can tell they're very worried, especially about his head. So of course I don't like leaving him at all. Actually, this is the longest I've been away, but Angela promised to come and get me if . . . if . . . She's marvellous, Beattie, honestly – well, *all* the nurses are. They hardly leave the patients for a moment. And if *I* slip out for any reason, I always say where I'm going. You see, I couldn't bear to . . .'

Beattie swallowed hard. 'Well, shouldn't we go back now? I . . . I'll come with you, if you want.'

'All right. But let me just sit here for a minute first. It's so . . . so *quiet*.' She closed her eyes, and Beattie took the chance to look at her again – worn down, washed out, defenceless.

'Look, why don't I make us a cup of tea?' she suggested. She had to do something useful; couldn't bear to sit here idly, witnessing this ghastly change in Elizabeth, and feeling guilty, guilty, guilty. Kim

366

had given her such hope, it was a bitter disappointment to hear that Hugo had injured himself so seriously. The word 'unconscious' was especially frightening, with its connotations of death.

Elizabeth opened her eyes and glanced around vaguely, as if uncertain where she was. 'What did you say?'

'I . . . I thought I'd make some tea.'

'Oh, tea . . . yes.' She gave a wry smile. 'It's funny you know, Beattie, they keep offering me tea, when what I'm really dying for is a cigarette. Oh, I know it sounds awful even to be *thinking* about smoking at a time like this, but you can't imagine what a strain it is being forbidden to smoke on the ward. In fact, the only place they let you smoke is in here and – would you believe it – I haven't any cigarettes.'

Beattie sprang to her feet. 'I'll go and buy you some.'

'No, it's all right, Beattie dear. I'm feeling a bit better now. They gave me some painkillers in Casualty and they seem to have dulled the craving along with the pain. Actually, I was worried about taking them. I was scared they'd make me sleepy, and I *mustn't* sleep. You do understand that, don't you? It would be terrible if . . .'

'Yes, of course. But that's why you should have some tea. If I make it nice and strong, it'll help to keep you awake.' She switched on the kettle and unstacked the loaded tray, soft-pedalling all her movements, so as not to jolt Elizabeth with the clatter of cups and saucers. The torrent of words appeared to have exhausted her, and the room was deathly quiet once more. It was almost a relief to hear the soft croon of the kettle slowly purring to a boil.

'Beattie?' Elizabeth said suddenly.

'Yes?'

'I . . . I haven't said this to anyone else, but you know, the . . . the worst thing of all is . . . is . . .'

'Yes?' Beattie said again, trying to model herself on Kim and sound encouraging but calm.

'Well, you see, I . . . I was really responsible for the accident.'

'*What?*'

'Yes. I feel such frightful guilt about it. But *I* was the one who persuaded him to go skiing in the first place. I thought it would be fun for him and . . .'

Beattie abandoned the tea-making and stared unseeingly at the carpet, her own guilt increasing even more. 'Because . . . because he had to go to Scotland on his own, you mean, and it would be something to cheer him up?' She didn't want to hear the answer. If Elizabeth said yes, how could she live with her conscience? In accusing herself, Elizabeth was unwittingly blaming *her* and, whatever Kim might say, she would have to shoulder that burden for ever.

'Oh, no,' said Elizabeth in a hopeless sort of whisper. 'Right from the beginning, when I thought I'd be going with him.' She suddenly began talking very fast again, the words spilling out in a rush. 'You see, I've got this schoolfriend I haven't seen for years. She lives in Aviemore, less than ten miles from the ski slopes. So I suggested Hugo went skiing while I spent a day with her. Oh, Beattie, the more I think about it, the more I blame myself. I mean, he wasn't even keen at first. He said from all he'd heard, skiing in Scotland could be pretty miserable – not much sun or . . . But I talked him into it. And to be honest, Beattie, it wasn't totally for *his* sake, but to give me a chance to see Cathy. You see, she isn't just any old friend. She used to live near me, and we were always very close. So when she moved right up to . . .'

Beattie could hardly believe her ears. So she *wasn't* guilty, *wasn't* to blame. This was her reprieve. She dared to look up at Elizabeth, shocked by her gaunt despairing face. 'Oh, Elizabeth, that doesn't make it *your* fault,' she insisted, repeating what Kim had said to *her*. 'It was an accident, that's all. Nobody's to blame.'

Elizabeth didn't appear to have heard. She was picking fretfully at the knobbly purple fabric of the chair-arm. 'If . . . if anything should happen, I'd never forgive myself.'

Beattie went to sit beside her, squatting on the carpet by her feet. 'It *won't* happen. We've got to trust. You told me yourself the nurses here are marvellous. Well, if everyone's doing all they can . . .' It sounded so lame, she broke off in embarrassment; tried another tack. 'Look, what I'm trying to say is, it's very early days yet. I mean, Hugo's only just had surgery, so you probably can't expect him to . . .' Again the words dried up. Elizabeth had been *married* to a surgeon, and would know all too well the risks and complications. 'These things are bound to take a while,' she added desperately, determined to fill the silence.

'But Beattie, it feels like months already, and I'm . . . I'm beginning to . . .'

'You mustn't give up hope – I shan't let you. It's only been two days, in fact, and any minute now, he'll open his eyes and say something. We'll *will* him to, both of us.'

368

Elizabeth pushed a strand of hair from her neck. Her bun was coming loose and shedding hairpins on the floor. 'That's what Angela suggested. She told me to keep talking to him because he may be able to hear, and it's important to give him the will to live. Apparently hearing is the last of the senses to go, and the first one to come back. Well, I talked to him the whole of last night, but . . .'

'Okay, so it's time for *me* to take over. That's why I'm here – don't you understand? I've come to help you, darling Elizabeth.'

'Oh, Beattie, thank you. I *am* so grateful, honestly.' Elizabeth was frowning, and looked anything but grateful. 'It's just that . . .' She gave an awkward laugh. 'Well, why *should* you help? I mean, I know you're not exactly fond of Hugo.'

Beattie locked her hands together, aware of the agitation in her voice. 'Elizabeth, listen – this is terribly important. I'm not going to lie to you. Yes, I *did* hate Hugo's guts. But not now. Things have changed for me. It's . . . well, difficult to explain, but I swear I'm speaking the truth when I say that the one thing I want most in all the world is for Hugo to . . . to pull through. I'll do anything I can to make that happen. *Please* say you believe me. I'll talk to him all night tonight, just like you did *last* night, and tell him he's *got* to live – he's got to. You probably weren't quite strict enough. I'm going to try a different approach. Don't worry, I'll be perfectly calm and reasonable, but I won't take no for an answer. I'll stay by his bed for *weeks*, if need be, until he opens his eyes and says, "Okay, Beattie, give me a break. I'm bloody well alive!"'

Elizabeth forced a smile, then immediately started crying again, sobbing almost uncontrollably. Beattie slumped back on her heels. She had failed – that was obvious – upset Elizabeth *more*. 'You don't believe me, do you? You don't even trust me enough to sit with him.'

'Oh, Beattie, of *course* I do! It's not that at all. I'm only crying because you're so . . . so wonderful.'

'Well, hardly,' she said sheepishly, secretly thrilled to bits by the praise. 'I'm shit-scared, if you really want to know. But we've got to think of Hugo. And he doesn't want you weeping all over his bed. He needs us to be strong – not to doubt for a single *second* that he's going to live and that you're going to be married and you'll both walk down the aisle together.'

Elizabeth leaned down and gripped her hand. 'Beattie, you *are* a darling. I can't tell you how much this means to me.'

Beattie squeezed the hand in response, too overcome to speak. It was a completely new experience being the good one, the strong one – wonderful, for God's sake! Yet all she'd done was repeat the loving, trusting things she'd learned from Kim. It was strange, though – just saying them made her believe them, and seemed to have changed her character. She stood up decisively. 'What I suggest, Elizabeth, is that you try and snatch a bit of sleep while I sit with Hugo. Then when you're feeling better, *you* can take over again. We'll take it in turns, okay?'

'Okay.' Elizabeth relaxed back in her chair and closed her eyes. 'I must admit I do feel rather peculiar. It must be those painkillers. I'm beginning to feel I could just float away on a cloud.'

'Right, you go ahead and float. But let's make you more comfy first.' She collected the cushions from the other chairs and was arranging them behind Elizabeth's head when there was a soft tap at the door. 'Come in,' she said, her confidence taking a nose-dive when she saw it was Staff Nurse MacGrath. She had been blithely offering Elizabeth help, without knowing if the staff would allow her into Intensive Care at all, when she wasn't even a relative.

Still, at least MacGrath was smiling. 'I see you've persuaded your friend to rest,' she said. 'That's marvellous.'

Elizabeth opened her eyes and looked anxiously from one to the other. 'I hope I'm not being a nuisance?'

'Not at all,' the nurse said. 'You should have put that foot up ages ago. Beattie obviously has magic powers! Actually, we do have a couple of beds upstairs for visitors to use, so if you'd prefer to have a proper sleep . . .'

'No, I'm fine,' Elizabeth murmured. 'Too comfortable to move.'

'And she says I can sit with Hugo,' Beattie put in quickly, 'so long as *you* have no objection?'

'No, that's quite okay. But are you sure you're not too tired yourself?'

Beattie shook her head. She *was* physically exhausted, yet she also felt an extraordinary new strength. She laid a hand on Elizabeth's arm, hoping the brief gesture would convey 'Sleep well,' and 'Trust me,' and 'Hugo will pull through.'

'Beattie, have you had a cup of tea?' the nurse enquired, lowering her voice so as not to disturb Elizabeth.

'No. I was just about to make one, but I never quite got round to it. At least the kettle's boiled, though.'

'*I'll* make it,' said the nurse, moving to the table. 'How do you like it – weak or strong? Milk and sugar?'

'Strong, please, with two sugars and just a dash of milk.'

'Okay, coming up! And by the way, do call me Jenny, won't you? We try to keep things informal here.' Jenny handed her the cup, then sat beside her, glancing with approval at Elizabeth, who had already fallen asleep. 'Have you ever been in an Intensive Care ward before?' she asked, leaning forward encouragingly.

'Er, no,' said Beattie, gulping the tea so fast she burned her tongue.

'Well, don't take too much notice of all the bleeps and things. They're just routine – you'll soon get used to them. And as far as Hugo's concerned, let me tell you what to expect. He'll have his head bandaged and a cradle over his legs, and there'll be a tube coming out of his mouth, attached to the ventilator, and quite a lot of other tubes as well. Oh, and he'll also have a . . .'

Beattie switched her mind to something else. She realized Jenny was trying to prepare her for the shock of Hugo's appearance, but it was almost worse to have the gruesome details spelt out in advance. Indeed, if they knew how terrified she was, they wouldn't let her in Intensive Care at all. However, she made a supreme effort to appear calm, as if she were merely relaxing over a cup of tea with a friend (and hoping the cup wouldn't rattle as she replaced it on the saucer with shaking hands).

'Well, if you're ready . . .' said Jenny, getting up from her chair.

Oh God! she thought, I'm *not* ready. I can't face it after all. She had suddenly remembered her own spell in Intensive Care, as a newborn baby, connected up, like Hugo, to a whole array of drips and tubes. Suppose the trauma of her first rebirth flooded back and overwhelmed her, right there in the ward? She might even faint or something, and upset all the patients. She would have to tell the nurse she'd changed her mind – and tell her *now* before she caused a scene.

She racked her brains for some excuse, some form of words which wouldn't sound too fatuous, while she followed Jenny out of the room and down yet another passage. This one was all too short.

'Look, I'm sorry,' she said, addressing Jenny's back and speaking in a desperate muffled croak, 'but I don't think I can . . .'

Jenny hadn't heard. 'Right, this is it,' she smiled, ushering her in to a large and glaring ward. 'Let's go and tell Hugo you're here.'

35

'Hugo, I've got a visitor for you. It's Elizabeth's friend, Beattie.'

Beattie stared in disbelief at the body on the bed. Why was Nurse MacGrath bothering to speak to someone who could neither hear nor understand, let alone reply? That *wasn't* Hugo – it couldn't be. There was absolutely nothing left of the witty talkative charmer who'd flirted with her in the golf club; the energetic sportsman who golfed and sailed and skied. She was looking at an *object*. The face was deathly pale, the eyes shut and covered with a transparent plastic shield, the hair completely covered by a bandage. A tube led from his mouth to a formidable-looking metal box, bristling with knobs and dials. Another tube protruded from his nose, held in place by a piece of sticking plaster. A tangle of wires sprouted from his hands and arms, linked to various plastic bags which dripped their contents into him. His chest was naked save for four or five electrodes, each with its own wire, which connected up to the box. From the waist down he was covered, but only with a sheet and one thin blanket. Who knew what horrors those coverlets concealed; what parts he might have lost in such a ghastly accident? The cradle over his legs was bad enough – a great ugly hump probably hiding mangled flesh.

She looked back at his face – expressionless, inert. A bomb could have exploded right beside his bed, or a fire swept through the ward, and he would just continue lying there, totally unaware. He seemed dwarfed by the machinery – a whole battery of smug machines pulsing and gibbering around him, as if to mock his own passivity. Above them, mounted on the wall, was a sort of television screen, with wavy lines and figures flashing continually across it. She was suddenly tempted to unplug it; to wrench out all those tubes and wires and free Hugo from this imprisonment. He was trapped there like a victim, with no power to say whether he agreed to such a mortifying ordeal. Of course, the nurses wouldn't see it in those terms – *they* would claim that they were using their miraculous technology to save him. So why did he look *dead*, despite it all?

She averted her eyes from the bulging plastic bags suspended from the side of the bed – bloody urine, by the looks of it, though *this* Hugo couldn't pee, any more than he could breathe or eat or walk or talk or flirt . . .

'Let me introduce you to Angela,' Jenny was saying with a smile. 'She looks after Hugo whenever she's on duty – which is mainly nights at present. Then Jo takes over in the mornings. We have what we call a named-nurse system here. It makes it much more personal, you see. Each patient is assigned two or three nurses who care exclusively for him or her.'

Beattie nodded mutely, wondering how an unconscious man could possibly tell the difference between Angela or Jo – or between Mother Teresa and Jack the Ripper, for that matter?

She said a dazed hello to Angela, amazed that anyone could actually *choose* to do a job like this: to sit all night, or day, with these wrecks, these all-but-corpses. She had hardly dared to look at the other patients as Jenny ushered her through the ward, but she only had to glance at the next bed to see another human vegetable; hooked up to similar hardware and festooned with the same hotchpotch of wires and tubes. Angela looked almost obscenely healthy in comparison. Her hair was thick and shiny, her cheeks glowing as if she'd been out in the cold, her stocky muscular figure suggesting she spent her free time in the gym.

'Hello, Beattie,' she said, getting up from her chair. 'Elizabeth was so pleased to hear you'd come.'

She sounded English, not Scottish. In fact, her soft and rather plummy voice was not unlike Elizabeth's. A pity Hugo couldn't hear it, Beattie thought. She found it impossible to believe that he could hear, whatever the nurses might say to the contrary.

'Well, I'll leave you with Angela,' Jenny said, with another of her reassuring smiles. 'Do ask her anything you want.'

Far from asking questions, she longed to follow Jenny as she walked briskly out of the ward. The only things she could think of to ask were just too terrifying: might Hugo lose his last shred of life at more or less any moment? And even if he *did* recover, would he be paralysed or brain-damaged? Besides, the machines were too dis-

373

tracting to encourage conversation. One of them was making a steady
rhythmic breathing noise, which seemed particularly grotesque. Poor
Hugo couldn't breathe himself, but never mind – a lump of metal
would do it for him and sound disconcertingly human in the process.

'That's the ventilator,' said Angela, following her gaze. 'They're
wonderfully sophisticated these days. If we adjust these dials, we can
change the length and pressure of each breath, or even . . .'

Beattie couldn't take it in. She was remembering Hugo's voice:
lively, jokey, always verging on a laugh; the life history he'd invented
to amuse her: born in Kwangchow, wasn't it? – his father the Celestial
Emperor.

'And let me explain the monitor,' Angela continued, pointing to
the television screen. 'That top line shows his heart-rate, and the
third line down tells us how much oxygen is circulating round his
body. And his blood pressure is recorded automatically.'

Beattie watched the orange lines trace their snaking curves; the
self-important figures scuttle across the screen. Where was the *real*
Hugo – the cultured Cambridge graduate, the connoisseur of art?

'Now if you'll excuse me for a moment,' Angela said, 'I'll just fill
in Hugo's chart. Do sit down, won't you?' She indicated the chair
beside the bed, while she sat on a padded stool and started pencilling
figures on a huge ruled sheet of paper, mounted on a special stand
at the far end of the bed.

Beattie subsided into the chair, wishing she could turn it round the
other way. She was far too close to Hugo now, and felt embarrassed to
be staring at him like a voyeur. Even seeing his naked chest seemed
something of an intrusion; Elizabeth's prerogative, not hers. The
chest was pale and rather flabby – nothing like a sportsman's – and
had a few coarse and grizzled hairs around the nipples. The nipples
themselves were pink and slightly puckered, with a scattering of
freckles spreading down to his stomach. She felt that she was prying
into Elizabeth's secret Hugo, and that she shouldn't really *know* such
things. But in Intensive Care you had no choice. Every patient was
exposed to public view; every confidential detail of their feeding and
excretion, their heart-rate and their breathing, blazoned on a screen.

She started as an alarm went off – not Hugo's, someone else's.
The noises in the ward were quite intimidating: a constant symphony
from the machines, of course, but also other sounds she couldn't
place, including a gruesome heaving and retching coming from
behind a screen. And one of the visitors was crying – a middle-aged

374

woman sitting by the bed of what looked like a young boy (or what remained of him). He was probably her son, although in this grim ward all relationships seemed severed. How could Hugo be Elizabeth's fiancé, or anybody's friend or colleague, when he'd been reduced to a carcass on a slab?

She watched the mechanical rise and fall of his chest and was suddenly reminded of a tableau she'd seen years ago in a children's museum: Sleeping Beauty lying on her bed in the castle, behind the tangled briar-hedge; dead to the world apart from the rising and falling of her breast. But Sleeping Beauty had looked enchanting, with rosy cheeks and cherry lips, whereas Hugo looked downright ugly. The lines on his face seemed deeper, and there was no seductive smile to redeem him, no once-blond hair or arty purple ties. She edged her chair away, still feeling she was gawping.

Angela looked up from her chart. 'All right?' she asked.

'Y . . . yes, fine.'

'Do hold his hand, if you want. Touch is very important, even for unconscious patients. They're probably aware of much more than we realize.'

Oh God, she thought, I only hope he's not aware of what I've been thinking all this time. It would be hypocritical to hold his hand, when she'd seen him as a vegetable, a carcass on a slab. She had even willed his *death*, for heaven's sake, though if she could have foreseen the horror of this ward, she would never have wished it on anyone, not in a thousand years. Here she was *surrounded* by death; the risk of it in every patient's chart, on every flashing screen. She was terrified of touching him in case his skin felt cold and corpse-like, as her mother's had done just before she stopped breathing. Gingerly she put out a hand towards him, but still shrank from making contact. Suppose she dislodged some tube or other and set off an alarm? Anyway, he might not want to be touched; might actually be recoiling from her somewhere in his mute immobile world.

No, she couldn't do it. His hand looked far too vulnerable: bruised around the thumb-joint, mottled red and purple. She would only hurt him, do him further damage. She slumped back in her chair. Hugo, forgive me, she said silently, blinking back her tears. Forgive me for everything.

Angela had finished writing and was now conferring with another nurse – an older one with short grey hair, whom she introduced as Lynn.

'We're going to give Hugo some suction,' she said. 'Lynn will give him a few deep breaths with the rebreathing bag, and I'll put a catheter down the tube which helps to clear his chest. Would you mind moving your chair to the end of the bed – that's it.'

The two nurses washed their hands at a small basin near the bed, then Angela pulled on rubber gloves and laid her gloved hand on Hugo's shoulder.

'Hugo, we're going to suction you out,' she said.

For a split second, Beattie imagined he might reply; sit up and say in his quietly cultured voice, 'Yes, go ahead, that's fine.' But there was no response whatsoever. Even so, she found it touching that they should bother to tell him what they were doing, rather than simply pitching in. Perhaps she was *wrong* about him not hearing. Otherwise, why would these highly trained professionals waste their time consulting him?

She watched the proceedings nervously. Lynn was armed with a sort of bellows thing which squeezed in and out across his chest, while Angela bent over his face and inserted a long piece of plastic piping into the ventilator-tube. The resulting noises were repulsive – sucking, slurping, gurgling sounds, which almost made her retch. Hugo remained totally oblivious. They could have been making pancakes on his chest for all the notice he took. And yet she had to admit she was impressed by the way they treated him; the respect and even graciousness they showed. She was pleased for Elizabeth's sake. This was the man Elizabeth loved, however damaged he might be.

She glanced at the next bed. All that was visible of its occupant was an impassive sallow face and one arm trailing tubes. His nurse had just returned to her chair with a handful of Maltesers, which she ate slowly, one by one, as she sat poring over the chart. The central table was well stocked with sweets and biscuits, and Beattie had noticed some of the staff helping themselves as they passed. It seemed almost blasphemous for them to eat when the patients they were looking after couldn't so much as open their mouths. Yet the smell of chocolate was tantalizing, and reminded her how empty she was.

The nurse looked up and saw her expression: slavering dog, deprived and jealous child.

'Sorry,' said Beattie hurriedly. 'You were making me feel hungry.'

'I can ask someone to fetch you a snack, if you like. What d'you fancy? Toast and Marmite?'

'No, honestly, I'm fine.' Beattie was even more embarrassed now. 'It's just that I've got this awful weakness for Maltesers!'

'Oh, really?' grinned the nurse. 'Well, you'd better have some then.' She got up to fetch the box and Beattie was just dipping in when suddenly an alarm went off, much louder than the previous one. Two nurses she hadn't seen before dived towards the corner bed and quickly drew the curtains round it. A third nurse hurried over, wheeling a small white trolley and looking anxious and grim-faced. From behind the curtains the sound of frantic sobbing could be heard. It was the woman who'd been crying over her son, now utterly distraught.

Even Angela and Lynn looked tense. They had completed the suctioning and were talking to each other in low but urgent tones. The whole atmosphere in the ward had changed, as if the staff were standing by for an earthquake or explosion.

'What's happening?' Beattie asked, the forgotten Maltesers melting in her hand.

'I'm afraid we've got an emergency,' said Angela. 'So I'll have to ask you to wait outside. There's a Visitors' Room just along the passage.'

Beattie stumbled to the door, all but colliding with three men in white coats who were dashing into the ward, followed by a swarthy man in theatre gear. She stepped back to let them pass, then bolted along the corridor. The Visitors' Room must be where she'd left Elizabeth, but she couldn't seem to find it. It was crazy to lose her bearings in one short stretch of corridor, but she'd been unnerved by the emergency, the panicky feeling that someone was about to die. She blundered back the way she'd come and saw the mother of the dying boy sitting on a chair outside the ward. She was no longer crying, simply staring at the floor in blank despair.

Beattie crept away, uncertain what to do or say. She was relieved to see a nurse approaching and, in response to her garbled request for directions, was escorted down the passage to a room she hadn't noticed, although the door was open and a television blaring out.

'Oh,' said Beattie disconcerted. 'I left my friend in *another* room – a smaller one with purple chairs and . . .'

'That's the Quiet Room,' said the nurse. 'It's just two doors along.'

'Thanks,' she said, walking towards it and opening the door a crack. Elizabeth was fast asleep in her chair, breathing very deeply, her hair tousled on her shoulders now, unloosed from its bun. Beattie longed to go in and join her, to press close to that warm body and shut out everything else. But it would be cruel to disturb her when she needed sleep so badly.

She trailed back to the Visitors' Room, wrinkling her nose at the smell of stale tobacco smoke. The room was empty, but a family row was in full flood on the television: father threatening, mother shouting, kids cowering in the corner. She turned it off and sank into a chair, looking in surprise at the mess of chocolate melting in her hand. She transferred it to her mouth, savouring its rich taste. As a child, she had always loved Maltesers: she would eat them very slowly, sucking off the chocolate first, then biting into the airy honeycomb, and finally using her tongue to search out any last remaining fragments. The ones in her mouth had long ago disintegrated, but she tried to eke them out as long as possible – a tiny comfort in this cheerless place. Though, to be fair, the room did at least look bright; the colours much less muted than in the Quiet Room. The walls were sunshine-yellow, with pictures of idyllic country scenes – thatched cottages and gambolling lambs – and there was a bowl of purple hyacinths on the sill. A great red hulk of a drinks machine hogged most of the end wall; 'ENJOY A COKE!' emblazoned across it, as if this were a disco or a leisure centre, rather than the grimmest of all hospital wards. Next to it was a pay-phone and, to the right, a book-shelf on the wall.

She licked her hand clean and got up to inspect the books. The selection was hardly inspiring: a dozen Mills and Boon, several dog-eared thrillers, some large-size children's picture-books and a set of leather-bound Walter Scotts which looked incongruous in such company. She picked out a Mills and Boon and opened it at random. 'His hands slipped under her nightdress,' she read, 'as his mouth sought out her parted lips with a searing soaring passion . . .' She tossed it back on the shelf and returned disconsolately to her chair. Sex had no place here. Her normal life, her nights with Max, belonged to another world entirely. She supposed she ought to phone Max and tell him where she was. But he would never understand, and would only have a go at her about throwing away her chances. Yes – he was right – that was exactly what she'd done. But how could she churn out jaunty pieces for the tabloids, with Hugo suspended between life and death? It put things in perspective, made her desire for fame and fortune seem petty, even crass.

All at once, the door burst open and a crowd of people trooped in – members of the same family, judging by their identical dark eyes and thick black wavy hair. They looked vaguely Middle Eastern, and were talking in some unrecognizable language. There was an ancient grandma dressed in black from head to foot; three younger women, obviously still in shock, two short and thickset men and a boy of six or seven, wearing an anorak on top of his pyjamas. They acknowledged her with a nod, then occupied the remaining chairs. Two of the women were sobbing to themselves, while the child stood by the window, staring at her with huge bewildered eyes. The men, for their part, were involved in some sort of argument, ranting and gesticulating and interrupting each other. She was glad she'd chosen a seat in the corner; even so, the tension was infectious and she sat rigid in her chair, wondering what had happened to cause such heated emotions.

By now, the child had started whimpering and one of the women switched the television on in an effort to divert him. Having flicked through various channels, she eventually settled for some cops-and-robbers thing, adding the brash American voices of a pair of hard-boiled detectives to the existing clamour in the room. Then a frenetic car-chase began, with the obligatory screeching tyres and shrilling sirens. And all the while the men continued their argument, shouting above the din.

In the crowded noisy room, Beattie felt even more alone. At least these people had each other – in their eyes, *she* was the foreigner. If only Elizabeth wasn't asleep, she could have gone to sit with her. Even if they didn't talk, it would be companionable and restful. She had a sudden mental picture of Elizabeth lying in Hugo's place, crippled by some fatal accident. It *might* have happened, if she'd gone to Scotland with him and he'd talked her into going skiing too. Elizabeth could be *dead*, she thought, and I would never have seen her again. She jumped up from her chair and grabbed another book from the shelf – anything to stifle such thoughts.

'Once upon a time,' she read, 'in a far-away country full of flowers and singing birds, there lived a beautiful princess with blue eyes and golden hair . . .' She looked around the room at the weeping women, the bellowing men, the sallow shrivelled grandma trying to comfort the child. Even the screen was full of violence and destruction: a gory close-up of a gangster dying in his mangled car.

Suddenly, she could bear it no longer. She slunk to the door and stood outside, wondering where she could go. She needed to be in earshot in case Angela called her back, so she couldn't stray too far. She began traipsing aimlessly up and down the corridor, keeping well away from the Quiet Room, so as not to disturb Elizabeth. To tell the truth, she envied anyone who could sleep just now – children tucked up safely in bed after their happy-ending fairytales; lovers snuggled close to each other. She had lost all track of time, but felt trapped in an interminable night, with no hope of ever emerging into morning.

A muted hubbub still issued from the Visitors' Room – the men's impassioned jabbering, a shrill female voice intoning in the background, and the mindless hype of television commercials.

After what seemed like hours of hanging around (counting the vinyl squares on the floor and playing a stupid game with herself that she mustn't tread on any cracks), she finally lost patience and marched back to the ward. At least there she could talk to the nurses instead of skulking in a passage. But her steps came to a halt as she spotted Angela emerging from the office with a folder in her hand.

'I . . . I'm sorry,' Beattie said. 'I know you told me to stay in the Visitors' Room, but I couldn't stand it any longer. A whole bunch of people turned up and it was absolute bedlam in there.'

Angela gave a sympathetic smile. 'Yes, we've had a new admission – a little boy – and his whole extended family came along as well. We couldn't have them all in the ward, so . . .'

She said no more, but Beattie sensed there might have been some contretemps between family and staff. 'And . . . and what happened to the other patient?' she asked, tactfully changing the subject. 'The emergency?'

Angela hesitated a moment. 'Sadly, he died,' she said, frowning. 'I'm afraid his heart stopped and the crash team didn't manage to revive him.'

Beattie kept her eyes down, staring at the floor. Only now did it dawn on her that she hadn't yet done a single thing for Hugo, despite her solemn promise to Elizabeth about willing him back to life. Any minute it could be too late. A patient had just died. Hugo might be next.

'Look, if you'd like a rest,' said Angela, 'why not join Elizabeth in the Quiet Room? I'm afraid I can't offer you the room upstairs because we may need it for the boy's parents later on.'

Beattie shook her head. 'No,' she said. 'I'd rather come back to the ward – if that's okay with you.'

'Of course.'

Angela led the way. The lights had been turned down, presumably to signal night-time, though it was doubtful if any of the patients here would be able to distinguish broad daylight from darkest night. The curtains round the corner bed were still drawn. Had they removed the corpse, Beattie wondered? It must be quite a business disposing of the dead without upsetting visitors or other (conscious) patients. Not that she could see either. 'Where's the little boy?' she asked, praying that he too hadn't died.

'We've put him in a side room,' Angela said. 'We normally do with children. It's easier for the parents then, if they want to stay all night.'

Beattie sat in the chair beside Hugo, pulling it closer to the bed this time. She glanced around the ward, averting her eyes from the drawn curtains, but darting surreptitious glances at the other patients: one with what looked like a knife-wound in his throat; another with lead weights suspended from both legs. At every bed, the machines were frantically busy – pumping, flashing, palpitating – in contrast to the torpid human beings whose existence they maintained.

Angela approached the bed with a pencil-torch and removed Hugo's plastic eye-shield. 'I'm going to shine a torch in his eyes,' she explained. 'It's one of the checks we do for consciousness.' She pulled up each eyelid in turn and flashed the light in briefly, telling Hugo what she was doing in a soft respectful voice. Beattie dared not ask the result of the test. What *she* must do was speak to him in that same unhurried caring way. It was no good being self-conscious or letting the machines upset her. She had to shut them out; ignore even Angela (who in any case had returned to her chart). If she was to be any use to Hugo, she had to concentrate on *him*; use the full force of her will to make him open his eyes.

She took a deep breath in, speaking in a barely audible whisper. 'Hugo, it's . . . it's Beattie.' She broke off in embarrassment, aware that she was blushing. It felt absurd talking to an unconscious man, though nobody was taking any notice – the nurses far too busy; the patients blind and deaf.

'I . . . I've come to sit with you for a bit,' she continued, 'while Elizabeth gets some sleep. Please don't worry about her. She hasn't gone away or left the hospital or anything. She just needs to rest her ankle.' Her voice petered out again. She wasn't meant to be talking about Elizabeth, but somehow it seemed easier. And anyway, Hugo

381

would probably like to hear about her. 'She was desperately tired,' she went on, 'so the sleep should do her good. And she was really pleased to see me. I must admit that was a great relief. You see, I . . . I wasn't sure how she'd feel about me coming. I hope *you* don't mind me being here. I drove up in my old car. It took me nearly all day. Actually, the journey was quite easy, much better than I expected.' God! What pathetic small talk – to someone struggling to escape the clutches of death. But what were you *meant* to say? She had never realized before how much normal conversation depended on feedback from the other person – a nod, a smile, a comment. Confronted with closed eyes and an impassive mask of a face, it was difficult to keep going.

Perhaps it would be better if she held his hand. It was still a terrifying prospect, but she was here to help, for heaven's sake, so her feelings were of no consequence. Nervously she reached out and, with the very tips of her fingers, made contact with *his* fingers. Nothing happened. She had somehow expected him to react, if only to recoil from her in distaste. Slowly she slid her hand down until, finally, it closed over his. It felt limp yet strangely heavy, and there was still no flicker of response, but at least the skin was warm to the touch; not chill and clammy as she'd feared. Encouraged, she began to stroke the fingers, feeling a sudden rush of pity for them – their stillness, their inertness, their bruised and swollen flesh. She remembered Hugo at the golf club, both hands in action then; one holding his glass of scotch, the other exuberantly sawing the air as he emphasized some point or other.

She sat silent for a while, stroking his fingers, and wondering what the tube was for, inserted into the back of his hand – what sedative or wonder drug it might be dripping into his body. She was aware that she had stopped talking, but it seemed pointless to keep wittering on about the weather or the journey. Besides, it was proving awfully difficult not to be distracted. She found herself gazing at the bandage now; its innocent whiteness presumably hiding some horrendous wound. It swathed his whole head like a turban, coming right down to his eyebrows. If the sight of it distressed her, how much worse it must be for Elizabeth. This was the man she planned to *marry*, in a matter of months, or even weeks.

All at once, she knew what she had to do: she must tell Elizabeth's fiancé, solemnly and officially, that she accepted the marriage – rejoiced in it, even – just as she had told herself, sitting in the car-park.

That would be the acid test, the proof she meant what she said.

She freed her fingers from Hugo's and clasped both her hands together. Now that she was back in contact with Elizabeth – a different and more vulnerable Elizabeth, an Elizabeth who needed her, who'd been thrilled to see her and even called her wonderful – it would be far more of a wrench to give her up. She shut her eyes, recalling all the things they'd shared; their marvellous day at Sandown, their happiness at Cheltenham which had drawn them so much closer, closer in every way. She longed to stay in that delicious world for ever; never to have to open her eyes to this hideous reality. But she had made a pact with herself – if she didn't accept the marriage and surrender her claim to Elizabeth, Hugo would die. And he was terrifyingly close to death already . . .

She *did* open her eyes, *did* hold his hand again, forced her voice to sound less hesitant. 'Hugo,' she said, letting her fingers gently brush his wrist, 'there's something I need to say – something terribly important.' She swallowed, cleared her throat. 'I . . . I love Elizabeth, just as much as you do. Maybe even more. But I want you to know that I . . . I'm *glad* you're going to marry her. I'm not enough for her. I accept that now. Though it's incredibly hard for me to admit it. Perhaps as hard as it is for you to come up from your coma or your . . . I'm sorry, I don't know the proper medical words. I don't even know what's happened to you exactly. But you *must* get better in time for the wedding. Hugo, listen! I'm going to say it again, in case you didn't hear the first time. I'm really pleased that you and Elizabeth are going to be married. I . . . I want you to be happy together.'

Angela got up and stood beside her chair. 'Beattie, are you all right?'

'Y . . . yes,' she stammered, despising herself for crying. She slapped her tears away, watching the nurse pick up her torch again and go through the same procedure as before: shining the light in each of Hugo's eyes in turn. Why was she checking him so often? Was that a good sign or a bad?

Angela's face gave nothing away as she replaced the torch in her pocket and scribbled something on the chart. Surely there must be some change, thought Beattie desperately, something to mirror her own stupendous progression from murderous hate to acceptance and almost-love. If Hugo could truly hear, as the nurses claimed he could, wouldn't her words have touched him, made some tiny tiny difference?

'Any change?' she whispered, her hand tightening its grip on his wrist.

Angela didn't appear to have heard. She was still bent over her chart, her full attention on its rows of hieroglyphics.

Beattie didn't repeat the question. Kim had told her to trust, and trust she would. Yes, of *course* there'd been a change: Hugo was slowly, surely, groping back to life.

36

'I have to admit I'm getting really worried.' Elizabeth stubbed her cigarette out and immediately lit another. 'The longer he's unconscious, the worse the outlook is.'

Beattie shifted position on the narrow lumpy bed. 'It's only been five days. That's not long,' she lied. It had been the longest stretch of time she'd ever lived through.

'Seven. The accident was Saturday.'

'Yes, but some patients are unconscious for *months*. Jo was telling me yesterday. And she said they can still pull through.'

Elizabeth was silent, but Beattie guessed what she was thinking: even if they did pull through, they would probably suffer permanent harm. 'We've got to trust,' she insisted, blocking out the images of brain-damaged paraplegics. 'And anyway, this is our night off. Sister gave us strict instructions to rest and take it easy.'

Elizabeth glanced down at her crumpled skirt and let out a sudden laugh. 'Good heavens, Beattie, I hadn't realized what a couple of tramps we look!'

'No wonder, the way we've been living. I suppose it's a bit like being stranded in an airport – cat-napping on chairs, and not knowing how long we'll *be* here, and that peculiar sense of losing track of time. I mean, night and day sort of merging into each other. And it feels so odd not having a proper base. D'you know, I haven't washed my hair since I arrived. It's disgusting! I suppose I ought to go and do it now and have a bath and . . .' She yawned and stretched, turning over on her side and curling up. 'No, sod it! It can wait. I'm just too tired to move.'

'We can't go to bed at half past six.'

'Why not? We can do anything we like. In fact we ought to get some sleep, in case Angela comes and gets us in the middle of the night, to tell us Hugo's sitting up and taking notice.'

'Oh, Beattie, *pray* he does! But I think I ought to *be* there, so that . . .'

'No. You need a break – we both do. And we've got to make the most of having *beds*.' They might lose those beds if another child was admitted. This was the only bedroom available for visitors, and parents of young children were given first priority. The parents of the Turkish boy had been using the room since Sunday, but he had died this morning, after a second operation on his stomach. There had been three other deaths as well, but she was trying not to think about them, trying to focus on the success stories: the man with the knife-wound – moved to a general ward; the attempted suicide – actually sitting up and joking with the nurses.

She leaned back against the pillows and surveyed the plain white walls, the well-worn carpet, patterned with both flowers and stains, the flimsy nylon curtain at the window. Okay, so it wasn't exactly the Ritz, but it still seemed the height of luxury to be able to stretch out full-length on a proper bed, made up with sheets and blankets, rather than doss down on a chair. And they even had their own washbasin and a small wardrobe for their clothes (which had been creased up in the car all week). 'Let's change into our night things,' she suggested, 'while we've got the chance.'

'Okay.' Elizabeth parked her cigarette in the ashtray and reached for her stick.

'No, wait. I'll give you a hand.' Beattie sprang off the bed and helped her out of her chair.

'I can manage, Beattie, honestly.'

'I *like* helping. Anyway, I've hardly done a thing for you.'

Elizabeth took her arm and looked directly into her eyes, demanding her attention. 'Beattie, you've been absolutely wonderful. No one could have done more. You've given up your time and your sleep without a word of complaint. And I hate to think of the jobs you've probably lost, and newspaper commissions and what-have-you. I just don't know how to thank you. I couldn't have coped without you here, that's certain.'

Beattie flushed with pleasure. That word 'wonderful' again, which she still felt she didn't deserve. It was much easier to be unselfish in this calm supportive environment, where everyone was caring and concerned. She was more used to people *bitching* about their work, or skiving off as early as they could, or taking three-hour lunches, then falsifying their time-sheets. Here, the nurses simply *missed* lunch if an emergency arose. It had made a deep impression on her; affected her own attitude to Hugo. She had started helping to look after him – only little things, admittedly, like filing his nails, or swabbing mouthwash on his gums, but it meant she had overcome her previous fear of touching him. And that in turn had changed the way she felt about him. It was difficult to hate someone you tended like a helpless baby, and who was totally in your power.

'Gosh!' said Elizabeth, wiggling the bare toes protruding from her bandaged foot. 'My toes are filthy again. I don't know how they get like that when I haven't been outside.'

'Sit down again and I'll wash them for you.'

'No, really, Beattie, *I* can do it.'

'Don't be silly. You'll overbalance. Anyway, I'm probably the world's best toe-washer.'

'Well, in that case . . .' Elizabeth submitted with a smile, returning to her chair (a monstrosity in olive-green leatherette which was too big for the room).

Beattie ran some water in the basin, then knelt at Elizabeth's feet with a hot soapy flannel. The leg was swollen above the bandage, and seemed no better than three days ago. She dabbed gently at the toes. 'I'm not hurting, am I?'

'No, Beattie, you're a fantastic nurse.'

'Right, I'll do the other foot then. Take your stocking off.'

Surprisingly, Elizabeth obeyed – unfastening her suspenders and rolling the stocking down.

Beattie slipped it off, tempted to run her hands along Elizabeth's bare legs; to *kiss* her toes, not wash them. It was so marvellous being alone with her, enjoying some real privacy, after five days of living on public view – although it was something of an irony that the two of them had drawn so close only because of Hugo's accident. At last they were sharing a sort of life together (even if they had to live it in shifts) and were now actually sharing a room. The gulf she'd always felt between them had diminished, almost vanished. Elizabeth *needed* her.

She dried the toes and powdered them, then handed Elizabeth her nightdress, turning her back tactfully to allow her to undress. Her feelings for Elizabeth were more confused than ever. One part of her still longed to touch her breasts, caress her naked body, yet another part recoiled, and without really knowing why. Perhaps because she seemed much older: a frail exhausted woman on a stick. No, she thought, that wasn't fair. Elizabeth would never be old, not in ways that mattered. And of *course* she was exhausted when she had so much to do – not just the vigil by Hugo's bed, but all the distressing phone calls to inform his friends and clients about the accident; their grief and shock added to her own.

'Beattie, dear, I want to write a letter before I go to bed. Where did you put the writing pad?'

'It's still in my bag, with the Crunchie bars. Hey, shall we have those now?'

'No, I'll do the letter first. Business before pleasure, as my father always says.'

'*My* dad said the opposite, though a lot of good it did him!' She bit her lip, wondering what her father was doing at this moment. She hadn't spared a thought for him since her abortive phone call from Mile End House. She gave Elizabeth the writing pad, then changed into her pyjamas and sat back on the bed, listening to the scratching of the pen. The letter appeared to be a tricky one, judging by the frequent pauses.

'Who are you writing to?' she asked.

Elizabeth looked up. 'A patient.'

'God! I'd forgotten all about your patients. They must be going spare.'

Elizabeth smiled. 'Don't worry, I rang a colleague before I left for Scotland and asked her to get in touch with them all and let them know I'd been called away. But this is one I'm rather concerned about.'

Hell, thought Beattie – as if Elizabeth hadn't *enough* on her plate. But a psychotherapist was trapped: whatever the crisis, her patients' needs came first. One or two were suicidal – she knew that for a fact – but Elizabeth couldn't even reassure them by saying she'd be back soon. There *were* no certainties. Neither the registrar nor the neurosurgeon had been able to provide hard facts, only 'maybes' and 'we hopes'.

'Any stamps left?' Elizabeth asked.

'No, you used the last one for Tim's birthday card. Damn! It's today, isn't it, and I meant to send a card myself. Happy birthday, Tim!'

Elizabeth folded the letter and put it in an envelope. 'I rang him first thing this morning and he was terribly upset about me missing his party. You see, when Hugo and I first planned the Scottish trip, we worked the dates around it, so he can't understand why I'm not back.'

'Doesn't he know about the accident?'

'Well, yes, but he doesn't realize how serious it is. Besides, his party's so important to him. He's been talking about it for weeks. They're having a magician and a special cake in the shape of a dinosaur.'

'You sound as disappointed as he is.'

'Mm, I suppose I am. I adore my grandchildren's parties! They remind me of when the girls were young and *I* was the one icing the cakes and blowing up the balloons. I remember when Harriet was five, she wanted those big heart-shaped balloons, which she'd seen at some smart London party. I couldn't get them locally, so I bought her fifty ordinary balloons instead, and then practically asphyxiated myself trying to blow them all up!'

Beattie laughed. 'How *are* the girls, by the way?'

'Okay.'

'Aren't they coming to see you? I thought one of them might have offered.'

'Oh, they did. But Caroline's got her hands full with the children, and Harriet's not well. And I don't want Emma travelling when she's pregnant. Anyway' – Elizabeth broke off and started fiddling with her pen – 'if I'm really honest, I prefer them *not* to come. Apart from anything else, I feel so stupid with this wretched ankle.'

'Well, it's hardly your fault. You didn't sprain it deliberately.'

'I know, but . . .' Elizabeth put the pen down and lit another cigarette. Away from the ward she smoked non-stop, as if to compensate for the hours of abstinence. 'It isn't only that. I haven't told you this before, Beattie, but I'm afraid the girls aren't exactly thrilled about the engagement. They think the whole thing's far too rushed.'

Beattie stared at her in surprise. Her own sentiments entirely, yet she hadn't had the slightest inkling that Elizabeth's daughters might react in the same way. In fact, when Sarah had phoned her last Saturday, she had talked about the wedding without a hint of disapproval.

Elizabeth frowned as she exhaled a curl of smoke. 'Sarah seems to mind the most. I suppose she feels I'm being disloyal to her father.'

'Elizabeth, for heaven's sake! *He* walked out on *you*!'

'Yes, I know, but she still misses him dreadfully. In fact, I think she dislikes poor Hugo simply because he isn't Jeremy.'

Yes, poor Hugo, Beattie thought, realizing that the two of them had something in common besides their love of Elizabeth. They were both resented for that love; shunned by Elizabeth's family. She sat up on the bed, hands clasped round her knees. 'Elizabeth?' she said.

'What?'

'*Will* you marry Hugo? Whatever happens? I mean, even if . . .' The sentence petered out. How could she complete so cruel a question?

'Beattie, I couldn't abandon him now. It would be unforgivable.'

That must be love, she thought – or utter lunacy – to shackle yourself for life to a man who might end up a dribbling idiot. She had learned a lot about love since arriving in Intensive Care, and it had nothing to do with the Mills and Boon variety, with roses and June moons.

Elizabeth rubbed her injured leg above the bandage, giving a sudden grimace of pain. 'And you know, I hadn't really realized before how few relatives he has – no brothers and sisters, no children. And his parents dead, of course. No one's been to see him.'

'But I thought you'd told people *not* to come.'

'Yes, but those were mainly casual friends, who're not meant to visit anyway. And I warned Anna off, of course. He was so livid with her over the divorce, I felt she ought to keep away.' Elizabeth gave a bitter smile. 'Actually, she seemed incredibly relieved to be let off the hook. She was just flying off to the Seychelles with her new man.'

'Heartless bitch!' said Beattie. 'Waltzing off on holiday and leaving Hugo in this state. I hope the bloody plane crashes.'

'Oh, don't say things like that, my love. I've seen enough horrors in this ward to last me several lifetimes.'

'Me too.' Beattie rummaged in her bag to find the Crunchie bars. She seemed to be continually eating sweets – as a source of comfort, probably, like Elizabeth's cigarettes. She bit into the crumbly chocolate, demolishing the bar in three large bites. 'Eating only makes me hungrier. I'm still starving. Are you?'

'Well, I wouldn't mind a snack. Though I don't really think I can face that canteen again. I had chicken nuggets last night, which I swear had never been *near* a chicken.'

Beattie screwed up the Crunchie wrapper and aimed it at the bin. 'Why don't I nip out in the car and *buy* us some stuff to eat? There's a Tesco's in the town which opens late.'

'But you'll have to get all dressed again.'

'No, I'll just put my coat on top of my pyjamas.'

'Well, if you're sure you don't mind . . .'

'Of course not. I'll be back before you know it. Then we'll have our little snack and be tucked up safe in bed by eight o'clock!'

'Shut your eyes, Elizabeth.'

'Oh good, you're back. I was getting rather worried.'

'Shut your eyes.'

'Why? What's happening?'

'Nothing. Just promise not to look.'

'What on earth are you doing?'

'Ask no questions and you'll be told no lies. My mother used to say that and it always drove me mad.' Beattie was busy emptying the Tesco carrier bags. She drew out the paper tablecloth first and spread it on the small table in the corner, then opened the various cartons and packets and arranged the food on paper plates.

'Can I open my eyes yet?'

'*No!*' She fetched the tooth-mugs from the basin and put them on the table; twisted the paper napkins into wobbly scarlet swans. 'Just give me a couple more minutes, okay? Oh – and can I borrow your matches?'

'What *are* you up to, Beattie? You're not *smoking*, are you?'

'Yes.' Beattie stifled a laugh. 'I'm afraid I've finally succumbed to the strain.'

'What*ever*'s going on?'

The only response was a series of huffing and puffing noises, then a sudden loud bang which made Elizabeth jump, followed by a muttered curse from Beattie.

'Beattie, *please*, the suspense is killing me!'

'Okay – you can open your eyes now.'

Elizabeth blinked in surprise at the sight of a bunch of heart-shaped red balloons hanging over the table, on which stood a birthday cake in the shape of a pink pig, with five lighted candles on top. Around it were plates of chocolate fingers, Iced Gem biscuits, gingerbread men, strawberry Pop Tarts, and two mugs of sparkling Bongo juice complete with stripey straws.

Beattie was standing by the table, holding the corpse of a burst balloon. 'I thought we'd have a party for Tim,' she explained, 'to sort of celebrate long-distance. I got all his favourite things . . . well,

391

except for the dinosaur cake. I had to settle for a pig. But he likes pigs, doesn't he? Oh, I know it's pretty daft, but . . .' She looked anxiously at Elizabeth, then handed her a mug of juice and squatted on the carpet at her feet. 'You see, it suddenly struck me as I was driving out of the hospital that we ought to be . . . well . . . thankful we're alive – actually rejoice in the fact that we can eat, and drink, and speak, and move and . . . I mean, when you think of those poor sods in the ward, lying in a coma and being fed through tubes . . . So I want to drink to *life*, Elizabeth – to Tim's life, and yours, and Hugo's . . .' She broke off in embarrassment. It sounded awfully pretentious, and anyway perhaps it was insensitive to have laid on balloons and party food when Hugo was so ill. In fact, maybe she'd only done it for her*self*. Children's parties hadn't been exactly thick on the ground when *she* was growing up.

She darted another glance at Elizabeth, relieved to see her raise her glass and repeat the toast, 'To life.' They clunked their mugs together and each took a sip of juice.

'And Hugo's life especially,' Elizabeth added, looking intently into Beattie's eyes. 'And now let *me* propose a toast.' She raised her glass a second time, holding Beattie's gaze. 'To my most loyal, devoted and very special friend.'

37

Beattie strode across the moor, her coat billowing out behind her, her ears aching from the wind. Despite the wild March weather, it was a huge relief to escape from the stuffy hospital and from the cramped and genteel guesthouse with its bad food and petty rules. She had a whole day's freedom ahead of her – alone – to walk, or drive, or sightsee, or treat herself to a slap-up lunch; perhaps take in a slushy film, or visit some romantic castle. Tomorrow she'd be back in the ward, continuing the grim vigil.

She broke into a run, exhilarated by the wind. It was buffeting the birds, ripping shreds off the swiftly-moving clouds, yanking at her hair with a sort of gleeful spite, as if to tear it from her head. The whole landscape seemed to be in motion, mocking Hugo's inertia. Even the staid town of Inverness had been harried by the gale: branches torn off trees, litter bowling along the streets, the River Ness churning in indignation.

She stumbled on a rock and just managed to keep her footing; slowing to a less reckless pace. This was dangerous country – only twenty miles from the ski slopes where Hugo had had his accident. He had been caught in a white-out and lost all sense of direction; the densely clouded sky barely distinguishable from the snow. It was now a fortnight since it had happened – thirteen days to be precise – and this weekend the clocks went forward for British Summer Time. Would she and Elizabeth still be here in the *real* summer; still staying at Marchmont Villa with the fussy Miss McPherson? God forbid!

She bore left to follow the course of the stream, which had swollen from a trickle to an obstreperous torrent, swirling over the stones. She stood watching the foaming water with its shellbursts of fine spray. Nature seemed attuned to her own mood: explosive, wild, impatient. She was *sick* of being good, sick of trying to rouse a man who remained stubbornly unresponsive.

'What you really need is a good fuck.'

Max's diagnosis when she'd spoken to him yesterday – and maybe he was right for once, although their long and rambling phone call had become distinctly acrimonious when she'd admitted that she wouldn't be back for the big do at the Savoy. She no longer even *wanted* to go – not with him, in any case. It was becoming increasingly clear that the thing with Max was over, though she was really scared of telling him. He was quite likely to turn nasty and call her an ungrateful bitch. Okay, perhaps she *was*, but she had to go along with her gut feelings. She was beginning to feel uneasy about the whole relationship, especially the fact that he was married. These last two weeks, she had witnessed the powerfully strong bond between ordinary married couples: they might have spent their lives bickering, like Max and Michèle, but the prospect of impending death often united them more closely, and to the exclusion of all others. She found herself thinking guiltily of Michèle (who after all had been unwell herself), conscious that her own nine months as Max's part-time mistress could hardly compare with a wife's thirty years' hard labour.

As far as sex was concerned, *yes*, she did miss it, but with Hugo so ill, it seemed wrong even to think of such a thing. Though she sometimes wondered secretly if Elizabeth was worried about that aspect of her future life with Hugo (if, indeed, he *had* a future). The doctors had mentioned the possibility of impairment to his brain, but might there not be other sorts of damage?

Her eyes were watering in the wind, as if she were weeping for Elizabeth. She had watched her, this last week, growing more and more dispirited as Hugo continued in the same corpse-like state. She too was losing heart. The nurses talked of 'progress', but the word grated on her nerves. It seemed over-optimistic, if not downright facile. Admittedly he'd been weaned off the ventilator and moved to a general ward, but only, she suspected, because they were short of beds in Intensive Care. If he were truly making progress, why did he still lie there like a vegetable, needing every last thing done for him?

She stopped to find a hankie, her shoulders hunched against the wind. It seemed to be doing its utmost to blow her off her feet, but she stood her ground, enjoying the sense of defiance. It was like standing up to Max – despite his bluster and annoyance, she had refused to give in and come back home, either to the Savoy or to his bed.

She forged on again, still following the stream, aware of the blood pounding round her body, glowing in her cheeks. Even her fingers were beginning to thaw, though her ears still hurt from the onslaught of the wind. No one else was out in this raw weather, but she took pleasure in that too. The whole moor was *hers* – her private estate, which she'd bought this morning for a cool two hundred grand, so she was free to wander wherever she chose. It was ironic to be staying in the Highlands for the first time in her life, yet have no chance till now to explore the countryside. She had seen tantalizing glimpses as she drove briefly into the town on various errands: a first faint flush of green contrasting with the mainly bare grey boughs; a yellow blur of catkins smoking from the dead brown undergrowth. She loved this time of year when spring and winter seemed to co-exist: lush bluebell shoots pushing through the sludge of last year's fallen leaves; glossy ivy wreathing naked elms. Here there were no trees – the moor was too exposed: a bleak and windswept wilderness, in keeping with her mood. And overhead the immense sky was indifferent to any paltry mortal like herself; too busy with its own concerns; great swollen clouds forming and re-forming, their colour changing as she watched from pale oyster to steel-grey.

She was so engrossed in looking upwards, she almost tripped on something lying on the ground: the half-gnawed corpse of a small animal. It was impossible to identify it from the few scraps of mangled fur and scattering of bones. Mesmerized, she stood staring at the remains, thinking of the dead bodies in Intensive Care. (Not that she'd actually seen them – they were spirited away in a special trolley with a wooden box inside, concealed beneath an innocent-looking sheet.) But here was death in all its gruesome detail: uncamouflaged, unsanitized. If Hugo died, this would be the reality: a heap of rotting bones.

'Hugo, you've *got* to live,' she shouted suddenly. 'For Christ's sake make an effort! You can't just lie there in a coma and expect everyone to wait on you for ever.'

Her words were shredded by the wind, drowned by the yammering stream, but she simply shouted louder, yelling his name at the top of her voice; repeating it over and over and over, as if that might

395

resurrect him from the dead. It was only now she realized how *furious* she was – furious like the weather, furious like the stream – enraged that one oblivious man could cause so much despair. It wasn't just Elizabeth who was racked with grief and worry, but the couple Hugo had been staying with in Scotland. They *also* blamed themselves, for failing to warn him about the treacherous conditions. And Elizabeth's whole family seemed to be foundering without her. Harriet was still unwell, and James about to have his operation, and Margaret had gone down with 'flu and couldn't cope with the visiting. And on top of everything else, the most disturbed of Elizabeth's patients was threatening to take an overdose.

'Hugo, *listen*, will you? Don't you *care* about all the misery you're causing? You've got to bloody well wake up!'

Her throat was hoarse from shouting, yet she felt strangely energized; blasted out of the torpor of the last few hopeless days, as if goaded on by nature itself.

She turned on her heel and raced back the way she'd come, lurching across the tussocky grass to where she'd left the car. Bugger her day off! – she had to get back to the ward. If love and kindness had brought about no change in Hugo, it was time for fire and fury.

Forty minutes later she swept into the hospital, hair tousled, shoes still caked with mud. Too impatient to wait for the lift, she hurtled up the three flights of stairs, only stopping for breath at the door to the ward. She peered in at the rows of beds – nineteen other patients; none as seriously ill as Hugo, but a miserable bunch on the whole; always moaning and groaning or causing some disturbance or other. She felt furious with them too, *and* their wretched visitors: Graham's garrulous relatives already clustered round his bed, jabbering in broad Scots. Further down, Elizabeth sat stiffly in her chair, as deathly pale as Hugo himself and decidedly more frail. Her ankle was still bandaged and seemed just as painful as ever. Did *nothing* get better in this bloody useless hospital?

'Excuse me, dear . . .'

A porter with a wheelchair was trying to manoeuvre his way past. Beattie stood back for him, then followed him into the ward. Several of the patients called out a hello, or acknowledged her with a smile. This was her new family: twenty sickly men. To hell with the lot of them! She'd had enough of illness in any shape or form. She marched along to Hugo's bed – the only one whose occupant showed no sign of life.

Elizabeth looked up in surprise. 'Beattie!' she exclaimed. 'What are you doing back so soon? I wasn't expecting you until suppertime.'

'Sorry – change of plan. Let *me* take over, will you?'

'But I thought . . .'

'I'll explain later, okay? There's something desperately important I need to say to Hugo and I'd rather do it on my own. How *is* he, by the way?'

Elizabeth gave a despondent shrug. 'I've been playing him some Berlioz – "The Royal Hunt and Storm". I hoped it might inspire him, but . . .'

Beattie leaned over and unhooked the headphones from his ears. He must listen to *her*, not Berlioz. She had bought the Walkman on one of her recent shopping trips, and a long list of cassettes suggested by Elizabeth. He was getting spoilt, that was the trouble – having so much fuss and attention not just from the pair of them, but from the whole array of surgeons and neurologists, radiographers and physios. It took three nurses simply to turn him, and he was turned a dozen times a day to prevent his getting bedsores. And given consciousness checks and brain scans, and all manner of other procedures.

'Hello, my dear. Nice to see you again!'

She looked round to see the hospital chaplain, the Reverend Hendrickson. He came every day to visit the patient next to Hugo, who had recently lost his wife and was now recovering from a hip replacement. *Damn*, she thought – how the hell could she say what she wanted with that sanctimonious Godman listening in? She mumbled a reply, then sat with her back to him while he launched into his spiel.

'Well, Ron, how *are* we today? Shall we say a little prayer together? "Jesus, our friend who suffered with us, thank you for this chance of knowing your presence in our pain." '

Our pain! she thought – that's rich. The chaplain positively glowed with health, his ruddy face contrasting with Hugo's ghastly pallor. She missed the remainder of the prayer because Hugo's special nurse appeared: an elegant woman called Laura, whose neatly swept-up chignon made Elizabeth's hair look even more unkempt.

'Hello, Beattie,' she said with a smile, as she checked the bag on the drip-feed. 'What happened to your day off?'

'Oh, I found I couldn't tear myself away.' Beattie winced as a raucous laugh erupted from one of Graham's relatives. They seemed to gather here more for their own amusement than for the sake of the ailing patient, who rarely got a word in. 'Look, now I'm back, Laura, is there anything I can do?'

'Well, you could give Hugo a freshen-up wash, and maybe clean his teeth.'

'Okay,' she said resignedly. It wasn't as easy as she'd imagined to bully Hugo back to life. There seemed always to be an audience: nurses, vicars, ward clerks, other people's visitors. She went to fill the plastic bowl from the washbasin at the end of the ward, pausing for a brief word with the old chap in the corner. She returned to Hugo's bed and took his soap and flannel out of the locker.

'Hugo, I'm going to wash your face and hands,' she said, as she'd said twenty times before. She had kept her promise and helped Elizabeth look after him, performing every task as lovingly as she could. Besides the purely practical chores, she also often read to him: newspaper articles, or extracts from his favourite books, even bits of poetry. And she had sat with him in Intensive Care through long exhausting nights, holding his hand and trying to talk him back to life. But *could* he really hear, or was it all a waste of time? She stood staring at his pale, still form, lying there as useless as a rag doll, apparently not breathing, and was suddenly struck by a horrendous thought: suppose he were actually *dead?* Holding her breath in terror, she moved the sheet aside and touched his bare chest with her fingertips. She was almost surprised to find the skin still warm; to detect the faint tremor of a heartbeat.

'So you *are* alive,' she whispered, daring to breathe again in relief. 'And, yes, maybe you *can* hear.'

She sponged his face gently with the flannel, washing deftly round the tube in his nose and trying to avert her eyes from the huge scar on his head. Now the bandage had been removed, it was exposed to view in all its gruesome detail. And almost worse was the uneven patch around it where they'd had to shave his head. The hair was beginning to grow back and looked stubbly and grotesque, like some animal recently operated on by a vet.

She rinsed the soap off and patted his face dry, then smoothed a little cream into the skin. It was like looking after a child – something she had never done, though it made her feel strangely protective, especially when she washed his hands, which lay pathetically limp in

398

hers. Touching a man's hands in a totally non-erotic way was another new experience. Up till now, her physical contact with men had centred only on sex. Perhaps that was her loss. She was becoming more aware of all the things she had lost out on: children, a loving partner, affection which didn't depend on her proficiency in bed.

She picked up the small child's toothbrush and inserted it into Hugo's mouth, which fortunately was open. Yesterday his teeth had been clenched together, which made things rather difficult. She did her best to manoeuvre the brush round the surfaces of every tooth, though there were a few she couldn't reach. Teeth-cleaning was the most intimate thing of all. She was more familiar with the contours of Hugo's mouth than if she had been his lover – the tiny chip off one front tooth, the fillings in the back ones, his coated yellowish tongue. Having wiped off the remaining toothpaste, she dipped a swab in mouthwash and stroked it over his gums, and finally smeared Vaseline on his lips. Throughout the whole procedure he lay completely passive: his eyes closed, his face expressionless. Of course it was childish to expect a reward for her pains, but she *did* feel extremely frustrated when she had tried so hard to rouse him (even phoning Kim one night to obtain new reserves of strength). Surely there should be some response by now – a word, a nod, a movement. Laura claimed to have seen him move his leg. It was supposed to have happened yesterday, but frankly she was sceptical. The nurses were so kind, they were probably simply trying to keep Elizabeth's hopes up, even if it meant massaging the truth.

She shrugged and returned to her duties, straightening the covers on the bed and putting all the toilet things away. Whatever else, the hospital had taught her to be tidy. Her parents wouldn't have recognized this new methodical daughter.

'Remember, Ron,' the chaplain was purring behind her, 'you can talk to the Lord whenever you want. And as soon as you're up and about, I'll take you to see our lovely little chapel . . .'

You might as well take Hugo, too, she thought, and perhaps *he*'ll talk to the Lord. He certainly doesn't want to talk to me.

She went to empty the bowl, nodding to Florence, who had just arrived with the lunch trolley. She hated mealtimes in the ward – the sight of the other patients slurping and munching all around only served to emphasize Hugo's catatonic state. (Not to mention being a depressing reminder of how much weight she'd put on:

399

wolfing Miss McPherson's porridge for breakfast every morning, then stoking up with canteen food later in the day. She seemed to *need* to eat in order to stay calm; to continue in harness day after tedious day.)

She returned to Hugo's bedside, relieved to see the chaplain getting up.

'God bless you, my dear,' he said to her, before bowling out of the ward, bestowing blessings left and right.

'Thanks,' she murmured, wiping down the top of Hugo's locker and listening to the clatter of the lunch trays. Often, she fetched herself a coffee at this time, but now the vicar had disappeared, she had something more important to do.

'Right, Hugo,' she said, positioning her chair as close to the bed as possible, so that her mouth was level with his ear. 'I want to have it out with you. If you think I'm going to put up with . . .'

The words faltered to a stop. There was no conviction in them. Her anger had given way to a feeling of futility. It had been easy enough to rage and bellow on the moor, shouting into the wind like some crazed character out of *Wuthering Heights*, but here she felt selfconscious and constrained. Anyway, there was just too much distraction: Florence padding to and fro, distributing chicken pie; the bossy ward clerk bouncing around, arranging X-rays or admissions; a patient being wheeled in on a trolley. It was Mr Ross, the man from the bed opposite, evidently back from theatre, and not too bright, by the sounds of it. Behind the hastily drawn curtains she could hear a doctor barking instructions at the minions, and then a woman rushed in – Mrs Ross, presumably – near-hysterical. The nurses told her she would have to wait outside, but she continued screaming and crying until they removed her forcibly. As she was escorted out of the ward, the big red-haired houseman appeared and swept inside the curtains – another voice added to the commotion.

Christ almighty! thought Beattie, it's worse than the night I arrived here: hysterics, drama, wailing relatives. If Hugo *did* remain unconscious for months, this would be the pattern: sitting by his bedside as spring crawled into summer, witnessing crisis after crisis. Could they take it without cracking up?

In a fit of fury she jumped to her feet and yanked the curtains round Hugo's bed, trying to cut herself off from the noise. 'Hugo, listen to me!' she shouted. 'I've had enough – more than enough. Unless you make some effort, I'm walking out. And I'm taking Elizabeth with me. This is *killing* her. She's barely eating or sleeping. So wake *up*, for Christ's sake!'

As she glared down at Hugo, she could feel her cheeks flaming; anger and adrenalin scorching through her body. And then she tensed in shock. His eyelids had moved – she was sure of it – an almost imperceptible flicker, but movement none the less.

'Hugo,' she implored, her voice sinking to a whisper as she clutched his hand, stared hard into his face. 'I *know* you can open your eyes. Please do it, Hugo – *now*. Not for me, but for Elizabeth.'

Nothing. No response. She almost cried with disappointment. Had she *imagined* the flicker – or simply not been angry enough? Maybe he responded only to threats.

'I warn you, Hugo,' she said in a deliberately aggressive tone, 'unless you open your eyes properly and show me you're awake, you'll never see me again. *Or* Elizabeth. So if you love her, you'd better prove it!'

Her eyes never left his face. She was *willing* the eyelids to move again, but there was not the faintest stir. She slumped back in her chair. The flicker had been so tiny – the merest hair's-breadth twitch – probably just an involuntary tic, not a sign that he was waking up. Anyway, what was the point of making empty threats? Of *course* they couldn't walk out, least of all Elizabeth, who was committed to this man for ever. She felt guilty now about her outburst. Anger was downright selfish – she ought to be bloody grateful that *she* wasn't the one lying here insensible. Or moaning with pain like Mr Ross, who, judging by the drama behind the curtains, was about to return to theatre.

She tried to ignore the hubbub and concentrate on Hugo. If this was to be home for the next few months, she might as well make the best of it. She picked up one of his poetry books and started leafing through it. 'I'll read to you, Hugo,' she said. 'Okay? How about "Fern Hill" again?'

Not the ghost of a response this time. Well, so what? Thirteen days wasn't actually that long, not compared with *some* cases. She settled back and read him the opening lines, hoping the lilting words would calm her.

'Now as I was young and easy under the apple boughs . . .'

Her father had occasionally recited poetry to her, but always in a histrionic tone and with grand dramatic gestures, as if he were playing to an audience of thousands instead of one uncritical child. She smiled wryly at the memory. He had always fancied himself a famous actor strutting on a West End stage, when the reality was bit-parts in provincial rep.

> 'The night above the dingle starry,
> Time let me hail and climb . . .'

She found herself slipping into her father's voice, copying his intonation – not that he ever read her Dylan Thomas. It had tended to be Sir Henry Newbolt, or Rudyard Kipling (or bits of 'The Ancient Mariner' – fixing her with his glittering eye and scaring her half to death). But she was warming to 'Fern Hill', now that she had read it several times. She skipped the third verse and launched into the fourth, her favourite, still parroting her father's fruity tones.

> '. . . the spellbound horses walking warm
> Out of the whinnying green stable
> On to the fields of praise.'

She paused to savour the words, glancing briefly at Hugo. She gasped. His eyes were open. No, she must be dreaming, or so desperate for some reaction she'd fabricated it. She blinked hard, then dared glance back. Open. Truly open – the eyes weak and slightly clouded, as if veiled in filmy gauze. But open, beyond all doubt, and actually looking at her.

For a centuries-long minute they held each other's gaze, then she bent and kissed him, her tears falling on his face. 'Hugo,' she sobbed, 'I *love* you for this. I'll love you for ever, even when you're married to Elizabeth.'

As if in answer, he made a sound in his throat: a strangulated croaking sound, which seemed to cost him great exertion – perhaps an avowal of his *own* love.

She leapt to her feet, almost overturning the chair, plunged through the curtains and went dashing down the ward. 'Laura!' she shouted. 'Quick, come and see! Hugo's awake! And he *spoke* to me!'

V

38

'Right, that's the lot.' Beattie handed over the folder of impeccably typed letters, and grabbed her white jacket from the peg. 'If you'd like to sign them, I'll post them on my way out.'

Greville uncapped his Mont Blanc pen. 'You obviously can't wait to get off.'

'Dead right!' grinned Beattie. 'I'm determined to get out of London before the rush hour starts, and on a Friday that means lunchtime.'

'Talking of lunch, we haven't had any yet.' Greville glanced at his watch and frowned. 'Can't I persuade you to change your mind and spend the weekend with *me*? We could have a leisurely dinner, spin things out a bit . . .'

'No, I'm sorry, Greville, I'm expected in Kent.'

'Am I allowed to ask who's expecting you?'

'Certainly. A great friend of mine – Elizabeth.'

'Oh, I see. Not your boyfriend, then?'

She laughed. 'I haven't got a boyfriend.'

'Yes, you told me that before, I recall. Which makes it all the more frustrating that you won't go out with *me*.'

'Greville, *darling*, we've been closeted together for the last three weeks, more or less non-stop.'

'Mm, that's work, though . . .' He was flicking through the letters, casting a quick glance at each before appending the high-speed hieroglyphic of his signature. 'I'm a busy man.'

'Yeah,' said Beattie. 'I've noticed.' She turned off the photocopier and put a new roll of paper in the fax. The quantities of hardware looked incongruous in such magnificent surroundings. The palatial room was furnished à la *Homes and Gardens* with floor-length velvet curtains, a huge chintzy sofa and matching chairs, an antique walnut dining-table (serving as her desk), and enough flowers to stock a hothouse. A suite at the Dorchester was certainly an improvement on the sort of humdrum office she normally found herself working in, but Greville's office proper was in Cape Town. He was here for just three months, investigating new British outlets for his company's wines and sherries.

She sealed the letters, picked the ripest of the peaches from the exquisite china fruit-bowl and put it carefully in her bag – for lunch. 'Right,' she said, 'I'm off. See you Monday week.'

'I don't know how I'll manage.' Greville pursued her to the door, laid his hand on her bare arm.

'You'll have Naomi.'

'I prefer *you*.' He remained standing far too close, his fingers creeping up to the hollow in her elbow.

'Greville, honestly, I've got to have a break. I've been here the *last* two weekends. And I've worked late every day this week, and . . .'

'Okay, I'm a slave-driver, but you shouldn't be so indispensable.'

'Is that a compliment?'

'Of course!'

She unlatched his hand and stepped resolutely out. Actually the gropings were harmless enough, and secretly she was flattered by his attentions – he was such a high flier, and not bad-looking either, with his dark eyes and rangy figure and superbly tailored clothes. But he was older even than Max, and married (naturally) – the 'little woman', as he called her, waiting patiently at home with the youngest of their teenage sons. Yet another unsuitable man to add to her long list. Still, the job itself was pretty good – long hours, maybe, but extremely well paid, and such incredible luxury. You could almost *taste* the opulence as you swept in through the revolving doors: the ostentatious Promenade with its marble columns and priceless works of art; the gold-encrusted Grill Room, as sumptuous as a sultan's palace.

She found her car waiting at the front entrance, brought round by a sniffy doorman (doubtless more used to Bentleys and Mercedes than fourth-hand 2CVs). She tipped him, Greville-style, then nosed out into Park Lane. Normally she came by tube, but there hadn't seemed much point in wasting time flogging back to the flat to fetch her car. Anyway, the car-park went on Greville's expenses and, given the casual way he picked up the phone and ordered anything from bottles of twelve-year-old malt whisky to Beluga caviar, another £20 was neither here nor there.

The traffic was already building up, although it was only half past one, but once she'd fought her way through New Cross and Lewisham, she started to relax and enjoy the drive. It was the sort of perfect June weather beloved of TV commercials: nature lushly green and fertile; the clouds fluffed up by some personal valet service, and the sky too smugly blue to be anything but fake. *Wedding* weather, she thought, noticing a bush covered in white blossom, and wondering if the date planned for Elizabeth and Hugo's wedding had actually come and gone. Impossible to ask.

She was making good time – had already crossed into Kent and was rattling along the motorway as fast as her car could go. Then came the best part of the journey, when she turned off into empty roads and the real untrammelled countryside: fields of rippling grass, damasked with a faint purple sheen; white-lace spokes of cow parsley clotting the dense hedgerows; the green shout of a beech wood dappled by the sun. When she'd left Kent just a month ago, the weather had been atrocious – grey and overcast, with two dramatic hailstorms and even a flurry of snow – in May! It had seemed to match the situation: Hugo moody and depressed, slurring his speech, forgetting people's names, and unable to concentrate on anything for more than a few minutes. He was supposed to be in a rehabilitation centre, but he'd discharged himself after just two days, refusing point-blank to return. Things had improved since then, thank goodness, and he'd agreed to attend the local hospital for various forms of treatment, though strictly as an outpatient. According to Elizabeth, he was making steady progress, although she was always rather vague about the details. It could be loyalty, of course – an unwillingness to elaborate on his remaining difficulties, or perhaps she simply felt that the accident had dominated their lives too much already.

Well, she'd find out soon enough. Here was the signpost to the village, and the ancient chestnut tree, now splendid in full leaf; embryo conkers sprouting on each branch. It occurred to her that she'd never seen Mile End House in the summer – in September, yes, but not flaming June.

The azaleas were a blaze of scarlet as she drew up outside the front door, with her usual feeling of excitement. Despite all that had happened in the last few months, this place was special for her – and always would be.

Harriet let her in with a less than welcoming smile. 'I'm afraid Mummy's seeing a patient. You're earlier than you said.'

Beattie bit back a retort. Harriet had *asked* her to come early: she was going to a wedding up in Durham and had a train to catch. 'Well,' she said equably, 'better early than late. And if you want to get off sharp yourself, I'll take over now.'

'Hugo's not here. He's gone to the hospital for his speech therapy and won't be back for at least an hour.'

'Oh, I see. I'd better go and unpack then.'

'Would you like a cup of tea first?'

'Mm, I'd love one.' Beattie wished the offer had been made less grudgingly. 'If you're sure you've got time, that is.'

'Yes, I'm not leaving until four.'

Roll on four then, she thought, following Harriet into the kitchen. Things had been tricky enough between them last month, when she and Elizabeth had brought Hugo back from Scotland and found Harriet ensconced at Mile End House. She had lost her job, given up her Bristol flat, and come home in despair. It was eventually decided that she should *stay* at home for a while and earn some money by looking after Hugo. It seemed a sensible solution: Elizabeth could get back to her patients, Harriet had a role in life, and there was no need to employ a stranger in the house.

Beattie stared despondently at Harriet's slender back, with its cascade of shining blonde hair. As far as *she* was concerned, a stranger would have been preferable. Harriet's presence as beloved daughter in residence had undermined her own role, and after a week of mutual resentment, she had finally upped and gone, returning to London and her temp work. It was only now she realized how successfully the job with Greville had kept her mind off all the problems here.

'How *is* Hugo?' she asked, as Harriet poured the tea.

'So-so.'

'Who's taken him to the hospital?'

'One of Mummy's friends in the village.'

Beattie spooned sugar into her cup. Harriet could hardly be described as chatty – at least not about Hugo. 'And how about *you?*' she enquired, determined to be sociable. Maybe Harriet would talk more freely about her*self.* 'Are you quite recovered now?'

'Yes, thanks.'

End of conversation. She gave a surreptitious glance around the

408

shambolic kitchen, and made a mental note to have a good clear-up once Harriet had gone. 'What time's your train?' she asked. 'I can give you a lift to the station if you like.'

'No, I've arranged a taxi, thanks. It'll be here in a few minutes.'

Beattie racked her brains for something else to say. Although Harriet was so much younger, her air of cool superiority was daunting, to say the least. 'Have you been to Durham before?' she asked. 'Or . . .'

The doorbell cut her short. Harriet got up languidly, leaving her tea untouched. 'Can you tell the cab I'm coming, please, while I go and fetch my case? And say goodbye to Mummy for me, will you. I've said it once already, but . . .'

Good riddance, muttered Beattie, as she waved the taxi off. She shut the front door and wandered into the drawing-room, hoping Elizabeth wouldn't be too long. Hugo's stuff was all over the place: a jigsaw puzzle half-finished on the table, magazines and papers scattered on the floor, dirty plates and glasses on every available surface. Harriet might be a good minder, but she was a pretty useless housekeeper.

She leafed through a couple of the magazines: the same mindless gossipy trivia Hugo had been reading *last* time she was here – a far cry from his usual *Art International*. And the jigsaw was one of Tim's: just twenty wooden pieces, with a picture of a steam train on the box. And there was the blue notebook, which had made her cry when she'd first read its crudely pencilled contents. 'Eight o'clock: get up and wash and dress and clean my teeth. Nine o'clock: eat breakfast, take my pills. Ten o'clock: go into the garden for a walk.' The urbane Cambridge graduate had been forced to write out a basic timetable and consult it hour by hour, to prevent him wandering around in his pyjamas all day, bewildered and unwashed.

There was still no sound from Elizabeth, so she took her case upstairs to Sarah's room. *Her* room, she had liked to think, once, though the whole house seemed Hugo's now – and not just because of the quantities of paintings, which had been sent down from his gallery and were stacked on every landing, still waiting to be hung. It was something more insidious than that: his disability had taken over everything, infecting the atmosphere with uncertainty and fear; questions hanging in the air never asked or answered: would he ever run a gallery again, ever marry his fiancée, ever . . . ?

Trust, she told herself, remembering her triumphant night with

Kim. He'd been right, in fact: Hugo *had* pulled through and, whatever happened subsequently, at least he was alive.

Suddenly she heard a door opening downstairs and a man's voice in the hall: the patient, leaving at last. She waited till the front door closed, then dashed down and clasped Elizabeth in a long affectionate hug. Elizabeth made no move to cut it short. Beattie could feel her warmth, in every sense.

It was *she* who finally pulled away, relieved to see that Elizabeth looked better; no longer so pale and drawn. She was wearing her therapist's gear: plain dark skirt and classic blouse in a simple navy print. She had her hair up in a bun – a style she'd adopted in Scotland, which made her look more a sedate grandmother than the girlish almost-rebel she had been at Ashley Grange. Beattie felt a sudden longing – for that original Elizabeth; the woman she had desired with such incredible intensity, even wanted naked in her bed. Strangely, the violence of those feelings had receded as her friendship with Elizabeth actually deepened and developed.

'Oh, Beattie, darling, it's so *good* to have you back. And gosh, you do look frightfully smart!'

'Well, I have to make an effort for the Dorchester.'

'Oh yes, of course – how's it going?'

'Fine. But how are *you*?'

'Okay.'

'And is Hugo any better? I think about him so much, you know, and sometimes I even *pray*. Mind you, I haven't a clue who I'm praying to, but I tell them to get their finger out and work a miracle. So, have my prayers been answered?'

'Well, I'm afraid things weren't too good this morning, but then he tends to have his ups and downs. It's all part of the process. But let's talk about *you*. I want to hear more about your South African millionaire!'

'Okay, there's loads to tell you. Why don't we go out for a walk? It's such a fantastic sunny day, and if we try and talk here, your wretched phone will ring and ring, or someone will pop in and we'll never get a moment to ourselves.'

Elizabeth looked anxiously at her watch. 'It's half past four already and I must be here when Mrs Phelps brings Hugo back.'

'Well, a *short* walk then – just down the lane and as far as the wood.'

They set off arm in arm, Elizabeth pausing outside the gate to light a cigarette. 'Now tell me about Greville,' she said, tossing the match into a bush. 'What do you think – is there any chance he could be Mr Right?'

Beattie laughed. 'No way! I've discovered he's married with three kids. In any case, he's far too old. I don't want a repeat of Max. Oh, by the way, did I tell you Max is going out with that French girl – the one he took to the Savoy instead of me? It's okay, I'm not that bothered. In fact I'm really rather grateful to her. She's let me off the hook. Oh, look, roses in the hedge!' she said, snapping off a pink rambler-rose and handing it to Elizabeth. It wasn't a wholly spontaneous gesture – she was hoping to forestall the awkward questions about journalism which were bound to follow from the mention of Max. She knew Elizabeth felt guilty about having kept her away so long from London and her contacts. True she'd lost a few commissions, but that wasn't just because of the time she'd spent in Inverness. She no longer *wanted* to write, at least not the sort of stuff she had been struggling to produce before Hugo's accident. The nine weeks at the hospital had changed her. Only a few months ago, getting into print had been her chief ambition – a way of *proving* herself – yet that all-consuming passion had now waned. She had proved herself in other ways, as Elizabeth was fond of telling her. Okay, she might not be solely responsible for bringing Hugo back to life, but she had certainly played her part.

She picked another rose, inhaled its scent greedily, then stuck it in her buttonhole. 'I've been writing a few poems,' she said, knowing *that* would please Elizabeth, and also divert her attention from the *other* sort of writing.

'Oh, marvellous, Beattie! Are you going to let me read them?'

'All right, if you want. They're mostly about the hospital. It's funny, you know, I can't stop thinking about it – I mean the gruesome things those nurses have to cope with, and their total dedication to it all. My own work seems so trivial in comparison. Even this job at the Dorchester makes me feel sort of . . . fidgety – typing reams of stuff about grape harvests or vintages, and queening it in such luxury, while Angela's suctioning out some car-crash victim in an overheated ward. In fact, when Greville's gone back home, I may think about retraining.'

'As a nurse, you mean?'

'Oh God, no!'

'Well, what then?'

411

'I only wish I knew. Perhaps I'll do a Miss McPherson and open Marchmont Villa Mark II, down here in the south! Anyway, enough of me – tell me about Hugo.'

Elizabeth drew on her cigarette, exhaling with a sigh. 'Well, he's seen the neurologist again. And they say he's doing well – as well as can be expected. His speech is definitely better. And his memory's improving, slowly. But I'm afraid he does get rather irritable. Or he might suddenly burst into tears, which is terribly distressing. I think it's just frustration – there are so many things he still can't do, and he must find that really galling. By the way, Beattie dear, if he *does* get upset in front of you, it's best not to react. The doctor advised us to ignore it, or change the subject – you know, give him a chance to calm down. Poor Hugo can't help himself, you see. He's not even aware that he's behaving any differently from normal. Head injuries *do* have that effect. It's to do with the frontal lobes of the brain, and it can change a person's whole behaviour, even their character, in some cases.'

'Oh, Elizabeth' – Beattie stopped and took her hand – 'I'm so dreadfully sorry. I just don't know what to say. It must be ghastly for you.'

'It's all right. I'm managing.'

'Honestly?'

'Yes, honestly. I've had so much help, you know. People have been wonderful, and Harriet's doing surprisingly well. In fact, I often feel guilty that I do so little for him myself. It's just that I seem to be so busy with my patients. I've even taken on two new ones.'

'Well, that's *good* – I'm sure it is. But you mustn't do nothing but work. Tell you what, let's walk on into the village and treat ourselves to a quick drink at the White Horse.'

'Oh, Beattie, we *can't*. Mrs Phelps is . . .'

'I thought you said you'd given her a key?'

'Well, yes, but . . .'

'That's all right then. She can let herself in. And they can always sit in the garden till we get back.'

'But Beattie, dear, it does seem rather *rude*, when . . .'

'Yes – frightfully rude. Which is why we're going to do it. You need taking in hand, Elizabeth. I haven't seen you for almost a month and you're getting far too dutiful again. Come on, gee up! Let's *run* to the village, and maybe we'll have time for steak and chips as well!'

*   *   *

'I'm so sorry, Mrs Phelps. I simply didn't realize the time.' Elizabeth hurried into the garden, where Hugo and his chauffeuse were relaxing in deck chairs on the lawn.

'That's all right, my dear. Hugo and I are enjoying the sun.'

Beattie hung back, staying close to the french windows, so she could observe Hugo without him seeing her. She was astonished at the transformation. His hair had grown again, completely concealing the scar; his deathly pallor was now replaced by an attractive tan, and he'd regained the weight he'd lost. To all intents and purposes he was a perfectly ordinary healthy man, relaxing in his garden. He was even *smiling*, for heaven's sake, as he chatted companionably with Mrs Phelps. She continued staring in delight, remembering the weak and listless invalid, hobbling around on crutches, too exhausted to do anything. Even the flamboyant Hawaiian shirt he was wearing seemed to reflect the enormous change; he looked as if he'd returned from some exotic foreign holiday, rather than a gruelling stint in hospital.

She stepped on to the lawn, holding out both hands to him. 'Hugo, I'm back. How *are* you? You're looking wonderfully well!'

Instantly his expression changed: suspicion darkening his whole face. 'I'm *not* well,' he retorted, flapping his hand at her irritably. 'I feel bloody terrible, if you really want to know.'

She flinched as if he'd struck her. He had sounded really hostile and cantankerous. But she tried to ignore his anger, remembering Elizabeth's advice. At least his speech was nearer to normal – only a trace of the slurring remained.

'How did you get on at the hospital?' she asked, speaking with deliberate calm.

'Oh, for Christ's sake, leave me alone! Can't you see I don't want to talk?'

Mrs Phelps looked embarrassed and muttered something about having to make tracks for home. 'He was quite all right with *me*,' she whispered to Elizabeth with a touch of smugness in her voice as she eased her bulky form from the deck chair. 'No trouble whatsoever.'

'I'm so glad,' Elizabeth smiled. 'It was extremely kind of you to take him. Can I offer you a drink before you leave?'

'No thank you, dear. But actually I would like a little word with you about the village fête. Eleanor said you had something rather special for a raffle prize?'

413

'Yes, a painting. It's only small, but it's a landscape of the country-side round here, so I thought it would fit the bill rather well. Would you like to see it now? It's upstairs on the landing.'

The two of them returned to the house, leaving Beattie alone with Hugo. He had got up from his chair and was pacing restlessly to and fro, kicking at the flowerpots on the patio. She was surprised how well he was walking, with only a slight limp.

'Shall we go for a tour of the garden?' she suggested. 'The roses look fantastic. I thought I might pick a few for my room.'

'I don't want to go anywhere. I've been out all bloody afternoon. Piss off and leave me in peace.'

She stopped dead in her tracks. In spite of Elizabeth's warnings, she was appalled by his sheer rudeness. How could she *not* take it as a personal rejection? As Mrs Phelps had said, he'd been perfectly all right until *she* appeared on the scene. It was as if he didn't even recognize her; had totally forgotten the hours they'd spent together at the hospital. She might have been an enemy, for God's sake, the way he was glaring at her so threateningly.

'What are you *doing* here again?' he demanded, his voice still more aggressive. 'I thought you'd gone for good.'

She bit her lip, determined not to cry. This was a different Hugo, a vindictive hurtful stranger, but she mustn't blame him, mustn't overreact. The accident had changed him. Anyway, it was far worse for Elizabeth, who had to cope with him every day.

Shakily, she backed away, suddenly catching sight of Boz, who was slinking round the side of the house under cover of the bushes. 'Boz!' she called in relief. 'I wondered where you'd got to.'

The cat approached her warily, without his usual welcoming purr. She was about to pick him up when Hugo strode over and aimed a kick at him.

'Hugo, *don't*! That's cruel.'

'Go away!' he shouted. 'I don't want you here, d'you understand? I've *told* you to get out.'

Tears welled in her eyes. Furiously she blinked them back. Boz had fled to the safety of the house. She turned to follow him, but stopped by the french windows. Hugo shouldn't be left on his own – not in such a state. He had snatched up his cigarettes and was striking matches, one after another, flinging each into the flowerbed, as if furious with them too. She watched him helplessly. If only she could *do* something – calm him down, somehow re-establish their

414

bond. However wounding he had been just now, she still felt closer to him in certain ways than to any other man. She had never washed or shaved or fed another man.

He had finally lit a cigarette and now sat slumped on the lawn, smoking morosely and staring into space. She could *weep* for him – that look of desolation on his face; the appalling change in a once normal sunny character.

He picked up one of the magazines scattered on the lawn and flicked through it aimlessly before tossing it aside. Then he stubbed his cigarette out in the grass, and dragged himself to his feet once more. He seemed incapable of keeping still and started prowling up and down again, yanking the heads off roses and crushing the petals in his hands.

'Hugo . . .' she murmured tentatively, trying to distract him, yet terrified he'd shout.

He swung round at the sound of her voice and strode towards her with such vehemence, she tensed, expecting a blow. Instead he grabbed her round the waist, his hands clutching her so tightly, it was difficult to breathe.

'Kiss me,' he pleaded. His voice had changed to a desperate sobbing whine, and before she could escape, she felt the violent pressure of his mouth ramming against her own.

39

Beattie heaved her suitcase out of the boot, then locked the car and let herself into the house. It wasn't often she felt so glad to be back (especially after leaving Kent), but the last week had been impossible.

She picked up her letters from the mat – mostly bills and junk mail – but among them was a fat blue airmail envelope with her father's writing on it. *That* would cheer her up. She'd read it over a leisurely cup of tea.

The mournful strains of Vince's guitar accompanied her up the three flights of stairs. She closed her door firmly, relieved to be alone: no Hugo shouting at her (or groping her), no embarrassed Margaret stepping in to help, only to be insulted in her turn.

She dumped her case on the bed and went through to the kitchen to put the kettle on. While she was filling it, the phone rang. 'Damn,' she muttered, returning to the hall.

'Beattie, it's Elizabeth. I was just phoning to make sure you got back safe and sound.'

'Yes, thanks. There was a lot of traffic in Bromley, but it's always bad round there.'

'Beattie . . . ?'

'Mm?'

'I . . . I wanted to say how *awful* I still feel – about Hugo.'

'Don't be silly. It's quite okay, I told you.'

'Yes, but when I think . . .'

'It's all right, honestly. I'm just sorry I was such a dismal failure.'

'Oh, Beattie – I *knew* you'd say that. That's partly why I'm ringing. How can I make you understand it's nothing to do with you personally? You've been absolutely wonderful – I can't tell you that enough. But poor Hugo's so unpredictable, and when he has these violent mood-swings he just takes it out on anyone and everyone. So you mustn't blame yourself.'

'I don't,' she said, 'not now.' At first she had wondered, wretchedly, if Hugo's aggression was directed only at *her*; that perhaps he some-how *knew* about her hatred of him, all those months ago, and that she had actually willed him to die. It was almost a relief when she saw him treating Margaret just as badly – at least that proved her fears unfounded. Though it was certainly disturbing, the way he could switch from spitting fury to pathetically fawning lust in the space of a few minutes. As well as pawing *her*, he had apparently made a grab for his physiotherapist, *and* a woman in the village shop. Poor Elizabeth had been continually apologizing, making excuses for his embarrassing behaviour – even now she was back on the same subject.

'Oh, Beattie dear, it *is* so difficult, when he doesn't even realize he's giving offence.'

'Yes, I know.' Beattie gave an impatient shrug. She would be glad of the rest from Hugo. Mile End House had become horribly like her childhood home: the air of constant worry centring round an invalid; the sullen moods and angry scenes.

'I'm awfully sorry, Elizabeth, but I've got something on the gas . . .'

She darted back to the kitchen, pounced on her father's letter and tore it open. The tea could wait.

Dearest George...

She smiled at his crazy handwriting – exuberant and all over the place, like *him*. What was she up to, he wanted to know. She hadn't written for so long, he assumed she must have made her mark in the newspaper world and was too busy being rich and famous to bother with her poor old dad.

Wrong, wrong, wrong, she murmured, feeling guilty that she hadn't been in touch.

Anyway, my darling, I've got terrific news! I've met this fantastic woman and she's asked me to move in with her.

Beattie jumped up to fill the kettle, running the tap with such force she sprayed water on the front of her blouse. Not *another* bloody woman! He was over sixty, for God's sake – would he never settle down?

She skimmed over the next page – more eulogies of Céline (*pretty name, isn't it?*): her gorgeous figure, smashing home, marvellous sense of fun, her equally adorable fourteen-year-old daughter Karen (who by all accounts had the body of Lolita and the brains of Einstein). It won't last, she brooded miserably, remembering her father's last two *femmes fatales*, who had stayed the course a mere four and six weeks respectively.

She's dead keen to meet you, Georgie, so I thought it would be a great idea if you came over for a visit, now you're in the money.

No thank you very much, she retorted. I'm damned if I'll play second fiddle to some sexpot with long legs and auburn hair. And anyway I'm *not* in the money – far from it.

In fact, if you weren't so busy in London, I'd suggest you came for keeps. It would be great if you could join our little family.

It's a bit *late* for that, she thought, tossing the letter on the worktop. Nice to have a sister, but not a stranger half her age who might detest her on sight. And as for stepmothers, well, they'd *never* had a good press.

She sloshed water into the pot and stirred the tea-bags moodily. Why on earth was she so worked up? – her father had meant no harm. Even so, his letter had stirred painful memories. As young as eight or nine, she had sensed there were other women in the background; that she and her mother were not the most important people in his life.

On impulse, she returned to the phone and dialled the Sevenoaks number. *Elizabeth* would help – her closest friend, who was trained to listen, trained to understand such childhood insecurities.

But it was Harriet who answered, with her air of snooty boredom.

'Oh, you're back,' said Beattie lamely. 'How was the wedding?'

'Fine.'

'And did you see a bit of Durham?'

'Well, naturally. I was up there a whole week.'

'Er, could I possibly speak to Elizabeth?' Why should she have to *beg*?

'She's seeing a patient.'

'On a *Saturday*?'

'Yes.'

No further explanation was forthcoming, so she said goodbye and rang off. Obviously Elizabeth was busier than ever. Well, who could blame her for taking on more work? Her patients *needed* her, and equally she needed *them*, to provide a reassuring structure to her day, a respite from the crushing burden of Hugo. And her training as a therapist seemed to have saved her from the extremes of grief. She

418

was *used* to difficult patients and could understand how Hugo had regressed; even retain a certain distance from him and just keep praying for some change.

Beattie drifted into the bedroom and sat down on the bed. She actually envied Elizabeth sometimes, for having such an important role in life – she *mattered* to so many different people: her patients, Hugo, all her friends and family. And soon there'd be yet more family. Emma's baby was due, and Sarah had decided to come home and work in England. She hadn't shared Elizabeth's pleasure at the news. With both Sarah and Hugo installed at Mile End House, she would have to face a barrage of hostility every time she visited, and there would be less and less chance of having Elizabeth to herself.

She unpacked her case and put her things away, then wandered aimlessly around the flat, making a half-hearted attempt at tidying up. Despite the strains of the last week, at least there had been company in Kent: people from the village popping in and out; the still convalescent James only too happy to chat, and Boz slowly regaining his trust in her (though still fleeing for dear life from Hugo).

She went into the kitchen and opened the other letters: she owed money to the gas board and BT; she had been nominated for a Sensational Prize Draw; the Laura Ashley catalogue was offering £5 off their summer stock, and the Royal Society for the Protection of Birds were desperate for her to join. She pushed them all to one side and picked up her father's letter again.

Funny, it didn't seem so upsetting now – in fact, the bit about Céline's home was actually quite enticing. Apparently she lived out in the suburbs, in a countryish sort of place, with dogs and cats and even a few hens.

It would be great if you could join our little family...

She stood at the window, staring out. Wasn't that what she'd dreamed of? A family – like Elizabeth's – somewhere she belonged. For all she knew, Céline might be *nice*; anyway, it was hardly fair to blame her for her gorgeous figure and naturally red hair. She had to admit she was jealous, and not only of Céline. She found it somewhat galling that her father had embarked on a romance at the ripe old age of sixty when *she* was on the shelf. But, jealousy aside, this could be her big chance. After all, she had made up her mind to look for a new job – even to retrain, perhaps – so why not a more radical change? In some ways it was perfect. She had been wanting a break with the past, without knowing how to go about it. And now it had arrived out of the blue: a new country, a new start.

Of course, it might not be as easy as it sounded. There was bound to be endless red tape, and they probably wouldn't even allow you into the country without a specific job to go to, or glowing testimonials from your bank. And anyway the whole idea was really rather frightening, venturing into the great unknown. And what about the fare? – that would be prohibitive.

Except a one-way ticket wouldn't be ... And if she worked for Greville night and day, she could clock up masses of overtime.

Her stomach rumbled through her thoughts. She had missed lunch at Mile End House, and it was now nearly four o'clock. She raided the biscuit tin, but found only two stale ginger nuts. There was nothing else to eat in the flat beyond a packet of pea soup and one lonely egg in the fridge. It might be a good idea to get some shopping in – at least it would take her mind off Melbourne. The more she thought about it, the more drawbacks occurred to her. Her father could be drinking still, or chronically hard up, and what if Karen resented him and made their lives a misery? Her *own* arrival on the scene could make things even worse. Besides, her fancy ideals about finding a worthwhile role in life might come crashing around her ears if she landed up without a job at all. No, it was crazy even to *think* of going. Why give herself more heartache?

She fetched her purse and keys and trudged downstairs to the street. She'd buy some Flash as well as food, and clean the flat from top to bottom. If she kept herself busy enough, she wouldn't keep chopping and changing. She had made her decision – to stay in England. Better the devil she knew ...

The sun was still wonderfully warm. In fact, Rainham Road looked very nearly attractive, with the new young trees planted by the council as yet unvandalized. For all she moaned about the area, she would miss it if she was the other side of the world. This was the nearest she had to home. The shops and pubs were comfortingly familiar, and she knew exactly where to go for the cheapest Indian takeaway, or the best bargains on the Portobello Road. She also liked the cosmopolitan atmosphere – the vast range of nationalities, the exotic food and smells, the buzz in the air which made the place so alive.

She stopped at the greengrocer's and bought half a dozen peaches – not quite Dorchester standard, but large and juicy, all the same. She took one out of the bag and bit into the flesh, strolling on to the bakery for her favourite Italian bread. Next door was a travel agent, its windows plastered with cut-price offers.

'CHEAPEST EVER FARES!' shrieked the largest of the posters. Her eyes flicked down the list of destinations: New York, San Francisco, Los Angeles, Hong Kong, Tokyo, Sydney, Melbourne . . .

She paused with her hand on the door-handle. She was staying in England, wasn't she, so why waste time going in? Apart from anything else, she couldn't bear to leave Elizabeth, or turn her back so callously on Hugo.

A huge cardboard kangaroo smiled down at her from the window. Above it were the words: 'AUSTRALIA – SO FAR AND YET SO NEAR . . .'

She hesitated a moment longer, then slipped guiltily inside.

VI

40

'Goodbye, Beattie darling. Good luck!'

'Oh, Elizabeth . . .'

'Don't cry.'

'I . . . I'm not.'

'You'll be all right once you get there. Remember, this is the most difficult part.'

Beattie nodded. 'I . . . I know. It's just that it's so . . . so awful to leave you.'

'Well, let me see you off *properly* then. Come on!' Elizabeth seized the luggage trolley and began manoeuvring it across the road towards the airport doors. 'It's a good two hours until your flight leaves. We can have a farewell drink.'

'*No.*' Beattie yanked the trolley to a halt just outside the entrance.

'Why not? It'll give us more time together. I've nothing to get back for. I told Hugo I wouldn't be home until half past one or two.'

Beattie turned to face her, still struggling to control her tears. 'Elizabeth, please don't be offended, but I need to be on my own. Just give me one last hug.'

They stood holding each other tightly, heedless of the crowds, Beattie clinging to Elizabeth as if to absorb some vital part of her – to take with her in her new life.

'G . . . give my love to Hugo,' she stammered. 'And to Harriet and . . .' She broke off, wiped her eyes. She had been through all that already, in the car. The farewells couldn't continue for ever. 'Look, I'm going now, Elizabeth, okay?'

'Hold on just a second.' Elizabeth extracted a bulky package from her Sainsbury's carrier. 'A little present for you.'

425

'Oh, *Elizabeth*! It doesn't look little at all. And you've already given me . . .'

'No, this is just a silly thing. To make you laugh! Open it on the plane.'

'Thank you – thank you for *every*thing. You'll never understand how much you . . .' But Elizabeth *did* understand. They had been talking the whole of the journey from Sevenoaks to Heathrow. Beattie squeezed her hand, forced a smile, then turned her back and strode resolutely through the doors.

The brilliant August sunshine instantly gave way to gloom. The ceiling was oppressively low; the serried banks of check-in desks uniformly grey. And there was barely room to move – queues at every desk, two raucous parties of schoolchildren standing just inside the entrance, and a large contingent of Japanese businessmen in near-identical dark suits. Everybody seemed to be *with* someone, and she felt a sudden surge of panic at having sent Elizabeth away.

But she refused to look back – simply took a deep breath in and walked towards the Qantas check-in. The queue was one of the longest, and she took up her position behind a pair of teenage lovers, their arms entwined, the girl's head on her boyfriend's shoulder. Looking at their tattered jeans, she felt distinctly overdressed. Greville's generous farewell 'tip' had paid for her new outfit: a snazzy little suit with a long double-breasted jacket and the shortest of short skirts. Not exactly the most practical choice for a twenty-five-hour flight, but she had a tracksuit in her hand-luggage to change into on the plane. The important thing was to look her best when her father met her the other end. She could still hardly believe that she'd actually be *seeing* him, after all this time – and living with him permanently, as she had longed to all her childhood. Admittedly she would have to share him with Karen and Céline, but they seemed far less daunting now she had received their friendly letters and seen their photographs.

She shunted her trolley along as the queue moved slowly forward. Her brand new luggage was a present from Elizabeth, who had insisted on real leather as being stronger and more special. Special was the word: a set of matching cases in a subtle shade of olive, with smart black trim and impressive-looking straps. It must have cost a fortune, but Elizabeth had shrugged off the expense, saying it was only a trifling recompense for her loss of earnings while she was up in Inverness.

She glanced along the length of the queue to inspect her fellow travellers – every type from ageing hippies to pin-stripe-smart executives to families like the one behind her, who looked like the cast of a sugar-coated TV commercial. However, by the time she reached the check-in, the idyll had been shattered – what with the parents' constant bickering, the infuriating bleeps and whines from the son's computer game, and the daughter's moans about wanting to go home.

'Are you travelling on your own, madam?' the woman at the desk asked.

Beattie nodded, now feeling only relief at the fact. Better alone than with companions like that.

'Don't worry – we'll look after you. Now, if you'd like to put your cases on the belt here . . .'

She heaved them off the trolley and watched excitedly as they were weighed and tagged and then juddered along the rollers. They were on their way – and so was she, to a new life in a new world. Her earlier fears had vanished, if only temporarily. Over the last few weeks, her emotions had seesawed disconcertingly from terror to elation, then back again. 'That's only normal,' Elizabeth had assured her. 'Change is always frightening.'

She stowed her boarding card in her bag, glad to be free of her luggage. Now all she had to carry was her flight-bag and Elizabeth's present, and both of those were light. She had two hours to kill before take-off, but that was quite okay – it was a welcome change to have time on her hands after the flurry of the last two months. As well as working flat out for Greville, she'd had masses of things to arrange for her departure: visas, money, references, insurance. Despite the pressures, it had felt quite liberating – disposing of her flat, her car, her debts. Having turfed out the old, she was ready to start again, anew.

She took the lift to the first floor and emerged into neon glare and still more crowds of people. She looked around at the array of shops and restaurants, wondering where to start. Perhaps there'd be time for everything – a drink, a snack, a browse in the bookshop, a quick tour of the boutiques. She would date her holiday from *now*, relish this new sense of freedom.

A display of hats caught her eye. Her father had always liked his women to wear hats – the more outrageous the better.

Right, she thought, making a beeline for the shop – she'd buy the most flamboyant one she could find. *That* would make him sit up and take notice.

'*Qantas Airways wish to apologize for the delay in the departure of Flight QF2 to Bangkok, Sydney and Melbourne. This is due to a technical problem . . .*'

Beattie put her parcels down. What was *that* supposed to mean? A bomb on board? A hijacker? The flight was scheduled to leave at one, and it was already ten past twelve. She had spent the last hour shopping. Not only had she bought a wild red hat, but also presents for her father, and for Karen and Céline: a crazy tie with 'cutie-pie' printed twenty times across its length, a medieval calligraphy set, four different Winnie the Pooh mugs and some rose musk scent from the Body Shop. Now her feet were aching and she was feeling uncomfortably hot – dressed as she was for the Australian spring rather than the current London heat-wave. She was dying to sit down, ideally with a cool drink and a book.

She wandered along to the bookshop and picked out a fat paperback: one in the best-seller list, with a string of rave reviews on the back. Then she bought a canned drink from a stall – the only place which didn't have a queue – and eventually found a seat in a bank of chairs opposite the Bureau de Change. She sank into it gratefully, easing off her tight shoes. Next to her sat an ancient turbaned Indian with a long white straggly beard, and on the other side an overweight Italian, perspiring in his cheap blue suit. Both of them were smoking, which meant she'd be subjected to cigarette fumes for the next half-hour or so. Well, at least it was a reminder of Elizabeth. *She* would be back home already, perhaps in the garden with Hugo. He was so much better now, thank God, they might even be having a reasonably normal conversation.

She wished *she* could talk to someone; chat about something mindless like the weather or the test match. She was beginning to feel isolated in the midst of so many strangers and so many foreign languages. The people sitting opposite had closed, expressionless faces. Her fellow human beings, yet it was hard to feel much affinity with them. Each person was confined in his own skin; unable to clamber into someone else's and view the world through *different* eyes. For all she knew, they might have suffered dreadful tragedies – accidents, like Hugo's; a child's death; a husband's suicide – all the horrors she had witnessed in Intensive Care. But they stared blankly back at her, as if she were an alien species, shut in her own cage. She remembered learning about parallel lines at school; condemned to run on side by side, yet always separate. She had asked if you could *make* them meet, maybe bend them out of shape. 'Certainly not,' Miss Branscombe had snapped, 'and kindly don't interrupt.'

She glanced up once more at the flight departure screen. Flight QF2 still said 'delayed'. How much *longer*, for heaven's sake? All this hanging about was making her introspective, and if they didn't get off soon, she'd start worrying again – about her father and Céline, and whether she'd be able to find a job.

She pulled out her book – reading would distract her. She skimmed the first few pages with a sense of growing disappointment. The style was very flat – she could have done better herself; certainly spiced the language up a bit. And the hero was a cliché on two legs: not only tall, dark and handsome, but also clever, cultured and seriously rich. Well, too bad – she was stuck with him, so she'd better stop complaining and enjoy his dazzling company all the way to Australia.

'*This is a further announcement for Qantas Airways passengers awaiting the delayed Flight QF2 to Bangkok, Sydney and Melbourne. Passengers are requested to go to the Granary restaurant, where they will be served lunch on production of their boarding card.*'

Beattie shut her book with a bang. Lunch was meant to be served on the *plane*, not in a stuffy airport restaurant with hundreds of fellow passengers fighting for non-existent seats. Still, there was no alternative, so she eased her shoes back on, gathered up her various parcels and joined the scrum surging towards the Granary. Her feet were really painful now, and her suit felt like a straitjacket. She couldn't face the thought of sitting for another hour in a mini-skirt and high heels.

She decided to change in the toilet, although it meant joining the inevitable queue. Emerging at last from the cubicle, she inspected herself in the mirror. Her top half – smart designer jacket – was wildly at odds with her bottom half – baggy track-suit trousers and battered brown suede moccasins. And, crowning it all, the red hat looked absurd. Well, who cared? So long as she could impress her father when she arrived the other end, the intervening hours didn't matter.

The queue for the restaurant tailed right back to the Sock Shop.

Even in more comfortable shoes, she refused to stand so long. First she'd go and get a drink – something with a kick to it. She trudged towards the Shakespeare Ale House, an olde worlde pub, complete with reproduction carriage-lamps, fake oak panelling and decorative beer-barrels devoid of any beer. It looked depressingly small and cramped, and a gaggle of salesmen were hogging the bar, their voices as loud as their suits. After an age, she was served with her vodka and tonic and took it into a corner, hoping to escape the noise of the aggressively loud music thudding from unseen amplifiers. There were no windows anywhere and the dim lighting was compounded by a low-beamed ceiling, which seemed to press down on her head. She had lost all sense of the English summer, or even of the outside world, and felt trapped in a sort of limbo, suspended between two time-zones and two homes. She could hardly wait to swap this claustrophobic congestion for the wide open spaces of Australia.

There were no seats – of course – and she had resigned herself to standing when she spotted someone getting up from a booth right at the back. She rushed to sit down, and found herself beside a dark-skinned woman, and opposite her two small sons. She smiled apologetically for disturbing them and was rewarded with a silent stare from three pairs of suspicious black eyes.

'Oh well – happy days,' she murmured, taking a large swig of her drink. She got out her book again, but it was hopeless trying to read with the thump-thump of the music and the intrusive buzz of conversation (although her three immediate neighbours maintained their sullen silence). Perhaps she'd open Elizabeth's present – at least it would give her something to do. Elizabeth had told her to wait until she was on the plane, but it was long past departure-time, so why not *now*?

The two boys eyed the package with interest as she put it on the table. 'Shall we see what's inside?' she asked them. Instantly they shrank away, but undeterred, she pulled the gift-wrap off, then unfolded several layers of tissue paper to reveal a pair of ducks – toy ducks made from felt, with button eyes and real feathers in their tails. She recognized the handiwork as Mrs Cunningham's – a WI stalwart who had made scores of inventive toys for last month's village fête. But the design was strictly Elizabeth's. One duck was small and green with a bandage round its foot and a cigarette stuck rakishly in its beak. The other was black and white with a scarlet beak and crest, and had a miniature copy of the *Daily Herald* tucked under one wing and a Qantas ticket under the other. And in case any doubt remained, each duck had its name embroidered across its chest.

Beattie sat staring at them. Sophie and George had died a natural death – or so she had assumed – along with the student sprees, the racing, the carefree days before Hugo's accident. But Elizabeth had resurrected them, even brought them wittily up to date.

She felt tears prick her eyes, tried furiously to blink them away. The woman with the boys got up, and someone else slipped into the seat opposite. He remained a blur through her tears, which were now streaming down her cheeks. She knew she shouldn't stay there making such an exhibition of herself, but she couldn't seem to move, and sat paralysed, clutching the two ducks.

'Oh God, don't cry.' The voice was male, unsteady. 'Or *I*'ll start.'

She looked up to see an out-of-focus face, the features crumpling, the eyes already wet. As she swallowed hard, struggling to regain control, he let out a sort of shudder, and then collapsed in silent grief, somehow worse than normal crying. He sat slumped over the table, his shoulders heaving, his face completely hidden, and through the shutters of his hands came strangled sobs and gasps. She realized to her horror that people were staring at them, probably assuming they belonged together, sharing some unspeakable grief. Yet surely he wasn't crying just in sympathy with *her*?

She felt she ought to say something, make an attempt to comfort him, but she was no more capable of coherent speech than he was. Wordlessly, he fumbled for his handkerchief, wiped his eyes and offered it to her. It was none too clean, but she took it thankfully. Her nose was running, her cheeks wet and flaming-hot, and when she saw streaks of black mascara on the hankie, she realized what a fright she must look. This morning she had started out as a smart successful woman – now she had degenerated into a snivelling urchin.

It was several minutes more before either she or the man looked up. Their eyes met for an instant, then glanced away, embarrassed. The man retrieved his hankie, blew his nose, and took a long draught of his beer. Then finally he found his voice and asked her what was wrong.

'It . . . it's these *ducks*,' she said, and all at once she was laughing as well as crying as she held George and Sophie out to him. The whole thing was so ridiculous – two complete strangers sitting sobbing their eyes out together.

He took the ducks from her carefully, fingering Sophie's bandage. 'You mean because this one's hurt its foot?'

'Yes,' she said, with another burst of laughter. 'But it's better now. And *I*'m okay, I think. How about *you*?'

'I'm not sure, to tell the truth. It's a bad day for me. I've just seen . . . someone off. To San Diego.'

'Hell, I'm sorry.' She wondered if the 'someone' (presumably his girlfriend) was worth so much emotion.

'Forgive me. I don't know what came over me. It's just that . . . goodbyes are so . . . upsetting. Look, can I get you a drink?'

'Thanks, that's very kind, but I haven't finished this one yet.'

'Nor have I. I've hardly started it.' He picked up his glass. 'Well – cheers! I don't even know your name. Unless it's Sophie?' he smiled, eyeing the green duck.

'No, I'm *this* one.' She picked up the black and white duck and gave it an affectionate pat. 'George.'

'Oh . . . who's Sophie then?'

'Well, it's a bit complicated, to say the least.' She decided not to explain. 'My real name's Beattie. Except *that*'s not true either. My *real* real name's Betty – Betty Cook.'

He looked more mystified than ever. 'So what do I call you – Betty? Beattie? George?'

'I don't mind. Take your pick.'

'Okay, I'll settle for Betty. I used to know a fantastic Betty at school. I was all of thirteen and I worshipped at her feet, but I'm afraid she never gave me a second glance. I suppose I was just too ordinary.'

Beattie looked at him. Yes, ordinary was the word: plumpish face, straight mousy hair and swollen red-rimmed eyes. His voice was rather ordinary, too – no pukka Hargreaves accent, just a faint south London twang. 'What's *your* name?' she asked.

'Bill.'

'Ah, like *this* place!'

'What d'you mean?'

'The *William* Shakespeare.'

'Oh, I see. No, I've never been a William, except at my christening, I suppose. Not that I remember it too well.'

She laughed. He had a sense of humour – that was *one* redeeming feature. His clothes were pretty dire though: crumpled chinos and an ill-fitting blue-checked shirt. She had become so used to Greville's tasteful elegance, most other men looked badly dressed in compari-

432

son. Though who was she to talk? Her present get-up was eccentric (to put it mildly), and her face must look a sight – make-up streaked, cheeks blotchy. 'And what sort of work do you do?'

'I'm a teacher.'

She might have guessed. 'What do you teach?' she asked, trying to inject a note of enthusiasm into her voice.

'Oh, a bit of everything. I work in a primary school.'

Worse and worse. In the glamorous world of her book, he'd have been an international banker, or a captain in the Foreign Legion, or at least an airline pilot. And if he *had* to teach, then he'd be something like an Oxford don or a professor of philosophy. Still, she'd got what she'd been looking for: someone to talk to, to help her pass the time. 'I'm flying to Australia,' she explained. 'But the wretched plane's delayed.'

'Oh, what a bind. Poor you. But I'm sure it'll be great when you get there. My brother went to Sydney a couple of years ago and he loved every minute of it.'

'I'm going to *live* there – permanently. In Melbourne. My father went out years ago and he's invited me to join him.' She broke off hurriedly as his eyes misted over again. 'Look, I will have another drink,' she said, pushing her glass towards him. She couldn't cope with more tears.

He was so long getting the drinks, she was half inclined to get up and go. But there was nowhere to go *to*. She could see the queue for the Granary still snailing past the pub. She might as well sit tight. At least a second vodka would deaden the pain of this awful interminable *waiting*.

'So why didn't you go *with* her – to San Diego?'

Bill put his burger down and wiped his greasy fingers. 'I . . . I suppose I realized it was over.'

'But you said she asked you to go.'

'Yeah, she did. But all we were doing was clinging to the past. You see, we've known each other donkey's years – since we were little kids at school, in fact – and it was a hell of a wrench to split up. But things were going wrong between us. So, even though it's painful, I know it's right for us to move on. Sometimes we need a good kick up the arse – if you'll forgive the expression – to force us to leave things behind and simply trust the future to work out.'

Beattie fiddled with the straw in her Coke, bending it this way and

433

that. 'You remind me of this guy I know called Kim. He's always going on about trusting and leaving things behind. "Writing a new birth-script" is the way he puts it.' She noticed Bill's puzzled expression, but she wasn't keen to explain rebirthing in a crowded place like this. 'I know it sounds a bit weird, and you'd probably think he had a screw loose if you heard *some* of his ideas. But he did help me through a bad patch in my life.'

Bill's face clouded in sympathy. 'What happened?'

'Oh, it's all over now, don't worry. And anyway, I'd rather hear about *you*. Wasn't Carla fearfully upset, after she'd bought the house and everything?'

'Well, yes, I'm afraid she was. But, you see, it wasn't until *that* stage I realized we were only going ahead because we were too shit-scared to stop. And anyway, I didn't want to live abroad – though I tried to kid myself about that as well. But deep down I knew I'd miss my friends – and England – the whole culture here and way of life, and my favourite parts of London, and our fantastic countryside. And even stupid things like the weather. I mean, we had hail and snow in May, for goodness' sake, and now we're sweltering in a heatwave! I like that – it's nicely unpredictable.' He picked up his burger and bit into it reflectively. 'Like *life*,' he added, smiling. 'Anything can happen – any time. Okay, Carla's gone and of course I'll miss her like stink, but – who knows – if I stick around and stop moping, I may meet someone else.'

Could he actually be *propositioning* her, Beattie wondered? A flirtatious note had crept into his voice and he was looking directly into her eyes. And what did he mean, 'Anything can happen – any time,' which he'd said with a sort of relish? Hastily she busied herself tearing open a sachet of brown sauce and daubing it on her chips. He could forget any idea of romance – *that* was a dead cert. Okay, so he was sensitive and decent and intelligent and all the rest, but she didn't feel the slightest flicker of desire for him. It was ironical in a way. For once in her life she had met a man her own age, with no wife or kids or hang-ups or commitments, but the basic chemistry just wasn't there, and she knew it never would be.

Well, she'd simply have to be grateful for small mercies: she had enjoyed his conversation and his company over lunch, and they were lucky enough to be sitting by a window – a whole *wall* of glass, in fact, which gave her a view of the outside world again, and also planes to watch. Yet all they'd done was move from the Shakespeare Ale

434

House to the burger place next door. True it was appallingly crowded, and the food was bad verging on diabolical, but who cared when there was daylight – even a high ceiling and a few healthy-looking plants. The place was largely populated by families; most of the kids wore Burger King cardboard crowns, and all and sundry were eating with their fingers out of paper bags and cartons. Her last meal out had been dinner at the Dorchester, the night before Greville flew back home to Cape Town. They'd had roast breast of quail with goose liver, eaten off bone china, with heavy silver cutlery, and a bottle of vintage Lanson in the ice-bucket. Now she and Bill were munching their way through Double Whoppers, washed down with Diet Coke.

'Hey, look at that!' Bill put his plastic cup down and gazed out, enthralled, at a huge grey metal monster taxiing towards them. 'I love planes. Don't you?'

'No,' said Beattie tersely. 'Not when I have to wait this long for them.' She swallowed the last mouthful of her flabby lukewarm burger and pushed her chips towards him. 'Do finish these if you want. I can't manage any more.'

'No, I'd better not. I'm going out this evening and there's bound to be loads of food. It's Mike's thirtieth birthday thrash. He's having it in a disused church in Lambeth. That's typical of Mike. I told you about him, didn't I?'

'Yeah, your atheist friend who teaches RE. But excuse me a second, will you? I really ought to check the flight again. It'd be awful to sit here chatting and find it's left without me!'

'Surely they'll announce it?'

'Yes, I suppose so. All the same . . .' She squeezed between the tables until she could see the flight-departure screens mounted on the wall, returning to her seat with a disappointed shrug. 'Still delayed.'

'Well, if it doesn't leave soon, you'd better come to the party *with* me. We can have a couple of quick drinks and still get you back in time to catch it.'

'Okay, you're on,' she joked. 'I can hardly wait!'

'Will passengers awaiting flight QF2 to Bangkok, Sydney and Melbourne please proceed to Gate 14. This flight is now boarding. We apologize once again for the late departure of this flight . . .'

'At last!' said Beattie, springing to her feet and snatching off her

Burger King gold crown. In its place she pulled on her new hat, then rummaged for her purse. 'Bill, could you be an angel and keep an eye on my stuff for a minute? I want to make a quick phone call.'

'Okay, but don't miss the plane!'

'Don't worry, it'll take ages for everyone to fight their way to Departures.'

She dashed out to the call-box, slotted in a couple of coins and dialled the Sevenoaks number. Damn! It was the answerphone.

'. . . Please leave a message after the tone and I'll phone you back as soon as I can.'

No you won't, she thought, I'll be high above the clouds by then. 'Elizabeth, it's Beattie,' she said breathlessly. 'I'm still at the airport, would you believe. It's nearly four o'clock and they've only just called the flight. There's been a terrible long delay – some problem with the electrics. I must dash now, but I just wanted to say thank you for those *wonderful* ducks. They're . . .'

The meter was running down – 4, 3, 2, 1 . . . She rammed in another 20p and continued almost without drawing breath. 'They're brilliant, honestly. George is a real work of art. I love his . . .' The words dried up – suddenly, inexplicably.

She stood listening to the eerie sound of her silence. All the commotion of the airport thrummed somewhere in the background, but it seemed muffled, far away. Her money was running out again. She took a 50p piece from her purse and pressed it slowly into the slot.

'Elizabeth, listen. I . . . I'm not going, after all. I'm staying here. In England.'

What in God's name was she *saying*? Of course she had to go. She couldn't disrupt everything at this stage; let her father down; change all her plans – and *his* – chuck hundreds of pounds down the drain.

I suppose I realized it was over. We were still clinging to the past.

Bill had made her understand – she too was clinging to the past; imagining she could run back to her father, to the myth of happy families, the past that never was. She *couldn't* be his little girl, his George. George was dead, even Sophie's George. But she still had Elizabeth, her closest and most loving friend, and her other friends – and England, and her favourite parts of London, and the fantastic countryside. And stupid things like the weather: hail and snow in May. And her determination to find a worthwhile job. She didn't have to cross the world for that. She could achieve it *here*, instead.

She put the phone down, still dazed by her decision, and began walking slowly back to Burger King. On an impulse, she stopped outside the bookshop and stood gazing in at the shelves and shelves of books: romances, thrillers, sagas, sci-fi. Then, suddenly, it came to her – she must write her *own* book, and it must start here, at the airport, with two strangers sobbing in the bar: a completely *un*romantic hero and an eccentric girl in a crazy scarlet hat. They'd confide in one another, but they wouldn't fall in love – oh no – nothing so predictable.

Words were flooding into her mind – a leaping shoal just waiting to be netted – exhilarating, gutsy words like the book she'd written at fifteen and a half. She *had* her answer – she'd known it all along; just lacked the will to do it. Writing for the papers had been a step along the way, but it had tied her down with deadlines and constraints. She needed much more freedom – freedom to be herself, to include her terrors and frustrations in her writing, even her failed affairs; put them to some use, at last.

Of course, journalism did *pay*, and she didn't fancy starving in a garret. But she could return to temping and insist on working shorter hours; devote every spare minute to her book.

The plot was already taking shape: her two unlikely protagonists would leave the airport together and go on to a party – a thirtieth birthday thrash in a disused church in Lambeth, given by an RE teacher who didn't believe in God.

She darted into the bookshop and bought a notebook and a pack of biros, impatient to get back to Bill. She was in his debt, and not just for a burger and a Coke. He had given her her basic inspiration – maybe given her far more than that. If, like him, she put the past behind her, wrote a different birth-script, trusted in herself for once, then she could make a complete new start. She might actually get published, even achieve a sort of fame, for heaven's sake!

Bill was still sitting by the window, watching for her anxiously, George and Sophie perched absurdly on his lap. He spotted her and half stood up, clutching the ducks to his chest. She laughed and ran towards him, dodging children, tripping over bags, his words singing in her head:

Anything can happen – any time.

Wendy Perriam

The Stillness The Dancing

Abandoned by God and her husband, the twin props of her existence, Morna Gordon has tried to live her life through her mother and
daughter, both plunged in crises of their own. But the priest's words
stir something in her soul, and meeting David – a man who believes
passionately in souls – stirs something more profound.

Emerging from her anger and bewilderment, she embarks on a
voyage of self-discovery, which takes her from the lunacy of
anything-goes California, to a remote northern island and another
century, to the fulfilment of scholarship and, finally, to furious,
fumbling but intoxicating love.

Exploring the lives of three generations of women with sensitivity
and perception, *The Stillness The Dancing* juxtaposes humour with
tragedy, sex with mysticism, faith with doubt, the grab-all twentieth
century with the hairshirt idealism of the Age of Saints in a giant
lifescape of a novel.

'Unashamedly sexual, yet profoundly spiritual . . . a remarkable
novel. It must be read'   FAY WELDON

'Perriam is bursting with ideas about sex, death, grief, celibacy, the
problems of old age, of guilt, of mother-daughter relationships. The
problems of women of all ages are described in a flexible lucid
style, while humour and exuberance help to make this novel hugely
enjoyable'   *Irish Times*

'An excellent novel which does not flinch from the grave and universal subject of death, yet manages intimacy and scale at once. The
wild and bitter comedy of life in America contrasts with the almost
poetic purity of life on a Scottish island. This novel is about the
utterly demanding nature of real love which can force a person
through darkness into light. Perriam's writing is as rewarding as her
theme'   BEL MOONEY, *Cosmopolitan*

ISBN: 0 00 654624 2

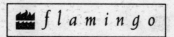

Wendy Perriam

Sin City

Norah Toomey and Carole Joseph have always been losers –
thrown together by chance in a seedy psychiatric hospital – until
Carole wins a holiday for two in Las Vegas. They take wing
together – eighteen-year-old Carole, with her seesaw moods and
explosive sexuality, egging on the shy, unworldly Norah, whose
only break from a lifetime of institutions has been the annual
day-trip to Littlehampton.

But Las Vegas isn't Littlehampton, as these two innocents
discover to their cost as they are plunged into a world of strip-
pers and gamblers, brothels and crime. The pair are both dazzled
and duped by America's glitziest – and saddest – hot-spot,
where sex-shows throb with phoney passion, Godmen tout for
cash, and Lady Luck rules and ruins lives.

Perriam's probing exploration of an extraordinary relationship,
and of the sin and shame of the city which seeds it, displays all
the rich uncensored gusto and exuberant humour which have
established her as exceptional among contemporary writers.

'Touching, funny and unblushingly outrageous. My eyes were
out on stalks!'   *Evening Standard*

'Religion and sex, stirred together by an uninhibited hand,
cannot fail to make a heady brew. Written with great energy and
verve, this is a deeply felt and vastly entertaining exercise'
                                                   Daily Telegraph

'Both poignant and funny. We get a wonderfully balanced birds-
eye view of the tawdry, neon world of Vegas. Fast, outrageous
and finally very moving, *Sin City* really is one of Perriam's best'
                                                   Woman's Journal

ISBN: 0 00 654623 4

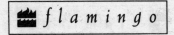

Wendy Perriam

Devils, for a Change

After twenty cloistered years in a Norfolk convent, Sister Mary Hilary casts off the spiritual strait-jacket of her medieval robes and returns to a world she can hardly recognize – one which is permissive, greedy, and amoral. Used to a life spent contemplating the mysteries of Christ – where 'self' is the enemy – she comes naked into the modern world, groping her way towards the as yet untasted pleasures of friendship, sensuality and love. But is Hilary ready for life outside the womb of the Mother Church – and can she ever be free from her burden of guilt and fear?

Devils, for a Change is the controversial and profoundly revealing story of modern society seen through the eyes of an innocent outsider in search of an identity.

'Compulsively readable. Perriam is a writer of authority and skill'
Sunday Times

'A stunningly readable, absorbing account of those enthralling lands where guilt ends, religion starts, and sex takes off'
Fay Weldon

'A joyous book . . . daring, provocative and brutally honest . . . a celebration of life and a triumph' *Time Out*

'Gutsy, punchy, pulsing with life' *Daily Mail*

'Thoughtful, provocative and scrupulous' *Books*

ISBN 0 586 08937 3

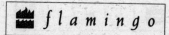 *flamingo*